William Milligan Sloane

Life of Napoleon Bonaparte

Vol. 3

William Milligan Sloane

Life of Napoleon Bonaparte
Vol. 3

ISBN/EAN: 9783337350390

Printed in Europe, USA, Canada, Australia, Japan

Cover: Foto ©Raphael Reischuk / pixelio.de

More available books at **www.hansebooks.com**

LIFE OF

NAPOLEON BONAPARTE

BY

WILLIAM MILLIGAN SLOANE,

PH. D., L. H. D.

PROFESSOR OF HISTORY IN PRINCETON UNIVERSITY

VOLUME III

THE CENTURY CO. NEW YORK
LONDON: MACMILLAN & CO., LIMITED
1896

TABLE OF CONTENTS

✤

VOLUME III

LIST OF ILLUSTRATIONS

✤

VOLUME III

LIFE OF NAPOLEON BONAPARTE

✤

CHAPTER I

THE DEVASTATION OF PRUSSIA

THE EFFECTS OF JENA AND AUERSTÄDT — DEGENERACY OF THE FRENCH
SOLDIERS — NAPOLEON'S ABUSE OF QUEEN LOUISA — THE OCCUPA-
TION OF BERLIN — CONDUCT OF THE FRENCH GENERALS — TURKEY
AND RUSSIA AT WAR — THE BERLIN DECREE — A RÒLAND FOR AN
OLIVER — ITS DISASTROUS EFFECT — NAPOLEON CONSENTS TO AN
ARMISTICE — TREATMENT OF MINOR GERMAN STATES — NAPOLEON AS
THE LIBERATOR OF POLAND — CONDITION OF THE COUNTRY.

THE moral effect of Jena upon Prussia was pitiful. All the years
of irresponsible government, of absolutism and militarism, seemed
revenged upon the monarchy at a single blow. The nation, with no
experience of independent action, was stunned, and did not run to arms,
except in a few abortive instances. In his flight Frederick William had
with difficulty kept together his royal state, and the day after Jena he
sent an envoy to ask for peace. But Napoleon declared that he would
dictate his terms only from Berlin, and his army continued its advance.
The Prussian court, with a few thousand men under Lestocq, retreated
through West Prussia and took refuge in Königsberg. So thoroughly
did Napoleon organize the pursuit, and so carefully did he estimate the
total result of his victory, that nothing escaped him. The French soldiers carried everything before them. A Prussian reserve corps was
easily beaten at Halle by Bernadotte, and fled for refuge to the unpro-

visioned fortress of Magdeburg. Lannes seized Dessau; Davout, Wittenberg; while Murat, Soult, and Ney proceeded to invest Magdeburg, which for those days was the strategic key of the Elbe valley. It resisted until November, but eventually fell, as did also Erfurt. In fact, the French ransacked the land. Even Hohenlohe did not escape them. Being overtaken by the infantry of Lannes and the cavalry of Murat, he was first driven from Prenzlau, and then, on October twenty-eighth, he surrendered, being a victim partly to the duplicity of Murat, who declared that a hundred thousand French were closing in on him, and partly to the stupidity of his own messenger, who asserted that the tale was true. Frederick William himself would have been captured at Weissensee but for Blücher, who brazenly declared to Klein, the French commander, that an armistice had been granted — a pure falsehood. Stettin capitulated to Lasalle's cavalry on the thirtieth, and Küstrin soon opened its doors. The fortresses of Spandau and Hameln followed their example, all four being surrendered with suspicious facility; in two instances the French and Prussian soldiers actually joined to hiss and execrate the governors, who were undoubtedly both recreant and venal. Blücher, after many gallant but fruitless attempts to collect a force, had reached Lübeck, through many dangers, with his cavalry; but driven thence after a gallant and exceptional resistance, he too surrendered. There remained no organized Prussian force in the lands between the Elbe and the Oder.

It had been accurate foresight which enabled Napoleon to say, in a decree issued from Jena on October fifteenth, that in the battle of the previous day he had conquered all the Prussian lands west of the Vistula. Before long the demoralization of the nation was as complete as the conquest of their country. The treatment of the people by the victorious soldiery was the climax of the long career of French officers and men as plunderers. As Napoleon's success kept pace with his ever-growing schemes of conquest, he laid less and less stress on the means to his end, ever more and more on its accomplishment. The army was once again scattered to obtain subsistence, and it left no opportunity for spoil neglected. As one of the most enthusiastic officers reluctantly declared: "From the moment Napoleon obtained supreme power the soldiers' morals changed, the union of hearts among them disappeared with their poverty, a desire for luxury and the comforts of life began. The Emperor considered it politic to favor this degeneracy. He thought it advantageous and shrewd to make the army absolutely dependent on him."

The shocking details of Prussia's treatment by Napoleon and his army have been often told. On October twenty-fourth the Emperor arrived at the Hohenzollern residence of Potsdam, and publicly visited the tomb of Frederick the Great. Uttering words expressive of profound reverence for the great general, he nevertheless sent the old hero's sword, belt, and hat as trophies to ornament the Invalides at Paris. "His intellect, his genius, and his affections were kin to those of our nation, which he so esteemed," was the pretext for this act of spoliation. He was equally unscrupulous in his shameful treatment of the unfortunate Queen. In bulletin after bulletin he heaped lying abuse on her devoted head. In one he depicted her as having a sufficiently pretty face, but little wit; in another he asked what mystery had led a woman hitherto absorbed in the serious occupations of her toilet to meddle with politics, stir up the King, and kindle everywhere the fire with which she was herself possessed. The answer, he insinuated, was to be found in the Czar's personal visits to Berlin.

On October twenty-seventh Napoleon made his triumphal entry into the Prussian capital with the utmost splendor he could devise, and at the head of the largest military force he could muster. Coignet, one of his soldiers, wrote of the scene: "The Emperor was grand in his plain clothes, with his little hat and a penny cockade. His staff, on the contrary, wore their dress uniform; and for strangers it was a queer sight to see, in the one man most meanly clad of all, the leader of so fine an army." To "show himself terrible at the first moment," as he had advised Joseph to do at Naples, an order was issued for the seizure of Prince Hatzfeldt, the most distinguished Prussian nobleman within reach. He was to be tried by a court-martial on the charge of being a traitor and a spy, his crime being that he had written to his King a letter giving an account of the French entry into Berlin. The epistle was so harmless in its nature that its writer had intrusted it to the mail, in which it was seized and then shown to Napoleon. The prince escaped the first blast of the storm by hiding; his life was afterward granted to the personal and tearful solicitations of his wife as an act of great clemency. As in Italy, the galleries, libraries, collections, and public monuments were stripped of their finest treasures to enrich Paris.

The French soldiers needed no example. Lübeck, which, as was

claimed, had been taken by storm, was handed over to the men to work
their will, just as Pavia had been. Wherever the troops were billeted,
they had but to demand from their terrified entertainers what they desired and their behest was done. They were not modest, and before long
both rapine and lust worked their will among the angry but helpless
populations. The French generals were too much like their men, and,
as in Italy and Austria, the gratification of their boundless greed met
the Emperor's approval. The castles of the nobility and the houses of
the wealthy citizens were of course chosen by them as quarters. It
would have been hard for their owners to refuse the unbidden guests
any object which met with their expressed approval, and the French
officers openly admired many valuable things. All these irregularities,
the Emperor believed, attached his generals to himself; and at the same
time a threat of examination into their accounts would, he knew, instantly check any manifestations of independence. Masséna was the
most avaricious of all; nothing but the love of money could influence
him, wrote Napoleon, and "where at first little sums sufficed, now mil-
liards are not sufficient." At another time he said, more generously,
that one must bow the knee before Masséna's gifts as a soldier, although
he had his faults like another. Bernadotte, on the occasion of a certain
surprise, lost the wagon which contained his Lübeck booty. He was
inconsolable, and it was considered a delicious joke when he explained
that he was so depressed because the loss "prevented him from paying
a gratification in money to the men of his corps." Davout before long
filled all Poland with the terror of his name. Napoleon's brother Jerome, finding a bin of choice Tokay in a Polish castle, loaded the contents in his baggage-train, and carried them away.

With Prussia thus shattered, disintegrated, and almost annihilated,
Napoleon proceeded without the loss of a moment to use his new vantage against both Russia and England. In the Oriental question he
could strike both with a single blow. As a result of the thorough
knowledge of the East obtained in 1803 through Sebastiani, he had virtually determined to assert his supremacy over Turkey. To this end,
however, he must for the present spare the sensibilities of Austria,
which, though humbled to the dust, was again rising to her feet; her
curiously assorted, heterogeneous peoples showed more spirit than the
Prussians, displaying resources and courage comparable to those of
France. During the summer of 1806, apparently of his own motion,

QUEEN LOUISA OF PRUSSIA

but in reality by French suggestion, the Sultan Selim III. had dismissed the viceroys of Moldavia and Wallachia, both of whom had made themselves conspicuous by their Russian proclivities. At once the Czar Alexander I. sent an army to the Danube. The Sultan was terrified, but on November eleventh, 1806, at the very climax of his peril, he was officially notified that Napoleon now had three hundred thousand men free to attack Russia and save Turkey; the Emperor would himself operate from the Vistula, and a Turkish army must simultaneously appear on the Dniester. The Sultan at once obeyed, and the Czar consequently sent eighty thousand men against the Turks. Austria, mindful, apparently, of Russia's desertion after Austerlitz, displayed neither resentment nor alarm at the course taken by France, and Napoleon felt himself a step nearer both to victory over Russia and to such a protectorate of Turkey as would be a serious menace to England's Eastern empire.

The particular bolt forged for England was the Berlin decree, which Napoleon issued on November twenty-first. It was the capstone to that structure of Continental embargo which for four years had occupied the attention of its author. England was the soul of every Continental coalition; France could answer only by continued Continental conquest. As England could be reached only through her trade, with Continental Europe in his hands Napoleon determined that he would strike his implacable enemy where she was vulnerable. "The British Islands," ran the decree, "are henceforth blockaded; all commerce with them is prohibited; letters and packages with an English address will be confiscated, as also every store of English goods on the Continent within the borders of France and her allies; every piece of English goods, all English vessels, and those laden with staples from English colonies, will be excluded from all European harbors, including those of neutral states."

As early as 1795 the Committee of Public Safety had considered the possibility of excluding English goods from the Continent. The idea of the Berlin decree was therefore not original with Napoleon, but the time and form of its application were; in particular, the final clause was thoroughly his own. These last words speak volumes. In reply to the principle of Great Britain that on the sea "enemy's ships make enemy's goods," he thereby retorted with "enemy's lands make enemy's goods," ordering all English wares found in countries occupied by his troops to be seized. But he went much further in his suicidal logic, and virtually

declared war to the knife by commanding that every British subject
found within the same limits should be held as a prisoner of war, and
that all property of individual Englishmen should be regarded as lawful
prize. These drastic measures, considered together, were intended as a
reply to Trafalgar, and to England's orders in council issued on May sixteenth, 1806, which announced a blockade of the Continent from Brest
to the Elbe for the purpose of utterly destroying French commerce.
The Berlin decree was also intended to be in the nature of reprisals for
the English practice of searching French ships and impressing French
sailors. Napoleon had himself been guilty of that discourtesy both to
war-ships and to merchantmen, but he had never been strong enough
seriously to annoy or cripple England as England had both annoyed
and crippled him by the practice. During the year 1806 three more
French agents were despatched into the Orient, and Joseph declared to
the Prussian envoy that his brother was contemplating an expedition to
India. Many years later the Emperor himself confirmed this statement
in a conversation with Dr. O'Meara.

No single scheme of Napoleon's contributed in the end so much to
his ruin as the Berlin decree. Colonial wares had become a necessity
of life to the populations of Europe, and to be deprived of them brought
irritation into every household, even the poorest; it was an attempt to
coerce Russia into adhesion to this ruinous policy which directly initi-
ated his fall.

As to Prussia, the ultimate arrangements were held in suspense.
Napoleon's first response to a request for peace had been that he would
make terms only in Berlin, and shortly after his triumphal entry negotiations were opened. The terms proposed by his ministers at the outset were far in excess of what the Prussian plenipotentiaries thought
reasonable; but as one fortress after another opened its gates the demands grew more and more exorbitant. Although other counsels
prevailed in the end, there was actually a moment when Napoleon contemplated the extinction of the Hohenzollern power, and the partition among his vassal states of that dynasty's variously acquired
and strangely assorted lands, which had so little territorial unity that
they extended in two separate parallel lines from northeast to south-
west. Voltaire said they stretched over Europe like a pair of garters.
The best offer that could be wrung from Napoleon — and, in view of
Prussia's absolute prostration, he thought his proposition not ungener-

ous — was for an armistice, during which the French should occupy all
Prussia as far as the Bug ; and Frederick William should order the now
advancing Russians off his soil.   The Prussian minister actually signed
this paper, but his sovereign, whose hopes were rising in proportion as
the Russian army drew nearer, refused to ratify it.

It is not difficult to conceive the desperation of Frederick William as
he learned the ominous disposition made of the lands belonging to his
allies.   The Elector of Hesse-Cassel had remained neutral in the war,
having requested and been refused membership in the Rhine Confederation.   The day after Jena he was informed that the Emperor had been
aware of his secret sympathy with the coalition, and that his feelings
had been evidenced by the permission granted the Prussian troops to
pass through his domain while his own army was on a war footing.
This conduct made it necessary to occupy his states.   Mortier, the
French commander at Mainz, was ordered to seize the prince and im-
prison him in Metz ; on November fourth it was curtly announced that
the house of Hesse had ceased to reign.   The fact was, the territories of
that house were needed for a new subsidiary kingdom, the formation
of which had been for some time in contemplation.   The Elector of
Saxony, whose troops had fought with the Prussians at Jena, was, on
the other hand, offered the privilege of neutrality, and, abandoning his
former ally, he eagerly accepted.   The dukes of Saxe-Gotha and Saxe-
Weimar followed his example, and obtained immunity by submission.
The Duke of Brunswick had withdrawn to his capital to die.   Thence
he appealed to his conqueror for mercy in behalf of his dominions.
Napoleon's reply was pitiless, recalling the duke's notorious proclamation of 1792 against the French republic, and declaring that it was
he also who had been the real instigator of the present war.   Brunswick, Hanover, Hamburg, and their domains were all occupied by French
troops and put under martial law.

In the treatment which Hesse-Cassel received, the Emperor of the
French was simply a despot.   In the case of Prussia he could not well
pose as a liberator, for as yet there was no wide-spread sense of oppression and little national spirit among the people.   In his dealings with
Saxony and the Saxon duchies he appeared in a better light, for among
their inhabitants there was a very extended sympathy with the liberal
ideas, both political and ecclesiastical, which he was still supposed to
represent.   But there was a nation of Eastern Europe which longed for

him as for a savior, and to whom he was far more than a representative liberal. Unhappy in her constitution, feeble in her political life, assassinated by a conspiracy of her neighbors, Poland was nevertheless still alive, and in her longing for a deliverer the majority of her people had fixed their eyes on Napoleon. From this fact he was anxious to draw the utmost advantage, and that right speedily, for the Czar with ninety thousand men was steadily marching toward the Prussian frontier. On November nineteenth a deputation of Polish nobility arrived in Berlin, and Napoleon, after treating them with impressive distinction, dismissed them with the statement that as France had never acknowledged the partition of their country, it was his interest as Emperor of the French to restore their independence and reconstruct a kingdom which, since it originated with him, would be permanent. A week later he proceeded to Posen, and, entering the city under an arch erected to "the liberator of Poland," awakened such enthusiasm that it far outran his own progress; a volunteer movement was almost instantly set on foot in Warsaw, which resulted in the enlistment of sixty thousand men as a national guard. It is idle to discuss whether Napoleon could or would have resuscitated Poland. Kosciusko and the more enlightened Poles believed not. Some of the Polish nobles demanded an immediate and formal recognition of their country's independence as the antecedent condition of their support. But among the masses the old ideals were revived, and the old spasmodic, misdirected energy was awakened in the service of the new Western Empire.

Such proceedings could not but arouse anxiety in Austria concerning the stability of her authority in the Polish lands under her crown. Andréossy, the French ambassador at Vienna, was instructed to say that such insurgent movements were a necessary consequence of the Emperor's presence in Posen, and that he had no intention of meddling with Austrian Poland; but that, nevertheless, if the Emperor of Austria felt uneasy, he might perhaps be willing to consider the acceptance of a part of Silesia as indemnity for the portion of Poland under Austrian rule. By this sly offer Francis was rendered powerless, for he could not accept Silesia, nor even a portion of it, without embroiling himself with England and Russia, and thereby entering into a virtual partnership with France. In spite of the unwearied efforts to stir up strife made by Napoleon's Corsican countryman, Pozzo di Borgo, who now represented the Czar at Vienna, Francis resolved to preserve a strict neutrality. The Poles were hopelessly divided, one party — that of Kosciusko — holding altogether aloof, a second under Poniatowski throwing themselves heartily on Napoleon's good will, a third under Czartoryski preferring to secure their country's resurrection through the Czar, who passed for an enlightened idealist. Here, as so often before, Napoleon concealed his intentions and movements behind the cloud of contradictory sentiments which he inspired in different classes of men by his assumed magnanimity, just as the octopus blinds all alike, the indifferent as well as the hostile, in the inky fluid with which it darkens the clear waters round about.

CHAPTER II

THE SEAT OF WAR—CHANGE IN THE CHARACTER OF NAPOLEON'S
ARMY—THE BATTLE OF PULTUSK—DISCONTENT IN THE GRAND
ARMY—HOMESICKNESS OF THE FRENCH—NAPOLEON'S MEASURES
OF REORGANIZATION—WEAKNESS OF THE RUSSIANS—THE ABILITY
OF BENNIGSEN—FAILURE OF THE RUSSIAN MANŒUVRES—NAPOLEON
IN WARSAW.

CHAP. II
1806–07

THE key to Napoleon's dealings with Poland is to be found in his
strategy; his political policy never passed beyond the first tenta-
tive stages, for he never conquered either Russia or Poland. After
Jena the Czar displayed great activity. In spite of being compelled to
detach eighty thousand men for service against Turkey, he had got together a second numerous army; Lestocq, with a corps of fifteen thousand Prussians, had joined him, and he was clearly determined to renew the war. For a time the French had no certain information as to
whether he would cross the Prussian frontier or not, and Napoleon at
first expected the city of Posen to be the center of operations. Before
long, however, it became evident that the Russians were drawing together on Pultusk. Displaying an astounding assurance as to the stability of his power in France, and without regarding the possible effect
upon conditions at home of a second war, at an enormous distance, Napoleon determined to meet them. With the same celerity and caution
as of old, the various French divisions were led first across the Vistula,
and then over the plains, until in the end of December they were concentrated before the enemy. During the three weeks consumed in these
operations much besides was done to strengthen the position of the
French and to assure their communications. The Russians were dislodged from Warsaw, and Thorn was besieged; the Vistula, Bug, Wkra,

Narew, and other rivers were bridged; and a commissary department
was organized. The seat of war was different indeed from any of those
to which Napoleon had hitherto been accustomed. It was neither as
densely settled nor as well tilled as Italy and Germany, the population
was far lower in the scale of civilization, and therefore fiercer. The
inhabitants could easily strip their villages of the little forage and
the few goods they possessed, and at that season the fields were bare.
The roads were of the worst description; the rivers were deep and
broad, often with swampy banks and treacherous bottoms. In these
circumstances it was almost impossible to secure reliable information,
for scouts and spies were alike at fault.

These new conditions of warfare were further complicated by a
change in the character of Napoleon's army. After Austerlitz many
men of German speech were to be found among the rank and file, and
after Jena the character of the soldiery grew more and more cosmopolitan. On the first appearance of the imperial eagles of France in Poland, Jerome was at the head of a whole corps of Würtembergers and
Bavarians; many Poles, Italians, Swiss, and Dutch were in others of
the French corps; and among the foreigners there were even Prussians
from beyond the Elbe. Some confusion was caused by this, and it was
not diminished by the fact that the French themselves had scarcely recovered from the orgies in which they had been indulging for the last
six weeks. Moreover, the determination of the Emperor to "conquer
the sea by land" had emphasized in his mind the necessity of an overwhelming superiority of numbers, and in November he demanded from
the French senate the eighty thousand conscripts who, according to
law, could not be drawn until September, 1807. This was the beginning of a fatal practice destined in the end to enervate France and de-
moralize the army. There was already little patriotism among the men,
except what served as a pretext for plunder; the homogeneity of purpose, principle, nationality, and age was soon to disappear.

In the preliminary operations this deterioration was not apparent.
The troops marched doggedly through the mud, worked hard when
called upon, and although their rations, which were supplied by rascally
contractors, were very bad and altogether different from those to which
they had become accustomed in the years just preceding, the men ate
them without murmuring. But when, on December twenty-sixth, they
joined battle, the old push and nerve seemed lacking. The preparations

had been made on the plan of concentration, but at the last moment Lannes was detached with his division to cut off the enemy's line of retreat over the Narew. Napoleon, as at Jena, believed the main army of his opponent to be where it was not, and he was incautious in thus dividing and weakening his force. Accordingly the battle had an irregular and indecisive character. Lannes came unexpectedly upon the mass of the Russian army, two columns forming the center and right, and engaged them from ten in the morning until two in the afternoon. At that hour a reserve arrived under Gudin, and attacked the Russian right. But Bennigsen, the commander of that column, had ready a fresh reserve, and with its aid the newcomers were repulsed. Lannes, who had simultaneously made a final onset, was also beaten off by the superior force of his enemy. On the same day, Murat, Davout, and Augereau reached the neighboring village of Golymin, expecting to find the Russian center there; on the left wing, at Neidenburg, Ney stood face to face with Lestocq and his Prussians. There was nothing but skirmishing at either place, for the French emperor could not drag his artillery through the mud swiftly enough to make it tell at the right time, and both Prussians and Russians drew slowly off. Soult was to have repeated the turning manœuvre as carried out before Jena, but the marching was so difficult, owing to a thaw, that he could not accomplish anything like the necessary distance.

The morning after this indecisive battle the entire Russian army was far away. For strategic reasons and for lack of provisions it had withdrawn to Ostrolenka. There was no pursuit. The natural question, Why? is still unanswered. Some declare that the French troops were too weary and bad-tempered; others, that Napoleon, in view of the quagmires to which the roads were now reduced, dared not abandon his base of supplies, as he was accustomed to do in summer weather and in fruitful lands. There is still a third answer, that nothing was to be gained; for of what use were the few miles of bare, flat land which the army, putting forth its utmost exertions, might have been able to traverse? All these reasons have validity. There was discontent among the soldiers, for there was no booty; not even a soldier's common comforts could be found. For the first time men of the line shouted insults after the Emperor, and with impunity; even the faithful guard indulged in double-meaning quips, but they on the other hand were at the proper time soundly berated. "The short campaign of fifteen days,"

MARSHAL MICHEL NEY

DUKE OF ELCHINGEN, PRINCE OF THE MOSKOWA

FROM THE DRAWING BY MEISSONIER

wrote one of them, " made us ten years older." There was also danger in advancing beyond reach of the commissary department,—deficient and contemptible as it was in the hands of unscrupulous speculators,— and there was indeed little to be gained by such a pursuit as was possible, except prestige, which at that moment and at that distance from France was not a valuable commodity.

This element of distance from home was weighty. In far-off Egypt and Syria, French soldiers had fought bravely ; an ideal will carry even the commonest Frenchman far, and they then believed themselves to be fighting for a principle. But since the armies of France had begun to fight for booty and glory, they must have both. Of the former there was little or none at all in the lands they now occupied ; the latter could be enjoyed only in the jubilations of their kinsfolk ; and although no account of any battle was more beclouded than that of Pultusk which the Emperor sent to Paris, the approbation of the fatherland could not reach Poland until long afterward, and in tones that were low and almost inaudible. It is an old French saying that next to the kingdom of heaven France is the most beautiful land, and every Frenchman believes it. The Emperor himself said that his French soldiers were unfitted for distant expeditions by their yearnings for home. In his mind, therefore, the one essential thing to restore the spirits of his men was rest. This opinion was strengthened when he endeavored to visit the posts. Although his carriage stuck in the mud and a saddle-horse could scarcely make its way, yet he got far enough to see that his men were suffering and destitute.

The measures adopted to secure a period of comfort and repose for the army were, unlike those taken for the campaign, apparently adequate. The Emperor proceeded at once to station the various corps along the Vistula, with provision and munition depots behind them. The commissary department was thoroughly overhauled and much improved. The line ran from Warsaw northwestward through Poland into Prussia, to the river's mouth near Dantzic. Bernadotte had eighteen thousand men ; Ney, sixteen thousand ; Soult, twenty-eight thousand ; Augereau, eleven thousand ; Davout, twenty thousand ; Lannes, eighteen thousand ; Murat, fourteen thousand ; and the guard numbered fifteen thousand—a total of about a hundred and forty thousand men. As conscripts and troops from various garrisons came in, a new corps of twenty-three thousand men was formed, and placed under the command of Lefebvre. At the same time, from his headquarters at Warsaw, the Emperor proceeded with the organization of a government for Poland, and with the training of her national guard. The two Russian columns had withdrawn to Szczyn, where they united under the command of Bennigsen, and the Prussians were at Angerburg under Lestocq. This left open the way to Königsberg, and early in January, 1807, Ney, overpowered by the temptation to relieve the miseries of his men, and to make a stroke on his own account by seizing the capital of East Prussia, set out from Neidenburg without orders, leaving Bernadotte's position at Elbing much exposed. Lestocq, however, managed to block Ney's path until the Russians under Bennigsen arrived and compelled the French general to return with his men to their quarters. Napoleon administered a severe reprimand; and well he might, for the advantage thus offered to the Russians had tempted Bennigsen to move, and the Russian army, once afoot, seemed determined to remain so. In this way were destroyed Napoleon's excellent calculations for the season of absolutely essential repose.

The action of Pultusk had made clear two serious defects in the efficiency of Russia's force. During the battle, Kamenski, the general-in-chief, a martinet and disciple of routine, had twice given the order for retreat, and it was Bennigsen's disobedience which made the conflict so indecisive that Russia claimed it as a victory. If a victory, it was a barren one, because a weak and venal administration of the commissary department had deprived the soldiers of sustenance at the critical moment. Kamenski, who was seventy-six years old, was retired on the ground of his health, and Bennigsen succeeded him, but the bad commissary administration was not remedied. The Russian army was strong in regular infantry, but weak in well-disciplined cavalry, although the latter defect was largely supplied by the Cossacks, a peculiar body of riders from the Volga and the Don, who paid the rental of their lands to the crown by four years' military service at their own charges. Then, as now, they fought with barbaric ferocity; they attacked in open formation, each man for himself, and gave no quarter until the Czar offered a ducat for every live Frenchman. They were known to ride a hundred miles in twenty-four hours, and their services in pursuing an enemy were invaluable.

The one remarkable and unique feature of the Russian army in every branch of the service has ever been its personal devotion to the Czar.

This feeling is a compound of religious fervor, patriotism, and dynastic loyalty; these elements, welded inseparably, form a sentiment of tremendous strength, which is a fair substitute for enlightened patriotism. The case is different with the Tatar hordes from Central Asia, who fight only for plunder, and at a pinch are often utterly unreliable. At this time both Cossacks and Tatars were in the field, the former in considerable numbers. The appointment of Bennigsen as commander-in-chief, and the results of Pultusk, awakened great enthusiasm among his hungry soldiers, who were now clamorous for a decisive battle. He had ninety thousand men,—at least on paper,—and was not disposed to leave the French in peace to recruit their numbers and physical strength in comfortable winter quarters. Unlike the Prussian officers, he had learned the lessons of recent campaigns, and had the strength of his character been equal to the cleverness of his strategy, he would have been a fair match for Napoleon. Moreover, the King of Prussia, shut up in Königsberg with a few thousand men, was in a most precarious situation, both Ney and Bernadotte being within striking distance. Finally, the garrison of the fortress at Graudenz was dependent on the precarious supplies which they received as Lestocq found an opportunity to send them.

Very soon, therefore, the Cossacks were sent out to scour the country. In their repeated skirmishes with the French light cavalry they showed such daring and address that their foes became timid and cautious. In this way the movements of Bennigsen's army were successfully concealed, and he hoped by a swift march to overtake and destroy Ney's isolated division; if successful he would secure access to Dantzic and a connection with Graudenz, Kolberg, and other fortresses, which would give him a position strong enough to jeopardize that of Napoleon at Warsaw. Accordingly, with about sixty-five thousand men he began a rapid and circuitous march northwesterly and around behind the impenetrable belt of dark forests, past Lake Spirding to Heilsberg, where he found Ney in full retreat on January twenty-second. But he had overestimated the strength of his Russians; they were too exhausted to strike quickly. Frost had set in, snow had fallen, and both Ney and Bernadotte made their escape to Gilgenburg, the latter after defeating the Russian advance-guard in a skirmish at Mohrungen. Bennigsen was compelled to retire in order to recruit the strength of his men.

The Emperor of the French was still at Warsaw. The Polish capital was gay and frivolous. New hopes had awakened the spirit of folly in the aristocracy, and the "liberator," now at the very height of his physical power, was often conspicuous in the revels. In the intervals of his serious labors Napoleon gave way to a life of sensuality, and the women were prodigal of their charms. One of them was the well-known Countess Walewska, a beautiful woman, who while yet a child had been forced into wedlock with an aged nobleman. She was now made to feel that the future of her country depended upon her captivating Napoleon, for he had singled her out as the most beautiful of all the crowd which pressed around him on his entry. Indignant when the proposition was first made, she finally listened to the flabby morality of her friends, and gave an unwilling consent. It is thought that her child was the first born to Napoleon, and that this fact, combined with his disgust for Josephine's incessant and inconsistent outpourings of jealous complaint as to his conduct, had much to do with his attitude concerning the political advantages of the divorce. Such was the young Polish noblewoman's eventual devotion to the father of her child, that throughout his subsequent life in Europe she ran every risk to be near her idol, and actually followed him to Elba.

A CARBINEER

CHAPTER III

CHECK TO THE GRAND ARMY: EYLAU

NAPOLEON'S PREPARATIONS — HIS CLEVER STRATEGY — THE PLAN DIS-
COVERED BY THE RUSSIANS — THE ARMIES AT EYLAU — FAILURE
OF NAPOLEON'S TACTICS — THE BATTLE INDECISIVE — THE FRENCH
ARMY DEMORALIZED — NAPOLEON'S ANXIETY — HIS ARMY IN WIN-
TER QUARTERS — THE EMPEROR'S ACTIVITY — REARRANGEMENT OF
HIS FORCES — AN ENVOY FROM THE SHAH OF PERSIA — REINFORCE-
MENTS FROM FRANCE AND GERMANY — THE NEUTRALITY OF AUSTRIA.

IT was not a very rude shock to his sensuous ease, however, when on
January twenty-seventh, 1807, Napoleon received the news of Bennigsen's march. In a general way he had been aware for some days
that the enemy was moving, but he believed they had no other intention than to derive what immediate advantage could be had from Ney's
rashness. In the absence of fuller information he had not changed his
opinion, but the army was nevertheless put in readiness, the trains were
equipped, and orders were issued for temporarily abandoning the siege
of Dantzic and for the complete occupation of Thorn. This step was
taken, as a glance at the map will show, to insure a new line of connection with Posen and Berlin, directly in front of his base, in case the ob-
lique one he was holding between Warsaw and Bartenstein should be
endangered by a flank movement of the Russians.

Believing that Bennigsen's plan was to reach Elbing and defend his
communication with Dantzic, Napoleon issued orders on January twenty-seventh for a countermarch in that direction, to engage him either
there or farther to the eastward. The orders given next day to Davout
and Augereau show that by swift movements he hoped to attack at
Willenberg, break through Bennigsen's center, and scatter his forces
right and left. Lannes had been taken ill after Pultusk, and was still

an invalid; Savary was therefore put in command of his well-tried corps, to bear the brunt of the battle. His business was to cover the line of the Narew for the purpose of assuring freedom of action to the main French army, and with that end in view to attack the Russian corps under Essen, which was menacing it. Three days after the orders

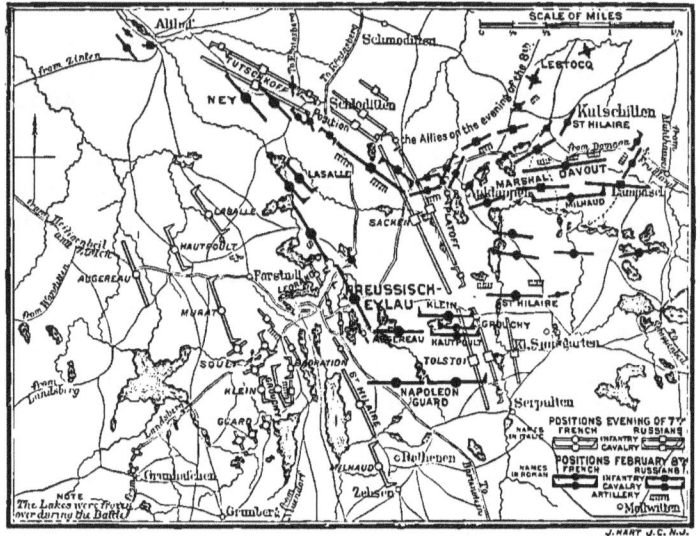

MAP OF THE BATTLE OF EYLAU.

of Napoleon were given, his army of a hundred thousand men was in position on a line running in general east and west within the space bounded by Willenberg, Gilgenburg, Mlawa, and Przasnysz, with one reserve of forty thousand on the left, to prevent the loss of Thorn, and another of fourteen thousand on the right. Everything was in readiness for an advance under the most advantageous circumstances, to take Bennigsen by surprise, strike him on his flank, and close the campaign in a single battle. On January thirty-first the final orders were issued for the advance, and the march began. As in Franconia, on the eve of Jena, it seemed as if the victory were already assured, won by the marvelous moving of great bodies of men, this time in the depth of winter.

On what a slender thread hang the fortunes of war! That day a French courier carrying to Bernadotte a particularly detailed account

of the Emperor's plan, and orders to advance to Gilgenburg, was caught
by the Cossacks. The precious papers were in Bennigsen's hands next
morning. The Russian troops were still in a wretched condition, badly
clothed, and sustaining life by marauding; moreover, they numbered
but sixty-five thousand, Lestocq not yet having come in from Mohrungen. The Russian general saw how he was entrapped, and that he
could escape only by a swift retreat. His conduct of the movement was
masterly, and on February sixth, though the French columns were not
far behind, he had reached Heilsberg. During the day the Russian rear-
guard was driven in, and Bennigsen, marching all night, found himself
next morning before the town of Eylau, or, more precisely, Preussisch-
Eylau, the spot he had selected for a desperate stand in defense of Königsberg. The Russian rear-guard was again overtaken, this time at
Landsberg, where Murat arrived with his cavalry on the morning of the
seventh. All day the Russians slowly resisted him, fighting bravely
under Prince Bagration, and receding steadily as far as Eylau, which
they held by a stubborn stand until induced to evacuate it voluntarily
by the considerations of gathering darkness and a foe superior in numbers. Their loss during the day was upward of two thousand. When
night fell the Russian lines were a short distance behind Eylau, and
stretched two miles, from Serpalten on the left to Schloditten on the
right. Lestocq, coming up with his Prussians, had reached Rositten,
between nine and ten miles away, where he received orders to hurry
onward. The French held the town of Eylau; in and near it were the
troops of Murat, Soult, Augereau, and just in their rear the Emperor
with the guard. Ney was farther to the north and west on the left,
with orders to cut off Lestocq.

When day broke on February eighth the general arrangement of the
hostile lines was such as to favor neither. Soult was before the town
on the French left, Augereau in the center, and Saint-Hilaire with one
division of Soult on the right. Behind the two latter was Murat with
the cavalry; in the rear, on rising ground, was the guard under Bessières as a reserve. Davout was far out on the right near Bartenstein.
The total number of French on the ground was about eighty thousand.
The Russian right was commanded by Tutschkoff, the center by Sacken,
the left by Ostermann-Tolstoi; their reserve was behind the center, under Doctoroff and Prince Galitzin. Their total number was about
fifty-eight thousand, but they were superior to their enemy in artillery.

Between the armies, in a low plain, lay several frozen ponds, and the ground was covered with snow. Napoleon's plan was to send Davout around the Russian left flank, while Saint-Hilaire engaged Tolstoi. Augereau and the cavalry were to be hurled against the center and to push toward the enemy's right; the combined onset would roll up Bennigsen's entire line and result in a rout; Ney would intervene, and make the battle not only decisive, but annihilating.

The combination did not work out correctly. It was a raw and bitter day; during the morning there were occasional snow-flurries, and at midday a heavy downfall. Bennigsen seized the initiative, and opened the battle by a cannonade. Napoleon, divining his plan, sent a messenger for Ney to come and strengthen Soult. At nine the Russian right advanced and drove in the French left, which was weak, to the town. At that moment the order was given for Augereau and Saint-Hilaire to move. In the driving snow they lost connection with each other, and the latter was repulsed by Russian cavalry, while Augereau's corps was almost destroyed by the enemy's center. The dashing horsemen of Galitzin reached the foot of the very hill on which Napoleon stood, and a panic seized all about him, not excepting Berthier and Bessières, who excitedly called up the guard to save their Emperor. The Emperor, however, remained calm, exclaiming, "What boldness! What boldness!" The pursuers fell back exhausted, and Murat in turn dashed with his cavalry toward the gap between the enemy's center and right. So worn out were both sides, however, that without a collision they ceased to charge, and began to fire.

About noon Davout at last arrived on the Russian left, and drove it from its position, while Saint-Hilaire again charged, and the two in combination effected the movement contemplated by the Emperor. In a few hours the Russians, who were receding in fair order and fighting fiercely, began to waver, and some of the formations broke into flight. In this crisis Scharnhorst arrived with five thousand Prussians; he had been compelled to make a long detour in order to avoid Ney, with whom Lestocq had been engaged. By nightfall the French were brought to a stand, and soon after they were driven back from the hamlets which they had seized in their advance. Night ended the fight. Ney had not received his orders until two in the afternoon, and arrived too late for service. The armies retained their relative positions, and both claimed the day. Neither had lost, neither had gained, the field. But the bat-

THE FOURTEENTH OF THE LINE AT EYLAU

tle was disastrous for both; from first to last the struggle had been desperate and bloody. The losses were virtually equal — about eighteen thousand men on each side. During the evening Napoleon began to arrange a retreat; in fact, Davout was about to begin it when he learned that there was a great commotion in the enemy's bivouac. Advancing as far as possible, the marshal put his ear to the ground and distinctly noted a diminishing rumble, which convinced him that the Russians were withdrawing. This was an agreeable surprise, and Napoleon, when informed of the fact, ordered his army to stand fast. The morning light displayed an abandoned Russian camp.

It is impossible to tell which army was in the worse plight; both were in the utmost distress. Augereau had been wounded, and, though not disabled, had left the field. This brought down on him the commander's displeasure, and inasmuch as his corps was nearly annihilated, it was disbanded; some of his regiments were virtually destroyed. The living were gaunt, exhausted, and ill with hunger; an eye-witness declared that but for the arrival, about noon, of some Jewish traders from Warsaw with four tuns of brandy, thousands would have perished from cold and fatigue. The dead were strewn thick over the field, and in some places were piled in heaps. On the white background of a Northern winter the carnage was terribly apparent; the prowlers who skulked from place to place in search of booty could be distinguished in all directions. Marauding began on a frightful scale, discipline was slackened by misery, and for miles around thousands of wretched soldiers stripped the scarcely less wretched peasantry of their few remaining bits of property.

The army was eager to be gone from these sickening sights. But Bennigsen had technically admitted defeat by his withdrawal, which the Prussians characterized as "a sin and a shame." Napoleon, therefore, waited to secure his victory, and formally despatched a few parties in pursuit. Murat advanced to within touch of Bennigsen, who had taken his position under the walls of Königsberg. At the same time the Emperor dictated a glowing account of the French triumph and of the admirable condition of the army. It was at once despatched for publication in the official journals of Paris. Soon afterward, on February thirteenth, a messenger carried to Frederick William proposals for either an armistice or a separate peace on most favorable terms. In these Napoleon set forth that the relation of Prussia to Russia was mere vassalage, and that her rehabilitation as an independent power was essential to the peace of Europe, agreeing to restore her lands as far as the Elbe, and saying that as to Poland he cared nothing whatever. The confident feeling of the allies was shown by the Prussian king's prompt refusal to accept such overtures, and by his determination to abide by the issue. On the other hand, the mere fact of the proposition was evidence of Napoleon's anxiety. It is said on good authority that the French emissary verbally offered the complete restoration of Prussia if she would desert her ally.

Stern necessity would wait no longer on Napoleon's bravado; in a few days his troops withdrew to the table-land behind the river Passarge. There they found better cantonments, but the food was neither better nor more abundant. The Emperor had only a thatched hovel for his headquarters at Osterode, and, as he wrote to his brother Joseph, lived in snow and filth, without wine, brandy, or bread. "We shall be in fine condition when we get bread," he said to Soult. "My position would be fine if I had food; the lack of food makes it only moderate," he wrote, on February twenty-seventh, to Talleyrand. This was true, because now the army was more concentrated than before; and when headquarters were moved in the spring to Finkenstein the Emperor was more comfortable. The movements culminating in Pultusk clearly prove that Napoleon could not until then adapt his means to the novel conditions of warfare he found in Poland. But in the movements antecedent to Eylau there are, in spite of virtual defeat, a clear apprehension of the difficulties, and an evident ability to surmount them. While Bennigsen constantly assumes the offensive, Napoleon always seizes the initiative, and in the retreat his choice of the plateau around Osterode as a rallying-point displays a continued mastery of all the conditions.

Around the camp-fires there was, during the remaining months of winter, a passive endurance, mingled with some murmuring about the horrors caused by one man's ambition. The Emperor set his men an example of uncomplaining cheerfulness. His health continued as exuberant as it had been for the year past, and his activity, though no longer feverish, lost nothing of its intensity. Savary thought he outdid himself, accomplishing in one month what elsewhere would have been, even for him, the work of three. Mme. de Rémusat remembered to have heard him say that he felt better during those months than ever before or after. This vigor of body, combined with the same iron de-

THE FOUNDING OF THE LINE AT CASE

termination as of old, did indeed work miracles, and this in spite of the
fact that his indefatigable secretary, Maret, was long at the point of
death.

To remedy the blunder of having left Dantzic behind in the hands
of the Prussians, Lefebvre was despatched with his new corps to be-
leaguer it. Savary drove the Russians from the Narew and out of Ostrolenka; Mortier threatened Stralsund and stopped the Swedes, who,
as members of the coalition, were finally about to take an active share
in the fighting. To strengthen the weakened ranks of the invaders,
new levies were ordered in both Switzerland and Poland, while at the
same time some of the soldiers occupying Silesia and besieging her fortresses were called in. Both Neisse and Glatz were still beset by French
troops, but the siege of Kolberg was abandoned, and still further reinforcements thus became available. In the daily skirmishes which occurred at the outposts the fighting was sharp; but the Cossacks were
as saucy as ever, and the French light horse could bring in little news.
Meantime Russia's difficulties, of which Napoleon remained ignorant,
kept her from reinforcing her army to the proper size. Her credit was
so low that she could raise no money on her own account, and when
she applied to England for a subsidy, it was refused. The Czar was
consequently furious, and strained Russia's resources to the utmost;
but he could give Bennigsen no more than enough funds and men to
restore his original strength.

The arms of Russia had been fairly successful on the lower Danube,
for the Turks had been paralyzed by an unforeseen danger. Great
Britain had sent a fleet to Constantinople, and the Sultan, though he
immediately declared war against England, was terrified. But Napoleon's emissary, Sebastiani, engaged the English admiral in negotiations
until the shore batteries were sufficiently strengthened to compel the
British fleet to retire. Filled by this success with new enthusiasm for
his Eastern projects, the Emperor of the French devised and set on foot
a scheme for the alliance of Turkey and Persia in order to checkmate
the ambitions of either Russia or Austria. About the end of April an
envoy from the Shah arrived at Finkenstein. He was received with
great demonstrations, and France was delighted to see the kings of the
East seeking, as she believed, her Emperor's favor. Napoleon's information with regard to the Orient was detailed and accurate; his knowledge of the Eastern character was fraternally instinctive. A treaty

was easily negotiated in which France promised to drive Russia from Georgia and to supply Persia with artillery; in return the Shah was to break with England, confiscate British property, instigate the peoples of Afghanistan and Kandahar to rebellion, set on foot an army to invade India, and in case the French should also despatch a land force against India, he was to give them free passage along a line of march to be subsequently laid out, together with means of sustenance. None of the Emperor's achievements during this eventful winter shows more clearly than this how he could rise above the discouragements of a doubtful situation, and how sanguine his disposition was when his health was really good.

Throughout the late campaign the Emperor Francis had occupied a position of non-intervention and hesitating neutrality similar to that of Frederick William the year before. If he had intervened any time during the winter after Eylau, his will would have been imperative. But as Prussia had held off in his hour of need, leaving Napoleon untrammeled, so now he let Prussia drink of the same cup, and remained nominally neutral. Andréossy reported, however, that Austria's strength was being rapidly recruited, and that her preparations foreboded a renewal of hostilities. There was a new prime minister, Count Stadion, remarkable for his energy and insight. Napoleon immediately began to make propositions for an alliance, intended merely to gain time. As he had the previous year called for the conscripts of 1807, so he now demanded those for 1808. The Confederacy of the Rhine was summoned to supply fresh troops, and even Spain, in which there had recently been symptoms of serious uneasiness, was called on for a large contingent of auxiliaries. Before the close of negotiations with Francis, Napoleon had virtually doubled his army; the new levies were kept in Silesia and central Prussia, apparently as a reserve, but they were not far from the Austrian frontier.

On May twenty-sixth, in spite of a gallant and persistent defense by Kalkreuth, Dantzic, the queen fortress of the Baltic, capitulated. This made Lefebvre's force available to strengthen further the army which still lay behind the Passarge. Napoleon again offered Silesia to Francis, this time entire and outright, as the price of an alliance; he was even willing to make an exchange for Dalmatia. On April twenty-sixth, at Bartenstein, Russia and Prussia had signed a new treaty, according to which they bound themselves to make no separate peace, and agreed

FREDERICK WILLIAM III
KING OF PRUSSIA

that they would endeavor to unite the Scandinavian powers with England, Austria, and themselves for a general war of liberation. The Viennese cabinet was again divided on the question of renewing hostilities,
and in the end proposed its services as a mediator, provided that Poland
should remain divided and Turkey unmolested, and that German affairs
should be rearranged. Napoleon coquetted with this proposal until
Russia and Prussia gave their reply, which was not an assent to Austria's proposition, but a request for Francis's adherence to the convention of Bartenstein. When Austria's offer was thus refused the French
position was virtually secure as against her, at least for the season.
Shrewd onlookers could hardly credit their senses, and thought that so
far from Francis's policy being one of neutrality, it was a favor of the
highest importance to Napoleon. The fact was that Austria knew Prussia's weakness and had little confidence in Russia's strength. Moreover,
France had powerful friends in Vienna, where Andréossy was influential, and Austria's own preparations were not complete. It would be a
serious matter if she should conclude a treaty with two allies who might
be beaten before she could herself take the field. Hence nothing disturbed the impenetrable front of the Danube power; her own plans
were maturing slowly but surely, and while the enormous French reinforcements in central Europe were in a sense a menace, she threw a
strong military cordon upon the frontiers of Galicia, and haughtily held
aloof from anything likely to fetter her own ambitions.

CHAPTER IV

AN INDECISIVE VICTORY: FRIEDLAND

THE STATE OF FRANCE — REMEDIES PROPOSED BY THE EMPEROR — NA-
POLEON'S SELF-INDULGENCE — PERPLEXITIES OF BOTH COMBATANTS IN
POLAND — OPENING OF THE CAMPAIGN — HEILSBERG — FRIEDLAND —
THE RESULT INDECISIVE — THE STRATEGIC PROBLEM — THE STATES-
MAN'S POINT OF VIEW — THE ARMISTICE — NAPOLEON'S RESOLUTION
— THE CZAR'S OBLIGATIONS TO PRUSSIA — HIS ATTITUDE TOWARD
NAPOLEON.

THE situation in Paris was even less satisfactory to Napoleon than
that in the rest of Europe. Then, as now, France was too much
like one of those interesting creatures called by the pleasant scientific
name of cephalopod — all head except a few tentacles; so we say Paris,
and not France. Imperial interests rested on two supports, Paris and
the rest of the world. When Napoleon withdrew behind the Passarge,
not all the fictions which his fertile brain could devise and his busy
agents spread were sufficient to deceive the astute operators of the
Paris exchange. Accordingly, the price of French government bonds
went down with a serious drop; England having announced soon afterward that she meant to land a great army on the shores of the Baltic,
public confidence was further shaken. A year before, the French
nation had been startled by the premature demand for more French
youth; the new call to anticipate the conscription filled them with
consternation. These were grave matters, and the roads from Paris to
Osterode and Finkenstein continually resounded under the hoofs of
horses and the roll of wheels as messengers sped back and forth with
questions and replies. The nature of this correspondence shows how
perfectly the government of France was centralized in Napoleon's
person, even in his absence at such a distance: the whole gamut of
administration was run, from state questions of the gravest importance

down to the disposition of trivial affairs connected with the opera and its coryphées. As to reviving the finances, the Emperor was at his wits' end, and in a sort of blind helplessness he ordered the state to lend five hundred thousand francs per month to such manufacturers as would keep at work and deposit their wares in a government store-house as collateral; nor did he disdain such measures as the founding of one or two factories of military supplies, or even the refurnishing of the Tuileries, in which he requested the women of his family to spend their money freely.

Of course he was absurdly unsuccessful; scarcely less so than he was in his attempts to restore general confidence by the publication of inspired articles in the newspapers. The censorship was more rigid than ever, and Fouché was instructed to stop indiscreet private letters from the army. Nevertheless, with no great difficulty the senate was bullied into approving the new conscription, and the volatile people soon listened without alarm to the siren voice of their Emperor, which said these boys would be only a national guard, children obeying the law of nature, the objects of his own paternal care. Louis, who was governing Holland with reference to its own best interests, and order-ing the affairs of his family rigidly but admirably, received a severe and passionate reprimand from the Emperor for his economy. What was wanted was pay for the troops, plenty of conscripts, encouragement for the Dutch Catholics, and a giddy court where men would forget more serious things, and where the gay young Queen Hortense could make a display. " Let your wife dance as much as she wants to; it is proper for her age. I have a wife forty years old, and from the field of battle I recommend her to go to balls; while you want one of twenty to live in a cloister, or like a wet-nurse, always bathing her child." In the absence of her bogy, Mme. de Staël, who said she loved the gutters of Paris better than the mountain streams of Switzerland, reappeared in the suburbs of that city. When Napoleon heard of it he grew furi-ous, and gave orders to seize her as an intriguer, and to send her back to Geneva, by force if necessary. It was done, but an awful present-ment took possession of the Emperor that she had appeared like a crow foreboding a coming tempest. As if to compensate France for the loss of the exile's literary powers and those of her friends, many means were devised and tried for the encouragement of an imperial literature. In his assumed and noisy contempt for ideals, Napoleon displayed his

fear of them : the Academy was ordered to occupy itself with literary
criticism; when in public assemblies mention was made of Mirabeau or
other Revolutionary heroes, the speaker was to be admonished that
he should confine himself to their style and leave their politics alone ;
the schools were ordered to train the children in geography and in history, but the instruction must be confined to facts, and not be philosophical or religious.

Napoleon's worst qualities and his growing weaknesses were made
manifest this winter in two exhibitions of self-indulgence most far-
reaching in their results. The first bad symptom was his notorious
license, which brought from the Empress expressions of the bitterest
reproach. Growing old at forty-three, not forty, as Napoleon gallantly.
but untruthfully wrote to Louis, the aging Creole dismissed from
memory the sins of her own youth and middle age, while in jealous
fury she charged her husband not only with his adulteries, but with
crimes the mere name of which sullies the ordinary records of human
wickedness and folly. She would have followed the Emperor to Poland, but his repeated dissuasions, although honeyed, were virtual
prohibitions, and she dared not. His unfriendly annalist, Mme. de
Rémusat, says he retorted to all Josephine's charges that he needed
but one reply, the persistent I : "I am different from every one else,
and accept the limitations of no other." Her continuous weeping, he
wrote to his consort, showed neither character nor courage. "I don't
like cowards; an empress should have pluck." The second sign of
weakness was the growing neglect of detail in his work. Life has always been too short for a despot both to gratify his passions and at
the same time to be a beneficent ruler, even under the simplest conditions. On the recovery of Maret, the Emperor relaxed very much in
his personal attention to detail, while his secretary sought to drown a
domestic sorrow and scandal in a feverish activity still greater than
that which he had always displayed. This conjunction gave the secretary an eminence he had not hitherto reached, and made him thereafter a power behind the throne whose influence was dangerous to the
Empire, to France, and to the peace of Europe.

In spite of the enemy's numerical inferiority, Napoleon had been
thwarted at Eylau by the weather, by the unsurpassed bravery of the
Russian soldiers, and by the able tactics of Bennigsen. The latter had
not been worsted in the arbitrament of arms, yet the Emperor's char-

acter for resolution and energy had virtually defeated the Russians, and had given him not only a technical, but a real victory. Although he fell back and assumed the defensive, feeling that without enormous reinforcements and the capture of Dantzic he could not resume the offensive, yet nevertheless he had remained for four months unmolested by his foe. Bennigsen's perplexities were great. The Russian court was rent by dissensions, affairs at Constantinople were occupying much of the Czar's attention, and the force available for fighting in the North seemed too small for a decisive victory : he remained virtually inert. There was an effort late in February to drive the French left wing across the Vistula, but it failed. A few days later Napoleon in person made a reconnaissance on his right, and this show of activity reduced the opposing ranks to inactivity. He had proposed to resume hostilities on June tenth, and had by that time increased his strength on the front to one hundred and sixty thousand men, all well equipped and fairly well fed. The reserve army in central Europe was much larger; there were about four hundred thousand men, all told, in the field.

Meanwhile, however, the pleasant season had mended the roads and dried the swamps. The Russians were refreshed by their long rest, and, children of nature as they were, felt the summer's warmth as a spur to activity. Bennigsen had by that time about ninety thousand men, excluding the Prussians, who now numbered eighteen thousand. By his delay he had lost the services of his best ally, the inclement weather; but he had now come to a decision, and forestalling Napoleon's scheme, advanced on June sixth to the Passarge, against Ney's corps, which was the French advance-guard. Ney retreated, and the seventh was spent in manœuvers which resulted in uniting his corps with the main army. Bennigsen, having hoped to cut off and destroy his division before attacking in force, felt compelled, in consequence of failure, to retreat in turn, and this movement left Lestocq at a dangerous distance to the right. At this juncture Napoleon determined to assume the offensive himself. On the eighth he began to concentrate his troops, and took measures to find the enemy in order to force a battle. Bennigsen had withdrawn beyond the river Alle : Soult and Lannes, with Murat in advance, were sent up its left bank to Heilsberg; Davout and Mortier were to pass farther on, as part of a general movement to surround; Ney and the guard were held in reserve, while Victor was despatched to block Lestocq.

The first shock occurred on the morning of the tenth, in the neighborhood of Heilsberg; for Bennigsen had sent a considerable number of his troops back over the river to feel the enemy. The Russians were slowly driven across the plain, fighting fiercely as they went, until by six in the evening they reached the heights near the town, which had been intrenched. Here they turned, and for five hours hurled back one advancing French column after another until eleven o'clock at night, when, fortunately for the attacking troops—so at least thought Savary, who was with them,— it grew too dark, even near the

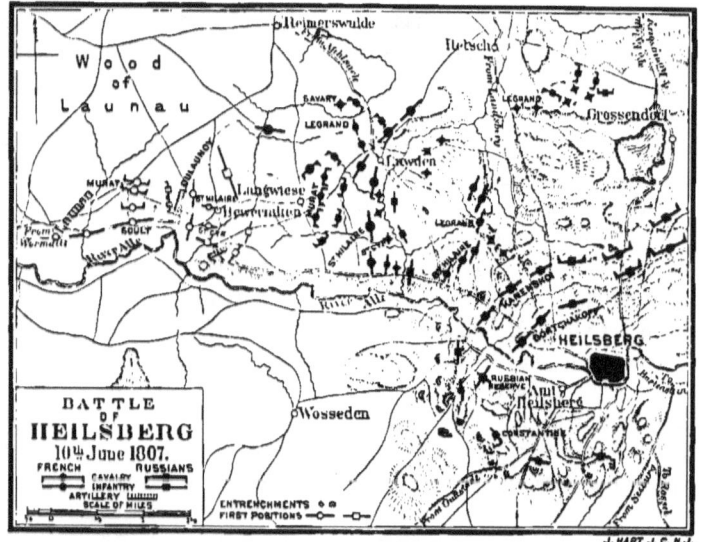

summer solstice and in those high latitudes, to fight longer. Next morning Napoleon woke after his bivouac and looked to see his enemy gone, as at Pultusk and Eylau. But this time a repetition of that pleasant experience was denied him. His losses had been so serious the day before that he spent the eleventh in manœuvers, further concentrating his army before Heilsberg, and despatching Davout to throw himself between Lestocq and Bennigsen, thus turning the latter's right and checking the former, if all went well. This movement determined the character of the whole campaign. It had the desired effect, and on the morning of the twelfth the trenches in front of him were empty. The

Russians had stolen away, and for two days they steadily retreated down the Alle in the general direction of Königsberg, until on the evening of the thirteenth they reached Friedland.

Bennigsen had expected to retreat still farther, hoping to reach Wehlau, and cross to the right bank of the Pregel for a strong defensive position before Königsberg. Lestocq with the Prussians was well forward on the extreme right toward that place. But at three in the morning of June fourteenth the head of Lannes's column appeared before Friedland, and the Russian commander, supposing he had to do with a single division, turned, and crossing to the left bank of the Alle, passed through Friedland in order to meet his enemy in the open. His evident intention was to follow the Napoleonic plan of overwhelming the attacking divisions one by one as they arrived. His right wing was stationed in the rear of the hamlet of Heinrichsdorf, his left rested on a forest known as the Sortlack. When his arrangements were completed it was nine o'clock in the morning. What information he had is unknown, but what he did remains inexplicable. Starting to seize Heinrichsdorf, he was, after a short conflict, repulsed; for Lannes had stretched his line far to the left for the same purpose, and had been reinforced by Mortier's vanguard. Bennigsen withdrew about noon to his first position, and stood there in idleness for three long hours, exchanging useless volleys with his foe. Having his entire force already on the field, he remained absolutely inactive while the enemy formed their line. In respect to his having massed his forces before the French could form, his position was exactly parallel to that which the latter had occupied at Jena with regard to the Prussians, and which was used by Napoleon with such vigor for a flank attack. But Bennigsen lacked the promptness and insight necessary to use his advantage, and the long delay was decisive. In the interval, Ney, Victor's artillery, and the guard arrived; at three the Emperor issued his orders for forming the line; and two hours later he gave the signal for Ney to attack on the right. The Russians had but shortly before learned that the main French army was in front of them, and were beginning their retreat with the intention of recrossing the Alle, many having entered Friedland, which lies on the left bank of the stream. In the first rush toward the town, Ney was repulsed with dreadful loss; but as Ney's corps rolled back to right and left, Dupont appeared with Victor's first division in the very middle of the breaking lines, and at the same moment Sénarmont pressed forward close to the Russian ranks with all Victor's artillery,—thirty-six pieces,—and began to pour in grape with shrapnel. This routed the enemy, who fled through the town and over the stream; but their right wing, being thus turned into the rear-guard, was caught by Lannes before it reached the crossing, and checked. The wooden bridge was set in flames, and before nightfall that portion of the Russian army which had not yet crossed was virtually annihilated.

About eighty thousand French and about fifty-five thousand Russians took part in this battle; the former lost seven thousand men, the latter sixteen thousand, with eighty field-pieces. It was the only one of Napoleon's great engagements in which he admitted his numerical superiority to his enemy. The same day Soult and Davout, with Murat's cavalry, drove Lestocq into Königsberg, and prepared to invest the town. But Lestocq's troops, with the garrison and the court, escaped, flying for refuge toward the Russian frontier. Bennigsen collected at Allenburg the troops he had saved, and, retreating in good order, crossed the Niemen at Tilsit four days later. He then had the option of awaiting Napoleon, who was close behind, or of making peace, or of withdrawing into the interior beyond the enemy's reach, as Alexander had done after Austerlitz. As a matter of fact, he confessed utter defeat. "This is no longer a fight, it is butchery," he wrote to the Czar's brother, the Grand Duke Constantine. "Tell the Emperor what you will," he said again, "if only I can stop the carnage."

The campaign of Friedland shows either less genius or more than any other of Napoleon's victories, according to the standpoint from which it is judged. If he is to be regarded throughout its duration merely as a general, then his conduct shows comparatively little ability. He came on his enemy where he did not expect a battle. Although he had ample time to evolve and execute an admirable plan, and his loss was trifling compared with that of his opponents, yet, nevertheless, Friedland was a commonplace, incomplete affair. It compelled the foe to abandon Heilsberg, but it did not annihilate him or necessarily end the war. Bennigsen found all Russia behind him after his defeat: twenty-five thousand men came in from Königsberg, Prince Labanoff brought up the Russian reserves, and thus was formed a substantial army. A retreat with this force into the vast interior would have left Napoleon as a general just where he was before. This in-

FRANÇOIS-JOSEPH LEFEBVRE

DUKE OF DANTZIC

SPECIALLY ENGRAVED FROM THE PORTRAIT IN THE COLLECTION OF BARON DE CHLAPIES

effectual result was entirely due to a single deliberate move which terminated his scheme of surrounding and annihilating the foe—the detachment of Davout against Lestocq on the enemy's extreme right.

But when viewed from the statesman's point of view, Friedland appears in a very different light. It is a strange coincidence that in the month previous a rebellion of the Janizaries had deprived Selim III. of his throne, and that, Sebastiani's influence being thus ended, France's position in the Oriental question was utterly changed. The

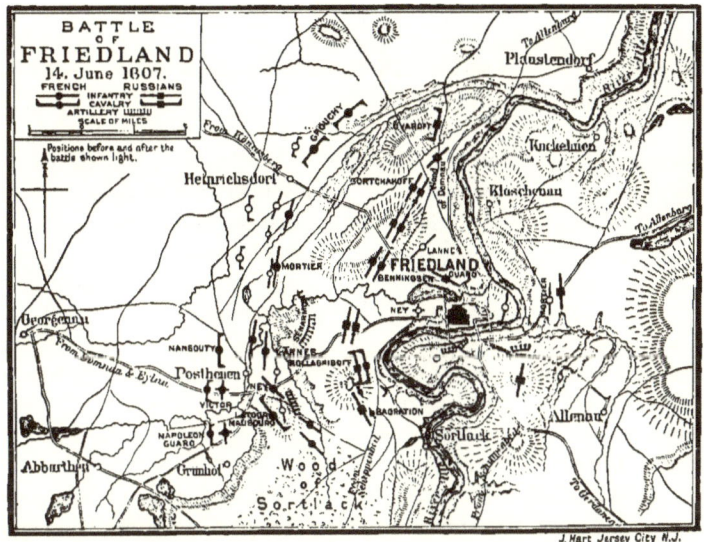

BATTLE
OF
FRIEDLAND
14. June 1807.
FRENCH　　RUSSIANS
INFANTRY
CAVALRY
ARTILLERY
SCALE OF MILES

Positions before and after the battle shown light.

J. Hart Jersey City N.J.

formal despatches announcing this fact did not reach Tilsit until June twenty-seventh or twenty-eighth, but there is a strong probability that it was known to Napoleon before the battle of Friedland. Is it possible that the Emperor intended Friedland to do no more than satisfy his army's eagerness for glory, and yet leave Alexander in a humor to unite with him for the gratification of those well-known Oriental ambitions of his which he had so recently seen jeopardized by the Franco-Turkish alliance and the consequent ascendancy of French influence at Constantinople? Such a hypothesis is by no means wild; nevertheless, a careful study of the campaign seems to prove that Napoleon, in suddenly changing from the defensive to the offensive, and so finding himself at Heilsberg face to face with defeat, took the quickest and easiest means to relieve a critical situation. It would have appeared something very much like bravado had Davout's corps penetrated between Lestocq's division and the Russian army, and thus have exposed itself to a rear attack. If the easy self-reliance Napoleon felt after a winter of robust health had been somewhat less, and if his intellectual acumen had been somewhat greater, the whole situation might have been foreseen and provided for. As neither was the case, he did as a general the best thing that was possible at the moment. Admitting this, we shall find the statesman making the most of the general's poor situation; for the treaty which followed Friedland is unique in the history of diplomacy.

There were forcible reasons on both sides for arriving at an understanding. It has been remarked that Napoleon never discharged the stings and darts of personal abuse at Alexander I. as he did at the persons of other enemies. When a proposition for an armistice was made by Bennigsen on June twenty-first, it was not only courteously but impressively accepted, and within a very short time things were moving as if the two emperors were no longer enemies, but rather as if they were already intimate friends, anxious to embrace. At least, even before their meeting, such was the attitude they assumed in their communications with each other and ostentatiously displayed to those about them. Some things are perfectly patent in the Czar's desire for peace. Prussia, although the principal in the fight, was but a feeble power. England, though reaping the harvest of Russia's commerce, had become niggardly in regard to subsidies, and had delayed the long-promised, much-vaunted Baltic expedition until it was useless. The King of Sweden was so hated by his own subjects that his efforts as an ally had been rendered almost futile. In Russia itself there was a strong party, led by the Grand Duke Constantine, which steadily denounced the war as one in the interest of strangers, and in it were included most, if not all, the Russian officers. It was evident that Alexander as an auxiliary would lose no prestige at home in withdrawing from a quarrel which was not Russia's, and in which he had more than paid any debt he owed to Prussia by the sacrifice in her behalf of his guards and of the flower of his army. Moreover, misery abounded among the survivors, and Russian finances were not exactly in a flour-

ishing condition. Such was the general discontent with the war that
men of importance — at least so it was said at the time — ventured to
remind Alexander of his father's violent death.

On the other side much also is clear. As the strategists say, Napoleon had won a battle, but not a victory, at Friedland. The situation
in Paris was highly unsatisfactory. The threatened English expedition
to the Baltic might arrive at any time. Contemptible as was Gustavus
of Sweden, he was in Pomerania with an Anglo-Hanoverian army of
ten thousand men. Most disquieting of all, there were movements
both of intellectual agitation and of active partizan warfare in Prussia
that presaged a speedy convalescence on her part. It is evident that an
alliance with Russia was better for France than one with Prussia as
regards both the Oriental and European plans of Napoleon. He therefore determined to suggest the most glittering prospects to Alexander's
messenger — nothing less than the partition of Turkey, and the Vistula
as the Russian frontier on the Baltic.

But all these reasons on both sides seem inadequate to explain
the extraordinary character of the events preliminary to the meeting of
the two emperors at Tilsit, of what occurred at that meeting, and of the
treaty there negotiated. When Bennigsen first proposed an armistice,
Napoleon demanded as a guarantee the three fortresses of Pillau, Kolberg, and Graudenz. His messenger returned with the reply that they
were not Russia's to give. Soon Duroc was despatched to the hostile
camp. Would the Czar make a separate peace? To do so would
be to betray Prussia by expressly violating the Bartenstein treaty.
Technically the document was invalid, for Austria had never signed
it, although she would gladly have done so when brought to face a
Franco-Russian alliance. Morally it would be base for Alexander to
negotiate separately, for Frederick William had refused a similar offer.
The young Czar, however, cared nothing for the royal Europe of
former days, and but little for the theory of a Western empire under
Napoleon. What he did care for was Russian influence in geographical
Europe under whatever name, for the dismemberment of Turkey, and
for the extension of his empire toward the west by the acquisition of
Finland from Sweden. Having failed to realize his purpose by a coalition of so-called legitimate sovereigns, and having heard the almost in-
credible suggestions which Napoleon had made to Prince Labanoff, his
messenger, he was overpowered by the temptation thus held out, and,

deserting Prussia, answered, "Yes." On the twenty-first an armistice
without serious guarantees was concluded between France and Russia;
but none was made with Prussia, for the terms offered to her were so
severe that, desperate as was her King, he could not endure the thought
of accepting them. She was no longer an equal with either France or
Russia, but a dependent on either and on both; her nomad court was
reduced to Frederick William, his minister Hardenberg, and a few followers who were here to-day and there to-morrow, wherever they felt
most was to be gained from the self-interest of either their former ally
or their conqueror. The Queen and royal family were at Memel, the
farthest outpost of Prussia's shattered domain.

The attitude of the Czar toward Napoleon was markedly different
from that of his predecessors in defeat. Frederick William's ancestor
had only a century before bought his title by supplying Prussian
troops to the German-Roman emperor, and, like Napoleon, had set
the crown on his own head. Francis I. of Austria was the grandson of
Maria Theresa, a powerful and masterful woman, who held her throne
in direct contravention of legitimist theories, because she had conquered
it. Both were nevertheless overpowered by the sense of their legitimacy and sacred aloofness. When Francis humiliated himself before
his conqueror after Austerlitz, his mien was distant and his salute
haughty; the miserable King of Prussia was, like him, dignified and
severe even in his beggary. The Czar was too close to the crime which
had set him on his throne to assume any airs of superiority with the
French Cæsar. Having taken the first step, he began to show a childish eagerness for a personal meeting with Napoleon. The Emperor
was far from averse, and made a formal proposal to that effect, which
was promptly accepted; the intercourse between French and Russian
officers grew warmer and closer every day, and the arrangements for an
interview between the would-be Eastern and Western emperors were
soon completed.

NAPOLEON DECORATING THE RUSSIAN GRENADIER AT TILSIT

CHAPTER V

NAPOLEON AND ALEXANDER AT TILSIT

The Floating Pavilion — Emperor, Czar, and King — The Two
Principals — Their Relation to Frederick William — A Diplo-
matic Novelty — Napoleon's Motives — Great Britain and the
World's Commerce — The Orders in Council — Napoleon's De-
crees — Russia as an Ally — The Ministers and the Negotiations
— Imperial Amusements — The Fate of Turkey — The Two
Friends — Work After Play.

ON the morning of June twenty-fifth, 1807, there lay anchored in
the middle of the Niemen, before Tilsit, a pavilion ingeniously
constructed by French soldiers from boats and boards. It was gaily
decorated, according to the taste of their country, with flags and gar-
lands. The front bore a large monogram composed of the letters N
and A interlaced. Within were two comfortable rooms, one for the
sovereigns, one for their suites. At a signal two skiffs put out, one
from each shore, amid the mingled cheers of the French and Russian
guards, drawn up in view of each other across the intervening stream.
The dull roar of cannon intoned the tidings of reconciliation. In one
boat was Alexander, suitably arrayed in uniform; in the other was
Napoleon, wearing the traditional gray coat and undress hat. The
Emperor of the French was first on board the float, and received his
guest with all that winning grace which he could so well command.
After a formal embrace he began an informal conversation, which then
continued without a break as the two schemers withdrew to the apart-
ment arranged for their interview. The staff, at a respectful distance,
could catch nothing of what was said; and although the interview
lasted nearly two hours, no words of it are known except the opening
phrases, reported by Napoleon himself. "Sire," remarked the Czar, "I

shall second you against the English." " In that case," was the reply, "everything can be arranged, and peace is made." Apparently nothing occurred to disturb the amiability of either monarch. It was doubtless agreed that they should form a dual alliance, absolute and exclusive. "I have often slept two in a bed," the suave but inelegant Napoleon was heard to say at a subsequent meeting, "but never three." Savary declared that the smiling and complacent young Czar thought the remark delightful. The meaning of the riddle, if riddle there be, was, of course, that Austria could no longer count as an equal in the Continental Olympus, the membership of which was thus reduced to two.

The Czar's conscience smote him in regard to his desertion of Prussia, but with no great effort he obtained material concessions for her from his new ally. The same afternoon an armistice was arranged with Frederick William, by the terms of which he temporarily kept his strong places in Silesia and Pomerania; but his propositions for an alliance were incontinently rejected. Next day there was another meeting on the same raft, but this was tripartite, for the King of Prussia was present. Napoleon was blunt and imperious, reproaching Frederick William with the duplicity of his policy, vindictively (the descriptive word he used himself), and with emphasis, demanding Hardenberg's dismissal. At parting he invited Alexander to dinner, but ostentatiously omitted to include Frederick William in the request. It was agreed that to expedite the final negotiations the three monarchs should remain on the ground; one half the town of Tilsit was neutralized and divided into three portions, each of the three parties to take up his residence in one. This closed the preliminaries, and the two emperors returned with mutual satisfaction to the respective sides of the river from which they had come. The sensations of Frederick William, who accompanied Alexander, must have been those of a patient under a capital operation in surgery. That very afternoon the Czar removed to the quarter of Tilsit appropriated to him. The King of Prussia took lodgings in the house of a miller, but spent only a part of each day in them, preferring the melancholy solitude of the neighboring hamlet of Piktupönen, where he and Hardenberg had last alighted.

Alexander was now thirty years of age, sanguine, ambitious, impressionable, and mature in proportion to his years. His features were well formed on Slavic lines, his look was sympathetic, and his form elegant. The many graces of his mind and person were natural. "My friend," wrote Napoleon to Josephine on the twenty-fifth, " I have just met the Emperor Alexander. I have been much pleased with him ; he is a very handsome, good young emperor; he has more intelligence than is generally thought." Napoleon himself was only eight years older, but his mind was more penetrating and adroit by a whole generation. The classic cast in his features, which only a few years before made sculptors mold him like the statue of the young Augustus, had nearly disappeared. A complete transformation had been produced in his bodily appearance by the robust health he had for some time enjoyed. He had become more of a primitive Italian and less of a Roman. His skin was now clear and of a rich, dark tint. His powerful frame was fully developed, and while fat, he was not obese; the great head sat on a neck which was like a pillar in thickness and strength. His expression was slightly sensuous about the mouth and chin, but his eyes were quick and penetrating in their glance. It was rarely that his gaze was intent. The good manners and polished courtesy in which he indulged at this time were an unwonted luxury.

Cobenzl said that the last step but one to universal conquest was to divide the world between two. At that moment there was little doubt as to which of these two would ultimately survive. Alexander was impressionable and eager for friendship. He was flattered by the attentive and considerate manner of the greatest man in Europe. The glittering, intoxicating generalities of Napoleon attracted his aspiring mind, while the fascination of the Emperor's person strongly moved his heart. On the other hand, the influence of the Czar on the Emperor was substantial. Beneath his frank and chivalric manners, behind his enthusiasm and romanticism, lay much persistence and shrewd common sense. The advantages which he gained were granted by Napoleon mainly from motives of self-interest, for Russia, strong, was the best helper in reducing Austria to impotence; nevertheless, they were secured largely through personal influence, and were substantial advantages which might be permanent in case of disaster to a single life. Frederick William was only two years younger than Napoleon. His development had been slow; he was well meaning but dull, proud but timid. Though destined to see a regeneration of Prussia under his own reign, he had as yet done nothing to further it, and in an access of resentment had declared a war in which she had been virtually annihilated. His former ally insisted that he should occasionally attend the conferences, but his presence was distasteful to Napoleon. Thus he sat, dejection and despair stamped on his homely face; haughty, yet a suppliant; a king, yet only by sufferance. Fortunately his queen, Louisa, the woman of her day, beautiful, virtuous, and wise, came finally to his support. Her hopes were destined to be rudely shattered, and her charm was to be used in vain; but it was her presence alone which gave any dignity to Prussia at Tilsit.

Both from the place and circumstances, from the station and character of the persons negotiating, as well as from the nature of the results, the meeting at Tilsit is the most remarkable in the history of diplomacy. The motives which disposed Napoleon to an armistice were plain enough; those which determined his later conduct can only be divined. Prussia had seemed to the French liberals of the Revolution to belong by nature to their system: they were quite as angry with her persistent neutrality as was either Austria or England, both of whom thought she should adhere to them, if only for self-preservation. Napoleon's repeated but vain attempts to secure a Prussian alliance before Jena, or a separate negotiation afterward, rooted this traditional bitterness in his mind. To secure the prize for which he was fighting he had only two courses open: either to restore Poland as the frontier state between the civilization of his empire and the semi-barbarism and ambitions of Russia, or else to negotiate with Russia herself.

The former course meant an interminable warfare with Russia, Austria, and Prussia, at a distance of fifteen hundred miles from Paris; for Russia would fight to the death rather than lose the only possessions which put her into the heart of Europe, and thus be relegated to the character of an Asiatic power. The Emperor of the French had already seen after Eylau how untrustworthy the grand army was, even in Poland; if dejected and insubordinate there, as he may well have recalled was actually the case, what would it be on the banks of the Dnieper, in the plains of Lithuania? Such considerations probably determined not only the fact of peace, but its character. In order to secure what he had gained in western, southern, and central Europe England must be brought to terms. Russia must therefore not only be an ally, but a hearty ally: as the price of her subscription to the Berlin decree, and the consequent closing of her harbors to English shipping, she could gratify any reasonable ambition, and might virtually dictate

THE GORGEOUS DRUM-MAJORS

FROM THE WATERCOLOUR BY F. GOELLER

her own terms. With an engine in his hands as formidable as Russia's adhesion to his commercial policy, he could act at the nick of time,— which, as he declared at this very season to Joseph, was the highest art of which man is capable,— could destroy England's commerce, and in a long peace could consolidate the empire he had already won. His empire thus consolidated, he would be virtual master of half the solid earth in the Eastern hemisphere. If ambition should still beckon him on, he would still be young; he could then consider the next step to universal empire.

It may safely be said that Great Britain was never more haughty than at this moment. Her king had turned the ministry of "All the Talents" out of doors; for after Fox's death the combination lost all dignity and power. The Duke of Portland was now prime minister. He was a blind but energetic conservative, his Toryism, unlike that of Pitt in his enlightened days, being of the sort which lay close to his sovereign's heart. England's monopoly of European commerce seemed assured: Sweden, Denmark, and the Hanse towns were the only important seafaring powers of Europe that retained a nominal neutrality, and it was only a question of time when they must accept terms either from France or from her. With every other European nation embroiled in the Napoleonic wars and deeply concerned for its own territorial integrity, the United States were her only real maritime rival, and she had bullied them into a temporary acquiescence in her interpretation of international law.

When colonies were first recognized as essential to the prosperity of European nations, the rule was universally observed that only the mother country could trade with her own. In 1756 France endeavored to break this rule by permitting neutral ships to engage in traffic between herself and her West Indian possessions. England at once laid down the "rule of 1756," that neutrals should not enjoy in time of war privileges of traffic which they were not permitted in time of peace; and this principle she was able to maintain more or less completely until 1793, when France declared war on her, and again invited neutral commerce to French colonial harbors. England, having regained her supremacy of the seas, reasserted in 1793 the rule of 1756, but nevertheless so modified it the following year that she permitted neutral traders to break in her own or in home harbors their voyages from or to colonial ports. In 1796 France notified all neutrals that she would treat them just as they permitted Great Britain to treat them, and in 1798 shut all her harbors to any vessel which had even touched at a British port. This state of affairs continued until the peace of Amiens. When war was renewed in 1803 between England and France the former again asserted the rule of 1756 as binding, while indirect trade between neutral ports and the ports of an enemy was again allowed, but under the new proviso that the neutral ship did not on her outward voyage furnish the enemy with goods contraband of war. This privilege of indirect trade was invaluable to American ship-owners, and for two years the ocean commerce of all Europe was in their hands. The fortunes they thus accumulated were enormous, while Great Britain saw her own manufactures displaced by those of Continental nations, and the colonies of her enemies prospering as never before. In 1805, therefore, she withdrew the privilege of indirect trade, and her flag being, after Trafalgar, the only belligerent one left on the ocean, proceeded both to enforce the new rule and to abuse the proviso concerning neutral vessels carrying contraband of war by ruthlessly exercising the right of search. Under the orders in council of September fifth, 1805, every neutral ship must be examined to see whether its lading was a cargo of neutral goods, or contained anything contraband. This could only mean that every American ship laden with other than American goods was to be seized; and in May of the following year, by the still more notorious order of the sixteenth, Great Britain declared that every European harbor from Brest to the mouth of the Elbe was blockaded. This was a distance of eight hundred miles, and even she had not ships enough to enforce her decree. Trafalgar had turned the heads of English statesmen.

This paper blockade was the challenge which called forth the Berlin decree from Napoleon. American ships, like those of the French, were for a time seized, searched, and detained by the British on the slightest suspicion that they were either leaving or were destined for a hostile port, while their sailors were pitilessly impressed. The government at Washington authorized reprisals, but American ship-owners found it more profitable to compromise than to resist, and Monroe came to an understanding with the English ministry; the prosperity of American shipping was again revived, and the merchants of the United States continued to prosper by carrying English wares under the American flag into harbors where the union jack was forbidden. By this evasion

Great Britain retained her commercial supremacy, and her prosperity was rather increased than diminished. She withheld a similar coöperation from Sweden and Russia until it was too late, her enterprise being chiefly concerned to open new channels for her commerce in Egypt and South America.

How was this leviathan, which was drawing the wealth of all Europe to its stores, and eluding or repelling all attack on its chosen element — how was this tyrant of the ocean to be slain? Clearly the Americans must be so harassed and annoyed that in the end the public spirit of the United States would be aroused to resent English control, and bid defiance to Great Britain's assumption of maritime supremacy. To this end the rigid enforcement of the Berlin decree would be well adapted in the long run, but in the interval much could be done: if its principle could be extended to the destruction of all smuggling, to the absolute exclusion of British commerce from the entire Continent—not only from the seaports, but from the markets—the end would be gained. With Russia's coöperation alone was this possible. Napoleon's present plan, therefore, was to secure France and the French Empire, as far as won, by compelling the world to a lasting peace through the immediate establishment of a counterpoise, the French and Russian empires against Great Britain, leaving time to do its perfect work of exasperating the rising naval power of the United States into open hostility against their parent land.

These, it seems, must have been the considerations which controlled the course of affairs at Tilsit. The deliberations were both formal, so called, and informal. At the former were present the three sovereigns with their ministers—Talleyrand for France, Kurakin and Labanoff for Russia, Kalkreuth and Goltz for Prussia; at the latter were sometimes all three of the monarchs, frequently only the two principals, for they found Frederick William a damper on their hilarity. The generals, the staff, and the men of the two great armies which had fought so bravely at Friedland harmonized in mutual respect; but the unwarlike King and his suite, both military and civil, were outsiders. Immediately after the formal and brilliant entry of Alexander into Tilsit, Napoleon began the exchange of prisoners, and despatched messengers commanding his forces in Germany to restore to their sovereign the territories of Mecklenburg, whose reigning house was kin to the Czar. For Frederick William there was scarcely a show of kindness — nothing, in fact, but a cold condemnation of Hardenberg, to whose influence, combined with that of the military party, the conqueror charged Prussia's declaration of war. This minister, banished at Napoleon's instance, was near by. It was a proposition outlined by him which brought forward the first vital question, the partition of Turkey. His sovereign's stateliest lands had been gained by the partition of Austria and of Poland; he now suggested that Russia and Austria should divide the Danubian principalities between them, that France should take Greece and her isles, and that Poland should be restored and given to the King of Saxony, who in turn should hand over his German domains to Prussia. The Czar accepted the paper, which was communicated to him as approved by the King, but kept silence.

A favorite amusement of the two emperors was playing with the French army. Napoleon delighted in the display of his condescension to the men, and in the exhibition of their enthusiastic affection for him. Their drill, their uniforms, the niceties of military ceremonial, the gorgeous drum-majors twirling their batons or marching in puffy state — every detail fascinated the Czar, whose house, said Czartoryski, was affected with the disease of paradomania.

At an opportune moment on one of these reviewing expeditions, Napoleon, surrounded by all the splendors of his power, was approached by a hurrying courier, who put into his hands despatches announcing the overthrow of the Sultan Selim. "It is a decree of Providence, announcing the end of Ottoman empire!" he cried. Thenceforth he talked incessantly of the Orient. As if inspired by prophetic fire, he sketched a missionary enterprise for the liberation and regeneration of Greece, and for the emancipation and reorganization of the lands and peoples on the Danube and in the Levant by distributing them among enlightened sovereigns. It was language identical with that which Catherine the Great employed to inspire her people and her descendants for Russia's policy. But the millennium must wait; for the present the barbarous Turks must be driven back, not by force, but by a steady, continuous application of the policy thus outlined; the consummation, when reached, would be permanent. For the moment more immediate and pressing matters must be settled; when Alexander should pay his promised visit to Paris they would have more abundant leisure to discuss ulterior plans. These dazzling prospects were a part of the Czar's consideration. He promised in return to conclude a sepa-

IN THE MUSEUM OF VERSAILLES

ENGRAVED BY PETER AITKEN

NAPOLEON RECEIVING THE QUEEN OF PRUSSIA AT TILSIT

FROM THE PAINTING BY NICOLAS LOUIS FRANÇOIS GOSSE

rate peace with Turkey, which, in the absence of French support, he doubted not he could make most favorable. But in case the Porte should prove obdurate, a provisional plan of partition was drawn up to indicate approximately what Russia might expect.

As the days passed, a routine life was gradually established. The two emperors met privately in the morning, and chatted about every conceivable point, pacing the floor or bending with heads touching over the map of Europe to consider its coming divisions. Alexander had said at the outset that his prejudice against Napoleon disappeared at first sight, and later he exclaimed, "Why did we not meet sooner?" He now repudiated any fondness whatever for the "legitimate" politics of Europe; he had visited the Bourbon pretender, the so-called Louis XVIII., at Mittau, and had found him of no account; he even accepted the light suggestion of his new-found friend that the Russian councilor Budberg should have no share in the conferences, as being possibly too closely wedded to old ideas. "You be my secretary," said Napoleon, "and I will be yours." In the afternoon the King of Prussia, with his staff, was generally invited to join their cavalcade for a ride. The Emperor of the French gave in later years a malicious account of these jaunts. Himself a fearless though awkward horseman, he spurred his charger to full speed, and the Czar followed with glee, while the King, as timid in the saddle as in the cabinet, jounced and bounced, often knocking Napoleon's arms with his elbows. The French and Russian officers paired in good-fellowship, while the few Prussians rode together. Constantine gathered Murat, Berthier, and Grouchy about him, and treating them on equal terms, displayed the strongest proofs of his regard. The dinners which followed, though always large and stately, were made as short as possible, for the emperors wished to be alone as quickly and as long as possible. The Czar was full of curiosity. How did Napoleon win victories? How did he rule men? What were his family relations? How did he regulate his inner life? The Emperor was full of good humor: he told again and again the tale of his victories, and expounded the principles on which he had won them; he explained with candor and in detail the structure and workings of his administrative machine; he opened his heart, and told how its strings had been wrung by the death of the "Little Napoleon," the eldest son of Queen Hortense.

In such pleasant converse the hours of ease rolled swiftly by, and then the work of negotiation began once more. Where differences appeared, Napoleon evaded close discussion and passed to other matters. Next morning early, the Czar would receive a carefully worded, concise note on the points at issue, together with an argument. Sometimes he replied in writing, more frequently not. When they met again, Napoleon sought, or appeared to seek a compromise, and never in vain. The council of ministers, in which there was not a single man of force except Talleyrand, received the conclusions from time to time, and elaborated the details.

CHAPTER VI

THE TREATY OF TILSIT

Two Equal Empires — Central Europe and the Orient — Prussia as a Second-rate Power — The Grand Duchy of Warsaw and the Kingdom of Westphalia — Napoleon and Frederick William — Queen Louisa of Prussia — The Meeting of Napoleon and Louisa — Courtesy and Diplomacy — The Bitterness of Disappointment — The Last Plea — Prussia's Humiliation — The Parting of the Emperors — Alexander's Disenchantment — Napoleon's Gains and Losses.

BY such hitherto unknown simplicity and address the diplomacy of Tilsit was rendered most expeditious. The negotiations were complete, the treaties drawn up, and the signatures affixed on July seventh. There were three different documents: a treaty of peace, a series of seven separate and secret articles, and a treaty of alliance. The first point gained by Napoleon was the recognition of all his conquests before 1805. The Czar admitted for the first time absolute equality between the two empires, and recognized the limits of the French system as it then existed: first, the Confederation of the Rhine, with any additions yet to be made; second, the kingdom of Italy, including Dalmatia; third, the vassalage of Holland, Berg, Naples, and Switzerland. There was a verbal understanding, it is said, that Napoleon might do as he liked in Spain and the Papal States, while the Czar should have the same liberty in regard to Finland. Subsequent events attested the probability of this fact. To illustrate Napoleon's attitude toward the recent, but now dissolved alliance, Prussia was given to understand that she owed to Russia what remnants of territory she retained; the stipulations with regard to her were therefore included in the treaty with Russia.

47

Still, there was to be a Prussia. Between the two great empires was to lie, in realization of a long-cherished plan, a girdle of neutral states like the "marches" established by Charles the Great. In this line Silesia was the only break. Prussia and Austria, one on each side of this mark, shorn of their strength and prestige, might await their destiny. France was to mediate for peace between Russia and Turkey, Russia between England and France. In case Great Britain should not prove tractable,—that is, admit the sanctity of all flags on the high seas, and restore all the colonies of France and her allies captured since 1805,—then Russia, in common with France, Denmark, Sweden, Portugal, and Austria, would declare commercial war on England, and complete the Continental embargo on British trade. Should Turkey refuse favorable terms, the two empires would divide between them all her European lands except Rumelia and the district of Constantinople. Alexander afterward declared that Napoleon gave a verbal promise that Russia should have a substantial increment on the Danube. The rumor was that Bessarabia, Moldavia, Wallachia, and Bulgaria were indicated to the Czar as his share.

No mention was made of Austria, which the treaty of Presburg had sufficiently dismembered. But Prussia? In order to complete the great "march" between east and west, Silesia was essential. At first Napoleon thought of combining it with Prussian Poland to form a kingdom. This would not restore the real Poland, but it would create a Poland, and give him a Polish army. It was already decided that the Elbe should form Frederick William's western frontier; to weaken his strength still further would destroy all balance between Prussia and Austria. Moreover, Alexander made a tender appeal, and adroitly suggested a distasteful counter-proposition. Accordingly it was settled that the great province should remain Prussian. This was a large concession to the Czar.

To make some pretense of fulfilling the lavish but indefinite promises made to the Poles, the lands of Warsaw and the province of Posen, with a considerable tract not now contained in it, were erected into the grand duchy of Warsaw. Under the influence of historical reminiscence this was given, not as a province, but as a separate sovereignty to the Elector of Saxony, who was simultaneously made king and a member of the Rhine Confederation. The Czar, in return for his cessions to the grand duchy of Warsaw, received the Prussian district of Bielostok. As a compensation for the Bocche di Cattaro and the Ionian Islands, Dantzic was restored to its position of a free city. The Prussian lands of the Elbe, together with Hesse-Cassel and many minor domains, were erected into the kingdom of Westphalia for the Emperor's brother Jerome. We have almost forgotten in our day how, less than a century ago, Germany was divided into insignificant fragments. It is instructive to recall that the formation of this new kingdom beneficently ended the separate existence of no fewer than twenty-four more or less autonomous powers — electorates, duchies, counties, bishoprics, and cities. It contained the all-important fortress of Magdeburg, the possession of whose frowning walls carried with it the command of the Elbe, and virtually made Prussia a conquered and tributary state.

This seemed to Frederick William the climax of his misfortunes. He had daily information from the Czar of what was under consideration, and the rescue of Silesia by his mediator gave him high hopes for the preservation of Magdeburg. But his poor-spirited behavior wearied even Alexander, who, willing at the outset to atone for desertion by intervention, became toward the end very cold. When the King desired permission to plead in person for Magdeburg, Napoleon refused. The Prussian case might be presented by counsel. Goltz was speedily summoned to the task, but though he was always about to have an interview with the French emperor, he never secured it.

It was at this crisis of Prussia's affairs that the King, after much urging, consented to summon his Queen. The rumors and insinuations concerning the Czar's undue admiration of her, so industriously spread by Napoleon, had made him over-sensitive; but as a last resort he felt the need of her presence. She came with a single idea — to make the cause of Magdeburg her own. She had suffered under the malicious innuendos of Napoleon regarding her character; she had shared the disgrace of the Berlin war party in the crushing defeat at Jena and Auerstädt; she had been a wayfarer among a disgraced and helpless people; but her spirit was not broken, and she announced her visit with all the dignity of her station. The court carriage in which she drove, accompanied by her ladies in waiting, reached Tilsit on July sixth, and drew up before the door of the artisan under whose roof were the rooms of her husband. Officers and statesmen were gathered to receive and encourage her with good advice; but she waved them away with an earnest call for quiet, so that she might collect her ideas.

In a moment Napoleon was announced. As he climbed the narrow stairway she rose to meet him. Friend and foe agree as to her beauty, her taste, and her manners; her presence, in a white dress embroidered with silver, and with a pearl diadem on her brow, was queenly. In her husband's apartments she was the hostess, and as such she apologized for the stair. "What would one not do for such an end!" gallantly replied the somewhat dazzled conqueror. The suppliant, after making a few respectful inquiries as to her visitor's welfare, and the effect of the Northern climate on his health, at once announced the object of her visit. Her manner was full of pathos and there were tears in her eyes as she recalled how her country had been punished for its appeal to arms, and for its mistaken confidence in the traditions of the great Frederick and his glory. The Emperor was abashed by the lofty strain of her address. So elevated was her mien that she overpowered him; for the instant his self-assurance fled, and he felt himself but a man of the people. He felt also the humiliation of the contrast, and was angry. Long afterward he confessed that she was mistress of the conversation, adding that she stood with her head thrown back like Mlle. Duchesnois in the character of *Chimène*, meaning by this comparison to stigmatize her attitude and language as theatrical. So effective was her appeal that he felt the need of something to save his own rôle, and accordingly he bowed her to a chair, and in the moment thus gained determined to strike the key of high comedy. Taking up the conversation in turn, he scrutinized the beauties of her person, and, complimenting her dress, asked whether the material was crape or India gauze. "Shall we talk of rags at such a solemn moment?" she retorted; and then proceeded with her direct plea for Magdeburg. In the midst of her eloquence, when the Emperor seemed almost overcome by her importunity, her meddling husband most inopportunely entered the room. He began to argue and reason, citing his threadbare grievance, the violation of Ansbach territory, and endeavoring to prove himself to be right. Napoleon at once turned the conversation to indifferent themes, and in a few moments took his leave. "You ask much," he said to the Queen on parting; "but I promise to think it over." The courageous woman had done her best, but her cause — if, indeed, it was ever in the balance — was lost from the moment she put her judge in an inferior position. Her majestic bearing was fine, but it was not diplomacy. She might, nevertheless, have succeeded had she been the wife of

NAPOLEON AND ALEXANDER AT TILSIT STUDYING THE MAP OF EUROPE

a wiser man. Long afterward Napoleon thought her influence on the negotiations would have been considerable if she had appeared in their earlier stages, and congratulated himself that she came too late, inasmuch as they were already virtually closed when she arrived.

The remainder of the day passed for the Queen in a whirl of excitement, receiving messengers from Napoleon with the pardons of Prussian prisoners and accepting polite attentions from his adjutants. She gladly consented to dine with Napoleon, and Berthier was chosen to escort her to his Emperor's lodging. On arrival she was received with distinction, and assigned at table to the seat of honor between the host and the Czar. The Emperor was all politeness, offering unwelcome consolations to Frederick William, and expressing astonishment at the Queen's courage. "Did you know my hussars nearly captured you?" he said to her. "I can scarcely believe it, sire," was the reply; "I did not see a single Frenchman." "But why expose yourself thus? Why did you not wait for me at Weimar?" "Indeed, sire, I was not eager." There is a tradition that Talleyrand, whose work the treaty really was, grew anxious and whispered to Napoleon later in the evening that surely he would not surrender the benefits of his greatest conquest for the sake of a pretty woman. Whether this admonition was given or not, the Emperor was respectful and polite, but non-committal. After dinner he conversed long with his fair guest. To her lady in waiting, the Countess Voss, he offered snuff — a singular mark of condescension. Next day, in a note to Josephine, he said that he had been compelled continually to stand on his guard; and the day following, July eighth, he again wrote to his Empress: "The Queen is really charming, using every art to please me; but be not jealous: I am like a waxed cloth from which all that glides off. It would cost me too much to play the gallant." The Emperor's courtesy had deceived the poor Queen entirely, and she is said to have returned to her husband's lodgings at Piktupönen in the highest spirits.

On that very night, immediately after the dinner, the step she so much dreaded was taken, and orders were given to conclude the treaty as it stood. At the last hour Goltz secured his interview to plead the expectations awakened in the Queen, but the Emperor coldly explained that his conduct had been politeness, and nothing more; the house of Prussia might be glad to recover a crown at all. Talleyrand showed a

completed and final draft of the treaty ready for signature, and said
that his master was in haste, that in two days the documents would be
signed. This was the news which greeted Louisa next morning. She
returned at once to Tilsit, her eyes swollen with weeping; but she appeared in a stately dress, and with a smile on her lips. Again she was
the object of the most distinguished courtesy from Napoleon's adjutants, but the expected visit from himself was not made. However,
she was again the Emperor's honored guest at dinner. The host at
once began to speak of her costume. "What, the Queen of Prussia
with a turban! Surely not to gratify the Emperor of Russia, who is
at war with the Turks!" "Rather, I think," replied the Queen, "to
propitiate Rustan," rolling her large, full eyes toward the swarthy
Mameluke behind his master's chair. She had the air, according to
Napoleon's account, of an offended coquette. After the meal it was
Murat who took the part filled the previous evening by the Emperor.
"How does your Majesty pass the time at Memel?" "In reading."
"What does your Majesty read?" "The history of the past." "But
our own times afford actions worthy of commemoration." "It is already
more than I can endure to live in them."

Before parting, Napoleon spent a few moments at her side, and at
the end, turning, pulled from a bunch a beautiful rose, which he offered
with gestures of gallantry and homage. Hesitating a moment, the
Queen at last put out her hand, and said as she accepted it, "At least
with Magdeburg." "Madame," came the frigid reply, "it is mine to
give and yours to accept." But he gave his arm to conduct her to the
carriage, and as they descended the stair together the disappointed
guest said, in a sentimental and emotional voice, "Is it possible that,
having had the happiness to see so near the man of the century and of
all history, he will not afford me the possibility and the satisfaction of
being able to assure him that he has put me under obligations for life?"
With solemn tones Napoleon replied, "Madame, I am to be pitied; it is
a fault of my unlucky star." Queen Louisa's own lady in waiting re-
lated that her sovereign's bitterness overcame her at the last, and as
she stepped into the carriage she said, "Sire, you have cruelly deceived
me." It is certain that next day she overwhelmed Duroc with reproaches; but she afterward frankly confessed that she could recall no
definite promise made by Napoleon. To Talleyrand she said, with fine
sarcasm, that only two persons regretted her having come to Tilsit—

be and she. Her duty, she believed, as a loving wife, as a tender mother, as the queen of her people, was fulfilled; but her heart was broken. Queen Mary of England said of the loss of Calais, "Should they open my heart, they will find the name of Calais inscribed in bloody letters within." Queen Louisa pathetically recalled this moan; she could say the same of Magdeburg.

The treaty with Prussia, signed two days later, did not modify in the least the terms arranged with Alexander, and for six years that country remained in a mutilated and conquered condition, compelled to obey with outward respect the behests of Napoleon. Every domain she had owned west of the Elbe went to the kingdom of Westphalia, the circle of Kottbus went to Saxony, the Polish provinces of south Prussia and new east Prussia to the grand duchy of Warsaw, the circle of Bielostok to Russia. Napoleon repeatedly urged the Czar to seize Memel and the strip of Prussian land east of the Niemen; but Alexander desired to be at peace with his neighbor, and firmly refused; moreover, he verbally stipulated for the evacuation of the Hohenzollern lands by French troops at an early date. Nominally, therefore, the King of Prussia regained sovereignty over less than half of his former territory. For this consideration he was to pay an indefinite but enormous and almost impossible indemnity, which was to cover the total cost of the war. To guarantee this a large portion of the French army was, in spite of Alexander's demand, still left quartered in the Hohenzollern lands, so that the Prussian people were daily reminded of their disgrace, as well as irritated by extortionate taxation. First and last, the war cost Prussia, in the support of the French army and in actual contributions to France, over a milliard of francs — about the gross national income of thirteen years. The process of Prussian consolidation begun three years before was thus hastened. What Pozzo di Borgo called a masterpiece of destruction turned out in the end to be the beginning of a new birth for the nation. But the royal pair were stricken down: the high-souled Queen died, three years later, of chagrin: the King lived to see his people strong once more, but in a sort of obstructing stupor, being always an uncompromising conservative. When he died, in 1840, he left to his successor a legacy of smothered popular discontent.

The treaties of Tilsit between France and Russia were signed on July seventh. The principal personages engaged on both sides in this grand scene of reconciliation were on that day reciprocally decorated with the orders of the respective courts, while the imperial guards of both emperors received food and drink for a great festivity. Next day Napoleon paid his farewell visit. At his morning toilet he had his valet loosen the threads which fastened the cross of the Legion of Honor to his coat, and as the Czar advanced to meet him he asked in audible tones permission to decorate the first grenadier of Russia. A veteran named Lazaref was summoned from the ranks, and with a wrench the Emperor tore off his cross, and fastened it on the breast of the peasant. The welkin rang with applause, while Lazaref kissed his benefactor's hands and the hem of his coat. Next day Alexander crossed the Niemen. Savary went with him as a French envoy, partly to keep up the Czar's courage and spirits, which would be endangered by the sullen humor of the court circles in St. Petersburg, partly to study the temper of the Russian people.

To the last moment of their intercourse the Czar appeared to be under the spell of Napoleon's seductive powers. He came as a conquered prince; he left with an honorable peace, with the friendship of his magnanimous conqueror, and with an unsmirched imperial dignity. He had saved his recent ally from destruction, and had secured a small increase of territory for himself; for the future there were Finland and the fairest portion of Turkey. But in a few days the magic began to pass. He had not secured Constantinople, and he had promised to evacuate Wallachia and Moldavia; he had not secured the complete evacuation of Prussia; he had risked a rupture with England; he had, above all, submitted to the creation of a state which, under the thin disguise of another name, was but the germ of a reconstructed Poland. It began to appear as if he had been wheedled. There is sufficient evidence that such bitter reflections made their appearance very soon; but they were repressed, at first from pure shame, and afterward from stern necessity, when England began to vent her anger. But the Russians themselves could not be repressed. Before long Savary was hated and abused by the public, the more because he maintained his ascendancy over the Czar. The reports sent home by the former police agent were clever and instructive, but their pictures of factional disputes and Oriental plots at court, of aristocratic luxury and general poverty, of popular superstition and barbarous manners, were not reassuring, and confirmed in his Emperor's mind doubts felt from the beginning as to

THE INCIDENT OF THE ROSE

the stability of the alliance consummated at Tilsit, an alliance out-
wardly fair, but, like all Talleyrand's diplomacy, more showy than
substantial.

Napoleon left for Königsberg the same day on which he bade adieu
to Alexander. His route was by way of Dresden. He was not in the
slightest degree deceived. The peace of Europe, he said, was in St.
Petersburg; the affairs of the world were there. But he had gained
much. The outposts of his empire were established, and from one of
them he could touch with his hand the enchanted East. He had secured the temporary coöperation of Russia, and with that as a beginning he might consolidate the Continent against England, and complete
the stage in his progress now gained. Above all, he could at once restore the confidence of France by the proclamation of peace and the up-
building of her prosperity. To be sure, he had forecast a division of
his prospective Eastern empire with Russia, he had left Prussia outraged and bleeding, and Austria was uneasy and suspiciously reserved;
but he had checkmated them all in the menace of a restored Poland,
while their financial weakness and military exhaustion, combined with
the reciprocal jealousies of their dynasties, might be relied on to prevent
their immediate hostility. Besides, while he had sung a certain tune
at Tilsit, in the future he would, as he sarcastically said somewhat
later, have to sing it only according to the written score.

CHAPTER VII

THE PATH OF NAPOLEONIC EMPIRE

NAPOLEON AND THE NEUTRAL POWERS — THE PROTECTORATE OF POR-
TUGAL AND THE END OF ETRURIA — ANNEXATION OF THE PAPAL LE-
GATIONS — SEIZURE OF THE DANISH FLEET BY GREAT BRITAIN —
THE DEGRADATION OF SPAIN — GODOY'S IMPOLICY — THE SPANISH
COURT AND THE HEIR APPARENT — EFFECTS OF THE RUSSIAN AL-
LIANCE IN PARIS — NAPOLEON'S COMMENTARY ON THE TREATY — HIS
ADMINISTRATIVE WISDOM — PUBLIC WORKS IN FRANCE — THE JEWS
IN FRANCE — THE SANHEDRIM — NAPOLEON'S SUCCESSFUL REFORMS —
WAR INDEMNITIES AND FINANCE — ANNOYANCES OF THE CONTINENTAL
SYSTEM.

BUT in order to fulfil the purposes and realize the possibilities which were indicated in the treaties of Tilsit, no time was to be lost. The fate of Sweden and the Hanse towns having been vir-tually settled, there remained three small maritime states in Europe which still maintained a nominal neutrality — Denmark, Portugal, and Etruria. One and all, they must choose between England and France. To each a summons was to be addressed, and Napoleon wrote the preliminary directions at Dresden. Between the lines of his despatches it was clear that the precious naval armaments of all three powers — ships, arsenals, stores, and men — must be put at the disposal of France. "A thing must needs be done before the announcement of your plan," was one of Napoleon's own principles, and it was his intention so to proceed in this case. At Dresden, also, was promulgated the new con-stitution of Warsaw. Modeled on that of France, it was far from liberal; but it abolished serfdom, made all citizens equal before the law, and introduced the civil code.

In 1804 Portugal had purchased her neutrality for the duration of

MEETING OF NAPOLEON AND TOLSTOI IN PARIS. 1807

the war with the sum of sixteen million francs. She was now ordered to close her ports to the British, to seize all their goods and ships, and finally to declare war against Great Britain. Junot, formerly imperial ambassador at Lisbon, was despatched with twenty-seven thousand men, designated as a "corps of observation," to be ready on the frontier to enforce the command. In reply, England seized the Portuguese fleet, and kept it in security until the close of the war. During the late campaigns in Poland and Prussia, King Louis of Etruria had died, and his helpless widow, the Spanish infanta, Maria Louisa, acting as regent for her young son, had admitted the English to the harbor of Leghorn. Prince Eugène was now ordered to take another "corps of observation" of six thousand men, and drive them out. He did so promptly. Duroc at once suggested to the Spanish minister that Napoleon would like some proposition for the indemnification of Maria Louisa for the loss of Etruria — say one portion of Portugal for her, and the rest for Godoy, the Prince of the Peace.

This "deformity" removed from the Italian peninsula, it revealed a still greater one — the fact that the Papal States disturbed the connection between the two kingdoms of Italy and Naples. Pius VII., returning disillusioned and embittered after the coronation ceremony, and finding that his temporal weapons had failed him, had taken a stand with his spiritual armor. It has already been recalled that he began to refuse everything Napoleon desired,— the coronation as Western emperor, the extension of the Concordat to Venice, the confirmation of bishops appointed in France and Italy by the temporal power, the annulment of Jerome's marriage, the recognition of Joseph's royalty,— except in return for a guarantee of his own independence and neutrality; in short, he feebly abjured the French alliance and all its works. There now came a demand from Napoleon that henceforth there should be as many French cardinals as Roman, that the agents of hostile powers should be banished from the Papal States, and that the papal ports should be closed to England. The Emperor was weary, too, of the petty squabbles in connection with the Church, of the threats to excommunicate him and declare his throne vacant. Did they mean to put him in a convent and whip him like Louis the Pious? If not, let the full powers of an ambassador be sent to the cardinal legate at Paris; in any case, let there be an end to menaces. At the same time Eugène showed to Pius a personal letter from his stepfather, which,

though marked confidential, was intended to be thus shown. It contained the threat that the Emperor contemplated calling a council of
the Gallican, Italian, German, and Polish churches to liberate those
peoples from the domination of Roman priests. The pontiff was terrified, and hastened to yield the most pressing demands made in the
message which he had himself received, among them the nomination
of a negotiator. But he childishly refused the letter of the Emperor's
demand, and commissioned, not the French cardinal legate at Paris, but
an Italian cardinal. Napoleon notified the See that he would treat only
with Bayanne, the French cardinal at Paris, and that longer dallying
would compel him to annex Ancona, Urbino, and Macerata to the kingdom of Italy. Pius yielded at once, nominating Bayanne, agreeing to
enter the federation with France, and promising to crown Napoleon;
but the annexation took place quite as expeditiously as the surrender
— was, in fact, complete before it!

Of the three minor sea powers, Denmark, commanding as she did
the gateway of the Baltic, was far the most important. Bernadotte was
already on her borders with an army. She was notified by him that
she must declare war against England immediately, or lose all her Continental possessions. Her government promised to obey, but procras-
tinated. It has been claimed that English spies at Tilsit had caught
scraps of the bargain contained in the secret articles, and that the
Portland cabinet, in which Canning was Secretary for Foreign Affairs
and Castlereagh for War and the Colonies, had divined the rest. It is
now known that Canning believed there were no secret articles, but
was convinced that the two emperors had reached a secret understanding hostile to England. During the summer the ministry received
what they called the most positive information — what was its extent
and how it was obtained have never been made known — that the
French intended to invade Holstein and force Denmark to close the
Sound to British commerce. The danger seemed imminent: the Danish
fleet contained no fewer than twenty ships of the line, eighteen frig-
ates, nine brigs, and a number of gunboats. Such a reinforcement of
the French navy would put it again on a war footing. The English
ministry, therefore, offered to defend Denmark, guarantee her colonies,
and give her every means of defense, naval, military, and pecuniary, if
only she would surrender her fleet to England, to be restored in the
event of peace. The Danish regent was already committed to France,

and did not accept. Accordingly the English army under Cathcart landed, and laid siege to Copenhagen, while the fleet bombarded it for three days, until the government agreed to their stipulations. This shameful deed of high-handed violence must be laid at Canning's door. It was the first step in the humiliation of a fine people, to their loss of Norway, and ultimately of Schleswig and Holstein. Moreover, it was impolitic in the highest degree, making the Czar a bitter enemy of England for four years. The wretched country, in distraction, threw itself into the arms of Bernadotte. Christian VII. had long been an imbecile, and his son, Frederick VI., though energetic and well meaning, turned Denmark into another vassal state of France by the treaty of Fontainebleau, signed October thirtieth, 1807.

In none of their many sovereignties had the incapacity of the Bourbons been more completely demonstrated than in Spain. With intermittent flickerings, the light of that famous land had been steadily growing dimmer ever since Louis XIV. exultingly declared that the Pyrenees had ceased to exist. Stripped of her colonial supremacy, shattered in naval power, reduced to pay tribute to France, she looked silently on while Napoleon trafficked with her lands, mourning that even the memory of her former glories was fading out in foreign countries. The proud people themselves had, however, never forgotten their past; with each successive humiliation, their irritation grew more extreme, and soon after Trafalgar they made an effort to organize under the crown prince against the scandalous régime of Godoy. Both parties sought French support, and the quarrel was fomented from Paris until the whole country was torn by the most serious dissensions.

When, in the previous year, Prussia declared war, and the French legions were about to face those trained in the school of Frederick the Great, a vigorous attempt was made by the Russian envoy in Madrid to win the support of Spain for the coalition. England, too, at the same moment, threatened to make the South American colonies independent if she did not consent. Godoy was persuaded that Napoleon had at last found his match, if not his master, and on October fourteenth issued a manifesto couched for the most part in ambiguous terms, but clearly announcing war as an immediate necessity. By a strange coincidence, its date was that of the day on which was fought the battle of Jena, and after hearing the news of that event the Prince of the Peace hastened to make his submission in the name of the King.

Napoleon turned pale as he read the news of the contemplated defection, which reached him at Berlin; he never forgave the treachery, although for the time he feigned ignorance of its existence. The renewal of Charles IV.'s submission gave him the opportunity to demand that the Spanish fleet should proceed to Toulon, that the King should send fifteen thousand men to oppose a possible English landing at the mouth of the Elbe, and at the same time undertake the sustenance of twenty-five thousand Prussian prisoners of war, while thenceforward he must rigidly enforce the embargo on English trade in all Spanish ports and markets.

These demands the weak and contemptible government could not resist. Godoy and the Queen resumed their scandalous living, while the King joined in a conspiracy to cut off his son Ferdinand from the succession. The young prince had the people's sympathy; but although he had sought Napoleon's favor, and wished to marry the Empress Josephine's niece, there was no response, and he remained impotent before an administration apparently supported by France. He was, in the sequel, arrested on a charge of conspiring against his father's life. Before the summer of 1807 closed, everything was ripe for Napoleon's contemplated intervention to "regenerate" Spain.

Such was the harvest of Tilsit in the field of foreign relations — a harvest which to the last the Emperor claimed that Talleyrand had sown. As to its effect in France, Metternich, then Austrian ambassador in Paris, declared that men sat in the cafés coldly discussing an entire reconstruction of Europe — two empires, and seventeen new kingdoms with new sovereigns either from or in the interest of the imperial houses! "Rhapsodies," he said, "which proved that all Europe might crumble without exciting a single emotion of sorrow, astonishment, or satisfaction in a people degraded beneath all others, beneath all imagination, and which, worn out, demoralized to the point where every trace of even national feeling is wiped out, by nineteen years of revolution and crimes, now looks on with cold-blooded indifference at what is passing beyond its own frontiers. Wise men think that the treaties, being as advantageous to Russia as to France, necessarily contain a germ which in developing will prove dangerous to the latter." In reality there was not now a state in Europe toward which the French empire did not stand in strained relations, not a nationality besides the French which did not feel its self-respect wounded, and resent the abasement.

NAPOLEON IN HIS STUDY.

This, however, was not the panorama which the Emperor unfolded in Paris. He reached St. Cloud quietly on the evening of July twenty-seventh. The people of Paris learned the news incidentally, and burst into spontaneous rejoicings, illuminating the city, and sending addresses in which the terms of adulation were exhausted. Napoleon was no longer an actor in merely human history: he was a man of the heroic age; he was beyond admiration; nothing but love could rise to his lofty place. On August sixteenth the Emperor opened the legislature in person. "Since your last session," he said, "new wars, new triumphs, new treaties, have changed the face of Europe." If the house of Brandenburg still reigned, he continued, it was due to the sincere friendship he felt for the Czar. A French prince would rule on the Elbe, and would know how to conciliate his subjects, while ever mindful of his most sacred duties. Saxony had recovered her independence, the peoples of Dantzic and the duchy of Warsaw their country and their rights. All nations rejoiced to see the direful influence of England destroyed. France was united to the Confederation of the Rhine by its laws, by the federative system to the countries of Holland, Switzerland, and Italy; her new relations with Russia were cemented by reciprocal esteem. In all this, he affirmed, his pole-star had been the happiness of his people, dearer to him than his own glory. He would like maritime peace, and for its sake would overlook the exasperations caused by a people tossed and torn by party strife. Whatever happened, he would be worthy of his people, as they had shown themselves to be worthy of him. Their behavior in his absence had only increased his esteem for their character. He had thought of several measures to simplify and perfect their institutions.

This picture of martial and political renown, painted by a master who had in one campaign changed the meaning of his title from its primitive sense of military ruler to its later and grander one of chief among and over princes, thus realizing the revival of the Western Empire, could not but please the fancy and arouse the enthusiasm of a generous, imaginative, forgiving people. The impression was heightened by their Emperor's activity in keeping faith as to their own prosperity. As after Austerlitz, his first care was now finance. The new commercial code was promulgated, and it proved scarcely less satisfactory to the merchants than the civil code had been to the people at large. The Bank of France was immediately compelled to lower its

rate of discount, and a council was held to consider how Italy and the
Rhine Confederation could be made tributary to French industry and
commerce. Recourse was also had to those measures of internal development by the execution of great public works which had been begun
after Austerlitz, but were suspended before Jena.

Before the last campaign the Emperor and Empress had been accustomed to visit various portions of France. During every halt the Emperor would mount his horse, and, attended occasionally by one or more
of the local officials, but usually only by Rustan or an adjutant, would
gallop hither and thither, gathering information, examining conditions,
and making suggestions. Immediately afterward he would throw off a
sketch of needed improvements: public buildings, almshouses, roads,
canals, aqueducts, town streets, mountain roads—anything, in short,
which would arouse local enthusiasm and benefit the country at large.
Many—most, perhaps—of these schemes remained inchoate; but
many of the grandest were executed, and Napoleon has left his impress
as indelibly on France itself as upon its society. The routes of the
Simplon and Mont Cenis, the great canals which bind together the river
systems, the restoration of the cathedral at St. Denis, the quays of the
Seine in Paris, the great Triumphal Arch, the Vendôme Column, the
Street of Peace, the Street of Rivoli, the bridges of Austerlitz, Jena,
and the Arts—these are some of the magnificent enterprises due to his
initiative. Such works were pushed throughout the summer of 1807
by employing large numbers of laborers and artisans, while local work-
shops were opened in every department to furnish employment to all
who could not otherwise find it. The political economist may lift his
eyebrows and shrug his shoulders in contemplating such shifts; but
they were imperial shifts, and created a high degree of comfort at the
time, while they satisfied in permanency that passion for beauty in
utility which does not enter as an element into economic science.

Closely connected with this policy was a measure of Napoleon's
already referred to, but little known. In some respects it was more
successful than any other; it certainly is most characteristic of the
man. The evil aimed at was cured at the time, and the permanent
question is less acute in modern France than in any other European
country. For years past there had been chronic distress among the
agricultural classes in some of the most fertile districts of France,
notably in the northeast. This was attributed to the presence of Jews

in large numbers. The stringent laws of the old régime had crowded that unfortunate people out of all occupations but two — peddling and money-lending. In both of these they became experts, and when emancipated by the Revolution they used their liberty, not to widen their activities, but to intensify the evils of the monopoly which they had secured. Since 1791 large numbers of Polish and German Jews had established themselves on the right bank of the Rhine; and reaching hands across that stream to their kinsfolk on the left bank, they combined to strip the French peasantry by the familiar arts of barter and usury, which need not be described here, until in a few years they were creditors to the extent of twenty-three million francs, and had become extensive landed proprietors. They were never seen to labor with their hands, and having no family name, they evaded the conscription laws with impunity, while the courts of justice became their humble servants in enforcing the collection of scandalous debts or in the foreclosure of inflated mortgages.

In 1806 a temporary decree had suspended all legal executions in certain districts, and many Jews of the better class made ready to bow before the coming tempest and come to the assistance of the government. Napoleon, aware that the Old Testament law was civil and political as well as religious, shrewdly asked advice from these and other men of the more enlightened sort. It was agreed to call a council. The Emperor summoned his prefects to name its members, and appointed a committee to represent the government at its sessions. Decisions taken by this assembly were to be submitted to a general Sanhedrim of all Europe. The assembly of French Israelites met in Paris during the latter part of 1806, and after due deliberation gave satisfactory answers to a carefully prepared set of questions propounded by the government commission. In 1807 the economic situation had nevertheless become graver. The Sanhedrim met early in February. Its members vied in flattery with the Roman priesthood, setting the imperial eagle above the ark of the covenant, and blending the letters N and J with those of the Jehovah in a monogram for the adornment of their meeting-place. On March fourth they issued a decree which is still the basis of religious instruction among Jewish youth. They forbade polygamy, and admitted the principle of civil marriage without anathema; they ordered all Israelites to treat those who believe that God is the Creator of heaven and earth as fellow-citizens and brothers: to obey the civil and military laws, including that of conscription, and to train their children to industry and handiwork ; they also invited them to enter the learned professions, and to attach themselves to the country by the purchase of public obligations. Usury was absolutely forbidden, the Israelite being enjoined as a religious precept to make no distinction in money transactions between Hebrew and Christian. The minutest details of the whole transaction were foreseen and regulated by Napoleon, and may be studied in his correspondence with his ministers.

A year later, after careful and mature deliberation, there appeared an imperial decree, not only organizing the Jewish Church and regulating its relations with the state, but defining the civil and political status of Hebrews. They were pronounced to be citizens like other men ; but they could not exact higher interest than five per cent., while if they should demand over ten they should be punished for usury. Every Jew in the northeastern department must have a license to do business, and a notarial authorization for pawnbrokerage. Any Jew not domiciled at the moment in Alsace might not thereafter acquire domicile in that department, and could do so in others only by becoming a landowner and tilling the soil. Every Jew should be liable to military service, and, unlike his Christian fellow-citizens, might not provide a substitute ; moreover, he must adopt and use a family name. This stringent law was rigidly enforced, except in Bordeaux, the Gironde, and the Landes, where no offense had been given. Its effect was steady and sure. Before long first one and then another Israelite was exempted from its rigors, until finally, in 1812, the department or the man still subject to its provisions was the exception and not the rule. From that day to this there has scarcely been in France what is known elsewhere as the Jewish question. Hebrews are found in every line of human activity ; they have the same civil, political, and religious standing as men of other blood and confessions ; they are illustrious in finance, in politics, in science, and in the arts. They are, moreover, passionate patriots, and to the casual observer scarcely distinguishable in mien and appearance from other citizens. The temporary contravention of the civil code, both as to spirit and letter, by the notorious decree above referred to has been so beneficent that it has for the most part escaped any criticism or even remark.

While in ways like these the clutch of the usurer was relaxed and

JEAN-ANDOCHE JUNOT

DUKE OF ABRANTES

the general well-being promoted, measures were taken to crown the
work by a stable system of finance. It will be recalled that two years
before the Emperor had saved the public credit by the direct expenditure of the Austrian war indemnity. It was his fixed principle that
France should not pay for his wars except with her children. He knew
too well the thrift of the whole nation and the greed of the lower
classes to jeopardize their good will either by the emission of paper
money or by the increase of tax rates. The panic of 1805 had been precipitated by the virtual failure of a bankers' syndicate which made advances to the government on its taxes and on the annual Spanish contri-
bution as well. In 1807 the war indemnity exacted from Prussia, Poland,
and Westphalia was used for a double purpose, the creation of two funds:
one to furnish an immediate supply of cash on the outbreak of war, the
other to replace the bankers' syndicate by making advances on the
taxes whenever required. There was therefore no increase in the rate
of taxation, work was abundant, and under the forcing process the
wheels were moving in almost every department of trade and industry.
The price of the imperial bonds on the Bourse rose to ninety-nine, a
price never afterward reached in Napoleon's day.

There was one sharp pinch. Coffee and sugar were no longer luxuries, but necessaries; and through the Continental embargo colonial
wares had become, and were likely to remain, very dear and very scarce.
Such substitutes as ingenuity could devise were gradually accepted for
the former; to provide the latter the beet-root industry was fostered
by every means. The Emperor kept a sample of sugar made from beets
on his chimney-piece as an ornament, and occasionally sent gifts of the
precious commodity to his fellow-sovereigns. The story is told that an
official who had been banished from favor recovered his standing entirely by planting a whole estate with beets. Such traits were considered evidence of plain, homely common sense by the people, who
enjoyed the sensation that their Emperor shared their feelings and
participated in their daily shifts.

CHAPTER VIII

THE NEW FEUDALISM

IMPERIAL FRANCE — THE ARISTOCRACY — THE VASSAL SOVEREIGNS — SUPPRESSION OF THE TRIBUNATE — THE RIGHT OF ENTAIL — EVASIONS OF LAW — THE NEW NOBILITY — TITLES AND EMOLUMENTS — STYLE IN THE FIRST EMPIRE — THEORY OF THE UNIVERSITY — ITS ESTABLISHMENT — THE LYCÉES — EFFECTS OF THE SYSTEM — REGULATION OF THE COURT — THE EMPEROR'S MOODS — MATRIMONIAL ALLIANCES WITH ROYALTY — GLOOM AT COURT — DECLINE OF TALLEYRAND'S INFLUENCE — HIS NEW RÔLE.

IT was not long before the people of Paris and of all France were in the best possible humor; they were busy, they were clothed, they were fed, they were making and saving money. With every hour grew the feeling that their unity and strength were embodied in the Emperor. Mme. de Rémusat was tired of his ill-breeding: it shocked her to observe his coarse familiarity, to see him sit on a favorite's knee, or twist a bystander's ear till it was afire; to hear him sow dissension among families by coarse innuendo, and to see him crush society that he might rule it. But such things would not have shocked the masses of plain burgher Frenchmen at all. When the querulous lady opened her troubles to the sympathetic Talleyrand, and bemoaned the sad fate which kept her at the imperial court to gain a living, his reply was not consoling. As time passed, the gulf between the ruler and his venal but soft-spoken minister had been widening, and the Prince of Benevento had oftentimes to hear taunts and reproaches in scenes of such violence as were unsuspected even by the complaining lady in waiting. But nevertheless Talleyrand replied to her that Napoleon still stood for the unity of France, and it was both his and her duty to endure and support their monarch.

No doubt the Emperor was perfectly aware of the situation. But he felt that what was a new aristocracy in truth, though not yet so in name, must be appeased as well as the people. He was furious at times with the venality of his associates. Talleyrand once admitted that he had taken sixty millions from various German princes. Masséna, Augereau, Brune, and Junot were not so colossal in their greed, but they were equally ill disposed, and very successful in lining their coffers. With Talleyrand Napoleon never joked; but when he wished to give a warning to the others he drew a bill for some enormous sum on one or other of them, and deposited it with a banker. There is no evidence that such a draft was ever dishonored. On one occasion Masséna disgorged two millions of francs in this way. Of the ancient nobility the Emperor once said, with a sneer: "I offered them rank in my army, they declined the service. I opened my antechambers to them, they rushed in and filled them." To this sweeping statement there were many noteworthy exceptions, but on the whole Napoleon never classed the estate of the French nobles lower than they deserved. Still they had a power which he recognized, and it was with a sort of grim humor that he began to distribute honors and the sops of patronage among both the old and the new aristocracy — a process which only made the latter independent and failed to win the affections of the former.

It was in the hope of securing the good will of the ancient nobility that he took two steps radical in their direct negation of Revolutionary principles: the destruction of the tribunate and the restoration of the right of entail. The connection between the two lies in the tendency of both: merging tribunate and legislature made it easy to substitute for an elective senate a hereditary house of lords. Feeling himself sufficiently strong, Napoleon clearly intended to gratify in others the weak human pride which, as Montesquieu says, desires the eternity of a name, and thereby to erect a four-square foundation for the perpetuity of his own dynasty. The brothers Joseph, Louis, and Jerome were now no longer Bonapartes, but Napoleons, ruling as Joseph Napoleon, Louis Napoleon, Jerome Napoleon, over their respective fiefs. Murat, the brother-in-law, was already provided for in the same way, and there were three reigning princes among the satellites of the imperial throne. All these could transmit their name and dominions in the line of hereditary succession. It may be read in the "Moniteur" of July, 1810, that, in whatever position they were placed by Napoleon's politics and the interest of his empire, their first duty was to him, their second to France. "All your other duties, even those to the people I may intrust to you, are only secondary."

Ten years earlier General Bonaparte had declared that what the French wanted was glory and the gratification of their vanity; of liberty, he said, they knew nothing. The Emperor Napoleon, in one of his spoken musings, applied the same conception to all Continental Europeans, saying that there were everywhere a few men who knew what freedom was and longed to secure it; but that the masses needed paternal guidance, and enjoyed it as long as they were comfortable. The asylum of this enlightened minority in France was for a time the tribunate; to many it seemed that, if free government be government by discussion, in the tribunate alone was any semblance of freedom left; its name had consequently retained a halo of nobility, and its mere existence was a comfort to the few who still recalled the ideals of the Revolution. But, in truth, the body itself had ceased to have any dignity whatsoever. The system of legislation was briefly this: from the throne came a message exposing the situation of the country, the council of state then formulated the measures set forth as necessary, the tribunate approved them in one or other of its sections, and the legislature gave the enacting vote. The suppression of the tribunate, therefore, appeared to the general public like final proceedings in bankruptcy. Some of the members went into the legislature, some into official administrative positions, and the right of discussion in committee behind closed doors was transferred to certain sections of the legislature. By way of compensation it was "decreed by the senate," as the formality was called, that no man could thenceforth sit in the legislature until he had reached the age of forty. Perhaps Napoleon remembered that his own fiery ambition had made him emperor before he was thirty-six. The measure was announced to the tribunes as a mere matter of course, and created no stir at the time. In later years it was recalled that the English Parliament under the Plantagenets had never entirely perished, and so was ready for powerful deeds in more propitious days. But in France's later crisis the French tribunate could not be revived; with it disappeared forever the last rallying-point for the scattered remnant still true to the Revolution.

The complement of this negative measure was the creation of the

THE EMPRESS JOSEPHINE IN THE PARK AT MALMAISON.

right to transmit together, and for an indefinite time, a title and the realty on which its dignity reposed. Though the restoration of this institution was slightly anterior in time to the other as to its beginnings, yet the final decree was not published until 1808, and logically it is complementary and subsequent to it. To this day many men of ancient and honorable name in France have not ceased to bemoan the destruction of primogeniture by the Revolution and the Code Napoléon. They are proud to transmit their title untarnished to their descendants, are ready to make serious sacrifices in its behalf, to exercise the rigid self-denials of family control for its sake, and to engrave the motto of "noblesse oblige" on their hearts in order to sustain it; but they bitterly complain that without the majorat, and the transmission of outward, visible supports in land and houses to strengthen it, the empty sound carries little weight. The compulsory subdivision of estates at the death of the owner enables every scion to live, if not to thrive, on the home stock. The failure of France in colonization is largely due to the absence of men from good families among the colonizers, while England sends her younger sons to the ends of the earth, there to found new houses and perpetuate the old line under favorable conditions. Hence, too, the petty dimensions of aristocratic French life: little fortunes, little ambitions, little establishments, little families, among that very class in society which by cultivating the sentiment of honor should leaven the practical, materialistic temper of the multitude. At the present time, when the burghers amass in trade far greater fortunes than the aristocracy possess, when the learned secure greater power by intellectual vigor, when the demagogues grow mightier by the command of votes, titles alone carry little weight, and the virtues of honor, of chivalry, of elegance, can with difficulty display their example.

No argument can ever restore general confidence in the institution of primogeniture, but it dies hard, even in England. In the United States the absolute liberty of testamentary disposition enables a wealthy father to found a family almost as perfectly as if the right of entail existed, and the bulk of large fortunes is constantly left by will to the most capable son, in order that he may keep up the family name, the family estates, and the family pride. But under the provisions of the Code Napoléon such a course is impossible. As the law-giver did not hesitate to contravene his own legislation in the case of the Jews, so he again disregarded it in order to consolidate that aristocracy of which he hoped to make another strong prop to his throne; for he already had the Church and the people. "The code," he said, "was made for the welfare of the people; and if that welfare demands other measures, we must take them." This was not difficult, because the imperial power had gradually shaped two instruments wherewith to act: one was the laws sanctioned by the legislature and pertaining ordinarily to abstract questions of jurisprudence; the other was the Emperor's personal decrees, which, though discussed by the council of state, were the expression of the Emperor's will, and covered in their scope the whole field of authority.

It was by the latter course that he had intended to create the new nobility. Ostensibly the measure was to be the last blow of the ax at the root of feudalism. The new dignities carried no privilege with them; they were, it was explained, a sort of civic crown to which any one might aspire, and their creation was therefore in no way derogatory to the principle of equality. The holders might become too independent and self-reliant, they might even display a class spirit; but the Emperor felt himself to be striving upward, these creatures of his would have to run fast before they could outstrip their master. At St. Helena the prisoner, recalling with bitterness the ingratitude of his beneficiaries, declared that he took the unfortunate step in order to reconcile France with the rest of Europe. He was by that time aware that though the Legion of Honor was, and would continue to be, an institution dear to the French heart, this one was not so, and needed an apology; for his imperial nobility had never been taken seriously or kindly by the people, who could not draw the nice distinction between a feudal and an imperial aristocracy. Even in the first steps of his enterprise he was made to feel the need of caution, and it was by statute, after all, not by decree, that the whole matter was finally regulated. So curious is popular fickleness that an Emperor who could boldly tyrannize in almost any other direction felt that he dared not take the risk of constituting himself a fountain of honor, such as legitimate monarchs were.

The system was for the world outside like some fairy wonder completed over night, since the duchies had been ready the year before. The Italian titles were the most honorable and the most highly endowed. They were either at once or later given as follows: Soult, Duke of Dalmatia; Mortier, Duke of Treviso; Savary, Duke of Rovigo; Bessières,

Duke of Istria; Duroc, Duke of Friuli; Victor, Duke of Belluno; Moncey, Duke of Conegliano; Clarke, Duke of Feltre; Masséna, Duke of Rivoli; Lannes, Duke of Montebello; Marmont, Duke of Ragusa; Oudinot, Duke of Reggio; Macdonald, Duke of Taranto; Augereau, Duke of Castiglione; Bernadotte, Prince of Ponte Corvo. In Germany there were created three similar duchies — Auerstädt for Davout, Elchingen for Ney, and Dantzic for Lefebvre. Berthier was made Prince of Neufchâtel. So much for the military officials. In civil life there were corresponding distinctions: Cambacérès, Duke of Parma; Maret, Duke of Bassano; Lebrun, Duke of Piacenza; Fouché, Duke of Otranto; Champagny, Duke of Cadore. The members of the senate, the councilors of state, the presiding officers of the legislature, and the archbishops, were all created counts. Each one of these titles was, like the others, richly endowed with land from the public domains in Poland, Germany, and Italy. But the distinction bestowed on the soldiers was marked in the difference between the accompanying gifts to them and those to civilians. The only portion of the great force which had returned to France was the guard, who were instructed to keep themselves as exclusive as possible. A most lavish pension-system, as it was considered even in that age of military splendor, drew from the army chest five hundred francs a year for soldiers who had lost a limb; officers received as high as ten thousand francs, according to the nature of their disabilities. But the marshals were showered with gold. Berthier had a million; Ney, Davout, Soult, and Bessières, six hundred thousand each; Masséna, Augereau, Bernadotte, Mortier, and Victor, four hundred thousand apiece; and the rest two hundred thousand. But even this was nothing to what some of them secured later by holding several offices at once. At one time Berthier had a yearly income of a million three hundred and fifty-five thousand francs; Davout, of nine hundred and ten thousand; Ney, of seven hundred and twenty-eight thousand; Masséna, of six hundred and eighty-three thousand. The ministers were able to secure salaries averaging about two hundred thousand francs, and ambassadors had incomes corresponding to their dignity. Caulaincourt, the ablest of all the latter class, had eight hundred thousand francs at St. Petersburg wherewith to support the imperial state of France. It is interesting to note from Napoleon's letters that he had occasionally to admonish some of these gentlemen to make use of their titles.

The Revolution had chosen to find its artistic expression in the correct and strict severity of classical forms. Napoleon had from the beginning of his career been under the spell of Greek and Roman examples. Thus it happened that the art of the First Empire was what it is — heavy, conventional, and reminiscent. With the ever-growing rigidity of censorship, literature sometimes took refuge in abstractions, or, what is much the same thing, in the contemplation of events so remote that their discussion could give no offense. Sometimes authors accepted the curious task of defending the external forms and results of the Revolution as expressed in the Empire, while combating every principle from which the movement had sprung. Able men like Chénier published some of their writings, and locked others in their desks against a brighter day. In religion the Emperor's principle was that his subjects should hate the English because they were heretics, and the Pope because he was a fanatic. The "ideologues" and "metaphysicians" were anarchists, for the public order was endangered by their teachings. The newspapers were not only gagged, but metamorphosed — the "French Citizen" into the "French Courier," the "Journal of Debates" into the "Journal of the Empire." Their columns were filled with laudations of the Emperor; their political articles were virtually composed in the Foreign Office; and there was not a symptom of anything like the existence of party feeling. A certain journalist having been allowed to make statements concerning the luxury at court, the editor of the offending paper was given to understand that the Emperor would tolerate no such criticism nor any remarks contrary to his interests.

But the crowning work of this period was the final realization of the plan for organizing public instruction in what was designated by the head of the state as the Imperial University. Though somewhat changed in name and character, it exists to-day virtually as it came from the maker's hand. Like the institution of the prefecture, it is a faultless machine of equalization and centralization, molding the mass of educated Frenchmen into one form, rendering them responsive and receptive to authoritative ideas from their youth upward, and passive in their attitude toward instruction. Joseph de Maistre used to preach that, all social order depending on the authority of beliefs as well as on the authority of behavior, no man who denied the supremacy of the Pope would permanently admit the sovereignty of the state. Napoleon

JEAN-JACQUES-RÉGIS DE CAMBACÉRÈS
DUKE OF PARMA

furnished a standing refutation of this thesis. The whole system of public instruction in France has under the third republic not merely been secularized, but it has been made, and for a quarter of a century has remained, substantially infidel. Twenty-five academic generations of living French citizens, reckoning each year's output as a generation, have come out from its laboratory with a minimum of faith; but state supremacy and state socialism are, in a moderate form, more prevalent among them than among any similar body of men elsewhere.

The University of France means literally the totality of all instruction in the country, organized by successive stages into a single system, and rigidly controlled from above. The outlines sketched in the law passed in 1802, and supplemented in 1806, were carefully followed by Napoleon in his final step, and neither the theory nor the method need be again discussed. It is significant that it was an imperial decree, and not a statute, which on March seventeenth, 1808, created the organism. There was an endowment of four hundred million francs, and a separate budget, " in order that instruction might not suffer by passing disturbances in imperial finances." In order, also, that its doctrine might not feel the influence of every passing philosophical fashion, the corporation was subordinate to, but separate from, the ministry, with a grand master, chancellor, and treasurer of its own, and thirty members, of whom ten were appointed for life by the Emperor, the rest being annually designated by the grand master. They made rules for the discipline, revised the text-books, and chose the instructors of all the institutions of learning in all France, except some of the great ecclesiastical seminaries and a few of the technical schools. At the outset it was ordered that all the masters, censors, and teachers in the great intermediate schools or lyceums should be celibates! The professors might marry, but in that case they could not live in the precincts of what was virtually a military barrack.

Liberal culture, so far as given, was provided in the lyceums, and they really form the heart of the University. Under the Empire their instruction was largely in mathematics, with a sprinkling of Latin. It is now greatly broadened and elevated. The pupils of the primary schools felt a quasi-dependence on the Emperor; those of the lyceums were the very children of patronage, for the cheapness of their education, combined with their semi-military uniforms and habits, impressed at every turn on them and their families the immanence of

the Empire. They entered by government examinations; all their letters passed through the head-master's hands; they were put under a
threefold system of espionage culminating in the grand master; the
one hundred and fifty scholarships and bourses in each were paid by
the state; the punishments were, like those of soldiers, arrest and imprisonment. With the acquisition of military habits the young *lycéen*
could look forward to military promotion, for two hundred and fifty of
the most select were sent every year to the military schools, where they
lived at the Emperor's expense, expecting professional advancement by
the Emperor's patronage. Others of less merit were detached for the
civil service, and in that also their careers were at the imperial mercy.
They were daily and hourly reminded of Napoleon's greatness, for
twenty-four hundred foreigners from the vassal states of the Empire
were scattered among these institutions, where they were turned into
Frenchmen and docile subjects at the Emperor's expense, while being
virtually held as hostages for the good behavior of their parents.
These powerful engines did not work in vain. During the comparatively short existence of the Empire their product assumed enormous
proportions, and largely modified the temper of society throughout
France. The youth educated by priests or tutors were found unable to keep pace with their favored contemporaries from the government schools, and from the first no prophet was needed to foretell
the destiny of private institutions and ecclesiastical seminaries. Little
by little they made way for or became annexed to the lyceums which
one after another were founded wherever needed. The charges of the
latter were, and are, very low; and thrifty fathers appreciate the fact.
The state is at enormous cost to support them; but public sentiment,
preferring indirect to direct taxation, approves of the expenditure,
while crafty statesmen, whether royalist, imperialist, or republican,
employ them to create citizens of the kind in power at the time.

Throughout the late summer and autumn of 1807 the imperial court
was more stately than ever before. The old nobility became assiduous
in their attendance, and, as one of the Empress's ladies in waiting is
said to have remarked, they "received good company." On his return
Napoleon had found Josephine's extravagance to be as unbounded as
ever; but he could not well complain, because, although for the most
part frugal himself, he had latterly encouraged lavishness in his family.
Still, it was not agreeable to have dressmakers' bills flung into his car-

AQUARELLE MADE FOR THE SOCIETY

FREDERICA CATHERINE SOPHIA DOROTHEA

PRINCESS ROYAL OF WÜRTEMBERG, QUEEN OF WESTPHALIA

AQUARELLE BY ERIC PAPE FROM THE PORTRAIT BY FRANÇOIS GÉRARD

riage when driving in state with his consort, and on one occasion he
sent an unprincipled but clever milliner to the prison of Bicêtre for
having disobeyed his orders in furnishing her wares to the Empress at
exorbitant prices. The person was so indispensable to the court ladies,
however, that they crowded her cell, and she was soon released. At
St. Cloud, Malmaison, the Tuileries, and Fontainebleau the social vices
of courts began to appear; but they were sternly repressed, especially
high play. By way of contrast, the city of Paris was at that very
moment debauched by a profusion of gambling-hells and houses of
prostitution, all licensed at an enormous figure by Fouché and produc-
ing great revenues for the secret police. The gorgeous state uniforms
of the marshals, the rich and elegant costumes of the ladies, the be-
spangled and begilt coats of the household, dancing, theatricals, concerts, and excursions—all these elements should have combined to
create brilliancy and gaiety in the imperial circle, but they did not.

There was something seriously amiss with the central figure. He
was often sullen and morose, often violent and even hysterical. To
calm his nervous agitation the court physician ordered warm baths,
which he spent hours in taking. Then again he was irregular in his
habits, being often somnolent during the daytime, but as frequently
breaking his rest at midnight to set the pens of his secretaries scamper-
ing to keep pace with the flow of his speech. With old friends he was
coarse and severe: even the brutal Vandamme confessed that he trem-
bled before that "devil of a man," while Lannes was the only human
being who still dared to use the familiar "thou" in addressing his old
comrade. To the face of his generals the Emperor was merely cold:
behind their backs he sneered—saying, for instance, of Davout that he
might give him never so much renown, he would not be able to carry
it; of Ney that he was disposed to ingratitude and turbulence; of Bessières, Oudinot, and Victor that they were mere mediocrities. Among
all these dazzling stars he himself moved in simple uniform and in a
cocked hat ornamented with his favorite cheap little cockade. It was
a well-calculated vanity, for with increasing corpulence plainness of
dress called less attention to his waddling gait and growing awkwardness of gesture.

The summer of 1807 saw the social triumph of the Bonaparte family, the sometime Jacobins, but now emperor and kings. Jerome
Napoleon was married on August twenty-second to the Princess Cath-

CHAP. VIII crime of Würtemberg. The Emperor had already spoken at Tilsit with
1807-08   the Czar about unions for himself and family suitable to their rank,
but the hint of an alliance with the Romanoffs was coldly received.
In the Emperor's opinion this, however, was a really splendid match.
The Rhine princes and subsidiary monarchs hastened to Paris, and one
of them showed his want of perspicacity by marked attentions to Josephine, which he hoped would secure her husband's favor. When men
of such lofty and undisputed lineage were joining what was apparently
an irresistible movement, the recusant nobility of France itself could
not well stand aloof any longer. It amused and interested the Emperor to see them obey Fouché's hint, and throng to be introduced in
the correct way to the new and undisputed sovereign, not merely of
France, but of western Europe.

KEY TO REGNAULT'S PICTURE "THE MARRIAGE OF JEROME."

1. Louis Bonaparte; 2, Princess Amelia; 3, Eugène Beauharnais; 4, Queen Hortense; 5, Joseph Bonaparte; 6, Princess Ellen; 7, Madame Joseph
Bonaparte; 8, Empress Josephine; 9, Emperor Napoleon; 10, Madame Mère; 11, Jerome Bonaparte; 12, Frederica Catherine of
Würtemberg; 13, Stéphanie Beauharnais; 14, Princess Pauline; 15, Senator Beauharnais; 16, Madame Murat;
17, Prince Borghese; 18, Marshal Murat 19, Prince of Baden; 20, Cardinal Fesch.

Moreover, they were no longer impertinent. They remembered the
fate meted out to Mme. de Staël for her solemn innuendoes, and did not
forget that the last item in the indictment on which Mme. de Chev-
reuse had been banished was a snippish remark to Napoleon's face.
Astonished at the splendor of her diamonds, he had in his own court
clumsily asked if they were all real. "Indeed, sire, I do not know,"
she replied; "but they are good enough to wear here." In consequence, therefore, of this new and now well-intentioned element the
court swelled in numbers and gained in grace, but not in joyousness.
The Empress was already foreboding her fate; there was the stiffness
of inaptitude about everything, even the amusement, and the languid
weariness of the ladies was an unforgiven imperial sin. The quick wit
of the Emperor remarked this annoying fact, and demanded counsel of
Talleyrand. The Prince of Benevento had by this time resigned his
position as minister, and the relations between himself and the Emperor were strained, but he was not rebuked when he ventured on the
old license of speech. "It is because pleasure will not move at the
drum-tap," was his answer, "and you look as if you would command

every one just as you do the army: 'Ladies and gentlemen, forward
march!'"

Talleyrand's numberless intrigues, his venality and self-seeking, his
cynicism and contemptuous airs, had finally destroyed his preponder-
ance with Napoleon, although he still retained much influence. No
one was better aware of the fact than he was. Thus far he had reck-
oned himself an indispensable factor in the administration of the Empire; now he saw that he was so no longer, that his time had come.

He had a sterile mind, and was destitute of principle. Constructive
politics were beyond his powers, and he was hopelessly ignorant of
social movements. The real Europe of his time was to him a closed
book; and while Napoleon was well served in every other function of
state, because he himself could assist and supervise, he was wretchedly
betrayed in the matter of permanent gains by diplomacy, in which he
was personally a blunderer and a tyro. Talleyrand was a distinguished
and typical aristocrat of the old French school, elegant, adroit, smooth-
spoken, and sharp. He was an unequaled courtier, influential by his
moderation in word, gesture, and expression, but a feeble adviser, and
utterly incapable of broad views. His character, being unequal to his
skill, was not strong enough either to curb or guide a headstrong master, for his intellect was neither productive nor solid. No treaty
ever made by him was lasting, and he must have known that even the
peace of Tilsit would begin to crumble almost before the papers were
signed. The balance of Europe was disturbed but temporarily by that
agreement, not permanently, as had been intended; the attempted se-
clusion of Prussia by Napoleon destroyed her old antagonism to other
German powers, and marked the beginning of amalgamation with all her
sister states for the reconstruction of an avenging German nationality.

Something may be forgiven to an adventurer in the storms of revolution, but Talleyrand trimmed his sails to every wind, outrode every
storm, and made gains in every port. He was a trusted official of the
Republic, the Consulate, the Empire, and the restored monarchy. Wise
in his day and generation, he had long before made ready to withdraw,
if necessary, from active life, by the accumulation of an enormous fortune, heaped up by means which scandalized even imperial France.
He had been embittered at the close of the Consulate by Napoleon's determination that his ministers should not be his highest dignitaries, his
arch-officers. The title of "prince," with two hundred thousand francs

a year, was a poor consolation when men like Lebrun and Cambacérès had the precedence as arch-treasurer and arch-chancellor, while — most unendurable of all — they drew salaries of three hundred and fifty thousand francs. Berthier, the Prince of Neufchâtel, had recently been made vice-constable to represent Louis Bonaparte, who, though still constable, had left Paris to become Louis Napoleon, King of Holland. This was Talleyrand's opportunity to resign from the ministry on his own initiative. He demanded a dignity for himself similar to that accorded to Berthier. The Emperor told him that, accustomed to power as he had become, he would be unhappy in a station which precluded his remaining in the cabinet. But the minister knew his rôle in the little comedy, and, persisting, was on August ninth made vice-grand elector, while Champagny, an excellent and laborious official, took his seat at the council-board as minister of external relations. Talleyrand's withdrawal had not the slightest influence on the Emperor's foreign policy; in fact, the quidnuncs at Fontainebleau declared that he was seen limping into Napoleon's office almost every evening. But he was so well known in every court, his circle of personal acquaintances was so large, so timorous, and so reverential, that superstitious men believed his retirement augured the turn of Napoleon's fortunes.

CHAPTER IX

THE EMPIRES OF LAND AND OCEAN

Diplomacy at St. Petersburg — Internal Politics of Russia — Alexander's Perplexities — War between Great Britain and Russia — New Orders in Council — The Milan Decree — Position of the United States — The Regeneration of Prussia — Napoleon's Repressive Measures — Austria's New Army — Diplomatic Tension between Russia and France — Designs of Napoleon as to Egypt — He Temporizes with Alexander — Caulaincourt and Tolstoi — The Czar's Demands — Napoleon's Visit to Italy — Limitations of his Ambition — Visions of Oriental Empire — Control of the Mediterranean — His Proposition to Russia — His Complete Program.

THE diplomatic intrigues at St. Petersburg were intensely amusing after the peace of Tilsit. Alexander coquetted with the English agents, and concealed his plans from the conservative Russians. His lips were sealed about what had occurred at the meeting with Napoleon, and the charge has been disproved that some of his suite blabbed enough to the British diplomats to enable them to divine the rest. Canning's acuteness and his conviction that Napoleon and Alexander had reached an understanding hostile to England sufficiently account for the bombardment of Copenhagen, and place the responsibility for it on his shoulders. But in the interval before that event the Czar cajoled the English embassy until they felt assured of a triumph, while almost simultaneously he assured Lesseps, the French consul-general, how precious Napoleon's society had been to him, and declared that if England did not yield the two allies would compel her. To the formal introductory communications of Russia concerning peace Canning replied by a demand for the secret articles of Tilsit, and despatched the

79

fleet to the Baltic. The successful stroke made in September at Copenhagen filled the Czar with solicitude; for, like his ally, he had hoped to gain time, and such promptness in imitating Napoleon's contempt for neutral rights dismayed him. It looked as though this were the first event in a maritime war which would end by destroying the shipyards at Cronstadt, or perhaps even St. Petersburg itself. But instead of further aggression came a new mission from the London cabinet asking for Alexander's good offices in appeasing Denmark, and offering every indemnity to that power except the restoration of the fleet. Great Britain, commanding the Baltic, could be magnanimous.

This conjunction of affairs destroyed Alexander's self-control. He had played the friend of England to no advantage, and England now asked for new and impossible proofs of his friendship. He could neither disclose to her the secret articles nor mediate in her behalf with a country which had already joined his own system. On the other hand, Savary, the French ambassador, and Lesseps, the French consul-general, were daily reminding him of his engagements to Napoleon. There was little need, for the alliance meant to him the attainment of his most cherished ambitions: the acquisition of Finland to the westward, and of the great Danube principalities of Moldavia and Wallachia to the south. In all contingencies he had to reckon with the wealthy Russian proprietors, whose prosperity demanded the easy export of their enormous produce in timber and grain by the same British ships which supplied them with essential articles that were not manufactured in Russia. To them the Continental blockade was a horror, and many in the army declared they would not shed their blood to undermine the national prosperity.

This tension could not last. The English secretly introduced into Russia a pamphlet charging that the peace of Tilsit had separated the Czar from both his people and his troops. Savary, mindful of his old detective arts, discovered its origin and adroitly laid the facts before Alexander, who burst into angry abuse of the "libel," and bemoaned the lack of able men to support him both in a wise foreign policy and in such internal reforms as the abolition of serfdom, which he was determined to accomplish. Moreover, Napoleon's conduct was such as to produce serious uneasiness. So far from evacuating Prussia, French troops still occupied all her harbor towns, and menaced the Russian frontier as if their commander were a foe and not a friend. The

JÉRÔME BONAPARTE
KING OF WESTPHALIA

agreement made with Kalkreuth for the gradual withdrawal of the French army from Prussia was held to be null, for the Prussians could not raise the indemnity of a hundred and fifty million francs computed as the direct cost of the war. To this was added the fact that no move was made toward the dismemberment of Turkey. The Emperor of the French had seized and fortified Corfu, but in a preliminary armistice between Russia and Turkey, due to his intermediation, not a word was said about the Danubian principalities; although the Russian troops were still in Wallachia, it was clear that French influence was daily growing stronger at Constantinople, and might grow strong enough to thwart the Czar's plans entirely.

Such were the disquieting considerations which finally brought to a climax the relations of Russia with England. On October twenty-sixth, Lord Leveson-Gower, the English ambassador, received a note from Count Rumianzoff to the effect that twice Russia had taken up arms for England's advantage, and had in vain solicited even such co-operation as would seem to have been in Great Britain's own interest. She had not even asked, said the writer, for reinforcements, but merely for a diversion, and had been chagrined to see that her ally, so far from maintaining the Czar's cause, had instead, like a cold observer of the bloody theater where war had been kindled at her behest, despatched expeditions on her own behalf to seize Egypt and to attack Buenos Ayres. After all this the Czar had still offered his mediation, but in vain: Great Britain had replied by an act of unheard-of violence, despoiling an ancient and dignified monarchy. Could the Czar apologize for such a deed? It was insulting to expect it. After reciting these grievances and asserting the principles of the armed neutrality, the paper announced a rupture of all diplomatic relations until reparation should be made to Denmark.

War was formally declared by Russia on November seventh, and England retorted by orders in council, issued on the eighteenth and twenty-sixth of the same month, which declared that every Continental port closed to her flag was thereafter in a state of blockade. The neutral states were each and all notified that she would exercise the right of search to the fullest extent; that all neutral ships must put into English harbors before proceeding to their destination, and pay a duty in case of reëxportation of their cargoes. An exception to this latter regulation was made in the case of the United States, they being graciously permitted to have direct commercial intercourse with Sweden, but with Sweden only. This, of course, meant that neutral states must either carry on England's trade under their own flags or abandon their commerce altogether.

This measure was in utter contempt of international law, even as then understood, and was a high-handed outrage against neutral powers, in particular against the United States. It was treating the ocean exactly as Napoleon had treated the lands of Europe. But it was a powerful weapon, for if successfully enforced it would destroy Napoleon's Continental system entirely. Accordingly, in pursuance of his policy that fire must be fought with fire, the Emperor retorted with equal ruthlessness, fulminating the terrible Milan decree of December seventeenth, 1807. In it he declared that any vessel which obeyed the orders of the English admiralty or suffered itself to be searched was and would be regarded as an English ship. It was essential, therefore, that any nation desiring exemption from the enactments of the Berlin and Milan decrees on the one hand and of the English orders in council on the other must make itself respected by force of arms. The Americans must either accept the humiliating terms of England or enter the French system and seek in a maritime war to capture the Continental markets for themselves.

Napoleon, as has already been narrated, intended to force them into the latter course immediately, but he was not well informed concerning American affairs. Jefferson was at that time in his second term as President of the United States. The Democratic party, of which he was the leader, was vastly more concerned with agricultural than with commercial interests. They were afraid to increase the public debt, cared little for the prosperity of New England commerce, and, seeking to avoid the dilemma arranged for them by England and France, passed the notorious embargo act forbidding all foreign commerce whatsoever. American ships must avoid foreign waters, which, like the land, had become the arena of a bloody duel in which the United States were not interested—so, at least, the Democrats fondly believed. Exports to England fell in a single year from forty-nine to nine millions of dollars. In other words, the embargo, though causing great distress, could not be perfectly enforced, since the Eastern merchants continued their humiliating submission to England for the sake of their lucrative speculations.

At the same time the farmers were suddenly awakened to the fact that in the end they suffered as much under the prohibition as the traders. In the resulting agitations Jefferson closed his public career without éclat. Madison wisely secured a modification of the embargo by the Non-intervention Act, which opened all foreign commerce except that with England and France. But the merchants of New England were rebellious and dissatisfied even with this. The Federalists wanted a navy and a place in the European system; in other words, a fair share in the world's carrying-trade for the seafarers of the Atlantic coast. Matters drifted on in general discontent and mutual recrimination until 1810. Napoleon in that year shrewdly announced that he had abandoned his policy, but for all that he actually continued to enforce it. This empty pretense of friendship embroiled the United States still further with England, and in the end led to their second war for independence.

The Czar had no sooner taken the decisive step of finally declaring war on England than the Napoleonic policy began further to unfold. Prussia was at once compelled to follow her protector's example, and before the ensuing season all her harbors were fortified and closed. In spite of the French occupation a national reform movement had begun in this land. In Königsberg was formed the League of Virtue, which focused the new morality and patriotism of the masses. The pens of Fichte, Schleiermacher, and other great writers continued to build up public spirit. Stein accepted office, stipulating that the privy council should be abolished, and then freed the serfs. Among other important reforms he destroyed the old distinction between land tenures, and made transfers simple. Self-government was granted to the cities. The schools were entirely reconstructed under the direction of William von Humboldt, and the University of Berlin was founded as a nursery for the new national spirit.

Under these influences the monarchy of Frederick the Great ceased to exist; the authority of the "yunker" class which supported it and had rashly brought on the war with France was temporarily eclipsed by a wholesome expression of national vigor, and the enlightened liberalism of Prussia became the stimulus for a similar movement in all Germany. As to the army, Gneisenau and Scharnhorst entered with zeal upon the task of reorganization, and the latter was a very genius of reform. Napoleon at length showed his true colors, forbade his victim to maintain more than forty-two thousand troops, and declared to the face of Frederick William's brother in Paris that the occupation of the fortresses had passed from the narrow domain of particular politics into the great field of general policy. He meant, of course, that he was thereby virtually holding in check not merely Prussia, but Russia and Austria as well. The limitation set by him to the active military force of the captive state was easily evaded by the subterfuge of substituting new recruits for those who had completed their training in the ranks; but the French occupation seemed to be virtually permanent.

The military reorganization of Austria was already complete, and Metternich wrote on July twenty-sixth, 1807, to Stadion, the minister of state, that as the peace of Tilsit had sown broadcast the germs of its own destruction, the wisdom of his correspondent's administration would one day bring Austria to the point where three hundred thousand men united under one will and directed to one goal would play the first rôle in Europe, "in a moment of universal anarchy, at one of those epochs which always follow great usurpations, and wipe out the traces of the conquerors; an epoch of which no one can foretell the date, but which nothing postpones except the life of a single man, and which all the genius of that man can so much the less postpone as he has not yet taken the first step to preclude its certain results." This reference to Napoleon's childlessness and the dependence of his system on his single life is clear enough. The Emperor of the French was himself thoroughly aware of the influence exerted by such a consideration upon the course of affairs, and in consequence his dealing with Francis was somewhat less peremptory than that with Frederick William. Nevertheless, the results were exceedingly humiliating to Austria's pride. In a treaty concluded at Fontainebleau on October tenth, 1807, with reference to the Italian frontier, her dominions were shorn to the quick. At Napoleon's suggestion, Count Starhemberg, her ambassador in London, intimated that England, in the interest of peace, ought to restore the Danish fleet and make terms with France. On the prompt refusal of Great Britain to listen, the envoy withdrew from London; but he did not leave the English cabinet in doubt as to the cause. He knew and broadly hinted that though his master dared not trifle with a Franco-Russian alliance, his heart was with the English cause. To all outward appearance, therefore, Austria was quite as subservient as Prussia to the mighty coalition of France and Russia.

THE PASSAGE OF THE FORD.

Almost immediately after the rupture with England, Alexander had the mortification of seeing his worst fears realized. Napoleon had opened to him at Tilsit a dazzling vista of territorial aggrandizement. Slowly but surely the desired effect was produced. Aware of all the dangers he ran, the Czar nevertheless sacrificed every other consideration, even that of his people's material comfort, in order to demonstrate his good faith. By declaring war he likewise paid in advance. But at the earliest possible moment, on November seventh, his ambassador to France, sent for the purpose, demanded the return—to wit, the two principalities of Wallachia and Moldavia. Simultaneously and in another quarter this same demand was made emphatic. Immediately after the meeting at Tilsit, Guilleminot, a French general, had been sent as mediator between Russia and Turkey to the seat of war on the Danube. An armistice was concluded under his direction at Slobozia, in which were two or three compensatory clauses promising that Russia would make restitution to Turkey of certain vessels and munitions of war which had been captured. The Czar professed to take great umbrage at these stipulations. Shortly afterward he rejected the whole paper, and the Russian troops remained in Wallachia. This conduct was intended to indicate his obstinate determination to have the vague promises of Napoleon defined, and then to secure their performance.

The Emperor of the French had been kept well informed by Savary, and knew that the Tilsit alliance, being distasteful to the Russian people, hung on the personal good will of their sovereign. He would have been glad to put Alexander off with some slight rectification of the border-line between Russia and Turkey and with further indefinite promises, but he dared not. Accordingly he devised the plea that the aggrandizement of the Eastern and Western empires must keep equal pace, not in the West, for that was his by right, but in those debatable lands wherewith Russia hoped to secure a permanent seat in the councils of Europe. He was confirmed in his desire to postpone the partition of Turkey by finding that Mustapha, the Sultan who had overthrown Selim in defiance of France, was now ready in turn to make friends with her and perform her behests. The hope of getting Egypt was again awakened, but the times were not ripe and delay must be secured.

In addition to these considerations there was that of immediate safety. The last two campaigns had seen Napoleon a victor, once over

Austria and Russia combined, again over Prussia and Russia combined;
but in each there had been moments when the coalition of the three
would have overwhelmed him. For this reason he would gladly have
declared at Tilsit that the house of Hohenzollern had ceased to reign,
in order thereby to preclude any future danger from a triple alliance.
This idea he had abandoned for the time in order to gratify Alexander.
His ally secure, he now returned or pretended to return to it. Prussia
was regaining her strength too rapidly; her embittered hostility was
an ever-increasing menace. On the plea that she could never pay the
promised indemnity, and was therefore to be treated as a bankrupt,
Napoleon declared at last that Russia could have the Danube provinces if France could take Silesia for the grand duchy of Warsaw.
" Prussia," ran Napoleon's despatch on this subject—" Prussia would
have but two millions of inhabitants; but would not that be enough
for the welfare of the royal family, and is it not in their interest to
place her without delay and with perfect resignation among the inferior powers, since all their efforts to restore the position she has
lost merely serve to distress their subjects and cherish idle regrets ? "
" What the Emperor would prefer," said this same memorandum, " is
that the Turks should remain in peaceable possession of Wallachia and
Moldavia; still he would hand over these provinces to the Czar in
return for a just compensation from Prussian lands; and finally,
though far from wishing a complete partition of Turkey, he desires
you not to condemn utterly the plan, but rather to dwell on the motives for postponing it. This ancient project of Russian ambition is a
tie which can bind Russia to France."

For the purposes of this difficult negotiation Napoleon had chosen
Caulaincourt, his devoted servant and most adroit diplomat. Having
been concerned in the expeditions to Strasburg and Ettenheim which
captured Enghien, the ambassador had been deeply, though unjustly,
involved in the disrepute of the execution, and that fact was a tie
which bound him to his master. The two seemed thoroughly to understand each other. Alexander had chosen an envoy who was the
very antipodes of the adroit and elegant Caulaincourt. Count Tolstoi
was a bluff soldier, selected in the belief that he would be uninfluenced
by the intrigues of Paris society, and could secure the utmost return
for the agreement of Tilsit by direct negotiation with the Emperor
himself, as one old soldier talking with another. This officer was

instructed to lay great stress on the liberation of Prussia, but to remember that the object of his mission was to cement harmony and
confidence. On the journey to Paris he paused at Memel to pay his
respects to Frederick William and his Queen. He found them, considering their station, actually in want, dependent on the Czar's gifts
of clothes and other necessaries for the little personal comfort they
enjoyed. This made a deep impression on Tolstoi's heart, and though
received at Paris with such distinction as had never been accorded to
any other ambassador, he was cold and distant with both the Emperor
and the court. At last there was positive disagreement between him
and the great personages of the capital; there was even a rumor that
Ney and he would fight a duel. The offensive remarks which led to
such tension were due to a statement by Tolstoi that Russia had been
beaten by accident, that Russian soldiers were invincible, and might
one day take their revenge.

Moreover, the ambassador could not even get on with Napoleon.
Both he and his staff avoided the splendors of Fontainebleau, preferring to frequent the drawing-rooms of a notorious actress whose name
had often been linked with that of the Emperor. Under such circumstances diplomacy gathered but little fruit. Napoleon offered both the
Danubian provinces for Silesia, or else the evacuation of Prussia proper
for that of Wallachia; he even mentioned the magic word "Constantinople" as part of Russia's share in an eventual partition of the whole
Turkish empire. Tolstoi wrote to St. Petersburg that France was
postponing the evacuation of Prussia for selfish purposes, meaning to
dismember her; and from that starting-point depicted the horrors of a
Napoleonic Europe. Such opinions dismayed Alexander, and although
he received Caulaincourt with distinction equal to that which had
been accorded to Tolstoi, he firmly refused the bargain offered by him.
He would not consent to a further dismemberment of Prussia, partly
for sentimental reasons, chiefly because he could not endure the
strengthening of the grand duchy of Warsaw, the new political organism which suggested the restoration of Poland. As to the principalities, these he would have. Russian society had for the moment repressed its hostility to the Czar and his treaty of Tilsit, and was
quietly waiting to see what would be the substantial results. No gain
less than the acquisition of Wallachia and Moldavia would reinstate
Alexander in their good will or make the French alliance endurable.

This was of course a serious crisis; but Caulaincourt, nothing dismayed, set himself, by the exercise of all those social arts of which he had such a mastery, to win the aristocratic circles of St. Petersburg.

In the month of December, 1807, Napoleon was on a royal progress through his kingdom of Italy, and the news of the diplomatic crisis in Russia reached him at Venice, which had become his as a result of Austerlitz and by the treaty of Presburg. Although he had gone thither for a serious consultation with Joseph, its fascinations were already weaving curious plans in the Emperor's mind. His rapid journey through Lombardy and a short visit to Milan, whence he fulminated his reply to the English admiralty, had convinced him of the firm sovereignty he exercised throughout these splendid realms. In the few days of his presence he had further strengthened his power by many generous and beneficent decrees. It was with a sense of security that he came to Venice; at once he yielded to her spell, realizing that at last his control of the Adriatic was complete, inasmuch as now he held both shores and commanded the entrance by the possession of Corfu. Just beyond was the brilliant East, ripe for conquest. Could he or should he lose the opportunity to use such a superb base of operations, win the gratitude of all Venetia by restoring the ancient glories of her capital, and thereby lay his hand at last on the bauble which had once before so dazzled him? Besides, Great Britain, his hated rival, scorning the terms he had offered, disdaining the Continental blockade, anchored in her strength by the control of Western seas, was vulnerable in India, and there alone. These considerations returned with overpowering allurement to his imagination, and four millions of francs were appropriated to improve the harbor and restore somewhat the splendors of Venice.

New Year's day found the Emperor again at the Tuileries, in time to receive a new courier from Russia with still more vigorous representations of Alexander's desires. The idea of a general partition of Turkish lands grew stronger, and in an interview with Metternich, Napoleon hinted that Austria should have a share. Instructions were sent to Caulaincourt that he should hold out hopes in order to gain time and to learn whether it was definitely impossible that matters should remain as the treaty of Tilsit, taken literally, had arranged them. This procrastinating attitude of mind had a twofold cause. One appears to have been a gradual realization in Napoleon's consciousness that

NAPOLEON DICTATING TO HIS SECRETARIES

dreams and schemes must materialize, that in the mystery of a life like his one step inevitably leads to another, that his career must encircle the vast globe, while he himself was but mortal, finite, and already verging to the utmost limit of his powers. A year before he had written to Josephine that he was of all men the most enslaved; "my master has no bowels, and that master is the nature of things." The other cause was the fearless and warlike attitude taken in Great Britain by both crown and Parliament and announced with threats of eternal war at the opening of the legislative session of 1807. It appears probable, likewise, that whatever answer should be given by Alexander to his pregnant question, he felt his only safety now to be in the alliance with the Czar.

Time, time, time — that was the prime necessity; there were only twenty-four hours in the day, and only a certain quantity of nerve force in his own system. Before the partition of Turkey, if Alexander's reply should make it inevitable, two weighty matters must be settled: first, the road to an Oriental empire must be secured; and second, the already existing Western empire of Europe must be rounded out by the "regulation" of Spanish affairs—the appropriation, if it should seem best, of the whole Iberian peninsula. Any tyro in geography could see by a glance at the map that as navigation was in those days—that is, by the propulsion of fickle winds amid the partly known currents of ocean and sea—the command of Gibraltar and Malta meant the control of the Levant, and the British held both places. With Spain in French hands, Gibraltar eventually might be taken, but the case of Malta was far different. In the possession of a seafaring nation like the English the island was impregnable. But was this in reality the only outlet for the French empire to the East? From France proper, yes; but from Italy, by the Adriatic, there was an admirable alternative, if not, indeed, the only true line of trade.

Since the first aspirations of his ambition, Napoleon had dreamed of supremacy in the Mediterranean, and every successive treaty made with Northern powers had looked to some strengthening of French influence on that sea. Now at last he had Corfu, and the English, straitened for troops, were withdrawing the forces which occupied Sicily to send them into Portugal. The squadrons from Brest, Lorient, and Rochefort were at once ordered to unite in the Mediterranean. This was the moment to seize Sicily, and with that island added to

Corfu, France would control the best road into Egypt. But the hostile fate which seemed to attend all Napoleon's undertakings by sea again checkmated him. English cruisers were found hovering about Corfu, and the landing in Sicily was temporarily abandoned in order to sweep the English from the waters of the Ionian Isles. In the event of success, the invasion of Turkey, the seizure of Egypt, and the gratification of Alexander would be easy. More remotely, the deadly blow at England could be struck in Asia. What a conception! What a debauch of the imagination! But there was one specter which, though laid for intervals, would not entirely down, and returned with stolid persistency: the existence of the Western empire hung on the thread of a single life; the very crowns of France and Italy had no heir. The situation was much discussed in court circles, sometimes even among the people, and was becoming acute. In order to solve the problem peace was essential, and not a remote, but an·immediate one, if possible. The Russian ambassador, returning from London, had reported on his journey through France that the English were not so envenomed as they seemed. It was only a straw, yet it was talked of. At once Napoleon seized it, and announced that his one aim, his most ardently desired goal, was—peace.

It was now the close of January; Tolstoi was invited to join a hunting-party, and in the heart of the forest Napoleon found means to be alone with him. After a long, vague, contradictory, but dramatic conversation setting forth the same three alternatives,—peace between Russia and Turkey without the principalities, or the principalities in exchange for Silesia, or the ultimate but not immediate partition of Turkey,—the great actor suddenly paused as if in an ecstasy of sincerity, and snatching his hat off his head with both hands, flung it on the ground as he said: "Hark you, M. Tolstoi; it is not the Emperor of the French, but an old general of division that is now talking to another. May I be thought the vilest of men if I do not scrupulously fulfil the contract I made at Tilsit, and if I do not evacuate both Prussia and the duchy of Warsaw as soon as you have withdrawn your troops from Moldavia and Wallachia! I am neither a fool nor a child, not to know what I stipulate, and what I stipulate I always fulfil." Leaving this objurgation time to work its effect, the Emperor of the French a few days later—on February second—wrote with his own hand to the Emperor of all the Russias. It was an innocent and

ANNE-JEAN-MARIE-RENÉ SAVARY
DUKE OF ROVIGO

kindly epistle, advising his friend to strengthen his army, and promising all aid possible in case he should feel that the border-line of Sweden was too near St. Petersburg. An army of fifty thousand men, Russian, French, perhaps a "little Austrian," marching into Asia by way of Constantinople, would not reach the Euphrates before England would begin to tremble. "I am strong in Dalmatia, you on the Danube. One month after an agreement we could be on the Bosporus. But our mutual interests require to be combined and equalized in a personal conference. Tolstoi is not built on the proportions of Tilsit. We could have everything ready, you and I, or perhaps Caulaincourt and Rumianzoff, before March fifteenth, and by May first our troops could be in Asia at the moment when those of your Majesty were in Stockholm. We would have preferred peace, you and I, but we must do what is predestined, and follow whither the irresistible march of events conducts us."

This letter was a masterpiece. It meant, first, a little European war, short and sharp, whereby Russia would get Finland as a sop and have her attention drawn off from Prussia and Spain; secondly, a menace which would bring England to terms and produce a peace; thirdly, the neutralization of Austria by inviting her to sit down at the feast; lastly, the consolidation of Napoleon's dynasty for the ultimate completion of his designs in the Orient either with or without Russia's aid. The alternative would be a war of hitherto unknown dimensions, including not only all Europe, but Asia Minor and northern Africa; out of such a conflict might result a permanent order the foundation and copestone of which would be French supremacy. England would of course rush to the assistance of Sweden, the only land now left in Europe that had never fallen into the orbit of the French system. At that moment Spain and Portugal, abandoned to their fate, must drop into French hands. If England should still prove resolute, then an expedition to Egypt would sail from Corfu, while simultaneously the united armies of Russia, France, and Austria would march to the conquest of Turkey and the seizure of India. It was a scheme so vast, so logical, so imperial, that it left far behind the dreams of a Corsican patriot or the visions of an ardent Frenchman. Successful as a soldier, the Emperor was carried by each new victory into widening circles of enterprise which could have no relation to narrow national limits.

CHAPTER X

FRENCH EMPIRE AND EUROPEAN NATIONALITY

DIPLOMATIC FENCING WITH RUSSIA—CAULAINCOURT AND RUMIANZOFF—
PLIGHT OF THE CZAR—NAPOLEON AND THE PAPACY—THE POPE A
PRISONER—THE HOUSE OF BRAGANZA—PARTITION OF PORTUGAL—
FLIGHT OF THE ROYAL FAMILY—JUNOT'S ASPIRATIONS—THE CON-
DITION OF SPAIN—THE COURT—THE CROWN PRINCE—THE POPU-
LAR FACTIONS—NAPOLEON'S PLANS—QUARREL OF CHARLES AND
FERDINAND—TRIAL OF FERDINAND—INVASION OF SPAIN—NAPO-
LEON AND LUCIEN AT MANTUA—NAPOLEON AND JOSEPH AT VENICE
—GODOY THWARTED—THE FRENCH ARMAMENT—THE HUMILIATION
OF SPAIN—FALL OF GODOY—ABDICATION OF THE KING.

THE instructions issued by Napoleon to Caulaincourt in this crisis reveal the writer's entire political system during the turning-point of his career: they show him at the height of his powers, promising, cajoling, suggesting, procrastinating, representing his own actions in the best light without regard to truth, using Russia as long as she could serve him, and abandoning her within a few days when she became re-calcitrant; all this to gain time and opportunity. The Czar had been from the outset instigated by the French ambassador to seize Finland, but feeling that success in that quarter would weaken his claims on the principalities, he hesitated. Court intrigue began to thicken about him once more. With every day the miseries and uncertainties of his position made him more wretched. At last he behaved with the incon-sistency of distraction and hesitation. Almost while soothing words were being uttered to the Swedish ambassador, Russian columns sud-denly burst into the Swedish province, and were not withdrawn. Alexander renewed his demand for the Danube provinces. Napoleon sent him exquisite presents, Sèvres porcelain or some specimen of choice armor. At last came the letter of February second. The first impression made on the Czar by its reading was one of exaggerated joy and enthusiasm: "Ha! the style of Tilsit! What a great man! What large ideas!" Such were his exclamations as he read. But calm deliberation awakened suspicions, and before long a defiant spirit led to a categorical request that any ultimate design on Silesia should be formally renounced, whereupon Caulaincourt replied: "The Emperor Napoleon demands that your Majesty shall not be more urgent with him than he is with you."

As a preliminary to the second personal interview between the two monarchs, suggested at Tilsit, and for which proposals were now renewed from Paris, the two ministers, Caulaincourt and Rumianzoff, finally began to discuss the terms of a partition of Turkey. The diplomatic gladiators were well matched; between offer and substitute, demand and excuse, feint and counter-feint, the days passed in a most entertaining manner, until suddenly the Czar became aware that time was flying and that he was not making headway. Somewhat petulantly the interview was postponed, for it was clear that the ministers would not agree by the time suggested, and without an agreement Alexander refused to attend. Meanwhile his troops in Finland had met with bitter and obstinate resistance. His army had been driven from eastern Bothnia, and his fleet lay blockaded by that of Great Britain under Admiral Saumarez. St. Petersburg was terrified by the presence of an English fleet in the Baltic. The Czar could not weaken his force on the Danube, lest he should lose the coveted provinces, and he dared not withdraw troops from Poland, for the French were still in Silesia. With the understanding that Bernadotte should be their active auxiliary, the Russian forces had rashly crossed the Swedish border with inadequate numbers; and in reality the marshal did set out to join them, but half-way on his march, for some unexplained reason, he had paused. Caulaincourt said it was because of the difficulties encountered in crossing the Belt; but the halt was, of course, one move in Napoleon's game. On April twenty-fifth the latter wrote to Talleyrand: "Was I to send my soldiers so lightly into Sweden? There was nothing for me there." Simultaneously the French forces in both Poland and Prussia were compacted and strengthened, while at the confluence of the Bug and the Vistula, in the grand duchy of Warsaw, over against the Russian frontier, were steadily rising the walls of a powerful fort above which waved the tricolor. What a plight was this for the White Czar, the grandson of Catherine II., the philosophic monarch educated by Laharpe, the beneficent despot! Behind him a disgusted nation, before him illimitable warfare; bound by the letter of an ambiguous treaty, occupied in a doubtful conquest, thwarted in his ambitions; in short, if not checkmated, put into a position very much like that known in the noble game of chess as stalemate!

Napoleon's treatment of the Czar makes the whole situation in northern Europe and Austria easily comprehensible; it is necessary to examine from the same standpoint, also, what occurred in the southern states of Europe, remote as they were; otherwise the course of affairs at the opposite extremities of Europe seems utterly mysterious. If the path followed at St. Petersburg was tortuous, what shall be said of the policy pursued in the Papal States, in Tuscany, in Portugal and Spain? During the diplomatic reconnaissance led by Caulaincourt, the statesmen of these countries had been busy at Fontainebleau. What Cardinal Bayanne seemed anxious to obtain for Pius VII.—namely, the inviolability of his territories — had been lost even before the concessions demanded from the Pope were made. The trembling prelate had consented to join the federation against England, to drive out the monks, to accept an increased French representation in the College of Cardinals, and to admit Venetia to the Concordat. But to use Napoleon's own expression in the decree issued from Vienna on May seventeenth, 1809, the Western Emperor had already "resumed the grant" of Charles the Great which had been used against his successor. There was no longer a hostile strip of land, stretching from sea to sea, which separated the kingdoms of Naples and Italy, for the three legations were occupied in December, 1807.

With this fulcrum Bayanne had been moved to negotiate a formal treaty containing all Napoleon's stipulations. The Pope was exasperated by the occupation of his lands, and refused his assent to the paper; he would not even enter the French federative system. This attitude appears to have been quite as agreeable to the Emperor of the French as one of submission would have been. Appealing to public opinion on the ground of necessity, he sent his troops on February second, 1808, into the city of Rome; in March, Ancona, Macerata, Fermo, and Urbino were consolidated with the kingdom of Italy; and before the end of April, the foreign priests were banished, the Pope's

ARMAND-AUGUSTIN-LOUIS DE CAULAINCOURT
DUKE OF VICENZA

FROM THE PAINTING BY FRANÇOIS GÉRARD

battalions were enrolled under the tricolor, and the guard of nobles was disbanded: the entire administration was in French hands. For a year the successor of St. Peter remained a fainéant prince shut up in the Quirinal. To a demand for the resignation of his temporal power he replied by a bull, dated June tenth, 1809, excommunicating the invaders of his states; thereupon he was seized and sent a prisoner to Grenoble. Napoleon, looking backward in the days of his humiliation, said that this quarrel with the Pope was one of the most wearing episodes in all his career. It undid much of the web knitted in the Concordat, by alienating the Roman Catholics both in France itself and in his conquered or allied lands.

During the same autumn months of 1807 another treaty was negotiated at Fontainebleau; namely, a secret compact with Spain for the partition of Portugal. The house of Braganza, like the other so-called legitimate monarchies of Europe, had fallen into a moral and physical decline. The Queen was a lunatic, and her son Don John, who was regent, though a mild and honorable man, lacked every element of greatness such as would have enabled him to swim in the troubled waters of his time. The land, moreover, was saturated with democratic principles. There had been a tacit understanding that on account of the enormous tribute paid to France for the acknowledgment of neutrality she would close one eye to the traffic with England, which was essential to the prosperity, if not to the very existence, of the little country. But the Berlin and Milan decrees were intended to be measures of serious war, and the Emperor now insisted that they should be enforced. Although the regent was the son-in-law of Charles IV. of Spain, yet after the peace of Tilsit the court of Madrid united with that of Fontainebleau in an effort to compel the closing of all Portuguese harbors and the fulfilment of the decrees to the letter, demanding the dismissal of the English minister, the arrest of all British subjects, and the confiscation of all English goods. The reply of John was a consent to everything except the arrest of innocent traders.

This partial refusal was a sufficient pretext; at once the French envoy at Lisbon was recalled, Junot was ordered to enter Spain and to march on Portugal, while the terms of partition were settled at Fontainebleau with Charles's minister, Izquierdo, in a compact which Napoleon must have looked upon as the great practical joke of his life. For fear he should be too quickly found out, he positively inhibited

Charles from communicating it to his ministers. The French ambassador at Madrid was also kept in ignorance of its terms. Under it the King of Spain was to be styled Emperor of the Two Americas; and in return for Etruria, which was at last to be formally incorporated with the kingdom of Italy, he was to have what he had so long desired, the virtual sovereignty of Portugal. Over one portion the young King of Etruria was to reign as a vassal; over a second, the generalissimo and high admiral of Spain, the Prince of the Peace, the Queen's paramour, the King's trusted servant, Manuel Godoy; a third was to remain unappropriated for Charles's disposal at a later date.

The treaty ended with the seemingly innocent stipulation that a new French army of forty thousand men should be formed at Bayonne, to be in readiness should Great Britain land troops in Portugal. It was not, however, to enter Spain without the agreement of both contracting parties. Meantime Junot, by his Emperor's command, was sending home maps, plans, topographical sketches, and itineraries of Spain. Although twenty-five thousand Spaniards were marching with him, he received orders, dated October thirty-first, three days after the treaty was signed at Fontainebleau, to seize all the strong places of Portugal, occupy them with French troops, and not to permit the Spaniards to garrison a single one. His first object, he had been already told, should be to capture the fleet lying in the Tagus and to take the regent prisoner. The clever and ambitious general marched swiftly, and on November twenty-seventh reached, with his exhausted troops, Abrantes, a town about eighty miles from Lisbon. The news of his arrival was unexpected in the capital; worse still, as it appeared to the dismayed court, were the evidences that he would receive an enthusiastic reception from many influential elements of the population, who still considered the word "French" a synonym for "democratic." Sir Sidney Smith, who commanded the British ships in the Tagus, addressed a letter to Don John promising that England would never recognize a rule in Portugal hostile to the house of Braganza, and strongly urging him to embark the royal family for the Portuguese dominions in South America. The prince had probably read what had been published in the "Moniteur" of November thirteenth : to wit — "The regent of Portugal loses the throne. The fall of the house of Braganza is a new proof of the inevitable destruction attending those who unite with England." At any rate the hard-pressed ruler was un-

THE FRENCH ARMY IN THE MOUNTAINS OF PORTUGAL

nerved, and issued a jerky, feeble proclamation, declaring that he would never submit to the tyranny of Napoleon, announcing his flight, naming a council of regency, and requesting those who were so disposed to accompany him. A very few faithful subjects joined themselves to the royal family, and with the mad Queen in their midst the little band embarked.

The fleet had hardly worked its way out of the river when Junot reached Lisbon with a small corps of panting, worn-out men. His prey had escaped, but so had the mad Queen, and from that moment he began to wonder why a crown would not sit comfortably on his own head. He had been Bonaparte's faithful confidant from the outset of his career, and could furnish a queen who boasted an ancestry no less distinguished than that of the Greek emperors of the Comnenian family. The people were most friendly, deputations from the powerful secret society of freemasons presented addresses, the regency made no resistance, the commander-in-chief and his army gave in their submission. But the French general showed no sign of organizing the liberal government which they so earnestly desired and fully expected. On the contrary, he established military provinces, seized all the public moneys, and sought to conciliate his master's debtors at his master's expense; for, instead of the forty millions indemnity demanded by Napoleon, he took his pen, like the unjust steward, and wrote twenty. In return the Portuguese radicals were to ask the Emperor that he should be made their king. Owing in part to Junot's insatiable greed and his appropriation of enormous private treasure,—an example which his army was quick to follow,—in part to the subsequent disenchantment and a general revulsion of feeling, the plan came to naught. Before long the Spanish general Bellesca seized the French governor of Oporto and began a rebellion in favor of Don John. The commander-in-chief, called from Lisbon to suppress the insurgents, left the city under a committee at the head of which was the Bishop of Oporto. The prelate at once applied to England for help, and in a short time the whole country had organized secret juntas in order to throw off the French yoke. England responded with alertness, sending troops from Sicily and from Ireland; but the strongest reinforcement of all was the general appointed to command them, Sir Arthur Wellesley. Before the middle of August, 1808, the Peninsular war was raging and the laurels were England's.

Meantime the contemplated upheaval had occurred in Spain. It is impossible to conceive deeper degradation than that into which the Bourbon monarchy of that country had sunk, and the court had carried the country with it in its debasement. The population had fallen to ten millions, and of a nominal army of a hundred and twenty thousand men not fifty thousand were really effective. The host of office-holders and privileged nobility which battened like leeches on an exhausted treasury was equaled in number only by the clergy, secular and regular, with nuns, novices, and servants, who lived on the revenues of the ecclesiastical estates, and on what could be extorted from an impoverished people. By a terrible form of primogeniture the lands which did not belong to the Church had gradually fallen into the hands of a few owners, who lived in state at Madrid and never laid eyes on their farms, forests, or pastures. The peasantry had no interest to improve what might be taken from them at the death of the proprietor, or by caprice be appraised at a higher value on account of their very efforts toward the amelioration of their lot. The grandees kept gloomy state in vast palaces filled with hordes of idle servants. The remnants from their lavish but poorly served tables supported the crowds of beggars that thronged their gates. Of social life they had little; they were gloomy, lonely, and sullenly indifferent. In their stables stood herds of mules and hung stores of gaudy trappings, but these were used only a few times each year to convey the owners in proper dignity to the great public functions.

On such a foundation stood the court: the King, generous-minded but deceived, and jealously attached to the crown servants, impatient of any annoyance, and always declaring a willingness to resign from his throne; the Queen, clear-headed and ambitious, but self-indulgent, extravagant, and vicious; Godoy, the Prince of the Peace,—so called from the treaty which he had negotiated at Basel to conclude the French and Spanish revolutionary wars,—the real ruler, soothing the King's sensibilities and gratifying the Queen's passions. To preserve his ascendancy this trimmer had thrown in his lot with Napoleon; but, faithless and perfidious, he would gladly have rejected that or any other protection to fly to one he believed stronger. In any centralized monarchy the administrative law is the backbone; in Spain the administration was feeble and corrupt, for every member of it was engaged in humbly imitating the example of its head, whose house was a depot of

plunder, whence toward the close of his career the spoils were transferred on pack-mules by night, no one knew whither. It was said, and
many sober men believed it, that Godoy had all the wealth of Spain.

Ferdinand, Prince of Asturias, and heir apparent to the throne, was
a young widower of good impulses but feeble character. His deceased
wife, married in 1803, had been the daughter of Queen Caroline of
Naples; having quarreled with her mother-in-law, Louisa, she had died
prematurely, probably poisoned. The prince knew the scandals of his
father's household and the abuses of Godoy's administration, but
thought the bonds of degradation too strong to be stricken off by a
weak hand like his own. His followers, however, headed by the Duke
del Infantado and the ambitious Canon Escoiquiz, his former tutor, were
numerous and enlightened. They understood how hollow was the protection vouchsafed by Napoleon to Godoy, and how faithless was the
pretended friendship of the latter for France. Their plan was that
Ferdinand should refuse the proffered hand of Godoy's sister-in-law,
demand that of a Beauharnais princess, and thus secure the interest
and aid of the French emperor. With such support they might hope
to overthrow the minister and reform the administration. No doubt
they also dreamed of power and place for themselves.

As time passed, the sympathies of the nation rallied more and more
to Ferdinand, until at last he became the leader and representative of
the solid elements in society. Between the waning power of Godoy and
the rising popularity of the crown prince, something like an equilib-
rium was at last established, and in 1807 the two embittered factions
stood like gladiators looking for a chance to strike. This situation was
made to Napoleon's hand; but as it gave rise to more and more serious
intrigues, a decision had to be taken promptly. Should he accede to
Ferdinand's desire, formally communicated in a letter sent by Escoiquiz
on October twelfth? Talleyrand and Fouché both urged the adoption
of the policy. What prompted Talleyrand cannot be surmised. After
Austerlitz he had urged moderation, but it was probably because he
was bribed by the vanquished. His judgment and interest may, however, have kept equal pace in that conclusion. He was most likely
influenced in this one by the Empress, whose position was becoming
desperate, for the Bonaparte family were now persistently and openly
urging a divorce. All Josephine's arts seemed unavailing against her
obdurate enemies, and her last hope was to obtain royal alliances for

her relatives, thus securing new support against those of the Emperor. She had a charming niece, Mlle. Tascher de la Pagerie, to whom she was ardently devoted; and to set on the throne of Spain one who was almost a daughter would both gratify natural affection and fortify her own position.

There is no indication, however, that Talleyrand's hand was crossed this time, though again his judgment coincided with his interest in sound advice. The country was utterly disorganized and a change must occur; the people were too haughty to endure their humiliation longer; it would be better to support Ferdinand as a reformer, and thereby secure for the French system not merely the kingdom proper, but all her colonial dominions. As Fouché put it, the King had so far been one of the best of French prefects, and if he were no longer efficient his legitimate heir had better be continued in the office. But the idea of securing the Spanish colonies for his Empire dazzled and allured the Emperor more than the assured support of Spain. Having determined for that purpose to put one of his brothers on the Spanish throne, he disregarded both the clamorous calls for aid from the King on one side and the approaches of Ferdinand on the other. All remonstrance from his own family was vain, and he proceeded with his scheme. A new conscription secured the forty thousand men for Bayonne, and General Clarke was ordered to fortify the frontier.

Exactly in the nick of time the intrigues at Madrid had come to a head. On October twenty-eighth an armed Spanish force seized the person and papers of Ferdinand. Godoy feigned illness and kept his rooms, while the Queen examined what was found. It was said that there was a cipher code for corresponding with friends; a memorial from Ferdinand to Napoleon charging Godoy with a design to seize the throne, and mentioning his mother's shame in covert terms; a memorial from Escoiquiz asking from the Emperor the hand of a French princess; and an order under the seal of Ferdinand VII., with blank date, to the Duke del Infantado, appointing him to the command of New Castile on the King's death. Two days later Godoy's connection with the seizure was proved; for, ill as he feigned to be, he was observed entering the Escorial after nightfall. Next day the King announced the discovery of this "conspiracy" in a proclamation to his people, and wrote a letter of similar wording to Napoleon, complaining that Beauharnais, the French ambassador, had been the center of the

THE ARREST OF FERDINAND

intrigue. The charge was strictly true, for this brother of the Empress's first husband, though a bluff, honest man, was blindly self-confident, and had fallen into the trap set for him in Paris. He was not unwilling to gratify Josephine, he despised Godoy, and his evident friendship for the crown prince had been largely instrumental in creating the popular confidence that France would regenerate Spain by means of the legitimate heir.

Charles also announced his intention of cutting Ferdinand off from the succession, and humbly requested Napoleon's advice. A commission of Castilian grandees was appointed to try the culprit, while simultaneously strenuous efforts were made to force a confession of conspiracy from him. The latter scheme failed, but the prince obeyed with alacrity the summons to appear. Exactly what occurred is unknown, but it can be imagined; some of the facts leaked out, and the result was a wretched compromise both at court and among the people. The prince asserted that he had written the suspicious order during his father's recent illness, basely denounced his accomplices, and by declaring that it was Beauharnais who had suggested his asking a wife from the Emperor strengthened the general belief that Napoleon had instigated his entire course. This was enough to cow the King and Queen. The offender was at once released, and wrote a formal request for pardon. His sire issued a proclamation granting the boon. His friends were formally tried, but Godoy dared not ask questions compromising the French ambassador, and they were acquitted.

During the trial the "secret hand" was indicated as being still unknown; some said it was that of the Queen, a few thought the grand inquisitor had been meddling. Napoleon sent a wily and misleading epistle declaring that he had never received a letter from the Prince of Asturias,— which literally was true, though he had been informed of its existence and of its contents,—and that he had heard nothing but the vague gossip of palace talk. This letter of Napoleon's was confided on November thirteenth to one of his shrewdest counselors, the chamberlain de Tournon, who was carefully instructed to bring home the most accurate information he could secure regarding the state of public feeling, and secretly to observe the condition in which he found the frontier fortresses of Pamplona and Fuenterrabia. On the same day orders were issued for Dupont to take advantage of the general excitement incident to the recent events, cross the frontier with his division, and advance to Vitoria, whence he should reconnoiter the surrounding country. As if to emphasize his own indifference, in reality to avoid unpleasant questions and with the most serious objects in view, the Emperor set out for Italy a few days earlier; and the day of his arrival in Milan was the date on which Dupont invaded Spain. During this visit to Venice, which has been referred to as the time in which Russia was brought to a standstill and the ultimate method of procedure in the Orient outlined, Napoleon met the Queen Regent of Etruria. She declared, as was expected of her, that she could not continue to reign where she did not rule, her dominions being occupied on the ground of large policy by French troops; accordingly she was despatched to Madrid with a royal train. Her sometime kingdom was incorporated with that of Italy, and the unsuspecting Beauharnais was instructed to have her new Portuguese realm ready against her arrival.

But the real object of that winter journey to Italy seems to have been the two interviews which the Emperor had with his brothers Joseph and Lucien, the former being beckoned from Naples to Venice, the latter from Rome to Mantua. The younger brother had, after the first juvenile heats of radicalism, become a moderate republican, holding his convictions resolutely. Having opposed a hereditary consulate for Napoleon, and unmindful of any reward he might have claimed for his services of Brumaire, he withdrew from public life to spend his time in study and the gratification of his literary tastes. On the death of his first wife, by whom he had two daughters, he married, in direct opposition to Napoleon's wishes, the beautiful and accomplished Mme. de Jauberthon. This was in 1803. Having been importuned to put her away and lend himself to the project of buttressing the Empire by accepting a crown and contracting a royal marriage, he had refused. By far the ablest and most courageous of the Bonaparte brothers, he was utterly indifferent to the rise of Napoleonic empire, for his principles were fixed. It was with reluctance that he came to Mantua. There are two accounts of what happened there: that which has long been accepted—of Lucien hotly refusing the crown of Portugal, with the hand of Prince Ferdinand for his daughter Charlotte; and that which makes Napoleon's first offer to have been Etruria. Both accounts agree, however, that the Emperor raised his bid to the promise of Italy—always on condition that his brother should divorce his wife and rule in the interest of the imperial power. Lucien disdained even this bribe, declaring that he would accept the crown, but that he would rule in the interests of his subjects, and that he would in no case consider a divorce. Angry words were spoken. Napoleon crushed in his hand a watch with which he had been toying, hissing out that thus he would crush wills which opposed his. "I defy you to commit a crime," retorted Lucien. Before parting there was a half reconciliation, and Napoleon requested that at least his brother's eldest daughter might be sent to Paris for use in the scheme of royal alliances. Lucien assented, and the child, a clever girl of about fourteen, was sent to live with Madame Mère. She was thoroughly discontented, and wrote bright, sarcastic letters to her stepmother, whom she loved, depicting the avarice of her grandmother and the foibles of her other relatives. These, like all other suspected letters of the time, were intercepted and read in the "cabinet noir"; their contents being made known to Napoleon, he sent the petulant, witty writer back to her father. Despairing of any support from Lucien or his family, Napoleon formally adopted his stepson Eugène, the viceroy, with a view to consolidating and confirming the Italian feeling of dependence on France.

Joseph's character also had ripened by this time. Experience had destroyed the adventurous spirit in which he entered on his career; he had become a gentle, philosophic, industrious monarch, careful of the best interests of his people, and he was accordingly beloved by them. Roederer had introduced order into the Neapolitan finances, his own administrative reforms worked smoothly, and the only discontented element of his people was composed of the nobles, who chafed at the repression of their power and the curtailment of their privileges. There is positive evidence that Joseph was summoned and came to Venice, but there is no record of the interview, except a marginal note written by Joseph himself in an existing copy of Miot de Mélito's memoirs, to the effect that Napoleon spoke of the troubles among the members of the royal family of Spain as likely "to produce results which he dreaded." The last word is underscored. "I have enough anxiety prepared," he said; "troubles in Spain can only benefit the English, who do not desire peace, by destroying the resources which I find in that ally to carry on the war against them." Over and above this information there is, however, a high probability that Joseph was then informed that since Lucien had proved refractory, he himself was now destined for Spain;

that the King expressed at first a decided unwillingness to accept the unwelcome task; and that, like Lucien, he departed under his brother's disfavor. Napoleon's offer had already been discussed at Tilsit as a contingency. Joseph was so accustomed to obey that a sober second thought led him to repent of his creditable hesitation; within a week, and before leaving Venice, he had despatched a confidential messenger to secure Alexander's formal compliance with his transfer to Spain. He was under the spell of the magician, for it was probably Napoleon who prompted his thoughts. After that of Charles the Great, the empire of Charles V. had been the most splendid in Europe, and Joseph perhaps dreamed that if not first he might be second, eclipsed only by his brother.

Godoy was an adroit diplomat. In reply to Napoleon's letter he personally asked and urged the bestowal on Ferdinand of a French princess in marriage, but at the same time he also urged the publication of what had been stipulated at Fontainebleau. The answer was most dilatory, and when it was written there was a new tone: Napoleon would gladly draw the bonds of alliance tighter by such a match as had been so often suggested, but could such a mark of confidence be shown to a dishonored son without some proof of his repentance? He added that it would be premature to publish the articles of Fontainebleau. In open contempt of that document, a decree was issued on December twenty-third, 1807, from Milan, appointing Junot governor of all Portugal. On February second, 1808, this paper was communicated to the King of Spain by Beauharnais, with the intimation that the treaty must temporarily remain suspended. The scales now fell from Godoy's eyes. His agent in Paris informed him that he had been coldly received by Champagny, the Minister of External Relations; and soon afterward Mlle. Tascher de la Pagerie was married to an unimportant member of the Rhenish Confederation, the Duke of Aremberg. It was thought at Madrid that the Emperor had abandoned both the court factions; public opinion, whether favorable to one or the other, was soon united in a common irritation against France, and before long it was current talk that Napoleon contemplated the dismemberment of Spain by the connivance of Godoy.

Meantime the new conscription had been carried through, and ever larger numbers of French striplings, dignified by the name of troops, appeared at Bayonne, and crossed the border. The sturdy Spaniards

AN EPISODE OF THE SIEGE OF SARAGOSSA

regarded them with amazement and contempt. There was no appearance as yet of any English invasion, and the army in Portugal was in no need of assistance; but Moncey followed Dupont with thirty thousand so-called men; Duhesme led an army corps to Barcelona at one end of the Pyrenees, while Darmagnac passed the gorge of Roncesvalles into Navarre with his division, and seized Pamplona; Bessières hurried on behind with the guard; and Jerome was ordered to levy forty thousand men in Westphalia. Figueras, San Sebastian, and Valladolid were soon in French hands. The "Moniteur" of January twenty-fourth explained that these acts were necessitated by plans of the English to land at Cadiz. Six days afterward the Emperor estimated that he had eight hundred thousand men under arms, and that he would soon have eighty thousand more. In the presence of such facts the Prince of the Peace was prostrated, while terror overpowered the feeble King and his wicked consort. Nor was their panic diminished when a second letter arrived from Napoleon, dated February twenty-fifth, which plainly showed a determination to quarrel. "Your Majesty asked the hand of a French princess for the Prince of Asturias; I replied on January tenth that I consented. Your Majesty speaks no more of this marriage. All this leaves in the dark many objects important for the welfare of my peoples." In a few weeks Izquierdo arrived from Paris and reluctantly explained the appalling truth: that the gossamer bonds of the treaty he had negotiated at Fontainebleau were blown away, and that Portugal was to be given entire to one of the Bonapartes. This was the explanation of the appalling armaments in northern Spain, beyond the Ebro. Godoy returned an answer refusing all proposals tending to such a conclusion. Izquierdo carried back this reply, and toward the close of March Talleyrand was appointed to negotiate with him under the pretense of finding some compromise.

Talleyrand was heartily sick of his inactivity, and eagerly seized the opportunity to reassert his importance. Abandoning utterly the position of semi-resistance to Napoleon which he had held for some time past, he now used his adroit and clever gift to further the Emperor's schemes. The document which was finally drawn up by him gave the French equal rights in the Spanish colonies with Spanish subjects, and proposed an exchange for Portugal of the great march north of the Ebro, which had once been held by Charles the Great and was now held by Napoleon. When Izquierdo heard the hard stipulations he cried out in dismay, but to every remonstrance came the cool reply that such was the Emperor's will. Early in March Bessières entered Spain with thirty-five thousand men. This raised the total number in the scattered divisions of the French troops now south of the Pyrenees to about a hundred thousand. The Spaniards were at last thoroughly awake to the fact of their humiliation. Excitement became more and more intense, until an eruption of popular violence was imminent.

At this crisis Napoleon took a step of great significance. Murat, Grand Duke of Berg, arrived at Burgos on March thirteenth, with full powers as commander-in-chief, and at once assumed command. Ordering a concentration of all the divisions, he slowly marched on Madrid. The Prince of the Peace and the King heard their hour striking. Godoy's first thought was to imitate the example set by the house of Braganza, and, flying beyond the seas, to establish the Spanish Bourbons in Mexico or Peru. The Queen was from the first ardent for a project which would prolong the semblance of power for herself and the favorite, but it was days before Charles could bring himself to such a conclusion. At last, on March fifteenth, the council was summoned to hear his determination, and orders were given to keep open the route to Cadiz. The populace felt that disgrace could go no further, and, denouncing Godoy, besought the King to remain.

They could get no satisfactory answer from Aranjuez, where the vacillating, terrified, and disunited court now was. One day followed another, and the streets of that town swarmed with angry men whose pride and scorn found expression in calls for Godoy's death. On the evening of the seventeenth they began to riot, and the wretched prince saw his house surrounded. Half clad and half starved, he tried first one door and then another; all were beset, and he was compelled to take refuge in the loft, where he remained hidden under a rubbish heap while the mob worked their will in the handsome rooms below. Next morning Charles yielded to the popular clamor, and deposed Godoy from his high offices. For thirty-eight hours the minister lay concealed. At last he could no longer endure the tortures of hunger and thirst; evading the attention of his own household, he reached the street, and on the nineteenth was taken in charge by the guards who held it. The rumor of his capture spread fast, and it required great courage on the part of the soldiers to protect their prisoner from violence. Their efforts were only partly successful; they had a bloody and fainting burden when they reached their barracks and withdrew behind the doors. In that moment, when it seemed as if the mob would finally break down even the strong entrance and seize its prey, Charles despatched his son to calm the storm.

The people adored the Prince of Asturias, and without difficulty he quieted the rioters and offered life to his enemy. The haughty grandee, broken by pain, fell on his knees and implored protection; but he retained enough of interest in the situation to murmur through his gory lips, "Are you already king?" "Not yet, but I shall be soon," was the reply. On a promise that the traitorous betrayer of his country's honor should be delivered to the courts and tried by the rigor of the law, the excited populace withdrew. At once Charles began preparations to carry Godoy beyond their reach; but the fact could not be kept secret, and once more rioting began. The populace of Madrid burned all the palaces belonging to the prince, except one, which they spared because they thought it was the property of their sovereign. The King submitted to what was inevitable, but determined to lay down the burden of his royal dignity. On the same day, the nineteenth, he signed the necessary papers and abdicated in favor of his son. Next morning, in the presence of a great council summoned to Aranjuez, he explained that he was overwhelmed by misfortune and the weight of government, and that for his health's sake he must seek the ease of private life in a milder clime.

CHAPTER XI

THE AWAKENING OF SPAIN

THE SPANIARDS AND THEIR DYNASTY—MURAT'S FATAL BLUNDER—LOUIS
NAPOLEON AND THE SPANISH THRONE—NAPOLEON'S SUBTERFUGE—A
TRAP FOR CHARLES AND FERDINAND—THE COURSE OF SAVARY—NA-
POLEON AND FERDINAND—DETHRONEMENT OF THE SPANISH BOURBONS
—QUARRELS OF FATHER AND SON—THE MADRID MASSACRE—FERDI-
NAND A PRISONER—NAPOLEON'S IDEA OF LEGITIMACY—THE SPANISH
CORTES AT BAYONNE—JOSEPH, KING OF SPAIN—THE SPANISH PEO-
PLE—AGITATIONS IN MADRID—UPRISING OF SPAIN.

IF there be a time when the turn of Napoleon's fortunes is evident,
it is the spring of 1808. Between the determination to complete
his system of commercial warfare in western Europe and the contempt
which he entertained for the Spanish throne, he fell into a deadly
snare—that of despising Spanish nationality. With the first manifestation of national sentiment in Spain began the process which
ended in his overthrow; Spain, Prussia, and Austria successively became aware that a dynasty is not a nation, that energy, high principle,
and organizing power reside after all in the people. This consciousness once awakened, the longing for unity grew to be a passion with
them as it had been with France; their dynasties became the ministers of the popular will, the forces of modern life were set free, and
the overthrow of Napoleonic imperialism became only a matter of time.
Ferdinand's first act as king was to request Napoleon's favor and protection. His letter was written on March twentieth, and intrusted to
an embassy of three grandees. Charles and Louisa had, however, re-
pented almost before the formalities of abdication were over, and the
newly arrived Queen of Etruria supported them in their fickleness.
With despicable inconsistency they too despatched an embassy, but

108

THE ENTRY OF FERDINAND INTO MADRID.

to Murat, imploring his interference on their behalf and his favor for Godoy. In reply, Murat, whether from slyness or from a desire to gain time, requested a formal, written demand to that effect. He was promptly furnished with a paper, signed by both King and Queen, declaring that they had acted under fear, and begging to be reinstated. This document was a precious arrow for Napoleon's quiver. Still, the perplexity of the French commander was great; he knew nothing of Napoleon's plans, he dared not acknowledge Ferdinand as king, and he dared not restore Charles, whose sovereignty he had been virtually menacing by his march. In this dilemma he despatched an aide-de-camp to Aranjuez with verbal messages of comfort, and, hurrying forward, entered Madrid with his army on the twenty-third.

Napoleon had frequently enjoined his brother-in-law to enter the city, recruit his supplies, and give his troops a rest; but with those injunctions he had likewise given strict commands to allay any fears in the court. These instructions had not contemplated the revolution of Aranjuez, and every condition was changed. Murat would have been wise if he had disobeyed the letter of his orders; but he did not, for new circumstances breed new ideas, and within twenty-four hours he had made up his mind. Here was a new kingdom; the other men of the family—Louis, Jerome, and Joseph—all had crowns; the grand duchy of Berg was very well, but a kingdom was better, and he might secure that of Spain for himself. For this end he must throw Ferdinand altogether into the shade, while placing the glory and power of France in the most brilliant illumination. It was a fatal step to occupy Madrid, more fatal still for the French general to exhibit himself in a martial splendor which sadly contrasted with the troops of beardless boys at his back. He was received by the inhabitants with cool contempt. Next day Ferdinand made his royal entry. The populace went mad with delight, and displayed a passionate devotion which augured ill for the schemes of Prince Joachim of Berg. A less egoistic man would have seen that a national uprising was imminent. But Murat was neither modest nor penetrating; he was a great and dashing cavalry general, at times an excellent commander-in-chief, but he was not a statesman. His conduct entangled the skeins of Spanish intrigue into a knot which only war could sever.

His course did not even ultimately lead to the goal, but to consequences far different   When on March twenty-fifth Napoleon received the despatch announcing the revolution of Aranjuez and Murat's neutral attitude, he replied in commendatory language, instructing his brother-in-law to keep the balance as it was, neither recognizing the new King until further directions, nor indicating by any action that the old one had ceased to reign. The same day, the twenty-fifth, a letter was despatched to King Louis at the Hague, asking for an answer in categorical terms as to whether he would accept the Spanish throne. Joseph had hesitated and was momentarily out of favor, while the perpetual smuggling of the Dutch had convinced Napoleon that the only means to secure the Continental embargo was to incorporate Holland with France. Three days later Murat received still higher praise, with a perfectly irrelevant clause interjected: "I suppose Godoy will come by way of Bayonne." This was, of course, a hint to send the Prince of the Peace into France. If the commander of the French forces should act on the suggestion, he would do the work thoroughly; and under the same date Bessières was instructed to treat the old King and Queen with distinction if they should pass his way. Publicly it was to be made known in Madrid that the long-talked-of visit by the Emperor would not be further postponed. Such was Napoleon's confidence in the quick apprehension of his subordinates that henceforward he regarded the whole royal household of Spain as his prisoners.

There is in existence what purports to be a letter from Napoleon to Murat, dated March twenty-ninth. It is undoubtedly by Napoleon, but it was either written at the time, for public effect, and not sent, or it was a later fabrication intended to mislead posterity, because its formal style is not used elsewhere in the correspondence. It explains to "His Imperial Highness" what was not known until ten years later, namely, that the Spaniards were a people with violent political passions, capable of indefinite warfare; that the nation could and must be regenerated only by careful management; and that nothing must be done precipitately. At the same time it gives the Protector, as Murat is designated, his own option in regard to a recognition of Ferdinand, expresses disapproval of the precipitate seizure of Madrid, and warns him that he must not create an irrepressible opposition. Whether the letter be authentic or not, whether it was sent or not, really matters but little as regards our judgment of the facts. The disorganization of Spain had been its own work; the court intrigues were already burning before they were fanned by Napoleon's agents in the hope that, like the royal house of

MARSHAL JOACHIM MURAT

GRAND DUKE OF CLEVES AND OF BERG, KING OF NAPLES

Portugal, the incapable Spanish Bourbons would fly to America. The revolution of Aranjuez was a bitter disappointment to the great schemer, and disconcerted his plans. But Murat's conduct and Ferdinand's character rendered difficult, if not impossible, any course which would combine the consummation of his fixed designs with even the slightest degree of popular good will in Spain. Nothing was to be gained at such a supreme moment by the ordinary brutal abuse which the Emperor was accustomed to heap on his brother-in-law for commonplace offenses; moreover, in view of the disappointing revolution, Murat's course was perhaps as good as any other. He must, however, bear whatever responsibility attaches to it, and that responsibility would have been his even without the supposititious letter which he never received. The contempt of the people for the boy-soldiers at whose head he had marched into Madrid, combined with disdain for his own pompousness and with fury at his subsequent cruelty, goes far to account for much that was disastrous to French prestige and to France in the sequel

In order to secure the Spanish crown it was now necessary that both the quarreling factions should be removed from the scene of their scandalous intrigues. Perhaps it would be possible, perhaps not. Napoleon set out on April second for Bayonne, accompanied by his Empress with a stately suite, and the adroit Savary was despatched to Madrid. Savary's memoirs indicate that his instructions for this memorable journey were very vague: the Emperor wished to see whether the Bourbons merited dethronement; in other words, whether they could be uncrowned. For himself, Savary naïvely declared that much of his own participation in the subsequent events was mere accident. Murat had obeyed both his verbal and his implied instructions. According to the former, Charles and his consort were in the Escorial, treated with all honor, but prisoners. Godoy, also, was aware that he must soon appear at Bayonne. But Murat had gone further, for he had slyly suggested to Napoleon that Ferdinand should appear at the same rendezvous. Beauharnais told Ferdinand to his face that he ought to meet Napoleon half-way on his journey, in order the better to make his peace.

This hint was quietly conveyed to Savary before his departure, and he was at the same time intrusted with a letter to Murat expressing a desire that the Prince of Asturias should either remain at Madrid or come out to meet the Emperor, who intended not to enter Spain for the present, but to wait at Bayonne. The careful plan worked admirably. No one knows on conclusive evidence what Savary said to Ferdinand, what hopes he held out, what promises he made in his master's name; but on April tenth the young King placed Madrid under the administration of a junta and set out, expecting to meet Napoleon at Burgos. He had been easily moved to this course, for Murat had so far coldly refused to recognize him, while Savary was prodigal of obsequiousness and addressed him as king. His ministers Escoiquiz and Cavallos declare, in their justificatory writings, that in addition to the impression produced by his conduct, Savary actually said, as if in a burst of military frankness, that the Emperor was already on his way to assure himself whether Ferdinand's dispositions toward the French system were as sincere as his father's had been, and would of course be favorably impressed if a personal interview should be sought by the young King before his guest could reach Madrid.

At Burgos Ferdinand learned that Napoleon was not yet within the Spanish borders; at Vitoria he was informed that the Emperor had not yet even passed Bordeaux. His people had utterly disapproved of the journey, but they acclaimed him joyously on the two days' progress to Burgos. Thereafter he remarked a change, and the nearer he approached the frontier the more they showed their irritation at his insensate folly. At Vitoria, therefore, he summoned Savary, whose carriage was "accidentally in the King's convoy," and reproached him with deceit. It was too late; divisions of French soldiers were scattered all about, among them the splendid cavalry of Bessières. To wheel and return would have been an open insult to the Emperor, which French soldiers would not have tolerated. The uneasy young King thereupon penned and despatched by a special courier a long letter recalling the facts, and begging the Emperor to terminate the equivocal position in which he found himself placed.

The reply was speedy and most insulting, for it studiously avoided the recognition of Ferdinand's sovereignty. The Emperor had expected before this to visit Madrid in person and institute some necessary reforms, but affairs in the North had delayed him, and the revolution at Aranjuez had changed the situation. He hoped Ferdinand would quickly put an end to any attempt at a trial of Godoy, for its revelations must necessarily dishonor the Queen. "Your Royal Highness,"

GODOY TAKEN INTO CUSTODY BY THE SPANISH TROOPS

he wrote, "has no other rights to the throne than those transmitted through your mother." Had the abdication been a free act or not? He would like to talk to Ferdinand as to whether or not it was forced by the riots of Aranjuez. His "Royal Highness" had behaved ill about his marriage, for he should not have acted without the King's knowledge, and every such approach to a foreign sovereign made by an heir apparent is a criminal act. If there had not been force at Aranjuez, there would be no difficulty in recognizing Ferdinand; moreover, a French marriage for him would be advantageous not merely to the Spaniards, but to the interest of the French.

The following day, April seventeenth, orders were issued to Bessières that if the prince should continue his journey there should be no interference; but if, however, he turned back toward Burgos, he was to be arrested and brought by force to Bayonne. Ferdinand hesitated as he read the insults, promises, and compliments which made up Napoleon's letter. His Spanish counselors advised a return; Savary laughed at such scruples, and was not only voluble in verbal commentaries on the ambiguous text, but profuse in promises. On the twentieth Ferdinand VII. of Spain, as his supporters called him, was at the gates of Bayonne. He was received, not with royal honors, but by his own legates, the three grandees whom he had sent to Napoleon; and they told him with mournful accents that the Emperor with his own lips had declared that the Bourbons could no longer reign in Spain. It was with dejected mien and shaky steps that the young monarch and his suite followed Duroc and Berthier to the wretched quarters provided for their residence. The Empress was, throughout the three months spent at Bayonne, both gracious and conciliatory, playing her part as hostess with grace, and alleviating with kindness the bitterness of her compulsory guests. On the evening of Ferdinand's arrival a handsome dinner was given at the château where the court was lodged, and the visiting prince was most decorously treated. His train grew more joyous and hopeful as the hours passed, although they noted that the Emperor did not address his guest as king. Still, that was a slight matter, and they returned in gaiety to their poor lodgings—all but one: Canon Escoiquiz had been asked to remain for a short private interview, while Savary escorted his master. It was an identical communication which was then made in the same hour to both minister and prince; short, terse, and brutal: to wit, the Bourbons had ceased to

reign in Spain, and Ferdinand would be indemnified by Etruria if he
would formally renounce a crown which was not even technically his,
since Charles declared that he had abdicated through fear. The document in which this was announced had already been printed and published at Madrid by Napoleon's command. He now summoned Charles,
Louisa, and Godoy to Bayonne.

Murat had found trouble in liberating the Prince of the Peace, for
the junta feared the populace if they should surrender the object of its
hate and scorn. But he finally succeeded, and in the last days of April
Godoy reached Bayonne, where by the thirtieth all the puppets were
assembled. Dejected and broken-spirited, the minister agreed to play
the part assigned to him. The honors of a royal progress had been
paid to Charles, and he posed for a few days as the King. Ferdinand,
whose character and behavior awakened the contemptuous scorn even
of Talleyrand, was the culprit at the bar, charged with dishonoring his
parents. The trial scene was a shocking exhibition of human frailty.
Ferdinand was summoned before a bench composed of his parents,
who claimed to be still sovereigns, and the French emperor; Godoy,
looking like a bull, as Talleyrand thought, sat sullenly by. The old
King demanded his crown. Ferdinand persistently refused to surrender it. Finally the trembling and invalid father rose on his shaky,
rheumatic legs and brandished his staff; the undutiful son remained
unmoved. A second demand was made by letter; it was to the same
effect, but the answer was different. Ferdinand agreed that he would
renounce his throne before the assembled Cortes at Madrid, but there
only, and to Charles IV. alone. At Napoleon's command Charles refused to consider the proposal, giving as a reason that Spain could be
saved only by the Emperor. This was Napoleon's opportunity. Two
days later an imperial decree was promulgated, which appointed Murat
dictator of Spain, under the style "lieutenant-general of the kingdom."

Meantime that intriguer had been making for himself a tortuous
approach to royalty. Nothing could more hasten the progress of events
than a riot in Madrid. The sensibility of the inhabitants of that city
had been rasped by the French occupation; they had seen the departure of their idol with irritation, and had been further exasperated by
Godoy's liberation. Murat set fire to the train of their passions first by
a new disposition of his forces, which so menaced the place as to make
it clear that he was no longer an ally, but a conqueror, and then by the

announcement that the infante Don Francisco was to be despatched to
Bayonne with his uncle and all the remaining members of the royal
family, including the Queen of Etruria and her children. On May
second the entire population rose to resist this insolent tyranny. Murat
was ready for the move; the conflict was short, but it was sharp, for
he lost several hundred soldiers, perhaps half as many as the patriots,
in whose ranks some eight hundred fell. The aspirant to royal honors
yielded with ostentatious grace to the first representations of the junta,
and promised a general amnesty; but he also thought it best to make
an example before the eyes of his future subjects, and in spite of his
plighted word two hundred of the insurgent patriots were seized and
shot. This very day, however, there was pronounced a decree of rude
disenchantment for him. It was on May second that Napoleon definitely wrote to him that the kingdom of Spain could not be his; he
might have Naples or Portugal. The Emperor was tired of Bayonne,
and longed to be back in Paris, where he could be active about the
business of perpetuating his empire and his dynasty. The stubborn
Ferdinand was therefore summoned once more, and charged with having instigated the upheaval of Madrid. He remained mute for some
minutes, and with downcast eyes. " If before midnight," came the cold
words of the Emperor, "you have not recognized your father as legitimate king, and notified the fact at Madrid, you will be treated as a
rebel." Some declare that there was besides a menace of death.

This ended all resistance. Ferdinand resigned his rights as king
into his father's hands, his rights as heir into those of Napoleon.
Charles had already assigned his rights as king to the same suzerain.
The complacent old man was actually cheerful and joyous, as his en-
tertainer desired he should be; but Ferdinand, in spite of the fact that
he was to have the château of Navarre with an income of a million
francs, in spite of promises that all the royal family would be liberally
pensioned, remained silent and gloomy. Napoleon was not pleased by
this behavior, and in commending him to the hospitality of Talleyrand,
at the splendid castle of Valençay, declared that his whole character
could be summed up in a single word — sullen. Poor Talleyrand! he
saw himself condemned to the "honorable mission" of turnkey to a
dispossessed monarch whose guard of honor was a troop of eighty
mounted police. By the Emperor's grace the young culprit was not to
be committed to jail, for he had voluntarily surrendered himself; but

Talleyrand was to watch and amuse him, and discover, if possible, some charming and marriageable girl to entangle his affections, so that in her society he might forget the delights of power, while time should weaken the promptings of ambition and revenge. In a few days Charles, Louisa, and Godoy were comfortably installed at Compiègne, while Ferdinand, with his brother, went sullenly away to "visit" at Valençay. The prisoner's character was soon displayed. The day of his arrival at his destination he wrote a cringing letter to Napoleon, and soon after not only congratulated the Emperor on the accession of the King of Naples to the throne he had claimed for his own, but even felicitated Joseph himself on his coronation as Catholic Majesty.

Napoleon knew the mysterious power throughout Europe of that charmed word "legitimacy." He despised the concept that it expressed, while he meant to make the most of its power. Having misunderstood the strength of Spanish patriotism, he now made the blunder of supposing that the Spaniards would receive as a legitimate prince whomsoever he chose to appoint as heir to the "legitimacy" which the Spanish Bourbons had just put into his hands. Louis, moreover, had but recently illustrated the force of a new environment under the notion of legitimacy. Replying to Napoleon's letter of March twenty-fifth, he had flatly refused the Spanish crown, on the ground that he had sworn a solemn oath to the Dutch. Joseph was immediately restored to favor and ordered to Bayonne. He came with apparent alacrity, due, as he claimed, to his desire to free his beloved brother Napoleon from embarrassment. Soon all was apparently ready for his inauguration.

The treaty of Fontainebleau had produced unexpected complications and disastrous results on its political side; the apparently insignificant military clauses had so far been successfully executed. One Spanish army was far away on the Baltic, held under curb by Bernadotte; another had been despatched to western Spain, and had remained there; in the mean while the north and the center of the country were occupied by the French. General Solano had made some movement to lead back his troops into the occupied territory, but was checked in his advance by instructions from the ministers of Charles IV. at Madrid. Uncertain as to their powers in a revolutionary crisis, he rendered only a half-obedience; but it was sufficient for Napoleon's object, and there was no body of Spanish troops within

JOSEPH BONAPARTE

KING OF NAPLES, KING OF SPAIN, COMTE DE SURVILLIERS

DRAWING BY THE PART FROM THE PORTRAIT BY FRANÇIS

striking distance of the capital. Accordingly, when the Spanish notables were summoned to Bayonne, they could not well refuse, and a hundred and fifty of them responded. On June sixth, 1808, the crown of Spain was offered to Joseph by this strange Cortes, and he accepted it. At the same time the new constitution, destined by Napoleon to regenerate the country, was laid before the same body, which discussed and adopted it. In the following month his Catholic Majesty presented himself, with this document and a cabinet of able ministers, to the people of Madrid. Charles IV. and his followers found Compiègne too cold, and soon moved, first to Marseilles, then to Italy. Murat became King of Naples. Ferdinand remained contentedly in France, licking the hand which had struck him down. Napoleon returned to Paris, uneasy at the attitude of the Spanish nation, but hoping that local discontent could be smothered by the strong hand, as he had seen it smothered in France, Italy, and the Orient. In this, however, he was to find himself sadly mistaken.

In the story of Spanish degradation at its worst two names must stand together as partners in political crime—those of Godoy and Escoiquiz, who sought to mask their own base ambitions behind the acts of their feeble creatures, the King and Ferdinand respectively. Throughout the whole vile complot moves also the figure of the Queen, whose counterpart must be sought in the annals of witches, furies, and hetæræ. But there were still left uncontaminated eleven millions of the Spanish people. They were indolent by nature, had been fettered both by tradition and by worn-out institutions, and had long groaned in the chains of corrupt administration. With the removal of the Bourbons all these paraphernalia were swept away. The brothers Napoleon believed, and no doubt honestly, that pure and capable administration under a modern system would soon produce order, industry, prosperity, and peace, and that a grateful nation would before long acclaim its preservers, and enroll itself as a devoted ally against the "perfidious and tyrannical" supremacy of Great Britain. It is useless to speculate how far this dream would have been realized but for the utter rottenness of the instruments with which the reformers worked: the King's senility, the Queen's lust, Godoy's greed, Escoiquiz's self-seeking, Ferdinand's unreliability, Murat's ambition, made a poor armory of weapons wherewith to accomplish a beneficent revolution. But the one vital blunder was, after all, not in the use of such tools: it was in the contempt for nationality shown first in making the treaty of Fontainebleau, then in its violation by the subsequent seizure of Portugal, and finally in the occupation of Spain by French troops. Declaring that more had been lost than gained by the events which occurred at Bayonne, Talleyrand says that on one occasion he icily observed to Napoleon that society would pardon much to a man of the world, but cheating at cards never. If this be true, it was a stinging rebuke and one which touched the heart of the whole matter.

To the bloody butchery and broken faith of May second, the day of the Madrid riots, may be attributed the turn of Napoleon's fortunes. How far he was responsible for each of Murat's successive acts cannot be known. With exaggerated conceptions of the Emperor's ubiquity, some attribute every detail in every step to the direct intervention of the master. This is unproved and highly improbable; but the spirit was his, and the use he made of each occasion as it arose is matter of history. The fires of rebellion were lighted thenceforth on every Spanish hearth. Madrid itself was dangerous enough, but Madrid was not Spain, as Paris is France, and the fine local enthusiasm of uncorrupted Spanish blood in every district was awakened into vigorous activity by the news of how faithless had been the French treatment, not only of the royal house, but of the citizens—men and women who were themselves true Spaniards, brothers and sisters of every other Spaniard. This possibility Napoleon had not foreseen, and he did not grasp the fact until long afterward, when years of bitter experience had rolled over his head. The Madrid riots, suppressed by Murat with such terrible bloodshed, were at the time, in Napoleon's mind, only a welcome leverage for moving Ferdinand to compliance, and that was all.

But the city had been full of provincials attracted from all parts of the country to swell the triumph of their idol Ferdinand on his accession to the throne. They returned to their homes inspired with hatred for the French and with bitter scorn for the pretexts on which Spain and Portugal had been torn from a commercial system that brought them considerable prosperity and many comforts, in order that they might be incorporated, under foreign princes, into another system, which not only required serious self-denial, but brought stagnation, disorganization, and the presence of an armed soldiery. One weakness of the Spanish monarchy had always been the absence of centralization, but that very fact had been the national strength in fostering local attachments. Into every city, town, and hamlet, each nourishing its own local pride by local patriotism, came the news from Madrid of how the invaders were trampling not merely upon Spanish rights, but upon every consideration of humanity and good faith. The national will was stirred as never before or since; its expression grew louder every day, until at last the conflagration of devotion to a national cause was kindled far and near. Every community formed its committees, and these organized such neighborhood resistance as was possible, while communicating with other juntas of the same sort to unite their little wars, or guerrillas, into a great combined and vigorous effort wherever the opportunity offered. Under the surface throughout all Spain the fires of resistance began to kindle; the crackling could be heard even while the assembly at Bayonne was adopting the new constitution.

CHAPTER XII

THE FIRST REVOLT OF NATIONS

The New Rôle of Spain — Guerrilla Warfare — The French Cowed — The Capitulation of Baylen — The French Retreat from Spain and Portugal — Complaints of King Joseph — Napoleon's Exasperation — Imperialist Sentiment in France — The Emperor's Determination — The Spirit of Prussia — The Work of Stein — The Revolution in Turkey — Austria's Anxieties — War Feeling at Vienna — Napoleon Turns to the Czar — Alexander's Hesitancy — Napoleon's Misrepresentations — Austria Warned — Talleyrand and the Czar — Napoleon's Allocution at St. Cloud.

THUS far in the history of Europe all politics had been in the main dynastic. The nations having been consolidated under powerful houses, it was the reigning family which seemed to constitute the national entity, not the common institutions, common speech, common faith, common territory, common aims, and common destiny of the people. Spain, like Italy, had a clearly marked national domain, and, in spite of some striking differences, a fairly homogeneous population. It was fitting and not entirely unnatural that the land of the Inquisition, the land of ignorance, the land of intolerance, the land, in short, which had sunk the lowest under absolutism, should begin the counter-revolution which, checking the excesses of Napoleon and the French Revolution in their disregard for nationality, ushered into the world's forum the nation and national sentiment as the strongest force of the nineteenth century.

This was exactly what happened in Spain. Napoleon's strategy had laughed at the military formation of Frederick the Great's system; the guerrillas of Spain laughed at the formations of regular

THE BURNING OF A PALACE OF GODOY BY THE POPULACE AT MADRID

FROM THE ENGRAVING BY MAURICE ORANGE

warfare in any shape. They rose to fight, and dispersed for safety, leaving their smarting foe unable to strike for lack of a billet. The occasional successes of the Spanish regulars showed, moreover, that the generals were not entirely ignorant of Napoleon's own system. When Joseph entered Madrid the whole land was already in open rebellion, except where French force compelled a sullen acquiescence in French rule. The long inactive, sluggish ecclesiastics suddenly seemed to feel the vigor to resist and the power to lead. They joined the insurgents, and invoked the orthodoxy of the nation so as to inflame the passions of the masses against the persecutor of the Pope. Irregular and undefined as were the elements of the uprising, it was nevertheless essentially a popular movement; as Napoleon himself later admitted, it was the people themselves who refused to ratify his new institutions, and who declared for Ferdinand VII. The sequel furnished ample illustration of this fact: the mountaineers of Asturias rose in united rebellion; the inhabitants of Cartagena threw open their arsenals to the volunteers of the neighborhood; the citizens of Saragossa beat off their besiegers, while those of Valencia first massacred the French who took refuge in their citadel, and then repulsed Moncey in a desperate conflict. When the Spanish leaders ventured into an open battle-field they were defeated; on the other hand, when they kept the hills and fought like bandits they were victorious.

So quick and general was the Spanish rising that the various French army divisions shut themselves up for safety in whatever towns they could hold: pretending to defy the national guards, who seemed to spring from the ground without, they were in reality awe-stricken before the wrath of the armed citizens within. A quick burst of Spanish anger, a sharp stab of the Spanish poniard—the frequency of such incidents began to create a panic among the French boy-soldiers. The seizure and sack of a city had for years been a traditional amusement of the grand army, connected in Italy and Germany with little or no loss of life, and enhanced by the acquisition of enormous booty. The young conscripts, who had heard the oft-told tale from their fathers' lips, found to their bitter disappointment that in Spain a sack meant much bloodshed and little, if any, booty. Sometimes the tables were more than turned. A French squadron put in at Cadiz to coöperate with a force despatched by Napoleon, under pretense of resisting an invasion threatened by the English, but really for the purpose of terrorizing southern Spain. The arrival of the troops having been delayed by the outbreak of rebellion farther north, the townsfolk of that ancient city rose and seized the fleet. The corpses of French soldiers, wherever found throughout the country, were mutilated by the furious Spaniards, and the wounded received no quarter.

At the end of May, Murat was in Madrid as commander-in-chief, with Moncey as his lieutenant; he had thirty thousand troops. Junot was in Portugal with twenty-five thousand. Bessières had twenty-five thousand more, half in Old Castile under himself, half in Aragon under Verdier. Duhesme commanded the thirteen thousand who were in Catalonia; Dupont stood on the Tagus near Toledo with twenty-four thousand more. In the first weeks of June four different skirmishes occurred between the French regulars and the insurgents in different parts of the country. Verdier at Logroño on the sixth, Frère in Segovia on the seventh, Lefebvre at Tudela on the eighth, and Lasalle near Valladolid on the twelfth, had all dispersed the hordes opposed to them. By the middle of the month a regular advance was ordered. It took the form of dispersion for the sake of complete occupation. While Lefebvre laid siege to Saragossa, Moncey started for Valencia with ten thousand soldiers, Dupont for Andalusia with nine thousand, and Bessières's division was distributed throughout Castile up to the walls of Santander, which closed its gates and prepared for resistance. Owing to the defiant attitude and desperate courage of the people, every one of these movements was unsuccessful, each failing in its own special purpose. Cordova was captured, but it had almost instantly to be abandoned. At once Napoleon changed his carefully studied but futile strategy, and determined to concentrate the scattered columns on the critical point, wherever it might be. By this time Palafox and others of the Spanish leaders had shown great ability as generals. The danger now was that a Spanish army would seize Madrid, and thither the French army must betake itself. On July fourteenth Bessières successfully overwhelmed the opposition made at Medina de Rio Seco by the Spaniards under La Cuesta and the Irish general Blake. The only corps left exposed was that of Dupont, to whom reinforcements had been promptly despatched; but the Spaniards under Castaños caught his army, now twenty-five thousand strong, in the mountain pass of La Carolina, among the Sierra Moreña mountains, and on July twenty-first forced him to capitulate at Baylen, where his whole corps laid down their arms.

Æt. 38]   THE FIRST REVOLT OF NATIONS   123   Chap. XII

1808

This was an awful blow, for Madrid was thereby rendered untenable. The Emperor gave orders to retreat behind the Duero, and directed Bessières to keep open the connection with Junot by way of Valladolid. In fact, he began to appreciate his task, for he warned his generals against any system of cordons in dealing with such an enemy, useful as a string of posts might be in checking smugglers; and besides this change of plan, there were indications that he would himself soon take charge in Spain. There was need of this, for his generals and boy-soldiers did not stop to hold the Duero; evacuating Madrid, they never halted until they were behind the Ebro, in what they considered a kind of French borderland. The siege of Saragossa was abandoned, and Duhesme evacuated Catalonia. Junot's situation was thus rendered most precarious, for when Wellesley landed early in August with fourteen thousand English troops, and found that the junta of Corunna had no need of him, he promptly advanced against the invaders of Portugal. Having driven in the French outposts on the seventeenth, four days later he attacked and defeated Junot at Vimeiro. At the very height of the contest, when victory seemed already secure, Burrard, a superior officer, arrived to assume command. This reduced Wellesley to the rank of an adviser, and, his advice not being taken, Junot escaped to the strong position of Cintra, whence, although entirely cut off from his base in Spain, he was able to dictate his own terms of surrender. He and all his troops had a free return by sea to France, but Portugal was to be evacuated.

Napoleon was at St. Cloud, near Paris, when the news of this disaster arrived. To some extent he was already aware of the situation. He knew that the Spaniards would not keep any stipulations they made, claiming that no faith was due to a hostile army which had entered their country under the guise of allies — an army, moreover, which stole the sacred vessels from the sanctuaries of their churches, and would not keep its promise to restore them. The letters of Joseph, who was now utterly disenchanted, had for some time been but one string of bitter complaints. He had asked the Emperor whether an end could not be made to the organized pillage of the churches, and had told him that the movement in Spain was as irrepressible as that of the French Revolution, emphasizing his hopelessness by the suggestion that if France had raised a million soldiers, Spain could probably raise at least half as many. He said, too, that men talked openly of assassinating him; that he had no friends but the scoundrels, the honest men and patriots being on the other side. "My generals," was the Emperor's comment on this querulousness, "are a parcel of post-inspectors; the Ebro is nothing but a line; we must resume the offensive at Tudela." "I have a spot there," he said, pointing with his finger at his uniform. To calm his brother's fears, he replied that the whole Spanish matter had been arranged long before with Russia; that Europe recognized the change as an accomplished fact; and that the priests and monks were at the bottom of all the trouble, stirring up sedition, and acting for the greedy Inquisition. "There is no question of death, but of life and victory; you shall have both. . . . I may find in Spain the Pillars of Hercules, but not the limits of my power." True to his old principles, Napoleon refused to "call off the thieves," as Joseph besought him, and declared that, according to the laws of war, when a town was captured under arms pillage was justifiable.

These were all brave words, but the Emperor was in the last stage of exasperation. The letters he wrote at the time betray something of the unutterable pain he felt. No one but himself could really know the difference to him: his glory was smirched, his Oriental plans and his scheme for peace with England were indefinitely postponed, his impatient ally was again put off, while Austria and Prussia were encouraged to revolt. Was the vast structure he had so laboriously erected now to fall in one crash at his feet? The news of Junot's surrender was further embittered by the receipt of information that the Spanish troops under General La Romana, which had slyly been posted first in Hamburg, and then sent to Denmark as Bernadotte's advance-guard, had at last revolted, and were embarking on English ships for home in order to join the movement of national redemption. By this disaster the demonstration against Sweden promised to the Czar was made impossible. This accumulation of misfortunes—defeat before Valencia, defeat before Saragossa, disaster and surrender at Baylen, disaster and disgrace at Vimeiro, retreat from Madrid, desertion of the Duero as a line of defense, exchange of the offensive for a weak defensive, and loss of the whole Iberian peninsula except the strip behind the Ebro — all this was shameful and hard to bear. Nevertheless, under favorable conditions the situation might have been retrieved. The conditions, however, were most unfavorable. The example and success of Spain were daily giving new comfort to Napoleon's enemies both in France and abroad.

THE CAPITULATION OF BAYLEN.

For the present, however, France might be trusted. The people as a whole had become imperial to the core. The republicans and royalists were so diminished in numbers, and so silenced by the censorship, that they were virtually impotent. The real ability of the country was no longer in retreat, but in the public service; the administration, both financial and judicial, had every appearance of solidity, and the industrial conditions were so steadily improving that the most enterprising and intelligent merchants began to have faith in the ultimate success of the Continental system as a means of securing a European monopoly to French manufactures and commerce. The perfect centralization of France kept the provinces in such close touch with Paris that there was no open expression of discontent in any part of the country. The people were not well informed as to the facts, and they were slow to apprehend the significance of what they learned. By this time the Emperor was France, and whatever he did must be well done. The gradual infusion of the military spirit into the masses had made them passive and obedient. There had been, they knew, some unpleasant troubles beyond the Pyrenees, but the season was not over, and before winter the Emperor's discipline would no doubt be successful. The grand army now pouring out of Germany across France into Spain evidently meant serious business, but there could be no doubt of the result.

The court remained solemn and dull in its weary round of ceremony. The moving spirit was now occupied elsewhere, and his constant absent-mindedness made the whole structure meaningless; for it was an open secret that the soft grace and beseeching eyes, the graceful and willowy form, the exquisite taste and winning ways of Josephine would avail her no longer. The little nephew, Hortense's son and Napoleon's darling, his intended heir, was dead; Joseph had only daughters, and there being no male successor to the throne, reasons of state made a divorce inevitable. The deference of others to the Empress and her condescension to them were but a mockery, the reality of her power having vanished. In this vain show the Emperor moved more dark and mysterious than ever. It was his will that nothing should be changed, and every courtier played his part as well as possible, the two leading actors playing theirs superbly. There was an outward display of confidence and kindness between them, which sometimes may have been real; there were quarrels, explanations, and reconciliations — a momentary return at times to old affection : but the resultant of the conflicting forces was such as to destroy conjugal trust and create general disquietude.

When Napoleon looked abroad he saw nothing to reassure him, and everything to create alarm. In Prussia there was a regeneration such as was comparable only to a new birth. The old military monarchy, under which the land had been repressed like an armed camp by its sovereigns, was gone forever. The Tugendbund, that "band of virtue" already mentioned, had ramified to the farthest borders; partizan warfare was abandoned; piety, dignity, purity, courage, and the power of organization were filling the land. The presence of the French could not quench the new spirit, but instead it poured oil on the flames of national hatred. Patriotic conventicles and every other form of secret meeting were held. Scharnhorst went steadily on with the training and reform of the army, while Stein, with a noble devotion, and under an unsympathetic master, was working to perfect his new administrative system. The churches were filled, and the hearers understood every allusion in the glowing sermons addressed to them by a devoted and patriotic clergy; schools, colleges, and universities swarmed with students, whose youthful zeal found every encouragement in the instruction of their teachers, which combined two qualities not always found united in teaching, being at the same time thoroughly scientific and highly stimulating.

At last, in August, Napoleon, who had looked and listened with deep interest, read with his own eyes in one of Stein's intercepted letters that the minister and his colleagues were aiming at a national uprising, not of Prussia alone, but of all Germany. The illustrious statesman, having emancipated the Prussian people, and having seen the reform of the whole political organism in that great land, was proceeding to extend his beneficent influence throughout all Germany. In September Napoleon demanded Stein's dismissal, and enforced the demand by sequestrating Frederick William's Westphalian estates, threatening at the same time to continue the French occupation of Prussia indefinitely. There was apparently no alternative, for the country, although rejuvenated, had no allies, and could not fight alone. Stein, therefore, resigned after an eventful ministry of about a year, in which he had prepared the way for every one of the changes which ultimately reconstructed Prussia.

The two movements which in Spain and Germany menaced Napoleon's prestige were national; there were two others, which, if not that, may, by a stretch of definition, be called at least dynastic. The first was a revolution in Constantinople. The Sultan Mustapha IV. had been from the beginning a feeble creature of the soldiers, who, after overthrowing Selim, had set him on the throne. Before long he became the contemptible tool of an irresponsible robber gang known as the "yamacks," who, under the guise of militia, held the Turkish capital in terror. The situation in Constantinople had finally grown unendurable even to the Turks, and the Pasha of Rustchuk appeared at the gates of the city to restore Selim III., who was still a captive in the Seraglio. When the doors of that sacred inclosure were forced open, the first object seen was the body of the murdered sovereign, killed by Mustapha in the belief that he himself was now the sole available survivor of Othman's line. But the soldiers ransacked the palace, and dragged from his concealment the young prince Mahmud, second of the name, and destined to be a great reformer. Him they proclaimed Sultan and set upon the throne, appointing their leader grand vizir. The new government was devoted to reform, contemptuous of French influence, and determined to repress the evils which seemed to have ruined its predecessor. This severity was more than the licentious capital would endure. At once every element of discontent burst forth again,—the Janizaries, the Ulema, or doctors of the sacred law, and the people,—some mistrusting one thing, others another, all alike unwilling to obey any master but their own will. Disintegration of what little administrative organization there still was, seemed imminent. The Turkish generals on the Danube began to make light of the armistice or truce of Slobozia, Napoleon's one reliance in his Eastern designs; they actually set in motion their troops, and prepared to take the offensive against Russia. This was in the hope that, before asking a separate peace from the Czar or returning to seize the leadership at Constantinople, they might secure some military prestige as a working capital. The whole outlook seemed to foretell the extinction of French influence with the Porte and a crash in the Orient before Napoleon was ready to take advantage of it.

But the events of Bayonne had been productive of greater alarm to the house of Austria than to any other power. In the humiliation of the Hohenzollerns, Napoleon had the sanction of conquest, though, in view of Prussia's rising strength, it was now commonly said that he had done too much or too little. While in weakening that nation he had rudely lopped the strength of an old French ally, yet he had not destroyed it, and he had exercised what all Europe still admitted to be a right—that of superior force. Austria, on the other hand, had been an old and inveterate rival of France in the race for territorial extension. Napoleon's treatment of her after Austerlitz had been bitter, but the Hapsburgs could not plead former friendship. Here, however, was a new development in Napoleonic ambition. The successive announcements that minor ruling dynasties had ceased to reign had all been made with the partial justification of either conquest or general expediency, or, as in most cases, of both. The Spanish Bourbons had been the Emperor's most obsequious and useful allies, obeying his behests without a question: for their degradation there was no plea either of expediency or of a right secured by conquest. The extinction of what still ranked as a great royal house was accomplished by chicane, was due to a boundless ambition, and was rendered utterly abhorrent to all divine-right dynasties by the specious pretext of reform under which it was accomplished. This gave Francis food for reflection.

In the territorial expansion of Rome her victims were first conquered, then made dependent allies, then at last destroyed, and their lands turned into Roman provinces. It appeared as if this, too, were, in general, Napoleon's policy; but in some cases he showed himself quite willing to dispense with any intermediary stage and marched direct to his goal. Austria, already irritated by the disposition made of Etruria and by the treatment of the Pope, could endure the suspense as to her own fate no longer. Her new military system was complete, her armies were reorganized and reëquipped, her administration was well ordered, her generals and statesmen were alike confident. The Emperor of the French had shown quite the same impatience with Austria in July as with Prussia in September, admonishing both to observe the Continental system with strictness; but his warning produced no effect at Vienna. On the contrary, the Viennese newspapers took a belligerent tone, and called for war; English goods poured in through the harbor of Triest; communications between the ministry at London and the cabinet at Vienna became more frequent and regular; the nation supported its monarch and assumed a warlike attitude. The disasters in Spain tied Napoleon's hands, and he did

CHARLES AND FERDINAND AT BAYONNE

nothing in a military way except to call Davout from Poland into
Silesia, and to strengthen Mortier in Franconia.

With the inconsistency of the highest greatness, Napoleon changed his whole political campaign in the twinkling of an eye, as he so often did his military ones. During the long months since the interview at Tilsit, Alexander had been kept in an agony of uncertainty, deprived of real French coöperation in regard either to Sweden or to Turkey, and actually menaced by the continued occupation of Prussia and the fortification of the strategic points in the duchy of Warsaw. Caulaincourt had found his mission of dissimulation and procrastination most difficult, partly by reason of Pozzo di Borgo's influence, partly because the conquest of Muscovite society was a task hitherto unknown to French arts, and experience had to be dearly bought. In this latter work his success was very moderate, but he became unconsciously an intimate friend and adviser of the Czar. This displeased Napoleon, who promptly recalled him to his senses by a warning that he must not forget that he was a Frenchman. Caulaincourt bravely repelled the insinuation, but the correspondence of Napoleon both with him and with the Czar became so voluminous that the Emperor was virtually his own ambassador.

The contents of these letters were partly personal and friendly; partly promissory, in preparation for what was about to be done at Bayonne; partly preliminary to the second interview between the two emperors, which had been mentioned at Tilsit and often discussed since then. But so far there was not the slightest change of front, no substantial fulfilment of the vague promises, no coöperation; the world was still under the system of Tilsit in the union of Russia and France —a union so far represented by the will of Napoleon. The events at Bayonne deeply affected Alexander. His ally knew they would, and on July tenth he wrote a long letter to St. Petersburg, lamely justifying his conduct. But, after all, the Czar cared little for ancient European dynasties, and, recovering from the first shock, he began to make sport of a king "who had nothing further to live for than his Louise and his Emmanuel," and then took a firm stand in approval of his ally's course. The French and Russian ministers had now completed their scheme for the partition of Turkey, and the Czar finally and unconditionally assented to the second meeting with the Emperor.

But before the details of the all-important interview could be arranged there was much to be done; in particular, Austria must be held in check. An English vessel had arrived at Triest with a deputation of Spanish insurgents who offered the throne of their country to the Archduke Charles. The armaments of Francis grew stronger day by day. No one could hold the Hapsburg empire in check except the Czar. Even amid the exhausting labors of Bayonne, Napoleon remembered this, and thought of the East, reorganizing his fleet in preparation for coöperation with that of Russia, and commanding reports to be made on the geography and military history of Persia. After the loss of Baylen, of which he learned in the first days of August, his ingenuity did not desert him, in spite of his heavy heart. A swift courier was despatched on the fifth, with a letter dated back to July twenty-first, and written as if in ignorance of events in Spain. He was enjoined to outrun the ordinary news-carriers, in order that, reaching St. Petersburg before them, he might present as an offering of friendship to Alexander the promise of a virtual evacuation of Prussia—even, in certain contingencies, of Warsaw. Twenty-four hours later another messenger was despatched, conveying the bad news in the mildest form, and expressing as the Emperor's greatest concern a hope that the Russian squadron which had been sent to Lisbon would escape, as he had reassuring news from its commander. It mattered not to him that this was untrue; the end was gained, and the real significance of Baylen was thereby largely concealed from the Czar, or at least the impression made on him by the news was weakened.

Waiting for these communications to produce their effect, the Emperor forwarded a formal remonstrance to Vienna, in his own name, against Austria's warlike attitude, and two weeks later categorically demanded a similar step from the Czar, opening out once more the vista of indefinite aggrandizement for Russia in the East if only the European conflagration were not rekindled. The Czar was charmed by the promises of Napoleon, but when it came to a menacing remonstrance with Austria he hesitated. The anti-French party in Russia were now repeating, like parrots: first, Spain is annihilated, then Austria, then we ourselves. Moreover, as Alexander himself felt, arrangements like those of Tilsit are but too easily overset by unforeseen circumstances, and in such an event what would Europe be without the Hapsburgs? In the end a feeble hint, backed up by a weak menace, was sent to Vienna. Peace, wrote the Czar, is the best policy for Austria. "May not the peace of Tilsit, which I made, carry some obligations with it?" The warning produced a momentary impression in the city on the Danube.

In this short interval every preparation was hastened for the interview which had now become indispensable to both parties. Napoleon had only one object—to draw the alliance closer in the eyes of all Europe for the conservation of his prestige. Alexander had several— the mitigation of Prussia's bondage, the successful occupation of Finland, and, what was the real bond of the alliance, the partition of Turkey. This was substantially what the Czar had been promised at Tilsit, but he had not yet obtained a single item of the list then agreed upon. In spite of Caulaincourt's caresses and Napoleon's cajoling, he was now in a determined humor, and meant to demand the fulfilment of his ally's engagement, not from good will, but from necessity. Talleyrand, wearied to distraction by the dull life of Valençay and the charge of the Spanish princes, had determined to regain his diplomatic power, and now began, by the agency of his many devoted friends in Paris, an extensive course of preparation for a return to public life and to influence. Through semi-official channels the Czar was informed that France, drunk with victory and conquest, now looked to his wisdom for protection from the further ambitions of her fiery ruler. Before long Alexander's own agents began to confirm this statement. The French nation, at least the reasonable portion of it, they said, was weary of Napoleon's imperial policy. If this were true, Spain and Austria might be used to hold France in check while Russia should work her will on the Danube. No matter now if her ally were faithless: compliance could be forced from his weakness.

This disposition had been partly foreseen by Napoleon; he was informed by Caulaincourt how steadily it was crystallizing into a fixed determination. To the observer the moment seemed critical, but the great adventurer was still able to ride the storm. Whence the impulse came is not easily determined, but he turned to Talleyrand as an agent likely to be useful in such complications. The intriguer came forward promptly, and, receiving the Caulaincourt despatches, together with a verbal explanation from the Emperor, was quickly in readiness for the duty of counselor, to which he was called. Napoleon himself assumed a lofty tone. On August fifteenth he held a levee at St. Cloud to which all the representatives of foreign powers were summoned; those of Russia and Austria stood near together. Again, as on the famous occasion before the rupture of the peace of Amiens, he uttered a public allocution in the form of a conversation; this time it was with Metternich, the Austrian ambassador, and he was calmer and more courtly. Reproaching the Emperor of Austria with ingratitude, he announced his political policy; to wit, that Russia would hold Austria in check, while he and Alexander divided the East between them without reference to Francis, unless the latter should disarm and recognize Joseph as king of Spain. Tolstoi remained frigid throughout the long harangue. It was he who had declared and repeated that eventually Napoleon, having humbled Austria, would attack Russia. A fortnight earlier, in an interview with the stern old Russian, the Emperor had asseverated the contrary, but to no effect: Tolstoi had shown no symptoms of faith or conviction. The address to Metternich was, therefore, a second string to Napoleon's bow in case he should fail at Erfurt to win Alexander. His general mien was undaunted and his tone loftier than ever. The tenor of his private conversation with Metternich and others was that he would rest content with what he had. Spain would no longer be a danger in the rear, Austria and Russia would be his allies, sharing in the mastery of the world, and England, the irreconcilable enemy of them all, would be finally reduced to ignominious surrender by the loss of her means of subsistence.

CHAPTER XIII

NAPOLEON AND ALEXANDER AT ERFURT

NAPOLEON'S IMPERIAL HOSPITALITY—THE INTERVIEWS OF NAPOLEON AND GOETHE—MEETING OF NAPOLEON AND WIELAND—THEIR CONVERSATION—THE GAINS OF RUSSIA—DANGEROUS ELEMENTS IN THE DUAL LEAGUE—AUSTRIA MENACED—NAPOLEON'S MARITAL RELATIONS—FOUCHÉ'S MACHINATIONS FOR THE DIVORCE OF JOSEPHINE—NAPOLEON'S PROPOSAL FOR A RUSSIAN PRINCESS.

THE second meeting of the two most powerful monarchs then living occurred at Erfurt on September twenty-seventh, and their
deliberations lasted eighteen days. It was Napoleon's greatest diplomatic engagement, and he was the victor. The town was his, and he was, of course, the host. Such splendid hospitality as he lavished would have touched a harder heart than Alexander's. The luxury and military display were barbaric on the one hand, while, on the other, Germany's greatest scholars and men of letters were summoned to flatter the Czar's intellectual pretensions. There was the same exhibition, too, of frank personal confidence and of imperial magnanimity as at Tilsit. Talleyrand and the Russian chancellor, Rumianzoff, held protracted conferences, the former, as he confesses in his memoirs, plotting against his master's interests, in order to see that Austria should suffer no harm. Day after day Napoleon and Alexander paced the floor of the great room in the palace which had been fitted as an office, examining details and bringing matters to a conclusion. There was intoxication in the very air. The kings of Bavaria, Würtemberg, and Westphalia were present with their consorts and attendant courtiers; so, too, were the Prince Primate and the minor rulers of Germany. The drawing-rooms, streets, and theaters of Erfurt were filled with the splendors of their gorgeous apparel and that of their bedizened atten-

dants. On October fourth the "Œdipe" of Voltaire was given at the playhouse before the assembled courts. At the words, "A great man's friendship is a boon from the gods," Alexander rose, and, grasping Napoleon's hand, stood for a moment in an attitude that typified a renewed alliance. The house thundered with applause.

More memorable still was the appearance on the scene of Germany's most transcendent genius, who came to lay the homage of his intellect at the feet of him whom he considered at the moment, and long after, not only to be the greatest power, but the greatest idealist, in the world. Goethe and Napoleon met twice—once in Erfurt, once in Weimar. On both occasions it was the man of arms who sought out the man of letters—*par nobile fratrum*. They talked of Werther and his sorrows; the Emperor appreciatively, and with a knowledge of detail. It is said that the latter took exception to some one passage in particular; which one is not known. The poet had probably just risen from penning the "Elective Affinities," and seemed to recognize his dazzling host as a creature familiar with such ties, transcending the bounds of nations, the trammels of commonplace human limitations, the confines of ordinary thought and speech. "A great man can be recognized only by his peers," is one of Goethe's own sentences. What to the poet were common men and the chains of political bondage, what were nations and their ambitions, in comparison with a society where mind and morals had the glorious license of Olympians and could follow the unobstructed paths of inclination in realms controlled only by fancy! Napoleon's greeting was laconic, "Vous êtes un homme." This flattered Goethe, who called it the inverse "ecce homo," and felt its allusion to his citizenship, not in Germany, but in the world. The nineteenth-century Cæsar then urged the great writer to carry out an already-formed design and compose a drama on the life of his own great prototype; such a work, he was sure, would be worthier of the theme than Voltaire's effort. At St. Cloud Napoleon had once paid a glowing eulogy to the power of tragic dramas, and, speaking of Corneille, declared that to his inspiration the French nation owed many of its finest impulses and its most brilliant deeds. "If he were here, I would make him a prince." To Goethe he now said that in art, as in politics, there should be rule and ordered beauty; apropos of the drama imitated from Shakspere, which mingles tragedy and comedy, the terrible with the burlesque, he expressed surprise that a great mind like Goethe's

NAPOLEON AND ALEXANDER AT ERFURT.

did not like clean-cut models—"N'aime pas les genres tranchés."
These two judgments, taken together, give a valuable picture of Napoleon's mind.

Amid the brilliant scenes arranged for the entertainment of Napoleon in the stately little town of Weimar, when surrounded by that
German aristocracy which he had humbled, he summoned to his presence the man who in the two periods of his career personified first
the strength and then the weakness of the German folk — the aged
Wieland. Indeed, the Emperor's conversation throughout that excur-
sion to Weimar was chiefly of learning, as if he bowed before German
knowledge, German science, German letters. He had studied much, he
said, in the barracks, "when I was a young lieutenant of artillery,"
and his cold, piercing glance seemed to search the very hearts of the
proud princes and dukes who crowded around and literally stood at
his chair in domestic service. It was at the ball given by the Grand
Duchess that he asked for Wieland. During the evening this gentle
and now temperate old man had been present while the actors of
the French comedy, brought among other decorative trappings from
Paris, had declaimed the "Death of Cæsar" from the stage of the
ducal theater; he had listened to Talma's significant utterance of
the words, "Rule without violence over a conquered universe," and
then, wearied by the excitement of these strange experiences, had
withdrawn from further revelry. The Grand Duchess of Weimar,
anxious to gratify her great guest, sent her carriage to fetch the author of "Oberon"; and rather than detain the illustrious dictator, the
poet started as he was, in his ordinary garments, with unpowdered
hair, wearing his little skull-cap and felt shoes. The meeting was
therefore most dramatic. The dancing almost ceased when Napoleon
advanced to meet his visitor, for the company crowded in a wide circle
to look on and catch what they might hear. But the conversation was
in a low tone.

Wieland would never tell or write what was said, and we know only
enough to feel that the great soldier's words were worthy both of his
genius and of the occasion. He had treated the German nobility with
haughtiness; this plain scholar he treated as an equal. Speaking of
the ancients, and defending the Cæsars against Tacitus, he discussed
the rise of Christianity and emphasized the value of all religions in
conserving morals. The poet replied, when needful, in broken French,

but soon felt at his ease, for the Emperor seemed disposed to engross the conversation, and in the manner of the times proposed questions. "Which of your works do you prefer?" Wieland disclaimed merit for any, but, under urgency, confessed that he liked best his "Agathon" and "Oberon." Then Napoleon asked the stock query which he so often put to scholars and men of letters: "Which has been the happiest age of humanity?" "Impossible to give a reply," said the poet; "good and evil, virtue and vice, continually alternate; philosophy must emphasize the good and make the evil tolerable." "Admirable! admirable!" said Napoleon; "it is not just to paint everything dark, like Tacitus. He is certainly a skilful artist, a bold, seductive colorist, but above all he aims at effect. History wants no illusions; it should illuminate and instruct, not merely give descriptions and narratives which impress us. Tacitus did not sufficiently develop the causes and inner springs of events. He did not sufficiently study the mystery of facts and thoughts, did not sufficiently investigate and scrutinize their connection, to give posterity a just and impartial opinion. History, as I understand it, should know how to catch men and peoples as they would appear in the midst of their epoch. It should take account of external circumstances which would necessarily exercise an important influence on their actions, and clearly see within what limits that influence wrought. The Roman emperors were not so bad as Tacitus describes them. Therefore I am forced to prefer Montesquieu; he is more just, and his criticism is closer to the truth." In discussing Christianity Napoleon said: "Philosophers seek in vain a better doctrine than one which has reconciled man with himself, and has guaranteed the peace and public order of peoples, as well as the happiness and hope of individuals." The talk lasted for two hours, and the interview ended by a movement, not of Napoleon, but of Wieland himself, who seemed weary with standing. "Go, go," said the Emperor, gently. "Good-night."

Such were the scenes which unrolled themselves before the eyes of Europe. Festival succeeded festival — plays, processions, parades, hunts, balls, and dinners. Onlookers sent broadcast to every quarter accounts of the millennial harmony which presided over all. Emperors, kings, princes, nobles, marshals, generals, historians, scholars, poets, players, diplomatists,— the most brilliant actors on the world's great stage,—were brought together at Erfurt in a group not often equaled.

MARSHAL BON-ADRIEN JANNOT DE MONCEY

DUKE OF CONEGLIANO

FROM THE PAINTING BY JACQUELINE'S · BARBIER-VALDIGNE

The stars of Russian decorations, the ribbons of the Legion of
Honor, glittered for the first time on breasts like those of Goethe
and Wieland, which were not accustomed to such distinctions. The
dual league of emperors appeared to the world stronger and more illustrious than before. In a sense this was true, for at the close Alexander
seemed to have obtained much, if not all, that he had demanded. The
two empires were still to act in unity for the reëstablishment of a general peace on terms which would guarantee to France her conquests
made in the south since Tilsit, and to Russia what she had secured in
the east and north. Things were looking brighter for the Czar in Finland, and of the Eastern acquisitions which he so ardently desired, Wallachia and Moldavia were already within his grasp. In other words,
England was to be forced into acknowledging the new order of things
established by France in Spain, and into acquiescing in Russia's seizure of Finland, Wallachia, and Moldavia. If Austria should ally herself with the Turks to defeat Russia's aims, France would intervene
for her ally, and, reciprocally, Russia would do the same in case the
cabinet of Vienna should declare war against France. In any case,
Francis was to be compelled to recognize the new kings of Spain and
Naples under the virtual compulsion of a united summons by Russia
and France. If England should again prove intractable, the two monarchs would meet a third time, and within a year, to concert further
measures. These were very substantial gains for Russia, and for the
time being the Franco-Russian alliance was, as it appeared to the
world, mightier and firmer than it had been.

But, on the other hand, it contained now what was wanting before
—active germs of dissolution. In the first place, Alexander and his
ministers had shown themselves so firm that more than once there had
been hot words even between the emperors, and the memories of these
were a source of the increased suspicions which Alexander carried back
to the Neva. The Czar had, moreover, been compelled to yield a very
important point. The treaty, as a whole, was to remain secret for at
least ten years. He might occupy and consider as his own the two
coveted provinces, but even they were not to be openly annexed until
England's answer was received. An Anglo-Turkish alliance, Napoleon
reasoned, would be disastrous, while a Russo-Turkish alliance, in case
of Russian victory, would give the ministers at St. James's too much insight into the agreement of Erfurt, and perhaps bring on some such

calamity as the seizure of the Danish fleet which the suspicions entertained at London concerning Tilsit had precipitated. The ultimate aim
of the treaty was to be indefinitely concealed. Another dangerous element in the affairs of Erfurt was that contained in the additional pro-
vocation given to Prussia and Austria. It is generally believed that
Napoleon urged Alexander to send troops and occupy not only Warsaw,
but parts of both Austria and Prussia. This would embroil him with
his neighbors, and make central Europe secure while France was fighting Spain. If this be true, it explains two facts. Prussia in her despair
had sent one agent after another to Paris in order to secure some mitigation of Napoleon's demands. The last had been Prince William, the
King's brother, who early in September had agreed that his country
should pay one hundred and forty millions of francs, surrender to France
the forts on the Oder, and reduce her army to forty-two thousand men,
in return for the withdrawal of Napoleon's troops and a reduction of
the indemnity by fourteen and a half millions of francs. On October
ninth, three weeks afterward, the prince was invited by Napoleon to
hunt hares on the battle-field of Jena! This incident, taken in connection with the demand for Stein's dismissal, seemed very significant
of Napoleon's attitude toward Prussia.

General Vincent had been despatched from Vienna nominally to explain away at Erfurt the Austrian armaments; in reality, to observe
what was going on. Although he found no difficulty in winning the
versatile Talleyrand to his cause, he was treated with scant courtesy
by Napoleon, and sent back with a letter from him to Francis containing bitter reproaches and menaces. Stein, after his withdrawal, found,
like Hardenberg, a refuge in Vienna. There he formed one of an influential coterie composed of Alexander's envoy, Pozzo di Borgo, and
others of like mind, who were steadily consolidating the war sentiment. The activity of these men explained a phrase in the letter to
Francis.—"The last rising in mass would infallibly have brought on
war if I could have supposed that that levy and those preparations had
been arranged with Russia,"—which hinted at Russia's possible interest in the military preparations; and one day at Erfurt, as Napoleon's grenadiers were marching by, the Czar had to listen while
their Emperor vaunted the courage they had displayed at Pultusk and
Friedland. Apropos of Napoleon's lack of delicacy, it is said that once
in the Tuileries he significantly addressed one of his court ladies, not re-

nowned for purity, with the words, "You are fond of men, I understand." "Yes; when they are polite," was the rejoinder. At Erfurt
Talleyrand gave the same explanation of his master's vagaries. "We
French are more civilized than our monarch," he said to Montgelas,
the Bavarian minister of state; "his is only the civilization of Roman
history."

But there was another incident at Erfurt more pregnant of ultimate
changes than any of these. Thanks to Fouché's Mephistophelian insinuations, and the details which leaked out concerning the quarrels
between Queen Hortense, representing her mother, and the Grand
Duchess of Berg, representing the Bonapartes, the subject of Napoleon's divorce had become common talk. The new position at Tilsit as the recognized head of Europe's kingly hierarchy seems as early
as that to have tempted the Emperor to a course distasteful to the
man; but what occurred there is uncertain, and did not commit him.
At Fontainebleau, the following autumn, his harsh and distant treatment of Josephine gave color to the suspicion that he was again under
temptation. Whom would he choose? asked the gossips. Sometime
during that year a list of marriageable princesses was prepared by the
Emperor's orders. It included Maria Louisa of Austria, aged sixteen;
Maria Amelia, niece of the King of Saxony; and the two sisters of the
Czar, the younger of whom was not quite thirteen. The general opinion seemed to fix on one or the other of the Czar's unmarried sisters.
This rumor soon reached St. Petersburg, and the scandal-mongers of
that capital promptly designated the Grand Duchess Catherine, for she
was of marriageable age, and they said she was learning French country dances. Alexander was in consternation; the Russian party would
be aghast if he should consent, while a refusal might endanger the alliance on which hung all his ambitions.

Some months previously, Fouché, aware of the conflict in Napoleon's
mind, had actually suggested to the Empress, and probably with her
husband's knowledge, that she should take the initiative. In reply she
ran with disheveled hair and streaming eyes to ask an explanation
from her lord in person. He consoled her with many protestations,
but he left for Italy without having entirely reassured her. On his
return from Milan he roundly abused his minister of police, and forbade his continued plotting. Nevertheless, the daring functionary persistently disobeyed, and by the month of March, 1808, the air of Paris

was thick with embittered and ardent pleas on one side or the other.
One evening the court was to attend a gala performance to be given in
the Tuileries. Their Majesties did not appear. Napoleon, in fact, had
not made ready; instead he had retired to his private apartments and
had sent for Josephine. She entered her husband's chamber in full
array of evening costume, to find him in bed, pale, worn, and weary. At
once he began the recital of his perplexities, pouring out, as it were,
his whole heart, and, though not uttering the request, he seemed as if
beseeching in dumb despair the decisive word from her. The Empress,
however, was inflexible. Was he, he said in fierce disappointment, to
be compelled to adopt his bastard children? Surprised and touched
by her signs of assent, the Emperor vowed never to desert her, and
there matters had remained.

At Erfurt the same vacillation overmastered Napoleon as that with
which he had been tormented since Tilsit. By his command Talleyrand and Caulaincourt were to drop the remark before Alexander that
the matter of the divorce was a European question; he wished to test,
he said, the temper of his ally. Both ministers suggested that a contemplated match between the daughter of Paul I. and the King of
Sweden had fallen through because of the confessional difficulties, the
latter being a Protestant, the former of the Greek Church. The Emperor
shrugged his shoulders in displeasure, and they discharged their task.
Apparently the Czar was not shocked, for, opening the subject himself,
he told Napoleon that his best friends looked with anxiety to see him
consolidate his work and his dynasty by a second marriage. This of
course led to a confidential talk, in which the possibility of a matrimonial as well as a political alliance was mentioned. If Napoleon had
demanded on the spot the hand of the Czar's marriageable sister,
Catherine, it is doubtful if Alexander would have refused. But the
imperial host still vacillated, for he had not taken the irrevocable
step; a hesitating mention was made of his guest's younger sister,
Anne, who was still a child, as an eventual possibility, and nothing
more was said. To stamp the success of the meeting, a joint letter
was sent to George III., asking for peace on the principle of "uti possi-
detis." The two monarchs parted with every manifestation of personal
devotion; but on Alexander's return to his capital his elder sister was
married with indecent haste to the Duke of Oldenburg.

NAPOLEON, GOETHE AND WIELAND

CHAPTER XIV

THE FAILURE OF THE SPANISH CAMPAIGN

THE GRAND ARMY IN FRANCE—THEIR ENTRANCE TO SPAIN—THE OP-
POSING FORCES—NAPOLEON'S STRATEGIC PLAN—FRENCH VICTORIES—
SIR JOHN MOORE—THE BRITISH AND SPANIARDS—NAPOLEON'S AD-
VANCE TO MADRID—HIS RETURN NORTHWARD—MOORE'S RETREAT
—NAPOLEON AT PARIS—DEATH OF MOORE—THE NAPOLEONIC CON-
STITUTION FOR SPAIN—SPANISH RESISTANCE—JOSEPH'S WEAKNESS—
ESTABLISHMENT OF THE NEW MONARCHY.

WHILE Alexander was hastening the preparations for his sister's
marriage, Napoleon was hurrying toward Spain, whither, too,
the legions of the grand army, released by the evacuation of Prussia,
had already been ordered. Baylen and Cintra must be retrieved at
any cost. As the splendid array of soldiers passed through France
they were received like men who had already conquered. The civil
authorities spread banquets for them, compliments rained from the
honeyed lips of chosen orators, poets sang sweet strains on the theme
of their glories. This appeared a spontaneous outburst to the troops,
and they marched with the elasticity of enthusiasm to their task.
The curious may read to-day what the army could not know—that
by Napoleon's personal decree the ministry of war had prepared every
detail of that triumph, that the prefects acted under stringent orders,
that three sets of warlike songs were written by commission in Paris,
and forwarded one each to various points, so that, as the Emperor
wrote, "the soldier may not hear the same thing twice." The success
of the plan was complete, and the jubilations had every appearance
of being genuine.

It was therefore not a tired and disheartened army which was gathered under the walls of Burgos early in November, but a body of

picked and energetic veterans. Joseph, to be sure, had done little in the interval to take advantage of the foolish and careless tumult into which the joy of victory had thrown the Spanish people. In spite of the minute directions which had been received almost daily from Na-

MAP OF THE SPANISH CAMPAIGN.

poleon, Jourdan, who, having been the King's military adviser in Naples, had come in the same capacity to Spain, gradually lost every advantage of position. But the French boys who had fought in the summer were older and more experienced. The defensive attitude of their leader had given them the training of camp life, and had secured the recuperation of their strength. When, therefore, they were mingled with the newcomers, they might be considered almost as good soldiers as those who had arrived from Germany.

Moreover, the best generals were now in command: Victor was at Amurrio, Bessières at Miranda on the Ebro, Moncey at Tafalla, Lefebvre near Bilbao, Ney at Logroño on the Ebro, Saint-Cyr at La Junquera, each with a corps, the smallest of twenty, the largest of thirty thousand men. Duhesme was shut up in Barcelona with ten thousand. There was a reserve of thirty-five thousand, the guard and cavalry, at Tolosa

and Vitoria. Mortier's corps of twenty-four thousand was in the rear,
and Junot, who had been better received in Paris than he expected,
was coming up with nineteen thousand more. In all, there were about
two hundred and forty thousand troops. Napoleon, reaching Bayonne
on November third, had it announced that there were between three
and four hundred thousand! With such a numerous and efficient fighting
force, there was no need of exaggeration. To oppose it Blake had thirty-
two thousand Spaniards at Valmaseda as the left wing of the Spanish
army, and La Romana, having disembarked at Santander, soon arrived
with eight thousand more; the center, twenty-five thousand strong,
lay between Calahorra and Tudela under Castaños; the right, seventeen thousand in number, was at and near Saragossa under Palafox.
Before Barcelona was Vives, with twenty thousand, and near Burgos
was a reserve of eighteen thousand under Belvedere—about a hundred
and twenty thousand men, all told. In addition to this regular army,
there was another irregular one of vast but vague dimensions, consisting of the entire nation.

Amid the exciting cares of Erfurt, Napoleon had still found time to
study the military situation in Spain with minuteness, and he finally
wrote to Joseph that he was coming in person to end the war by one
skilful stroke. This hope was founded on the position held by Blake,
advanced as it was beyond the Spanish line, and remote enough to be
exposed. By a swift blow that general's army might therefore be cut
off from its support, and annihilated; the center and right would
successively meet the same fate. This plan had been jeopardized by
the rashness of Lefebvre. On October thirty-first Blake had advanced
from Durango for an attack. He had not only been routed, but in
the heat of victory had been thrown far back to Valmaseda by the
overzealous French general. Although the Emperor had hoped for
something quite different, having given orders to draw him forward
toward Biscay and Navarre, he still did not abandon his strategic
plan. The Spaniards had grown warlike in a day, but their victories
had intoxicated them, and of military science they had only what they
had learned by experience. There was no harmony among the generals — not even a preconcerted plan of operation. Accordingly the
mass of the French army was directed toward Burgos to cut off
and overwhelm Blake, while two corps under Soult were directed to
intercept his retreat.

Burgos fell almost without opposition on November tenth; Blake was defeated the next day at Espinosa, and his scattered columns, turned but not captured by Soult, fled into Asturias, where they joined the force of La Romana. Without a moment's hesitation Ney was now despatched to the southeast in order to fall on Castaños's rear, while Lannes was to unite Moncey's corps with Lagrange's division and attack his front. The Spanish general was posted, as has been said, on the Ebro between Calahorra and Tudela. Before the twentieth the two moves had been executed and all was in readiness. The Spaniards fled before Lannes's attack on the twenty-third, but Ney with his cavalry remained inexplicably stationary, and did not cut off their retreat. They were therefore able to reassemble at Siguenza, while Palafox withdrew to Saragossa. This was seemingly an easy triumph for Napoleon's matchless strategy; his plan worked without real resistance, for his self-sufficient and ignorant enemy was scattered. Nevertheless, it will be observed that the execution was deficient and the result disproportionate. Neither Soult on the right nor Ney on the left showed such vigor or promptness as of old; there was no general surrender by the Spaniards, nor was any portion of their force annihilated. All that was gained — and for a common general it would have been much — was the ability to take another step.

The capitulation at Cintra, the affair at Bayonne, and the uprising of the Spaniards, had combined to intensify rebellion in Portugal. She was now in full sympathy with Spain, and her people were scarcely less bitter or less active than the Spaniards. The easy terms secured by Junot had infuriated England, and not only Dalrymple and Burrard, but Wellesley himself, had been recalled to give an account of their conduct. The last was triumphantly vindicated; but while the others were not convicted of dereliction in duty, they were virtually withdrawn from active life. Sir John Moore was now in command of the English troops in the Peninsula. He had been reinforced with ten thousand men, and feeling sure of Portugal, had advanced into Spain. To Napoleon it seemed evident that his intention was to seize Madrid.

This was a mistake. The jubilant Spaniards, expecting to treat Napoleon as they had treated Dupont, had summoned the English to join them. Moore's orders were to assist them, and he prepared to obey, although he well knew what would be the consequences of Spanish hallucination. With one column he reached Salamanca on No-

NAPOLEON AND THE FRENCH TROOPS REACHING THE CONVENT
AT THE SUMMIT OF THE GUADARRAMA MOUNTAINS

vember thirteenth; the head of the other was at Astorga. His own division numbered only fifteen thousand men; the other was even smaller — ten thousand at the most. It was on that date that he learned of Napoleon's victories. Accordingly he halted to await the next move of the French. That move was against Madrid. Saragossa was besieged by Moncey, Lefebvre was thrown out to guard the right flank, and Ney to protect the left of the advancing columns; the march began on November twenty-eighth.

The first obstacle was the mountain-range of Guadarrama, which had to be crossed by the pass of Somosierra. This defile was found to be strongly guarded; there were not only infantry stationed on the heights, but artillery also, sixteen guns being below the turn of the pass in a most advantageous position. In the early morning of the thirtieth the French infantry began to climb the cliffs on each side of the narrow gorge, and as the mists were heavy their movements were successfully concealed until the Spanish bivouacs were reached, surprised, and dislodged. Simultaneously a regiment of Polish light horse was launched against the battery. Their charge was magnificent, and the gunners could fire only a single round before they were overpowered. By the ordinary breakfast hour the pass was free. On the evening of December second the whole army—infantry, cavalry, and artillery— was united on the heights of Chamartin before the gates of Madrid. Two days later, after a gallant resistance by its little garrison and the undaunted inhabitants, the city yielded to the superior strength of Napoleon, and proposed terms. After some parley these were accepted, but under the circumstances the Emperor felt that mildness must be seasoned by menace. There were disorders in the streets, incident to the new occupation by the French, and that fact he used as a plea to declare the capitulation null and the Spanish officers prisoners of war. Their men had escaped the day before.

The military operations of the campaign were of course not yet ended, for Moore had not appeared in the valley of the Tagus, marching, as it was believed he would, toward Madrid. The first task was to find him. The different corps were sent out in all directions, but it was not until the middle of the month that the British position was even approximately ascertained. Napoleon was surprised by what he learned, and concluded that the English were about to abandon Portugal in order to secure Ferrol as a base of supplies. His first impulse was to march out himself and prevent such a disaster; on the twentieth half of his army set forth from Madrid, and on the twenty-second he led them through the snows of the Guadarrama.

Meanwhile Moore had made his decision. It was to attract the attention of the French, draw them toward him, and then slowly retreat northward, thus leaving Andalusia free from interference, and giving the southern Spaniards time to organize once more and equip themselves for a second Baylen. To this end he prepared on the twenty-third to attack Soult, but learning of Napoleon's rapid advance, he promptly changed his plan and began his retreat; three days later he led his troops safely across the Esla. Then began a famous chase. The Emperor hurried forward, marching on foot through cold and snow to encourage his tired men. He was eager to strike a blow at his enemy's rear before they should get too far away, and Soult was urged onward to Mansilla, to flank the retreating column. On the twenty-ninth the French cavalry reached the Esla and were driven back by the English rear-guard, while Moore stopped only long enough to destroy the magazines at Benevento, and then hurried on to Astorga.

For two days longer the retreat continued. Moore, after many successful skirmishes, reached Corunna, where he hoped to embark. Soult crossed the Esla at last, and on New Year's day, 1809, the Emperor found himself at Astorga. He believed there was an English fleet at Ferrol; the weather was bitter, and his health was jeopardized by the severity of the cold; moreover, disquieting letters arrived, and he determined that this game was not worth the candle. Soult was intrusted with the pursuit, Ney was stationed at Astorga as a reserve, and Napoleon, putting himself at the head of his guards, set out for Valladolid, which he reached on the sixth. After a rest of ten days, new and more disquieting despatches made clear the urgent need for his presence in Paris, though his task in Spain was far from ended. On January twenty-third he reached the Tuileries.

The tale of Moore's splendid retreat, of his courage and calmness in loss and disaster, of his superb control of his men in their disappointment when Corunna was reached and no fleet was found there, of his brave fight with Soult on January sixteenth, of the mortal wound which struck him down in the hour of victory, and of the self-forgetfulness which enabled him in the agonies of death to make all necessary arrangements for his men to embark on the belated ships—all this is a

ANTOINE CHARLES LOUIS COLLINET, COUNT OF LASALLE.

brilliant page of English history, perhaps the finest record in its entire course of glory won in retreat, of patience, moderation, and success in the very hour of bitterest disappointment. It was the spirit and example of Moore which made possible the victories of Wellington.

The French interests in Spain were left in a most deplorable condition. The populace of Madrid had received the hero of the age with coldness, and shut themselves up in their houses to avoid forming a crowd or creating any enthusiasm in the streets. They would not even come out to see the gorgeous military parade which was arranged for their benefit. The gentry and nobility had been alike distant and cold. It was clear that Spain could neither be wheedled, cajoled, nor threatened into even passive acquiescence in the new conquest. It was essential, therefore, that another course should be tried. On December fourth, Napoleon, in the rôle of reformer-statesman, pronounced and issued from Chamartin a series of the most thoroughgoing edicts. All feudal privileges, all interprovincial customs dues, were swept away; the Inquisition was abolished, and the number of convents was reduced to a third. These measures were in themselves most salutary, and struck at the very root of the upas-tree under the baneful shade of which Spain had been slowly perishing. But to do good they must be enforced; there must be a complete military conquest of the country, and a capable administration.

There was neither. The Spanish army had been defeated, but, severe as had been its punishment, its power of resistance was not destroyed; the occupation of the country was also sadly incomplete, and it made no difference whither French soldiers marched, or what strategic points they held, some kind of Spanish fighting force, no matter how irregular, sprang up behind them and on their sides. The complete military centralization of Prussia had made Jena decisive for the whole loose-jointed territory of that kingdom; the compact territory of Spain and the local independence of her peoples made regular victories utterly fruitless so far as the open country was concerned.

Moreover, Joseph, although he had been driven from his capital, and had enjoyed neither power nor consequence except as the general of Napoleon's armies, now asserted that he, and not his brother, was the king of Spain. He was hurt by the Emperor's assumption of superior sovereignty, and angry. He was the one, he felt, who could best deal with the Spaniards, win their affection, and consolidate his power. To be shouldered off his throne, and compelled to stand by while such radical measures were taken, embittered him. Shame, he said, covered his face before his pretended subjects; he renounced all rights to the throne, preferring honor and honesty to power so dearly bought. This angered Napoleon, and he threatened to divide the land into military provinces; but, like his gentler brother, he himself recoiled before the utter annihilation of a nationality so ancient and dignified as that of Spain.

As the price for the evacuation of Madrid, the people of the capital swore to accept Joseph once more as their king. Similar oaths of allegiance came from all the provinces occupied by the French. Although these oaths were not considered binding by those who took them, inasmuch as they held themselves to be acting under compulsion, yet at least the shadow of Joseph's monarchy reappeared under the imperial protection, and a so-called liberal constitution, modeled on that of France, was given to the people as a boon. "It depends on yourselves," was the Emperor's language, "to make this charter yours. If all my endeavors prove vain, and you do not justify my confidence, then I have nothing left but to treat you as a conquered province, and create another throne for my brother. In that case I shall put the crown of Spain on my own head, and teach the ill-disposed to respect it; for God has given me the power and the will to overcome all obstacles."

ENGRAVED BY R. SOPP

SIR JOHN MOORE

FROM A MEZZOTINT ENGRAVING

CHAPTER XV

THE TRANSFORMATION OF AUSTRIA

DANGERS IN NAPOLEON'S REAR — THE STATE OF PARIS — AUSTRIA WAR-
LIKE — THE CZAR'S POLICY — NATIONAL MOVEMENTS IN GERMANY —
NAPOLEON'S TRUE POSITION — TALLEYRAND'S RESPONSIBILITY — THE
NEEDS OF FRANCE — THE CONSCRIPTION AGAIN ANTICIPATED — THE
ARCHDUKE CHARLES — WAR DECLARED BY AUSTRIA — CHARLES'S AP-
PEALS TO NATIONAL SENTIMENT — IMPERIAL EXCESS AND DYNASTIC
MODERATION — THE UPRISING OF THE TYROL — AUSTRIA'S SUCCESSES.

THE news from central Europe which reached Napoleon in Spain
was of a most alarming character, and made certain considerations so emphatic that all others became insignificant. It mattered
not that he must leave behind him a half-accomplished task; that while
his strategy had been successful, he had lost the opportunity to annihilate the English, which, though he did not know it at the time, he
had really had in the tardy arrival of their transports at Corunna; that
the national uprising was not suppressed by his carefully devised measures; that the oaths of allegiance sworn to Joseph and the constitution had been sworn under compulsion by a minority, who, pious as
the people were, did not, for that reason, consider even themselves as
bound, much less the nation as a whole — all this was serious enough,
but it was paltry when compared with what had taken place in German lands while he had been absent from Paris.

During the campaign of Marengo there had been a knot of active,
self-seeking, and traitorous men who, having risen by Bonaparte's help,
schemed how best to sustain themselves in case of his death. This
same group, under the leadership of Talleyrand and Fouché, had been
again arranging plans for their guidance should misfortune overwhelm
Napoleon in Spain. Such was their activity that even Metternich had

been deceived into the belief that they had a large party of French patriots behind them, who, weary of the Emperor's incessant calls on France for aid in enterprises foreign to her welfare, would gladly be rid of him. So grave did the Austrian ambassador consider the crisis that late in November he left his post and set out for Vienna. Vincent's reports about the friction at Erfurt had already found credence in the Austrian capital among the war party, and the belief was spreading that the Franco-Russian alliance was hollow.

Stein's absence from North Germany had only intensified the sympathy of the people with his policy. Even at Königsberg, the seat of government, public opinion demanded the measures he had desired. Prussia was not only strong once more, but was ardent to redeem its disgrace. The reflex influence of the popular movements in Prussia and Austria upon one another had intensified both, until the more advanced leaders in the two countries cared little whether the process of German regeneration was begun under Hohenzollern or Hapsburg leadership. Into this surcharged atmosphere came Metternich with his exaggerated statements about the great reactionary party in France. The effect was to raise the elements. He declared, besides, that the Spanish war had absorbed so much of Napoleon's effective military strength that not more than two hundred thousand men were available for use in central Europe, and that Austria alone, with her new armaments, would be a match for any army the French emperor could lead against her, at least in the first stages of a war. Austria had been negotiating for an English subsidy, without which her troops, fine as they were, could not be maintained; but Great Britain refused a grant until they should actually take the field. This fact was an inducement so strong as to put a climax on the already hostile inclinations of the Emperor Francis; and as his minister Stadion had long felt that Napoleon's power must not be allowed time for further consolidation, the government concluded to strike while the difficulties in Spain were at their height.

Although the Czar had left Erfurt in an anxious mood, he was nevertheless clear in his mind that through Napoleon alone could his ambitions be gratified. He was equally convinced that, while the European system should not be further upturned, it must for the present be maintained as it now was. On his homeward journey he had time to reflect on the situation, and as he passed through Königsberg the

warlike temper of Prussia was so manifest that he thought Frederick
William, for a while at least, should be removed from its influence.
Accordingly he pressed the King to pay a visit to St. Petersburg. The
invitation was accepted, and the Czar's efforts were so successful that
when his visitor left for home his feeling was as unwarlike as it had
ever been. He informed Austria that his interests were those of Russia, that there should be no offensive warfare, and that any conflict
must be confined to repelling an attack. The Czar declared on March
second, in response to an inquiry from Vienna, that if Austria should
begin a war he would fulfil his obligations to Napoleon; but six weeks
later, seeing how determined was the war sentiment at Vienna, and
how complete were the preparations of Francis, it seemed best to
throw an anchor to windward, and he so far modified his attitude as
to explain that in the event of war he would not put his strength
into any blow he might aim at Austria.

The cabinet of Vienna was perfectly aware that neither Alexander
nor Frederick William represented the national feeling of their respective peoples. They knew that Austria's opportunity to lead a great revolt against Napoleon was to be found in the support of the powerful
conservatives of Russia, in the enthusiasm of all Prussia, where Arndt
was already crying, "Freedom and Austria!" and in the passionate loyalty of her own peoples, not excepting the sturdy Tyrolese, who, chafing under Napoleon's yoke, were ready for insurrection. On March
eighteenth, 1809, the French minister at Vienna wrote to Paris that in
1805 the government, but neither army nor nation, had desired war;
that now the government, the army, and the people all desired it. The
Austrian plenipotentiary was ordered, in requesting a subsidy from
Great Britain, to state that in the event of victory his government
hoped to secure such internal vigor as Austria had enjoyed before the
treaty of Presburg. As to the neighboring states, she desired some
minor rectifications of her own frontier, with indemnifications to the
younger branches of her dynasty for their lost domains. These might
be found either in Germany or in Italy, and if she should succeed in
destroying Napoleon's system of tributary powers, she meant to restore
all their territories to their rightful owners, not excepting those of the
German princes who had been hostile.

To suppose, as many do, that no inkling of all these stupendous
schemes reached Napoleon in Spain is preposterous. Bavaria was his

faithful subordinate, and Poland still hoped everything from his successes. Both were in the heart of Germany, and through a carefully organized system of spies, information of the most reliable nature was regularly received in both countries. The same historians who assert that after Marengo Bonaparte left Italy for Paris to cloak his defeat, and that he fled to Malmaison to conceal his direct connection with Enghien's death, expect us to believe that Napoleon fled from Spain merely to throw the responsibility of failure on Joseph. Most men in any crisis act from mixed motives. Such a charge displays skill in combining facts, but Marengo, whether a defeat or a victory, secured France to the general who commanded there; the retreat to Malmaison did not induce the Consul to deny his responsibility for the execution at Vincennes; and it would have been simply an intervention of the supernatural if Napoleon, for purely subjective reasons, had left Spain to return to Paris just at the very instant when his presence was absolutely essential there, not only to check those who, although ostensibly his supporters, were in reality his deadly foes, but also for the warlike preparations to meet the storm which was about to burst. His secretary has asserted that the letters which reached him at Astorga contained all this disquieting news, and there is absolutely no proof that they did not. The probability is all on the side of the account which was universally accepted until attacked by the group of over-credulous French historians whose zeal for the Revolution is such that they feel bound to deny every statement of the equally biased school of Napoleonic advocates.

Moreover, it was from Spain that the Emperor warned the princes composing the Confederation of the Rhine to have their contingents ready. His language is guarded—whether the cabinet of Vienna had drunk from the waters of Lethe or from those of the Danube, he himself would be ready. Besides, his actions could have but one meaning. The moment he reached Paris, significant looks and conduct warned Talleyrand to beware. "Is Joseph," the Emperor said, in an interview with Roederer, "to talk like an Englishman or behave like Talleyrand? I have covered this man with honors, riches, and diamonds; he has used them all against me. At the first opportunity he had, he has betrayed me as much as he could. He has declared during my absence that he kneeled in supplication to prevent my enterprise in Spain; for two years he tormented me to undertake it. . . . It was the same with regard to Enghien. 1 did not even know him; it was Talleyrand who brought him to my notice. 1 did not know where he was; it was Talleyrand who told me the spot, and after having advised the execution he has groaned over it with every acquaintance."

At the same time the columns of the "Moniteur" were filled with half-true accounts of the Emperor's success in Spain, and the French people knew everything that was favorable; but there was a complete suppression of all the rest. As Austria desired war to secure her subsidies from England, so France was again in need of funds which her own resources could not provide. Because of the failure to paralyze Spain by a single blow, Napoleon had, for the first time in his history, returned after a "successful" campaign without an enormous war indemnity. Once again, after temporary patching, French finances were in disorder, and there was urgent need to repair them. The people desired peace for their enterprises, but the Continental blockade so hampered commerce that any peace which did not include a pacification of the seas would avail them little. It was a customary formality of Napoleon's to put the entire responsibility of war on the enemy, and it was announced in February that negotiations with Austria had failed. This was in a large sense true, although the particular effort referred to was perfunctory, and was intended technically to secure the help of Russia, which was to fight only in case Austria should be the aggressor.

Gradually, therefore, the war spirit revived in France. No one remonstrated when once more recourse was had to the fatal policy of anticipating the annual conscription. Not only were the conscripts for 1810 called out, but the number was stretched to the utmost, and those who from immaturity or other causes had been unavailable in 1806, 1807, 1808, and 1809, were now collected. The total of the youths thus swept together was not less than a hundred and sixty thousand. To render available their slender efficiency, they were divided among the various regiments already in the field, in each of which these raw and boyish recruits constituted a fifth battalion.

Since the Archduke Charles had been again at the helm of military affairs in Austria, not only had a transformation been wrought in the army as a fighting instrument, but the general staff had likewise been completely reorganized. For two years, therefore, Austria's occupation had been not only forging a sword, but practising, as well, the wielding of it. The lessons taught her by previous experience in Napoleonic warfare were thoroughly learned. It was consequently a very different strategic problem which the Emperor of the French had to solve in this campaign.

For two years the Archduke had been studying his task, and that in the light of ample experience. The conclusion he reached was that he would attack and overpower Davout in Saxony; then, by an appeal to their German patriotism, raise and use the peoples of northern and central Germany for an overwhelming assault on Napoleon. But as the time for action drew near, the moral influence of those annihilating blows which the French armies had struck once and again began to assert itself and to create hesitancy. Count Stadion, the minister of state, knew that diplomacy had reached the limit of its powers and could gain at most only a few weeks. These he felt sure the enemy would use to better advantage in strengthening himself than Austria in her poverty could do. He was therefore urgent for prompt action. Charles, on the other hand, hesitated to face the miraculous resources of Napoleon without a finishing touch to some of his preparations which were still incomplete. He therefore began in January to procrastinate, and consequently it was not until February that Francis demanded an advance. In this interval the whole plan of campaign was changed. The main army, under Charles, was to be collected in Bohemia, ready for action in any direction, so as to thwart whatever course Napoleon might adopt. Hiller was to guard the line of the Inn, the Archduke Ferdinand was to march against Warsaw, while the Archduke John was to enter the Tyrol from Italy and excite the people to revolt. On April ninth all these movements were well under way; Hiller had reached the Inn, and Charles declared war.

Ostensibly this war was to be unlike any other so far waged. The secret instructions given to the imperial Austrian envoy in London clearly indicated that the Hapsburgs hoped by victory to restore their influence both in Italy and Germany; for that was the meaning of "restoration to rightful owners" and the "slight rectification of their frontiers," or, in other words, the restoration of European conditions to what they had been before Napoleon's advent. This was the dynastic side; the national side was also to be used for the same end. "The liberties of Europe have taken refuge under your banner," ran Charles's proclamation to the army; "your victories will break their bonds, and your German brethren still in the enemy's ranks await their redemption." To the German world he said, "Austria fights not only for her own autonomy, but takes the sword for the independence and national honor of Germany." Another manifesto, written by Gentz, the ablest statesman in Vienna, declared that the war was to be waged not against France, but against the persistent extension of her system which had produced such universal disorder in Europe.

The tone and language of these papers have an audible Napoleonic echo in them: if an upstart house, represented by a single life and without direct descendants, could win success by appeals to the people, and gain the support of their enthusiasm by identifying its interests with theirs, why might not an ancient dynasty, with vigorous stock and numerous shoots, do likewise? Moreover, Napoleon no longer respected the limits of natural physical boundaries, or the restrictions of birth, speech, religion, and custom, which inclosed a nation: his empire was to disdain such influences, to found itself on the universal brotherhood of man, and to secure the regeneration of humanity by liberal ideas of universal validity. Austria would offset this alluring summons by a trumpet-call to the brotherhood of Germans, to the strong forces of national feeling, to the respect for tradition and history which would animate her soldiers and justify her course.

If she needed a concrete illustration she could point to the Tyrolese. Since the treaty of Presburg their chains had chafed their limbs to the raw; at this very moment they were again in open rebellion. The administrative reforms introduced by Maximilian of Bavaria were in reality most salutary; his determined stand against priestly domination over the Tyrolese people proved in the end their salvation. But the evils of feudalism were always least among mountaineers, and relations of patriarchal tenderness existed between the aristocracy and the peasantry. The devotion of both classes to their institutions, their habits, their clothes, their customs, their local names, was intense. They had no mind to see the name of their country disappear forever, to lose their pleasant, easy-fitting institutions, or to submit to the conscription and join in the great leveling movement which compelled them to serve in the ranks as ordinary soldiers. With their local assemblies they meant to keep their military exclusiveness as scouts, skirmishers, and sharp-shooters, in all of which lines they excelled.

The more enlightened citizens of the towns were well pleased with

Bavarian rule, but the impulsive, ignorant, and superstitious peasantry were the glad instruments of Austrian emissaries. When they learned that war was inevitable and would soon be formally declared, they at once rose, seized Innsbruck, and held it against the Bavarian troops. When an Austrian garrison marched in, their reception was enthusiastic. This was in the middle of April; simultaneously the Archduke John defeated Prince Eugène in Italy and drove him back upon the Adige, while Ferdinand overpowered all resistance in Poland, and on the twentieth occupied Warsaw. Such successes were intoxicating; the great general had, it seemed, been caught napping at last, and the advantage of a successful opening appeared to be with his enemy.

FIGHTING IN THE STREETS OF ESSLING

FROM THE PAINTING BY P. H. PERBOY.B

CHAPTER XVI

THE FIFTH WAR WITH AUSTRIA — ECKMÜHL

STRATEGIC PRELIMINARIES—FINAL ORDERS—THE DEFENSIVE PLAN OF
AUSTRIA—BERTHIER'S FAILURE—NAPOLEON'S ARRIVAL AT DONAU-
WÖRTH—THE HEIGHT OF NAPOLEON'S ABILITY—THE AUSTRIAN
ADVANCE—THE FIRST COLLISION—CONCENTRATION OF NAPOLEON'S
ARMY—THE AUSTRIANS DIVIDED—THE AUSTRIANS AT ECKMÜHL—
THE BATTLE—CHARLES'S RETREAT—THE FIVE DAYS' FIGHT—ITS
RESULTS—CHARLES AT THE BISAMBERG—NAPOLEON AT VIENNA—
THE GERMAN RISINGS DEMORALIZED—DISCRIMINATION OF THE PEO-
PLE—NAPOLEON'S UNSUCCESSFUL APPEAL TO HUNGARY—PIUS VII.
LOSES HIS SECULAR POWER—NAPOLEON'S ACTIVITY—CHARLES'S
SLUGGISHNESS—PLANS OF BOTH GENERALS—NAPOLEON ON THE
LOBAU.

IT was Napoleon's pride that in his campaigns no enemy should lay
down the law to him. He did not ask, How will my foe behave?
What must I do to thwart him?—that was defensive warfare. For his
purposes he must ask, Whence can I best strike? This question he
now answered by selecting the valley of the Danube as his line of approach, and Ratisbon as his headquarters. He had before him the
most difficult task he had so far undertaken. The concentration and
sustenance of his troops must be made along the line of very least resistance. Davout had four divisions—one each in Magdeburg, Hanover, Stettin, and Bayreuth; he was also in command of the Poles and
Saxons. Bernadotte had two divisions distributed in Hamburg, Bremen, and Lübeck; Oudinot had one in Hanau; the soldiers of the
Rhine Confederation were scattered in all its towns. Two other divisions were just starting for Spain. In the beginning of March Berthier
was again appointed chief of staff, and the Emperor's orders were

issued. They were as clear, concise, and adequate as any of his best; he was once more on familiar ground, under ordinary conditions, facing a well-known foe, whose strength was greater than ever before, but whose identity was still the same. Davout was to collect his troops at Bamberg, the Poles were to remain in Warsaw, the Saxons in Dresden. To the latter capital Bernadotte should lead his army and then assume command. Oudinot was ordered to Augsburg, where he was to be reinforced. The departing divisions were brought to a halt and sent back to Ulm for Masséna's command, while two fresh ones were gathered in France and sent to Strasburg. The Rhine princes were to have their contingents ready and await orders.

A glance at the map will show that, as Napoleon said, he could then in an emergency reach Munich like lightning. But he expected no move from his enemy before the middle of April. By that time he hoped to have his German army gathered, equipped, and ready; in the interval the forces already on the ground could hold Charles in check; by the end of March there would be a hundred thousand French in Bamberg, Ulm, and Augsburg, with thirty thousand Bavarians under Lefebvre about Munich; before the outbreak of hostilities he hoped to have a total of two hundred thousand available fighting troops. "Should the Austrians attack before April tenth," were the orders given on March twenty-eighth, "the army shall be collected behind the Lech, the right occupying Augsburg, the left resting on the right bank of the Danube at Donauwörth." Then followed the most minute instructions to Berthier, explaining every move, and setting forth the reasons why Ratisbon had been chosen as headquarters. This would assure control of the Danube, keep open a line of communication, and enable the writer so to control space and time that he could open the campaign much as he chose.

These dispositions had already compelled another change of plan by the Austrians. They had expected a repetition of Moreau's advance by Munich; instead, they were called on to defend their capital a second time. Two divisions were left to watch the Bohemian Forest; the rest of the army, with Charles at its head, set out, by the circuitous route through Linz, to join Hiller and assume the offensive in the Danube valley. In case of a battle the two divisions were to come up by the short, direct route through Ratisbon, and add their strength to the main army. On the declaration of hostilities the Austrians at once

crossed the Inn and began their march; it was the sixteenth before
they reached the line of the Isar. Had the Archduke not been so sparing of his troops, wearied as they were by the circuit through Linz, he
might have changed the course of history. Napoleon had not yet arrived, and Berthier, who was but human, had proved unequal to the
execution of his commander's orders.

It had been the object of Napoleon to gather his army on a certain
definite, well-connected line, and thence use it as necessity demanded.
Instead of obeying the letter of his instructions, Berthier had struggled
to obey their spirit, and had failed. The command on the left bank
had been assigned to Davout; that of all the troops on the other side
had been given to Masséna; the latter was to concentrate on the Lech,
the former at Ingolstadt. So far all was good; then Berthier lost his
head (the critics say he never could have learned strategy, if he had had
ten lives), and, swerving from the clear letter of Napoleon's orders, he
attempted a more rapid combination — not that behind the Lech, but
one directly at Ratisbon. Davout was to march thither and remain
there; the other divisions were successively to join him. The result
was that three days elapsed before any army was gathered at all; the
two portions, one at Ratisbon, the other at Augsburg, being for that
time widely separated, and each exposed to the separate attack of an
enemy without the possibility of coöperation by the other half.

When the Archduke Charles learned the general situation of his
enemy he determined to do exactly this thing — that is, to attack and
overwhelm each portion of the French army separately. For this purpose he crossed the Isar, and, turning to the right, marched directly on
Ratisbon to attack Davout's command with his superior force before
Masséna's scattered divisions could reach the positions assigned to
them. But he was too late. The semaphore telegraph then in use
had flashed from station to station its signals of the declaration of war
and of the enemy's advance over the Inn, until the news reached Napoleon in Paris on the twelfth. On the sixteenth, after four days' almost unbroken travel, he reached Donauwörth. The confusion into
which Berthier's orders had thrown his carefully arranged plans infuriated him; but when he heard, as he descended from his traveling-
carriage, where the enemy was, he could not believe his ears. When
assured of the truth he seemed, as eye-witnesses declared, to grow
taller, his eyes began to sparkle, and with every indication of delight

he cried: "Then I have him! That 's a lost army! In one month we are in Vienna!" The enemy's first decisive blunder was the march by Linz; the second was yet to be made.

Napoleon's strategy during the following days was, both in his own opinion and in that of his military commentators, the greatest of his life. Such had been Berthier's indecision when he saw his blunder that one general at least—to wit, Pelet—charged him with being a traitor. In twenty-four hours his puzzled humor and conflicting orders had more or less demoralized the whole army. But Napoleon's presence inspired every one with new vigor, from the division commanders to the men in the ranks. Promptly on the seventeenth the order went forth for Davout to leave Ratisbon and challenge the enemy to battle by a flank march up the right bank of the Danube to Ingolstadt in his very face. Lefebvre was to cover the movement, and Wrede, with one Bavarian division, was held ready to strengthen any weak spot in case of battle. Next day Masséna was ordered to set out from Augsburg for the same point, "to unite with the army, catch the enemy at work, and destroy his columns." To this end he was to march eastward by Pfaffenhofen. In a twinkling the scattered French army seemed already concentrated, while scouts came one after the other to announce that the Austrians were separating.

The Austrians had crossed the Isar in good order, Charles himself at Landshut. If they had kept directly onward they might have still wedged themselves between Davout and Lefebvre. But the Archduke grew timid at the prospect of swamps and wooded hills before him; uncertain of his enemy's exact position, he threw forward three separate columns by as many different roads, and thus lengthened his line enormously, the right wing being at Essenbach, the center advanced before Landshut to Hohen-Thann, the left at Morsbach. At four in the morning of the eighteenth Lefebvre received orders to fall on the Austrian left, while flying messengers followed each other in quick succession to spur on Masséna with urgent pleas of immediate necessity. It was hoped that he might come up to join an attack which, though intended mainly to divert the Austrians from Davout, could by his help be turned into an important victory.

The Archduke during the day collected sixty-six thousand men at Rohr for his onset, and thirty-five thousand men at Ludmannsdorf to

ARRIVAL OF NAPOLEON AMONG THE BAVARIANS AND SAXONS.

cover his flank, leaving twenty-five thousand at Moosburg. That night
Davout's last corps, that of Friant, came in, and he began his march.
Masséna, who had collected his army and was coming from Augsburg,
was ordered to turn, either left toward Abensberg, in order to join Davout, or right toward Landshut, to attack Charles's rear, as circumstances should determine. Lefebvre was now commanded to assume
the defensive and await events at Abensberg. Throughout the morning of the nineteenth Davout and Charles continued their march,
drawing ever closer to each other. At eleven the French van and the
Austrian left collided. The latter made a firm stand, but were driven
in with great slaughter.

A considerable force which had been sent to strike Davout on
the flank at Abensberg was also defeated by Lefebvre. Before evening the entire French army was united and in hand. Davout was on
the left toward the river Laber, Lefebvre, with the Bavarians and
several French divisions, was in the center beyond the river Aben,
while Masséna had reached a point beyond Moosburg. Within
sixty hours Napoleon had conceived and completed three separate
strategic movements: the withdrawal of the whole army toward Ingolstadt, the advance of his right to strengthen the incoming left, and
the rearrangement of his entire line with the right on his enemy's base
of operations.

"In war you see your own troubles; those of the enemy you cannot
see. You must show confidence," wrote the French emperor about
this time to Eugène. How true it was of his own course! On the
morning of the twenty-first he declared that the enemy was in full retreat. This was over-confidence on his part, and not true; but it might
as well have been. As a result of the preceding day's skirmishing and
countermarching the Austrian army was almost cut in two; one division, the right, under Charles, was pressing on to Ratisbon, while the
other, under Hiller, was marching aimlessly behind in a general northwesterly direction, and the whole straggling line was not less than
twenty miles in length. Lannes, the sturdiest, most rough-and-ready
of all the marshals, had arrived from Spain the night before. His
presence increased the army's confidence that they would win, and
next day he commanded a division formed from the corps of Morand,
Gudin, and Nansouty. Davout received orders to hold the enemy in
front; Masséna was to spread out along their rear from Moosburg

down the Isar, ready to harass either flank or rear with half his strength, and to send the rest, under Oudinot, to Abensberg.

On the morning of the twentieth the Emperor himself, with Lannes and Wrede, set out to sever the enemy's line. They had little difficulty. The thin column dispersed before them to the north and south. Hiller was driven back to Landshut, whence he fled to Neumarkt, leaving the Isar in possession of the French. Davout advanced simultaneously against the Archduke's army, which, although very much stronger than Hiller's division, nevertheless retired and occupied Eckmühl, standing drawn up on the highroad toward Ratisbon. At Landshut the Emperor became aware that the mass of the Austrian army was not before him, but before Davout. Leaving Bessières and two divisions of infantry, with a body of cavalry, to continue the pursuit of Hiller, he turned back toward Eckmühl at three in the morning of the twenty-second. Here, again, a great resolve was taken in the very nick of time and in the presence of the enemy. With the same iron will and burning genius, the same endurance and pertinacity, as of old, he pressed on at the head of his soldiers. It was one o'clock when the eighteen-mile march was accomplished and the enemy's outposts before Eckmühl were reached.

Meantime one of the Austrian divisions left in Bohemia had arrived at Ratisbon. Charles, strengthened by this reinforcement, had determined to take the offensive, and at noon his advance began. Vandamme seemed destined to bear the force of the onset, but in the moment before the shock would have occurred, appeared Napoleon's van. Advancing rapidly with Lannes, the Emperor rode to the top of a slight rise, and, scanning the coming Austrians, suddenly ordered Vandamme to seize Eckmühl, and then despatched Lannes to cross the Laber and circumvent the enemy. Davout, having learned the direction of the Austrian charge, threw himself against the hostile columns on their right, and after a stubborn resistance began to push back the dogged foe. In less than two hours the French right, left, and center were all advancing, and the enemy were steadily retreating, but fighting fiercely as they withdrew. This continued until seven in the evening, when Lannes finally accomplished his task.

This destroyed all resistance. The Emperor weakly yielded to his generals' remonstrance that the troops were exhausted, and did not order a pursuit. Charles withdrew into Ratisbon. During the night and

MARBOT AND LABÉDOYÈRE SCALING THE WALL AT RATISBON

FROM THE AQUARELLE BY LUC OLIVIER MERSON

early morning he threw a pontoon bridge across the stream, which was already spanned by a stone one, and next day, after a skirmish in which his outposts were driven into the town, he crossed the Danube; three days later he effected a junction with his second division, left in the Bohemian Forest, and stood at Cham with an effective fighting force of eighty thousand men. The result proved that Napoleon's judgment had been unerring; had he pursued, in spite of all remonstrance and in disregard of the fatigue of his men, he would have had no mighty foe to fight a few weeks later at Wagram. Some time thereafter he told an Austrian general that he had deliberated long, and had refrained from following Charles into Bohemia for fear the Northern powers would rise and come to the assistance of Austria. "Had I pursued immediately," he said at St. Helena, "as the Prussians did after Waterloo, the hostile army crowded on to the Danube would have been in the last extremity."

"Labor is my element," he remarked on the same dreary isle almost amid the pangs of dissolution. "I have found the limit of my strength in eye and limb; I have never found the limit of my capacity for work." This was certainly true of this five days' fight. "His Majesty is well," wrote Berthier on the twenty-fourth, "and endures according to his general habit the exertion of mind and body." Once more his enemy was not annihilated, but this contentment and high spirits seem natural to common minds, which recall that in a week he had evolved order from chaos, and had stricken a powerful, united foe, cutting his line in two, and sending one portion to the right-about in utter confusion. To the end of his life Napoleon regarded the strategic operations culminating at Eckmühl as his masterpiece in that particular line. Jomini, his able critic, remained always of the same opinion. French history knows this conflict as the Battle of Five Days; Thann, Abensberg, Landshut, Eckmühl, and Ratisbon being the places in or near which on each day a skirmish or combat occurred to mark the successive stages of French victory.

The results were of the most important kind. In the first place, Austria's pride and confidence were gone. She had lost fifty thousand men, and her warfare was no longer offensive, but defensive. Charles called for peace, but the Emperor would not listen. The Archduke John, moreover, was compelled to abandon the Tyrol, and when he found himself again in Italy, he was no longer confronted by Eugène alone, that excellent youth but feeble general, whom he had so easily defeated: Macdonald was associated with the viceroy in the command. In Poland, also, Ferdinand's easy successes had carried him too far in pursuit of Poniatowski, and he began to retreat. Lefebvre with the Bavarians was stationed at Salzburg to prevent an irruption of the Tyrolean mountaineers toward the north; all the rest of the Emperor's army was immediately ordered to march on the Austrian capital.

The advance was scarcely contested. Hiller, commanding Charles's left wing, had paused in his retreat, and crossing the Inn with his thirty thousand men, had successfully attacked Wrede at Erding. He had probably heard that Charles was marching to Passau, but the news was false. Learning the truth, he turned again and recrossed the Inn; thence he continued to withdraw, stopping an instant at the Traun to avail himself of a strong position and hold the line if Charles were perchance coming thither to join him. At Ebelsberg, on May third, he made a splendid and momentarily successful resistance, but was overwhelmed by superior numbers. Hearing of his leader's slow advance, and being himself in despair, on the seventh he led his army at Mautern across to the left bank of the Danube in order to effect a junction with the disheartened Archduke, and then destroyed the bridge behind him. The forces of Charles and Hiller met and halted on the slopes of the great hill known as the Bisamberg, which overlooks Vienna from the north shore, and commands the fertile plains through which the great river rolls past the Austrian capital.

Day after day, with unimportant interruptions but no real check, the French ranks marched down the right bank of the stream. On May tenth they appeared before Vienna. Then, as now, it had no efficient fortifications, and its garrison consisted of a citizen militia, strengthened by a small detachment which Hiller had sent forward to reinforce and encourage them. The defenders were commanded by the Archduke Maximilian. There was a brave show of resistance; all the suburbs were evacuated, and the populace gathered behind the old brick walls which had been erected two centuries before against the Turks. At first Napoleon thought there would be a second instance of such embittered and desperate resistance as he had encountered at Madrid. But a feint of the French to cut off the communication of the town with the river, together with a few cannon-balls, quickly brought the unhappy capital to terms; Maximilian marched out at

DOMINIQUE-JOSEPH-RENÉ VANDAMME
COUNT OF UNEBOURG

midnight on the eleventh, and on the twelfth Napoleon returned to the neighboring palace of Schönbrunn, where he had already established his headquarters. The news which arrived from day to day was most encouraging. Poniatowski was again in possession of Warsaw, which the Archduke Ferdinand had evacuated in order to rejoin his brother Charles. The Archduke John, flying before Macdonald, had passed the Carinthian mountains into Hungary, where the liberal movement threatened Austrian rule. The Bavarians, after desperate fighting under Lefebvre, had driven the Tyrolese rebels from Innsbruck. It seemed a proper time to complete, if possible, the demoralization of the whole Austrian empire before crossing the Danube to annihilate its military force. Francis had sown the wind in his declaration of war: he must reap the whirlwind.

From the beginning Napoleon had made the most of his enemy's being the aggressor. There were no terms too harsh for the "Moniteur" to apply when speaking of the hostile court and the resisting populations. The Emperor's proclamations reveled in abuse of the Tyrolese and of Schill. The latter was a Prussian partizan who, having distinguished himself after Jena, was now striving to use the Austrian war in order to arouse the North Germans. He had already gathered a few desperate patriots, and in open hostility was defying constituted authority with the intention of calling his country to arms. The news of Eckmühl had destroyed his chances of success, and he was soon to end his gallant but ill-starred career in a final stand at Stralsund, whither he had retreated. He was stigmatized by Napoleon as a "sort of robber, who had covered himself with crimes in the last Prussian campaign." In repeated public utterances the Emperor of Austria was characterized as cowardly, thankless, and perjured, while the Viennese were addressed as "good people, abandoned and widowed." The last acts of their flying rulers had been murder and arson; "like Medea, they had with their own hands strangled their own children."

This policy of wooing the people while abusing their rulers had been successfully undertaken in Italy, and continued with varying results from that day. No more effective revolutionary engine could have been devised for Europe in Napoleon's age. The specious statements of the Emperor were based on truth, and while the idea they expressed was distorted and reiterated until its exaggeration became falsehood, yet France and the Napoleonic soldiers appeared to fight and suffer enthusiastically for what they still considered a great cause. Even the dull boors, whose intelligence had been nearly quenched by centuries of oppression, felt stirrings of manhood as they listened to the Emperor's fiery words; the middle classes, though not deceived, had no power to refute such language from such a man; and among the few truly enlightened men of each nation who were aware of their country's abasement under dynastic absolutism, a tremendous impression was often created, at least temporarily.

This fact had already been well illustrated in Poland. Austria had another appanage whose people cared little for the prestige of their foreign kings and much for their own liberties. The Hungarians were a conservative, capable race; many of them were ardent Protestants, well educated and well informed, successfully combining in their institutions the best elements of both civic and patriarchal life. To them Napoleon issued a proclamation on May fifteenth which was a masterpiece of its kind. It set forth that the Emperor Leopold II. in his short reign had acknowledged their rights and confirmed their liberties; that Francis I. had sworn to maintain their laws and constitution, but had never convoked their estates except to demand money for his wars; that in view of such treatment, Hungary should now rise and secure national independence. The proclamation produced some effect, but as a whole the Hungarians stood fast in their allegiance.

Four years earlier Napoleon's proclamation declaring that the Bourbons of Naples had ceased to reign was launched from Schönbrunn. Now another, to which reference has already been made, equally famous, was dictated within its walls, though dated, May seventeenth, from the "Imperial Camp at Vienna." It was a document even abler than that addressed to the Hungarians. Citing the abuses which had from immemorial times resulted from the confusion of temporal with spiritual power in the papacy, it revoked the donation of Charles the Great to Hadrian I. (made a thousand years before!), declared that Pius VII. had ceased to reign, and that, as an indemnity for the loss of his secular power, he was to receive an annual increase of income amounting to two million francs. In time of peace this decree would have produced throughout Europe a tremendous stir; but in the interval between the two acts of a great campaign, men were much more occupied with speculations about the decision of arms than with a change which was, after all, only another phase of a protracted, tiresome struggle in

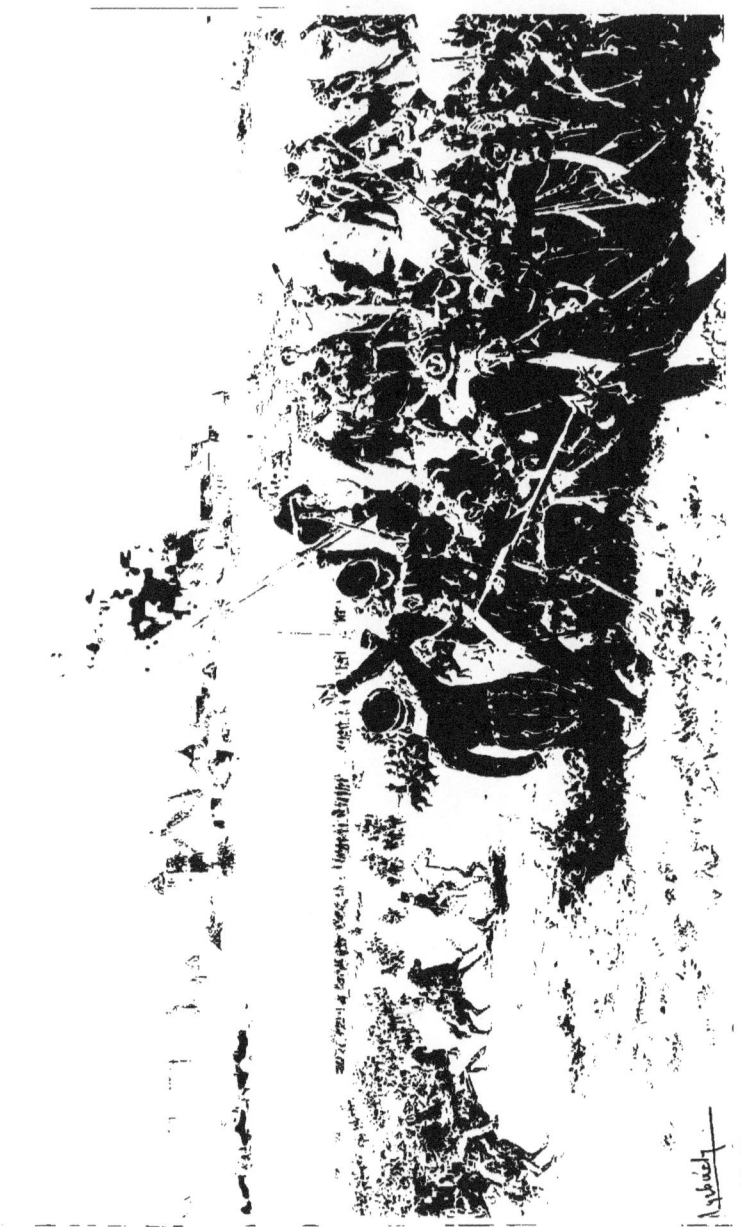

REAPPEARANCE OF NAPOLEON ON THE FIELD BEFORE RATISBON.

which the papacy had long since fallen from its pinnacle. It was, however, an element of terrific demoralization in the house of Austria, which thus saw the consolidation of Italy under the Napoleon family complete, and their last hope to regain their European influence by enlargement in that peninsula extinguished.

Such was the scenic diversion provided for the great world in the pause of a few days after the occupation of Vienna. These moments were likewise occupied by the greatest military activity. Morning, noon, and night secretaries wrote and messengers ran; the roads of central Europe resounded beneath the feet of tramping infantry and the hoofs of horses which were dragging provision-trains and artillery carriages, or bearing despatches to distant points.

The Archduke Charles was a fine strategic theorist, in his age second only to Napoleon. After the fatal division of his army before Landshut, he had wonderfully retrieved his strength in seizing Ratisbon, crossing the Danube, and standing at Cham eighty thousand strong, as he did after his reinforcement by the division which he called in from the Bohemian Forest. But again he became the victim of indecision. Calling for peace negotiations, he loitered long at Budweis, failed to join Hiller so as to throw their united force across the French advance to Vienna, and when at last he brought up on the slopes of the Bisamberg he seemed for an instant aimless. Thus can the hope of peace paralyze a great general's activity. But when, having offered to open negotiations with his adversary, he received no answer, when he learned that the Austrian ministry also was determined to fight the struggle out, he was himself again. His plan was the greatest perhaps ever devised by him: so great, indeed, that four years later Napoleon made it his own at Dresden. It was to free Vienna by threatening the French communications.

The idea was old enough; the novelty lay in the details. Kollowrath was to detach twenty-five thousand men from his own force, and to seize Linz with its bridge; the Archduke John was to join the Army of the Tyrol, which had retreated to the head waters of the Enns, and then march with fifty thousand men to the same point. But Masséna was already master of the Enns valley, and Bernadotte was sent to assist Vandamme at Linz. The Emperor had already divined the plan, and thwarted it by the rapidity with which his orders were transmitted and distant divisions summoned. The communications were threatened, but not broken, and Napoleon gave his whole attention to the problem of crossing a great river in the face of an enemy. He had done it before, but never under circumstances so peculiar as these which confronted him in the size of the Danube and the strength of his foe.

The mighty stream follows for the most part a single channel until it enters the plains which face Vienna on the north, where, at intervals, it divides into several arms, inclosing numerous islands. These branches are nearly all substantial streams; many of them are navigable. It was determined to choose two such points, one above and the other below the town, to build bridges at both, and to select whichever one should prove more feasible when the task was done. The enterprise above the town failed entirely through the vigilance of the Austrians. Masséna had better success at the other end, and succeeded in gathering sufficient material without great difficulty; his bridges between the two shores by the island of Lobau were ready on May twentieth. In this interval Charles advanced, and occupied a line farther forward in the great plain, stretching from hamlet to hamlet — from Korneuburg, Enzersfeld, Gross-Ebersdorf, to Strebersdorf. Eugène and Macdonald had reached Villach, whence they could march direct to Vienna; the Archduke John was at Völkermarkt, on his way down the Drave toward Hungary. Two days before, eight hundred French soldiers had crossed into the island of Lobau to drive out the Austrian scouts; on the nineteenth Napoleon arrived, and the necessary fortifications were constructed; on the twentieth the passage began, and Masséna, with Lannes's light cavalry, was sent out to reconnoiter.

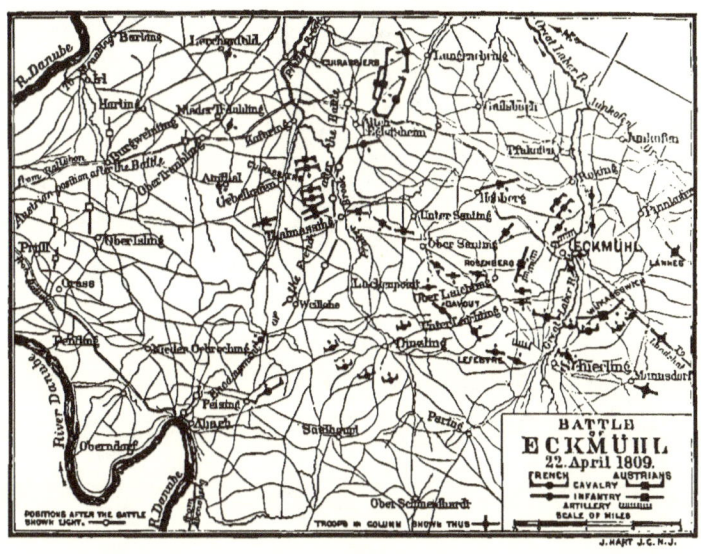

BATTLE OF ECKMÜHL 22. April 1809.
FRENCH · AUSTRIANS
CAVALRY
INFANTRY
ARTILLERY
SCALE OF MILES
POSITIONS AFTER THE BATTLE SHOWN LIGHT.
TROOPS IN COLUMN SHOWN THUS

J. HART J.C. N.J.

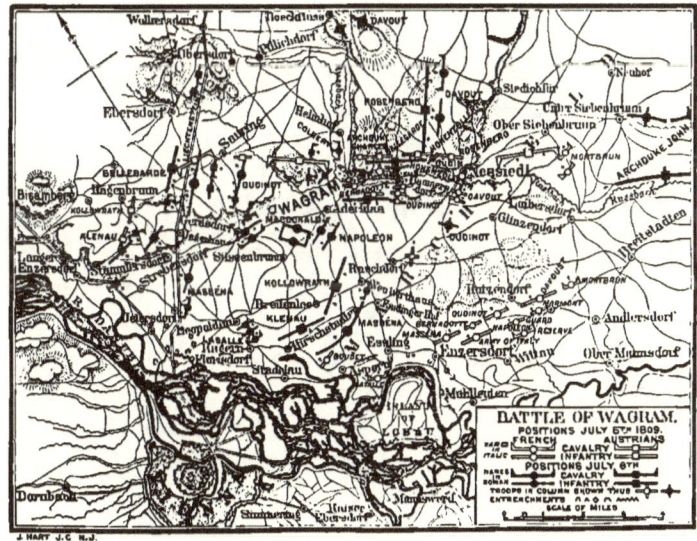

BATTLE OF WAGRAM.
POSITIONS JULY 5TH 1809.
FRENCH · AUSTRIANS
CAVALRY
INFANTRY
POSITIONS JULY 6TH
CAVALRY
INFANTRY
TROOPS IN COLUMN SHOWN THUS
ENTRENCHMENTS
SCALE OF MILES

J. HART J.C. N.J.

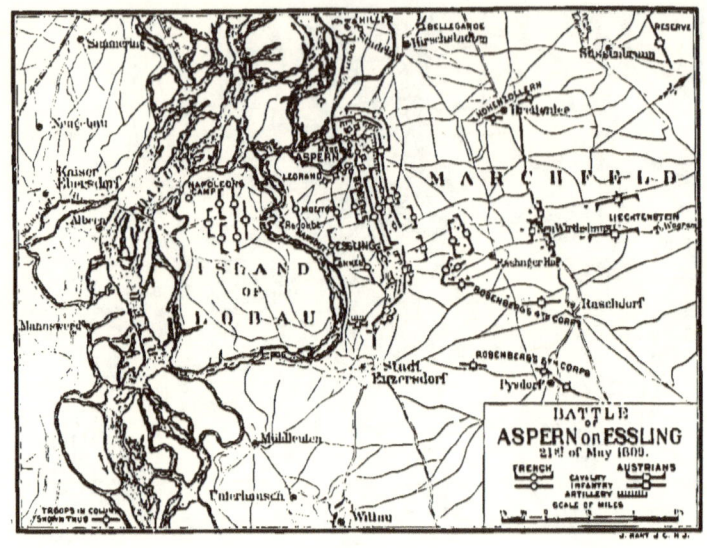

BATTLE
of
ASPERN or ESSLING
21st of May 1809.

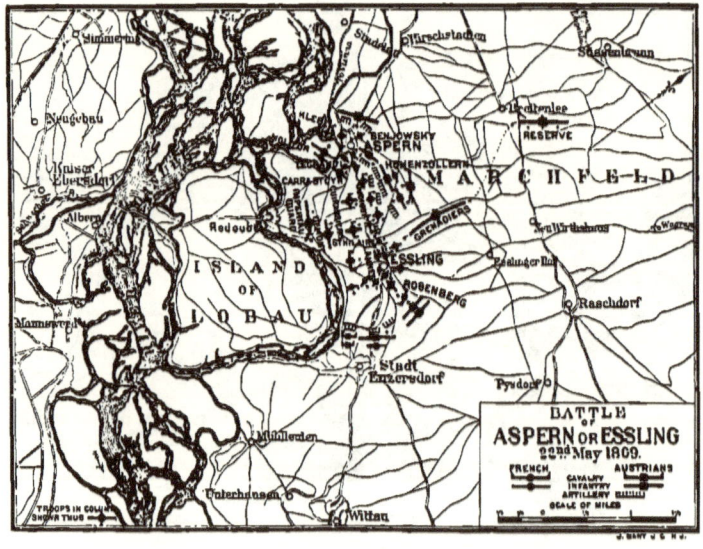

BATTLE
of
ASPERN or ESSLING
22nd May 1809.

CHAPTER XVII

ASPERN, ESSLING, AND WAGRAM

THE MARCHFELD—TACTICS OF THE TWO ARMIES—THE BATTLE IN ASPERN AND ESSLING—THE INDECISIVE RESULT—NAPOLEON'S RETREAT—CHARACTER OF THE BATTLE—DISCONTENT IN THE FRENCH ARMY—THE SPIRIT OF AUSTRIA—PREPARATIONS TO RENEW THE CONFLICT—THE FRENCH ARMY ON THE LOBAU—NAPOLEON'S NEW TACTICS—THE FIRST DAY OF WAGRAM—NAPOLEON'S USE OF ARTILLERY—THE SECOND DAY OF WAGRAM—THE VICTORY DEARLY BOUGHT—A FRENCH PANIC—NAPOLEON'S DILEMMA.

CHARLES, having apparently determined to let his enemy cross unmolested, and to fight the decisive battle on his own ground, had advanced meantime to still another line of hamlets—Strebersdorf, Gerasdorf, Deutsch-Wagram. On the morning of the twenty-first Napoleon's army was partly across the main stream, some of his troops being yet on the Lobau, some entirely over on the left bank, but a large portion still on the right bank. His cavalry was again sent to clear the Marchfeld of the Austrian light horse, who were coursing from one vantage-point to another; and he himself, in order to survey the country, advanced to the first slight rise beyond the low meadows which border the river. Near where he stood was the comfortable hamlet of Aspern, composed like the others round about of one-story stone houses and high stone barns, some of which are of great size, with walls many feet thick. The farmsteads and churchyards are inclosed with ordinary masonry walls. At a short distance to the eastward lay Essling, which, like Aspern, had a few hundred inhabitants, and farther still, but easily visible, the somewhat larger village of Enzersdorf. The plain, though not rolling, is yet not perfectly flat, and small watercourses traverse it at frequent intervals, their direction marked by the trees growing on their banks. The most important of these, the Russbach, was some miles north of where he stood. Turning to Masséna, after scanning the ground, he said: "I shall refuse on the left, and advancing on the right, turn in the Austrian front to the left." That is, he would leave his own left on the river, turn the Austrian left, and rolling up their line, inclose them with their rear to the Danube. His success would be their annihilation, for they had no means of crossing in retreat.

To men of less daring this would have seemed a mad plan. A careful general would, without hesitation, have seized and strongly garrisoned Aspern, Essling, and Enzersdorf, in order that his own line of retreat might be secure, and sufficient room be assured in which to deploy. Pelet, in his memoirs, declares that the Emperor's orders were "to cross the river and march against the enemy." Be this as it may, there were as yet only three infantry divisions on the left bank of the Danube, and Aspern was but weakly garrisoned. Charles was determined to maintain if possible his superiority of numbers. The river was somewhat swollen and he sent floats laden with stones down the main channel to crash through Napoleon's bridges. The attempt met with only slight success, though it weakened the most important bridge. Meantime the Austrians were advancing in five columns, one by Breitenlee against Aspern, one by Aderklaa against Essling, one direct on Enzersdorf to their left; the two others were cavalry, and bore in the general direction of Breitenlee toward Aspern. They appeared in full sight about one o'clock, the column destined to attack Napoleon being nearest. Napoleon's over-confidence disappeared at once, and while the Austrians deployed for the attack, and occupied Aspern, he sent in Molitor's division to seize and hold that hamlet, Masséna being in command. The divisions of Legrand and Boudet were in the rear, on the right and left respectively. Bessières, with the cavalry of Lasalle and Espagne, stood between Aspern and Essling; the division of Carra Saint-Cyr arrived later and was held in reserve. Lannes and Boudet, with a small force, were ordered to hold Essling. Enzersdorf was abandoned, and quickly occupied by the Austrian left.

The fighting at Aspern was awful. The French pushed in, were driven out, then turned and seized the place again. Once more, and still once more, the same alternation of success and defeat was repeated, the thickest of the fight being at the churchyard in the western end of the

NAPOLEON BONAPARTE IN 1800

village. At Essling the fore-post about which the battle raged was a great barn with mighty walls and vaulted cellars. Meanwhile the Emperor was calling in his troops as fast as possible from behind, but at three in the afternoon his main bridge over the chief arm of the Danube gave way before masses of rubbish brought down from the hill-country by a freshet, which was hourly increasing in volume. The Austrians were from first to last superior in numbers on the battle-field; their enfilading batteries were able to sweep the French lines for several hours, and the carnage was dreadful. At last Bessières succeeded in dislodging them from Essling, and by great exertion that place was held until dusk, when the Austrians drew off to bivouac. But at Aspern the numbers engaged were greater, Legrand being sent in toward nightfall. The Archduke intended to take and hold the village if possible, and the fighting continued there until midnight. Weakened and inferior in numbers though the French were, they understood better than their foes the defense of such a place, and when firing ceased they still held half of the long main street.

By midnight the French bridge was again repaired, and Davout, in response to Napoleon's urgent orders, began to bring up reinforcements, especially artillery, holding them on the south shore of the main stream in readiness for crossing. At two in the morning the Austrians made still another effort to drive out the enemy from Aspern; soon afterward they again attacked Essling. Masséna called in Carra Saint-Cyr to Aspern; within an hour both attacks had been repulsed, and the latter hamlet was entirely cleared of the enemy. While the desperate struggle again went on, the Emperor once more surveyed the field; and when at seven in the morning Davout sent word that a portion of the reinforcements was already on the Lobau, Napoleon determined to break through the enemy's center, and for that purpose threw forward the troops already on the ground. But once more the weakened and patched structure over the Danube gave way, and the arrival of reinforcements was stopped; the available French force was immediately drawn back, and stationed to hold the line from Aspern to Essling. The enemy was encouraged and pressed on to the attack with renewed vigor; in the former village the scenes of the previous day were repeated, first one and then the other contestant holding it for a time. In the center, where the Austrians almost broke through the line, Napoleon quickly brought together his recently arrived artillery and Bessières's cavalry:

after terrific struggles they succeeded in holding the Austrians in check. On the right Essling, after being captured and recaptured several times by each side, was taken and long held by the enemy's left; it was then retaken at about three in the afternoon, by a portion of the French reserve, Napoleon's "young guard." Thereupon, from the sheer exhaustion of both sides, the conflict ceased, nothing being heard but desultory discharges of artillery. The French were in possession of both Aspern and Essling. At seven the Emperor called a council of war; the generals advised recrossing the Danube and a retreat into Vienna. "You must mean to Strasburg," said their chief; "for if Charles should follow, he might drive me thither, and if he should march to cut me off at Linz, I must march thither, too, to meet him. In either case, I must abandon the capital, my only source of supplies." There was no reply, and it was determined to withdraw into the Lobau, and hold it until a stronger bridge could be constructed and Davout bring over his entire force. After two days of terrific defensive fighting,—so terrific that the Austrians were several times on the point of retreat,— Napoleon was obliged to abandon the field.

The night of May twenty-second was the beginning of such bitterness for the French emperor as he had not yet tasted. His enemy's forces numbered about seventy thousand, his own perhaps forty-five thousand; but this was entirely his own fault, due largely to overweening confidence in himself and a weak contempt for foes who, after a long and severe novitiate, now fought like veteran Frenchmen, and were led by one who had learned the lessons of Napoleon's own strategy. Five times Essling had been lost and won; how often Aspern had been captured and retaken could only be estimated. Both hamlets were now abandoned by the French. The last Austrian charge against the center had been made and repelled with fiery valor, but in it Lannes was mortally wounded. The grand total, therefore, of the two days was a loss of gallant troops by the thousand, and of this marshal, Napoleon's greatest division general, the friend of his youth, and the only surviving one that was both fearless and honest. Worse even than this, the "unconquerable," though not conquered, had been checked, and that, too, not in a corner, as in Spain or at Eylau, but in the sight of all Europe, on a field chosen by himself.

As the war-sick Emperor passed the litter on which lay his old comrade, he threw himself on the living but maimed and half-conscious

form in an agony of tenderness; and that night, as he sat at table
before an untasted meal, briny tears rolled over cheeks which did
not often know the sensation. But the bulletin which he dictated
ran, "The enemy withdrew to their position, and we remained masters
of the field." This latter clause was exactly as true of the French at
Aspern as it had been of the Russians at Eylau—the affair was a technical victory, a moral defeat. The Austrians celebrated the battle as
their victory, the honors of which they accorded to the last cavalry
charge under Prince John Liechtenstein; and in the peaceful churchyard at Aspern lies the effigy of a majestic lion stricken to the heart,
as a reminder to patriotic Austrians of those two days' victorious
fighting, which literally drenched the spot with blood. "We could not
use the victory," wrote Charles's chief of staff on the twenty-fourth;
"for the enemy's strong position made pursuit impossible." This he
well knew, because the night before the Austrians had tried with signal
failure to dislodge the French army from the Lobau.

The respective feelings of the two forces are mirrored in two facts.
On the twenty-third Napoleon again visited Lannes, who was now fully
conscious and aware that he was doomed. He was as fearless as ever,
and with the stern candor of an old republican poured out to the Emperor all that he felt. The army, he said, was weary of bloodshed, the
nation of its sense of exhaustion; for both were alike aware that they
suffered and bled no longer for a principle, but for the boundless ambition of one man. The veteran marshal refused all sympathy or consolation, and turned his face to the wall. Both Marbot and Pelet
declare that this story of Cadet de Gassicourt is an invention; if so,
it is a clever one, for we know from other sources that the language
ascribed to Lannes expressed the sentiments of the soldiery. As there
was little chance for booty in such rapid marching and constant fighting, the youth and the poor were disheartened. The great fortunes
won by the officers were of little use while peace was denied for their
enjoyment; the millions of Masséna did not save him from the ex-
posures and hardships of the battle-field, and he confessed that he
loved luxury and immoral self-indulgence. Such voices had created an
undercurrent of discontent.

The feeling of Charles and his soldiers was not greatly different.
There was nothing possible as the result of their victory but to take up
a more comfortable position on the same Marchfeld which had wit-

nessed their losses. Before them were the bodies of ten thousand dead and four times that number had been wounded; losses which were about equally divided between their brethren and their foes. The Archduke urged that now was the time for diplomacy. The battle of Aspern had softened Napoleon, he said, and Austria might secure an advantageous peace. But Francis had not changed his nature; he would await the final decision. His brother Ferdinand would soon arrive from Poland, and John was already in Hungary. To Frederick William III. he had offered Warsaw if Prussia would only come to his assistance. But the King of Prussia was stubborn. Fearing lest Austria should secure German leadership, and expecting in the end to gain more from Russia, he refused, in spite of the earnest advice of all his ministers, to assist his rival. It was only when he was assured that Alexander intended to remain neutral that he consented to a secret armament, but then it was too late. The insurrection in Westphalia, to assist which, Schill, in disobedience of orders, had led his battalion of hussars from Berlin, was easily suppressed. This fact, with Napoleon's signal success in Bavaria, seemed to justify Frederick William, and the failure of Francis to secure any advantage after Aspern confirmed the opinion. Such, however, was the temper of the Prussian people that, under moral compulsion, their King finally proposed formal terms of alliance. Austria's real spirit appeared in her vague answer. She first asked England for more assistance, but failing to secure it, turned ungraciously and with indefinite proposals to Prussia. Her envoy of course found no response. Thus it was that Charles and Napoleon lay for weeks watching each other like gladiators, each ready to take advantage of any false step made by the other, and both steadily gathering strength to renew the struggle in the same arena.

Napoleon seemed to make his preparations with a determination to risk all in the next encounter. His line of communication with the west was abandoned altogether; the Tyrol, too, was virtually evacuated, and Lefebvre, with the Bavarians, relieved Vandamme and Bernadotte at Linz, so that both the latter might at once advance within striking distance. Eugène had reached Bruck in Styria, and was therefore at hand; Marmont with ten thousand men was called from Illyria. Being thus safe toward the south, the Emperor sent two divisions to watch the Austrians at Presburg. Before June tenth he had compacted in and about Vienna an army of two hundred and forty thou-

NAPOLEON AND MARSHAL LANNES AT ESSLING

FROM THE PAINTING BY L. LELOIR

ENGRAVED BY W. B. CLOSSON

sand men. On the thirteenth the Archduke John, having turned and advanced toward Raab, was attacked, defeated, and driven back into Hungary by Eugène, who had learned, if not generalship, at least obedience, and having carefully obeyed his stepfather's injunctions, had thus won an important victory.

Meantime all was activity on the Lobau. A new and solid bridge was built across the main stream. To forestall another such accident as had occurred before, this structure was not only protected by piles, but guarded by rowboats which were armed with field-pieces and manned by artillerymen. The enemy had withdrawn behind the Russbach in a line from Deutsch-Wagram to Markgrafneusiedl, leaving only a corps to fortify the old line from Aspern to Essling. In consequence the Emperor entirely changed his plan. The island of Lobau was first strongly fortified, and then, not one, but numerous bridges were constructed to the mainland on the left bank under cover of the guns. Lower down similar measures were taken. In this way the French troops could effect their passage very rapidly and much farther eastward than before, avoid the Aspern-Essling line, and reaching Enzersdorf under protection of their own forts, turn the enemy's left almost in the act of crossing, and so roll up the left wing of his line, which was strongly posted on high ground behind the Russbach, from Markgrafneusiedl through Parbasdorf toward Wagram, where it was connected with the center. These arrangements were all completed by July first, on which date the Emperor left Schönbrunn for the Lobau. During the fighting at Aspern he had observed the field from the swinging rungs of a rope-ladder fastened to one of the tall trees on the island. This time he brought with him a long step-ladder, one of those used in the palace gardens to trim high shrubs. The Archduke John was now in Presburg; the Archduke Charles had raised his numbers to a hundred and thirty thousand men. On and near the Lobau were a hundred and eighty thousand French soldiers; twenty-two thousand more were behind.

It was the fifth before all the preliminary moves were successfully taken. The passage had been safely accomplished during the previous night exactly as had been planned, a feint against Aspern having thrown the Austrians on a false scent. In the morning, therefore, the two lines were arrayed opposite, but somewhat obliquely, to each other, the French right overlapping the Austrian left beyond Enzersdorf as far as Wittau, so as either to prevent the approach of Archduke John or to outflank the Austrian left according to circumstances. The French center was thus in front of the Austrian left, and Masséna, with the French left resting on the Danube, was to attack the Austrian center at the village of Gerasdorf, while Bernadotte and Eugène were to throw themselves on Charles's left, which stretched behind the Russbach from Wagram to Markgrafneusiedl. Napoleon waited for some hours while scouts reconnoitered toward Presburg. Being assured about five that John had not left that city nor given any signs of moving, he prepared his columns, and about seven in the evening ordered the onset.

Masséna made a vigorous effort to hold the enemy's center and right, while Napoleon launched his own center and right against the positions held by his opponent's left. For some hours there was vigorous fighting, but Charles saw the Emperor's manœuver, and swiftly throwing his reserve from behind Gerasdorf into his left, gained time to call up reinforcements from his right at the Bisamberg. Bernadotte moved slowly, and did not render his force effective at the crucial moment. Napoleon was much incensed by his apparent sluggishness. An attack made at seven against Wagram by Oudinot failed. This hamlet was the key of the Austrian position, forming as it did the angle of their line, and the fighting there was desperate. By nine o'clock the French were thrown back all along, and compelled to resume the positions they had held in the morning. At eleven a last attempt was made by Eugène and Bernadotte on Wagram, but like the other it was bloody and useless. At the council-fire that evening the leaders of the French left and center were ordered to move farther to the right, and to concentrate next morning on the positions behind the Russbach. About dawn the change was made, and before sunrise all was ready, the Emperor having passed a sleepless night on his tiger-skin behind the bivouac fire in front of his tent.

But Charles did not wait to be attacked. With new courage and added confidence he ordered his right, under Klenau, to follow down the Danube against the enemy's weakened left, which might thus be turned, while with the break of day his center advanced against Masséna. For a time the Austrians carried all before them, and Masséna retreated step by step until it appeared as if the tables would be turned and Napoleon overwhelmed by his own tactics. Both Aspern and Essling were taken, and then, turning north, the united Austrian center and right entirely surrounded the French left and attacked it on the flank. They thought themselves victorious, when unexpectedly the heavy artillery on the Lobau opened fire upon them, and they began to waver. At this crisis the great artillerist brought into action the strong batteries of his own arm which he had so carefully prepared. Lauriston was chosen to carry out the decisive movement, and his splendid conduct not merely secured the victory, but made it overwhelming. According to the most conservative estimate, there were under his command one hundred field-pieces,—sixty from the Guard, —and these were supported by cavalry and cuirassiers; some estimate the number of guns at four hundred, but this is manifestly a wild exaggeration. As the artillery rolled up and unlimbered, volleys of shot, shell, and shrapnel began to follow in swift succession, and in a short time the enemy's pursuit was not only stayed, but with the approach of Macdonald's infantry to form a new flank it was turned into retreat. The Austrians made one gallant stand, but were finally forced back to the foot of the Bisamberg.

Meantime Davout had attacked the left. While he fought he was steadily reinforced, until at one time, about midday, over a third of the army was concentrated under his command. The Austrians opposed to them could not, even with their vantage of high ground, withstand the ever stronger pressure, and slowly rolled back northward in a curve. Eugène captured Wagram, and then turned in that direction to unite with Macdonald, whose division had joined that of Wrede, and had been steadily pushing back the enemy's line toward the same point. They were supported by Davout and Oudinot. The Austrians on the right were then once more dislodged and compelled to withdraw on the highway to Brünn. It was about two in the afternoon. Davout had been ordered to wait for a signal to make the decisive advance. It was given, and as Oudinot rushed up the heights at Parbasdorf, his comrade appeared from Markgrafneusiedl, driving the enemy before him. A breach in the opposing line was made at once, and the whole Austrian wing, being thus disorganized, hurried back to reform if possible beyond Wagram, cross the Russbach, and join the main army. They were successful. The French right halted just beyond the village which gave its name to the battle. Lasalle, a brilliant light-horse general, was killed in the last charge, and both armies bivouacked for the night. Next morning Charles withdrew toward Znaim, Masséna.

Davout, and Marmont following with the van of Napoleon's army. Several skirmishes took place between portions of the Austrian rear and various corps of the French van, in which the latter were decidedly checked. Marmont was obliged to assume the defensive under the walls of Znaim. The Austrian losses at the battle of Wagram were computed at twenty-four thousand, including seven hundred and fifty-three officers. Those of the French were certainly not less, if we include seven thousand who were taken prisoners. They lost, moreover, twelve standards and eleven guns.

In the early hours of July sixth, Charles had despatched an adjutant to Presburg with orders to the Archduke John to march at once and attack the enemy's rear. The story at first accepted was that the messenger found the bridges over the river March destroyed, and arrived six hours too late for his errand to be successful. There were, however, many at the time who attributed criminal negligence to John, among them his own brother, the commander-in-chief. For a time, by means of court intrigue and persistent misrepresentation, the blame was put, not on John, but on Charles, but eventually the former was found guilty and banished to Styria. Had the latter's plan succeeded, Napoleon would have had a different task — a task so difficult that the issue of the battle might well have been doubtful, if not disastrous. As it was, the victory was dearly bought, and the Austrians were not demoralized.

On the other hand, in the very hour of victory the French, who had halted to take breath, were thrown into a panic by the appearance of a few Austrian pickets from the Archduke John's army, then coming up, and thousands of the victorious soldiers fled in wild demoralization toward the Danube. John, whose appearance but a short time earlier would have turned his brother's defeat into victory, drew back his thirteen thousand men in good order to guard Hungary. As Napoleon himself had been in a dangerous condition of over-confidence before Aspern, so now his soldiery were clearly in the same plight. Self-conceit had made them unreliable. Bernadotte's corps had displayed something very much like cowardice and mutiny at the last. The army still fought in the main like the perfect machine it was, but the individual men had lost their stern virtue. They believed that victory, plunder, and self-indulgence were the fair compensations of their toils. Ungirt and freed from the restraints of discipline, they gave signs that

MARSHAL JEAN LANNES
DUKE OF MONTEBELLO

the petulance, timidity, and unruliness which had been manifested in Poland and Prussia were not diminished.

Their Emperor, if his vision had been unclouded, would have understood that endurance, suffering, and privation would make such men an untrustworthy dependence in the hour of need. How changed he was himself is clear from the fact that Bonaparte would never have rested until his foe was disorganized and overpowered, while Napoleon saw himself forced to treat with an opponent who, though beaten, was still undaunted and active. If the victor had been fighting for life, his position would have been morally strong; fighting as a world-conqueror, it was illogical; fighting as equal with equal to repel aggression, it was comprehensible. This last was the attitude into which he was forced by the campaign of Aspern, Essling, Wagram. Francis, whose power he had meant to crush, upon whom a few short weeks before he had heaped insult and abuse, had turned out a most dangerous foe. Technically conquered, it would not be well for his opponent to try conclusions with him again in the still uncertain position of the Napoleonic power. Rather reap the field secured, the daunted conqueror reasoned, than risk devastation by grasping for more. This, and no other, is the explanation of that remarkable somersault in Napoleon's diplomacy which followed in the next few weeks.

CHAPTER XVIII

THE PEACE OF SCHÖNBRUNN

SCHILL AND THE DUKE OF BRUNSWICK — ANDREAS HOFER — THE AR-
MISTICE OF ZNAIM — THE NORTHERN POWERS ADHERE TO FRANCE
— WELLESLEY'S SUCCESSES IN THE PENINSULA — THE WALCHEREN
EXPEDITION — NEGOTIATIONS FOR PEACE — AUSTRIA A SECOND-RATE
POWER — ATTEMPT ON NAPOLEON'S LIFE — HIS GREAT UNEASINESS
— THE TYROL SUBDUED — THE POPE A PRISONER.

NAPOLEON'S course was probably somewhat influenced both by the mutterings of national discontent in France and by the actual insurrections which were taking place in Germany. Schill, after leaving Berlin, had been successively harassed by the Dutch, the Westphalians, and the Danes, until in despair he threw himself into Stralsund in hope of coöperation from an English fleet. The city was immediately beleaguered, and on May thirty-first it fell. The King of Prussia had already denounced the gallant adventurer and his companions as a robber band of outlaws. As has been told, the daring patriot was killed in the assault, and only a hundred and fifty of his comrades escaped. The officers who fled into Prussia were court-martialed, and punished by a light sentence of imprisonment. Those captured in Stralsund were taken to Brest and sentenced to penal servitude. Frederick William, the young Duke of Brunswick, deprived by Napoleon of his throne, and determined to avenge his father, had raised, during the progress of the French campaign in Austria, a corps of Bohemian and other adventurers, which was soon famous for its extraordinary exploits, and became world-renowned as the Black Legion. With this force, assisted by that of the Austrian commandant in Franconia, General Kienmayer, he defeated the Saxons at Nossen, a French army under Junot at Berneck, and repelled King Jerome of Westphalia; he then seized Dresden, Leipsic, and Lindenau, holding at the time of Wagram a considerable portion of Franconia. Napoleon's victory rendered his situation desperate, but with fifteen hundred men he cut his way northward through Leipsic, Halle, Halberstadt, and Brunswick, defeating the Westphalian, Saxon, and Dutch troops which sought to intercept him, and reached the shores of the North Sea at Elslfleth, where, seizing a merchant flotilla, he embarked with his men for England. He was received in London with jubilation, and was richly pensioned for his heroic adventures.

Almost simultaneously the Tyrolese, taking advantage of Lefebvre's withdrawal, rose again. The exploits of their hero, Andreas Hofer, form a romantic episode of history, but they very indirectly affected the central story, if at all. In the five weeks intervening between Aspern and Wagram, that able and devoted man had virtually reorganized his country and cleared it of intruders. Even the double invasion of French and Bavarians, on one side from Klagenfurth, on the other down the valley of the Inn, was successfully repelled. The tactics of Hofer's men were most effective against regular troops, who, marching in thin lines through mountain defiles, were cut down by sharp-shooters, overwhelmed with rocks hurled from high ledges over the precipitous walls of ravines, entrapped by ambushes, or slaughtered by the scythes, clubs, and pitchforks of the peasantry.

Leaving Eugène to hold the Marchfeld, Napoleon and his army pressed on after Marmont in pursuit of Charles. Before Znaim, which was reached on the eleventh, the vanguard had just suffered something very like a repulse, and the Emperor made ready for another battle if it should be necessary. In the very midst of the preparations came a proposition from Charles for an armistice. After a long discussion by the French generals, Napoleon accepted it. "You must fight only when the hope of any fortunate turn is gone," he wrote about this time; "for in its nature the result of a battle is always doubtful." The Archduke's motive was to gain time. The Emperor Francis had accepted a plan proposed by John for a reunion of the Austrian armies on the confines of Hungary to continue the war, and he was still hoping to retrieve the blunder he had made in not negotiating on equal terms with Prussia. He therefore acquiesced in Charles's proposal, though not intending the armistice as a preliminary of peace. Napoleon affected uncertainty, and demanded an enormous cession of territory

CHAP. XVIII   as the price of a truce. Francis in turn demurred, but finally yielded.
1809   To this again Charles, confident in his ability to carry on the war, would not listen. His quarrel with Francis and John was growing more bitter; and the Emperor felt that in order to compose the family difficulties and allay jealousies, time must now be gained at any price. Francis therefore persisted, Charles resigned the command, and the former assumed it himself.

The Austrian Emperor's first step was to open negotiations in the hope of prolonging them until he could rearrange the control of his army and recuperate his strength, trusting that in the interval the kaleidoscope of European diplomacy might entirely change. He was not disappointed in the fact of a change, but the change was far different from what he had expected. The King of Prussia now definitely withdrew the propositions which he had half-heartedly made before Wagram. He thought it was better to reign behind the Oder than not to reign at all. The Czar kept the promise made at Erfurt most unwillingly; but having at last secured Finland, he felt bound to fulfil the letter of his engagement. Prince Galitzin had been put at the head of thirty thousand unwilling Russians, and sent to invade Galicia. Crossing the frontier, his officers declared their distaste for the task, and knew they were reflecting the sentiments of an overpowering majority of their own nation. The invasion turned out a farce, and was rather in the nature of a friendly reception by the inhabitants.

Francis therefore hoped for something from Alexander's lukewarmness. The latter, however, would do nothing, for nominally, and in occasional skirmishes really, he was fighting Turkey, and meant, after the peace, to claim the fulfilment of Napoleon's promise. It would be impolitic to jeopardize his whole ambition by any deviation from the letter of the Erfurt agreement. Francis therefore was informed that he must make the best terms with Napoleon that he could. As to Great Britain, the chances seemed better. In the seas that bordered Italy and the Ionian Isles, off the coasts of Spain and Portugal, on the waters of the Baltic, her flag was seen. Wellesley had been landed in the Iberian peninsula, and, driving Soult before him, had not only expelled the French from Portugal, but had defeated Victor at Talavera, and was preparing for the invasion of Spain. The English government had in readiness another army of forty thousand men and another fleet of thirty-five ships of the line. Where best could they employ them?

DEFENCE OF THE GRANARY AT ESSLING.

After long deliberation the selfish policy was adopted of using them, CHAP. XVIII
not to cripple Napoleon, but for England's immediate advantage. They   1-09
were not sent to reinforce Wellesley and insure the conquest of Spain,
nor to save Schill, nor to strengthen Austria. By any one of these
courses the European uprising against the French emperor would have
been inaugurated that very year.

As it was, they were despatched to destroy the dockyards of the
Netherlands, where it was said, and perhaps believed, that Napoleon
was building ships to dispute British supremacy at sea. After dis-
embarking on the island of Walcheren, the army combined with the
fleet in a successful attack on Flushing, which fell on August fifteenth.
This was their only success. Fouché raised an army of national guards,
and Bernadotte, who, having incurred the Emperor's displeasure at
Wagram for his slowness and lack of success, had been sent home in
disgrace, was induced to put himself at its head. The army and navy
officers of the English disagreed as to how they should meet him.
The result was separation and disaster; the fleet sailed back to England
and the army withdrew to Walcheren, where it was held in check while
the swamp-fever devastated its ranks. About the same time a plague
also broke out in the Austrian army, and, as was claimed, destroyed
its efficiency. Wellesley, unsupported, saw himself threatened by a
flank movement of Soult and drew back, while, in August, Sebastiani
defeated a division of the Spanish army.

These were the circumstances which turned the pretended peace
negotiations of Francis into reality. When proceedings first began at
Altenburg they were simply farcical. Napoleon really needed peace, if
Prussia and Russia were meditating war; but the first proposal made
by Austria he scorned, and talked of Francis's abdication, with a partition of Hapsburg lands among the new Napoleonic states. When the
nominal plenipotentiaries, Champagny and Metternich, actually met, the
former still scouted anything like reasonable terms, demanding for his
Emperor the lands occupied by French troops. The Austrian, anxious
to gain time, replied with equally impossible propositions. But as the
summer passed, and Francis's hopes of support grew fainter and fainter,
he sent a personal representative, General Bubna, to Napoleon, and this
plenipotentiary began to display sincerity. Thereupon the Emperor
of the French manifested his earnest desire for peace. So far he had relied on the Czar, who stood by the alliance in the face of his people's

opposition. How much longer, Alexander must have asked himself, could this state of things continue? It was praiseworthy in him that he cared nothing for popular opinion, but he might not be able to hold out against it much longer. It was very significant that in a formal note just received from St. Petersburg by the hand of a Russian officer, Alexander advised peace. To this messenger, when speaking of the chances for renewing hostilities, Napoleon exclaimed in undisguised horror, "Blood, blood, always blood!" And then, with a sudden change of manner, he said: "I am anxious to get back to Paris." Like his generals, the Emperor of the French was plainly sick of war. His sad countenance, like theirs, was an open book in which the Russian could clearly read this important fact. Indeed, the anxious, war-worn, unsettled Napoleon actually contemplated an alliance with Austria. It was clear that if her territories were left intact she would gladly join in one. He had need to be done with her in order to settle his affairs in Spain and elsewhere. But he feared Francis, and hoped that such a vacillating temporizer might abdicate in favor of some thoroughly trustworthy successor. Napoleon confessed to Bubna that he admired the Austrian troops; they were as good as his own, and under his leadership would be victorious. Champagny's demands, he admitted, were not final, but certain territories on the south, on the west, and in Galicia he must have.

With this understanding, full powers were given to Prince Liechtenstein, and he went direct to Schönbrunn. The terms of peace turned out very hard indeed. A war indemnity of a hundred million francs was first incorporated in the treaty itself; but afterward, in a secret article, Francis was required to reduce his army to a hundred and fifty thousand men, and the indemnity was diminished to eighty-five millions. This would have been an awful burden to lay on the empire even as it had been, and Austrian territory was now to be seriously diminished. Salzburg, Berchtesgaden, and the Inn quarter went to the Confederation of the Rhine, New Galicia to the grand duchy of Warsaw, along with a large district in East Galicia and the town of Cracow. A small strip of the same province was reserved for Russia. But the most deadly blow was the constitution of a subsidiary government, to be known as Illyria, by the surrender directly to France of Görz, Monfalcone, Triest, Carniola, Willach in Carinthia, and Croatia east of the Save. This made Austria not only a second-class, but an inland power, cutting her off entirely from the sea; but she was, nevertheless, to enter the Continental system against England, and recognize all that Napoleon had done or might do in Spain, Portugal, and Italy. These were the hard but imperative conditions which the Emperor laid down. Liechtenstein accepted them subject to his sovereign's approval.

But the conqueror was in haste. On October twelfth there had been a great review of his troops at Schönbrunn. In the crowd was a youth, scarcely more than a child, who pressed forward to gain access to Napoleon. His urgency attracted the attention of Berthier, and he was seized by General Rapp. On his person was a large knife, and he openly avowed his purpose of assassination. He was confronted with his intended victim. His name, he said, was Staps, and he was the son of a Protestant pastor at Naumburg. The Emperor coldly asked what he would do if pardoned. "Try again to kill you," was the culprit's reply. He avowed no penitence, but declared he had no personal feeling. He would gladly have reasoned with Napoleon, he further said, if he could but have gained an interview; if unsuccessful in his plan, he would have thought it a deed of honor to smite down the world's oppressor. The would-be assassin was secretly shot, and the police had instructions to say, if there should be much talk, that he was crazy. This event seemed deeply to impress the intended victim with the intensity of feeling among the common people of Germany, and he was anxious to be gone. His fears were well founded; assassination was in the minds of many unbalanced men. A captain in the Austrian army actually sought a furlough, giving as his reason that he desired to kill Napoleon.

This mania for assassination completed the depression of spirits which for some time past had been noticeable in the French emperor. Severely wounded in the great toe at Ratisbon, he had there been compelled to exercise enormous self-control to prevent a panic in the army. Knocked senseless by a fall from his horse on the road to Schönbrunn, he had for the same reason been forced to enjoin silence on nearly two hundred persons who were aware of the fact. At Essling he had thought it necessary to throw himself into the bullet hail to sustain the morale of his troops, and having saved Lannes from drowning during a preliminary reconnaissance of the Danube banks, he had finally lost him under the most distressing circumstances. To cap the climax of these experiences, it now seemed as if his own life were in constant jeopardy. When, therefore, the official articles of the peace were drawn up on the fourteenth, and Liechtenstein departed to lay them before Francis, the French cannon did not wait for formalities, but proclaimed the peace as already made. The next night Napoleon was on his way to Paris.

The armistice of Znaim had utterly crushed the hopes of the Tyrolese, but they continued to fight in despair. The peace of Schönbrunn set free the entire French army to overwhelm them. A second double invasion was organized. Prince Eugène offered amnesty to the insurgents, and the Austrian ministry advised them to cease resistance. But Hofer had by this time convinced himself that his mission was more than earthly. After some hesitation, he refused to accept Austria's advice, and the conflict was renewed. The Tyrolese were now alone, and after a vain resistance the combatants dispersed among the mountains. The land was again reduced to submission. Hofer remained safely hidden for some time, but he was eventually betrayed, captured, and sent to Mantua for the formality of a trial. Napoleon's directions to Eugène were very concise. Whenever the order should reach him, the viceroy was to name a court-martial, try the prisoner, and have him shot. Throughout suffering and imprisonment the hero displayed the greatest firmness, and met his death with lofty devotion. In the previous spring, when at Austria's instigation the Tyrol had risen, he had been ennobled; ten years later the title and estates of Passeyr were bestowed on his family. Among the eastern Alps the name of Andreas Hofer is like that of William Tell among the mountains of Switzerland. His rugged virtues are celebrated in verse, and tradition lingers about his haunts.

Napoleon's decree of May seventeenth, depriving the Pope of his secular power, reached Rome in due time, and Murat proceeded without delay to execute it. There were no difficulties, for it will be remembered that in February General Miollis had occupied the city. A committee of administration was immediately named, whose duties were to prepare the way for incorporation with Italy. On June tenth formal proclamation was made that Pius VII. was no longer a secular prince, his dominion having passed to the King of Italy. He was still to reside in Rome as spiritual head of the Catholic Church. That night the Pope promulgated a bull excommunicating Napoleon and his adherents, favorers, and councilors. Unlike similar instruments of his predeces-

THE BATTLE OF WAGRAM

sors, it contained a clause declaring the punishment to be purely spiritual, and prohibiting every one from using it as a sanction for attack on
the persons of those against whom it was issued. On the night of July
fifth a French general with his guard forced the doors of the Quirinal
palace, and demanded from Pius a formal renunciation of his secular
power. The Pope having firmly and quietly refused, he was informed
that he must make ready to leave the city. At three the next morning he was placed in a carriage with a single cardinal, and on a second
dignified and solemn refusal to comply was carried to Florence. There
he was separated from his one companion and put in charge of the
gendarmes. Traveling by day and night, sometimes in a litter, sometimes by sea, the aged man was finally brought to Grenoble. The devout French of that city could not understand the secrecy and haste
of his journey, and hastened to pay him homage. So great were the
crowds and so intense was the feeling that very soon his presence in
France was considered dangerous. He was therefore carried back to
Savona, where he remained a state prisoner under rigid supervision
in decent but plain apartments until 1812, when he was conducted
to Fontainebleau and lodged like a prince.

CHAPTER XIX

NAPOLEON'S FATAL DECISION

NAPOLEON'S EXPLANATIONS TO ALEXANDER—HIS NEW MANNER—SAD
PLIGHT OF JOSEPHINE—THE DIVORCE ANNOUNCED AND CONFIRMED
BY THE SENATE—NEGOTIATIONS FOR THE CZAR'S SISTER—NAPO-
LEON'S IMPATIENCE—HIS DESIRE FOR A GREAT MATCH.

THE treaty of Schönbrunn was a flagrant violation of the agreement made between Napoleon and Alexander at Erfurt, inasmuch as it materially enlarged the grand duchy of Warsaw and thus
menaced Russia with the reconstruction of Poland. "Clearly," said
Rumianzoff to Caulaincourt, "you want to be rid of the Russian alliance, and to substitute for it that with the grand duchy." Alexander
was very angry, but, though in the strict observance of forms he had
been irreproachable, his conduct in the real support of his ally had not
been sincere. His people were more embittered with the French alliance every day, and Napoleon knew how both the nation and the Czar
would feel when they were informed that provinces occupied by Russian troops had been assigned to Poland. Francis, wroth as he was,
had not dared to disturb the popular joy so loudly expressed over Napoleon's premature announcement of peace. Accordingly, on October
twentieth, 1809, the very day on which the papers were signed and
ratified, an explanation was sent to Alexander by the Emperor of
the French. It pleaded that he could not abandon a friendly people
to Austria's vengeance, but declared that he would guarantee their
good behavior under Saxon rule; as for the names of Poles and
Poland, for all he cared, they might disappear from history. The
Czar accepted the excuse with what grace he could, for the partition of Turkey was not yet accomplished. But the peace of Schönbrunn marked the initiation of a policy which dissolved the peace of

Tilsit. There could now no longer be any serious question of marriage between members of the two courts. Compelled by circumstances to choose between a dual alliance with a first-rate power which must share on equal terms in the dominion of the world, and one with a second-rate power whose armies were surpassed by none, Napoleon had deliberately chosen the latter, as the shortest way to absolute and complete supremacy, to the assertion of a sovereign will over a conquered universe.

Napoleon's return to Paris was celebrated in the manner usual after a victorious campaign. The departments of government issued the most fulsome addresses; subsidiary and vassal kings crowded to offer their congratulations; there were the ordinary manifestations of popular joy, and no one seemed to remember that the Emperor had been smitten by the papal bolt. But men remarked a great change in his bearing and expression. Cambacérès said that he seemed to be walking in the midst of his glory. Moreover, he withdrew from the capital, and held his court in Fontainebleau. The air was all surcharged. The Duc de Broglie tells us in his memoirs that he had seen the Empress early that year, surrounded by the brilliant throng of " ladies in waiting, ladies of the court and palace, accompanied by the train of 'readers,' which composed the harem of our sultan, and enabled him for a time to endure the painted old age of the former sultana." The truth which underlies this is notorious, and the scene over the divorce before the Emperor's departure for the campaign just concluded bears witness to the depth to which Josephine had fallen in her desperate attempts to retain both her place and some portion of Napoleon's tenderness.

Napoleon himself had long since announced that he was superior to plain virtues, and the list of his paramours was daily growing longer and better known. But all this self-abasement on the part of Josephine and all the self-indulgence of Napoleon could not do more than postpone the judgment day. "My enemies," the Emperor was accustomed to cry out—"my enemies make appointments at my tomb." He could not rest content with an empire for himself which he knew would break of its own weight on his death unless he left a legitimate heir. On his return from Austria his resolution to divorce the Empress was taken, and Eugène was summoned to convey it to his mother. Josephine, though forewarned, was still unable to realize the fact. She behaved well; her own long career of intrigue, license, and extravagance forbade recriminations, and besides, she was to enjoy the title and state of an empress for life. Still, as women under the Directory loved, she loved her husband, and there had been much tenderness between them, neither taking very seriously the infidelities of the other. To the end, even after the moderate beauty and great physical charm of her middle age were transformed into the faded colors and form of old age (for she was old at forty-five), and when the arts of the toilet could no longer conceal the ravages of time and license, there still continued to exist between the Empress and her second husband a mutual good will and a feeling of comradeship engendered by the memories of adventure, risk, plots, and gains, encountered side by side through a married life of thirteen years. She had little intellect and not much character, but she had much feminine sweetness and many soft, winning ways. Her only weapon, therefore, in the hour of defeat was tears, and those she shed abundantly. When the paroxysms of grief were over, the Emperor made a display of tenderness, and the Empress manifested a gentle and affecting courage.

On December fifteenth, 1809, before the grand council held in the Tuileries, the divorce was pronounced, and the next day it was confirmed by decree of the senate. Josephine withdrew to Malmaison to drag out her remaining years in empty state, for the support of which she had a grant of two million francs a year. To the hour of her death, five years later, she asserted her love for Napoleon, and in general she displayed great anxiety for his welfare and success. Posterity has always felt a certain tenderness for the unfortunate woman who was raised so high and then cast down so suddenly. She was not virtuous, she was not strong, she was not even very beautiful. Her wrong-doing was like the naughtiness of household pets, impulsive but not malicious, deceitful but without rancor, determined but quickly deprecated. For this reason her misfortune has veiled her weakness and softened the harshness of men's judgment.

Almost a month before the formal divorce Caulaincourt had received instructions to address the Czar on the question of marriage between his sister Anne, now sixteen years of age, and the Emperor of the French. The ambassador was to make no formal demand, but was to ask for some expression of general intentions and feelings. Alexander was in the provinces, and did not return until the middle of December. Meantime Caulaincourt, after careful inquiry, had learned that

BUILDING THE BRIDGE AT THE ISLAND OF LOBAU.

the young princess was frail in health and not yet of marriageable age. The letter to his master conveying this information was crossed by one of Napoleon's making a formal demand. The difference in confessional adherence was of no account, he said, and an immediate answer was desired. "Take as your standpoint that children are wanted." This put the Czar in a serious dilemma. An alliance with France was still near his heart. By the treaty of Friedrichshamm, which had been signed on September ninth, 1809, he had secured Finland at last, but of the other splendid projects suggested at Tilsit and confirmed at Erfurt not one was realized. Aside from the chagrin he had felt at the war with Austria, and its menacing results in the enlargement of Poland, there was now an additional cause of anxiety; for in the conflict with Turkey his troops had but recently been driven back across the Danube. If he broke with Napoleon he might even lose Moldavia and Wallachia, and realize nothing further. A few weeks had softened the displeasure he felt after Schönbrunn, and he now began to shower favors on Caulaincourt, expressing the greatest anxiety for the match. The youth of the princess was, however, a serious obstacle, and he must consult his empress-mother. Of course the dowager made every objection to the marriage; she was an ardent sympathizer with the old Russian party, and hated Napoleon. There is little doubt that she was entirely right, moreover, in declaring at last as an insuperable obstacle that her daughter was too young. Alexander then turned his whole attention to cajoling the French ambassador in order to gain time. He had always been more Napoleon's friend than his ally, he said; surely the Emperor would grant a delay for a few months.

But this was exactly what the suitor would not do. His dignity forbade him to abide the empress-dowager's time; the divorce had been pronounced, and state reasons made his marriage imperative. "To adjourn is to refuse," he replied; "and besides, I want no strange priests in my palace between my wife and me." This was apparently a complete somersault, for it meant that either Alexander must yield or the alliance would be jeopardized. No one can divine from the evidence exactly which alternative Napoleon desired; but in view of his general character, of the treaty he had made with Francis, and of subsequent events, it was probably the latter. He could have used the Czar's compliance to found his dynasty, but he seems to have made up his mind that Austria was the better dependence. Besides, he had very serious reasons of state for urgency. He recognized at every step of his career that his power rested in the popular will, not on tradition or theories. Hence, at every moment two purposes were immediate: first, to keep the popular favor; second, to transform his tenure of power by the infusion of a dynastic element.

In the winter of 1809 the people of France were not comfortable. The promised peace with England seemed again postponed; the war in the Spanish peninsula was still raging; the Continental system was steadily undermining public prosperity. There was stagnation in the great French seaports; hand in hand with commerce, both industry and trade were languishing. The great southern towns, deprived of their Spanish market, were nearly bankrupt. In addition the clergy and their adherents were thoroughly roused by the treatment of the Pope. On the other hand, the Emperor's personal popularity was also suffering serious ravages. In the new administrative system the places which led to promotion had now for a long time been given to members of the old nobility; the recipients looked on them as their right, and neither they nor their families were grateful, while the sturdy democracy felt slighted and injured. Even the new nobility grew more unmanageable with every day. In full possession of their estates, titles, and incomes, they felt their independence, and refused to be longer guided by the hand which had led them into their promised land. They had allied themselves with the oldest families in France, and the haughtiness of family pride led them to feel condescension for the great adventurer whose blood so far flowed in no aristocratic veins. It seemed to Napoleon that in order to secure popular good will he must restore prosperity, which was not easy, and to assert a moral ascendancy over his court he must make a suitable match, which was easy enough. Neither must be half done; his prestige required a great stroke, and it was better to make the match first, and thereby ease the tension until England could be brought to terms—with Russia's aid if possible, without it if necessary.

CHAPTER XX

THE AUSTRIAN MARRIAGE

ANXIETIES OF THE AUSTRIAN COURT — THE PLAN FOR A MATRIMONIAL
ALLIANCE WITH NAPOLEON — OPENING OF FORMAL NEGOTIATIONS —
THE DELIBERATIONS IN PARIS — NAPOLEON'S DECISION — THE CZAR'S
INDIGNATION — THE CEREMONIES AT VIENNA — NAPOLEON'S PREPA-
RATIONS — HIS MEETING WITH MARIA LOUISA — THE WEDDING —
GIFTS AND REJOICINGS — IMPRESSIONS OF THE NEW EMPRESS — THE
NEW DYNASTY.

THE court of Vienna had regarded what were apparently preparations for a matrimonial alliance between France and Russia with
nothing less than consternation. Such an arrangement would, if consummated, temporarily seal the political bond already existing, and
might guarantee it indefinitely. The empire of Austria, already shorn
of so many fair territories, was no longer a first-rate power. The language used by Napoleon after the armistice of Znaim about Francis and
the necessity for his abdication, had made a deep impression in view of
the events at Bayonne. Was the ancient monarchy really to be humiliated and remain permanently dismembered? Not if an imperial alliance was the only thing necessary to secure Napoleon's favor. There
was an archduchess of the proper age, and the house of Hapsburg was
far more ancient and splendid than the house of Romanoff.

Among the many confidential agents of Napoleon concerned in
formulating the treaty of Schönbrunn was a certain Alexandre de Laborde, who had once been in the Austrian service and knew Vienna
well. Remaining behind after his employer's departure, he wrote a
memoir in December, 1809, which, though sent to Maret, was intended
for the Emperor himself, and was seen by him. In it is detailed a conversation with Metternich, in which the latter had first vaguely and

then distinctly spoken of a match between Napoleon and the Arch-duchess Maria Louisa. This, it was explained, was to be considered only in case the divorce should take place, and the Austrian minister declared that his master knew nothing of the project. There is no reasonable doubt that Laborde's statement was substantially true, for as long as there was glory in being the author of the suggestion Metternich claimed the credit of it and, in a letter of September eleventh, 1811, categorically asserted that it was his; but after Napoleon's fall he declared that the scheme originated in France, and it was then said that Napoleon had himself taken the initiative, on a hint from Schwarzenberg, the new Austrian ambassador in Paris. Whether Napoleon or Francis was the suitor, it soon transpired that both were willing. When, therefore, the former learned that the fate of the Russian alliance was in the hands of the empress-dowager, he gave the surly answer already quoted, and turned toward Austria. During the pathetic scene of the divorce he formally asserted that having lost hope of offspring by his well-beloved spouse, he was about to sacrifice the tenderest emotions of his heart for the welfare of his people. Being but forty years old, he might still hope to bring up children and train them in his own ideas. Josephine gave her consent to the dissolution of her marriage, because it was an obstacle to the well-being of France, in that it stood in the way of her country's future government by the descendants of a great man.

To emphasize this thought, the Emperor employed two devices. The first was to produce an effect intended for home consumption. After the battle of Wagram, Stadion, the Austrian minister of foreign affairs, who had advocated the war, resigned; Metternich, who had been called from the embassy at Paris to negotiate the peace on his master's side, remained in Vienna to succeed Stadion, and Prince Schwarzenberg was appointed to France. But the Countess Metternich was still in Paris. The Beauharnais family—Eugène with the Austrian ambassador, Josephine and Queen Hortense with Frau von Metternich—opened the negotiation for securing Maria Louisa as the second Empress of France. To remove all religious scruples, the bishops' court of Paris met, and on January fourteenth pronounced Napoleon's first marriage null.

The second device was to lay before an extraordinary council the two alternatives and ask their decision. Murat, Cambacérès, and prob-

BATTLE AT ZNAIM, JULY 11, 1809

ably Fouché, voted for Russia. Fouché, like Talleyrand, had long been suspected of playing not for Napoleon's, but for his own interest. A certain independence of conduct and language which he had displayed in raising the national guards to repel the Walcheren expedition had awakened further suspicion in the Emperor's mind, and there had been plain speaking between them. The Minister of Police, according to one account, now declared that there were only two parties in Europe —those who had gained and those who had lost by the Revolution; that Russia belonged to the former, and was the true ally for the French empire. It was believed that this argument was an endeavor to regain the Emperor's favor, for the words have a Napoleonic ring. The majority of the council, however, was under Maret's leadership, and after a long, vague harangue from Talleyrand, in which he seemed to concur with Maret, expressed itself in favor of Austria. From immemorial times she had been the pivot of every Continental coalition against France. She was now irritated, and must be soothed.

Napoleon's friends assert that he himself really favored the Russian alliance, but looked on the request for delay as a covert refusal, and considered himself the victim of circumstances. This is not probable, for Maret was still his confidential man; at any rate, the Emperor accepted the decision of the majority. Accordingly, a family council was next called, and the matter was laid before them. There was no doubt as to the conclusion: they declared for the Austrian marriage. The formalities of arrangement were speedily concluded. Berthier, the Prince of Neuchâtel, was named ambassador extraordinary to marry the Archduchess by proxy at Vienna, and the date was fixed for March eleventh, 1810. The news was received at the Austrian capital with jubilation. The populace had already lost much of its bitterness against the French, for they had convinced themselves that in the last war their own cabinet had been the aggressor. Stadion's resignation was probably to many minds a confession of the fact, though in reality it merely marked a change of policy. The French wounded were nursed by the Viennese with tender care, and even under the lash many turned to regard the strong hand which wielded it as probably the only power able to restore peace and bring back its blessings. In judicious minds the French alliance, even if not a high-spirited course, was popular because it guaranteed Austria on the east against Russia and on the west against France. If her identity were not destroyed, she might hope at some distant day to regain her strength and her place in Europe.

At St. Petersburg the news produced different effects. The conservatives were not greatly disturbed, for now they were freed from the possible disgrace of an imperial marriage with the Bonapartes, and they could put up with the insult if only it should break the bonds which tied them to the hated Continental system of Napoleon. But the Czar was outraged; he had been personally insulted, and his policy was toppling. He had secured nothing, he would be the laughing-stock of his people, and he could no longer justify himself in resistance to popular tendencies. He was likewise true-hearted enough to feel the loss of a friend, and proud enough to smart under the feeling that he had been duped. Much of this he concealed, although his suite thought they could discern all these emotions. In the face of both Austria and France he could not attack the deed itself. Caulaincourt assured him in Napoleon's name that the match had no political character, and changed nothing in the personal friendship which his Emperor continued to feel. He insinuated that the real cause of the decision was the religious difference. But this Alexander would not accept. "Congratulate the Emperor on the choice he has made," was the reply. "He wants children; all France wants them for him. The decision was the one which should have been taken, but it is fortunate that the matter of age stopped us here. Where would we have been if I had not spoken of it to my mother? What reproaches could she not have heaped on me? What must I not have said to you? for it is clear you were dealing in both quarters. Why," he concluded, "has anything been said about the difference in religion, when at the outset the Emperor declared it would be no obstacle?" Thus was reached the second stage in the dissolution of the famous alliance of Tilsit.

The scenes in Vienna were brilliant in the extreme. On the one hand, they marked the Austrian approach to democracy, because for the first time the tricolor was displayed in the streets, and the rigid etiquette of the Hapsburgs, preserved from hoary antiquity with pious care, snapped at every turn which Berthier took. On the other hand, they marked the approach of France to absolutism. Napoleon ordered that his bride should receive the same presents as those which Louis XV. had ordered for Maria Leszcynski, the splendors of the ceremonial were to be royal, the new Empress's train was arranged according to the same model, the itinerary of her journey was marked out as a royal progress. The civil contract was signed on the tenth; the religious ceremony occurred on the eleventh, as appointed; and then followed a banquet where Berthier was absolved from all the ceremonies considered obligatory upon one of his rank in the Hofburg. Three days later the new Empress was handed to her traveling-carriage by the Archduke Charles, and amid salvos of artillery, mingled with the cheers of the populace, she set forth. There were a few signs of discontent among little knots who collected to curse their national humiliation, and the aristocracy were not reconciled to see Prince Esterhazy in the rôle of guide to the Prince of Wagram, as Berthier had now been styled by imperial decree in Paris. But, on the whole, Europe was impressed with a sense of Francis's sincerity. The father went forth a day's journey to spend an evening alone with his daughter and bestow in parting his paternal blessing on a child who had saved her country. Her journey through Bavaria and Würtemberg was one long ovation, for these countries believed their welfare to be bound up with that of France. On the twenty-sixth her cortège, having passed by way of Strasburg, was moving toward Soissons.

After the divorce Napoleon had withdrawn in solitude to the Trianon at Versailles, as if to mourn his widowhood the appointed and decent time in silence. The spot chosen had a significance with reference to the coming celebrations. For a week he spent his days in the unaccustomed but truly royal occupation of field sports. Once he visited Josephine at Malmaison. The next months he had spent again in Paris conducting the matrimonial negotiations and arranging every detail of the etiquette to be observed in the cumbrous ceremonial which he had devised for the celebration of his marriage in France. When all was completed to his satisfaction he left for Compiègne to supervise the arrangements made for the reception of his new consort, and spent the last week of waiting there. Of all his family the giddiest and most worldly was his sister Pauline. She and his sister-in-law, the sensible and charming Queen of Westphalia, were chosen to advise and counsel regarding matters of dress and behavior. The latter wrote to her brother a full account of the Emperor's passionate expectation. During these days his occupations were singularly human. Much of the time was spent in trying on gorgeous clothes: gold-laced coats, and embroidered waistcoats, which had been sent by Paris tailors. Some of it

was passed in the acquisition of accomplishments, notably in learning to waltz.   Every day he sent a letter with flowers to meet the
new Empress at every stage of her progress, and every day he received
a reply from her written in correct French.

At last she reached the close of the final stage, and her bridegroom
went out to meet her.   Half-way between Soissons and Compiègne
were pitched three splendid pavilions.   Her suite was to remain in
that nearest their last lodging, his in that nearest the palace, the bridal
pair were to meet in the central tent, where, according to the custom
of feudalism, she was to kneel and pay homage to her liege as his foremost subject.   But when the Emperor heard that his bride was so
near, his impatience seemed to break through all bounds.   Entering
his carriage without ceremony or warning, and attended by only a single
companion, the King of Naples, he drove far past Soissons until the
carriages met, when he stepped out of his own, tore open the door of
the other, and entered with the eagerness of a youthful lover to embrace his bride.   The prearranged stops were countermanded, and the
same evening, at ten, the wedding-train reached Compiègne.   Such was
the lover's ardor that he again flung propriety to the winds, and, claiming the validity of the procuratorial ceremony at Vienna, slept under
the same roof with his bride, instead of in the chamber furnished for
his use in one of the administrative buildings.   As an excuse for this
conduct he pleaded the example of Henry IV.

Next day the ladies and gentlemen of the Empress's court were presented, and formally took the oath of office.   On the morrow St. Cloud
was reached in the imperial progress; and two days later, on April
first, the civil ceremony of marriage was performed in the presence of
all the great dignitaries of the empire, including all the cardinals but
two.   Excepting only those who pleaded their age or infirmities, the
entire college had been transplanted from Rome to Paris shortly after
the seizure of the Pope.   There was the usual festival at night, accompanied by salvos of artillery, with illuminations of the palace grounds
and fountains.   The weather, like the date, was untoward, but the
Parisian populace streamed out in spite of pouring rain to get a fore-
taste of the more magnificent spectacles soon to follow.   The solemn
procession of the bridal pair into the capital occurred next day, and the
religious ceremony was celebrated in the great gallery of the Louvre,
before an assembly declared at the time to be the most superb ever

DETAIL FROM THE RELIGIOUS MARRIAGE OF
NAPOLEON AND MARIA LOUISA

seen in France, except for one ominous fact—the twenty-seven cardinals were absent. They protested that their absence was an empty form, due only to the circumstance that Pius VII. had not sanctioned the divorce. But Napoleon was as keenly sensitive to the effectiveness of forms as any Roman prelate; the offenders were banished from Paris, stripped of their great revenues, and forbidden to wear the color or insignia of their office. The popular speech dubbed them black cardinals.

In the first outburst of enthusiastic loyalty, Paris and the nation could not sufficiently manifest their joy. The illuminations were lavish, the crowds exuberant, the presents to the Empress superb. Among the latter was a complete toilet service of silver-gilt, including not merely small vessels, but large pieces of furniture, such as an arm-chair and cheval glass. Apparently the French people felt assured that they had exchanged an old, worn-out dynasty for a new and vigorous one. They were jubilant at the thought of peace and safety, which seemed to a generation cradled under royalty to be even yet impossible in Europe except in connection with a great conquering family. It was for this they poured forth their sentiment and their substance, not for the affection they bore the new Empress.

Measured by a certain standard, Maria Louisa was beautiful. Her abundant light-brown hair softened the high color of her brilliant complexion, her eyes were blue and mild, her features had the pretty but uncertain fullness of her eighteen years, her glance was frank and untroubled; but her lips were full and heavy, her waist was long and stiff, her form was plump like a child's, and her timidity and self-consciousness were uncontrollable. The French taste inclines to lines in the human form which suggest a lithe and sinewy figure; the French instinct seeks in the expression signs of quick emotion, not to say passion; the French eye knows but one standard of taste in dress: that alone is natural to French feeling which is the product of self-control and consummate art. In all these respects the Austrian archduchess was woefully deficient. She was pious, and, as her letters declare, had spent much of the previous winter in praying that Providence would choose another consort for Napoleon. But with the resignation of her faith, which some call fatalism, and with the obedience which German life demands from all women, even those of the highest station, she had accepted her destiny. These qualities, combined with her capacity for motherhood, soon gained a courteous and affectionate support from her husband, and together they defied both irreconcilable royalists and radical republicans, who, in spite of their ever-waning influence and ever-thinning ranks, still annoyed the Emperor by significant whisperings and glances. Both were in despair because the strongest indictment they had urged was now quashed. One pretext of England, Napoleon declared, had been that he intended to destroy the ancient dynasties of Europe. Circumstances having opened the way to his choice of a consort, he had used the opportunity in order to destroy the flimsy plea under which Great Britain had disturbed the nations and had stirred up the strife which had inundated Europe with blood. Metternich heard people wondering in Vienna whether a new French dynasty was really to be established for the peace and welfare of France, or whether the alliance was intended to throw the strength of a hitherto implacable and courageous foe into another Napoleonic combination for the conquest of Europe and the world.

The solution of this enigma has never been found. There was at the moment a lull in the storm; for a time it seemed as if it would lengthen into a prolonged calm. During the ceremonies at the Louvre the Austrian ambassador, who had taken to himself the credit of what was passing, and had impressively accepted the congratulations showered on him, caught up a wine-glass from the breakfast-table, and, appearing at the window, announced in a loud voice that he drank to the "King of Rome," a title reserved under the Holy Roman Empire for the heir apparent. It was but a short time since Schwarzenberg's proud master had renounced his proudest style, that of Roman emperor. The crowd knew that the toast as now given was intended for Napoleon's issue, and they burst into cheers at this new sign of Austrian amity. The captive Spaniards at Valençay were not to be outdone. They chanted a "Te Deum" in their chapel, and drank toasts to the health "of our august sovereigns, the great Napoleon and Maria Louisa, his august spouse." Ferdinand set a climax to his disgusting obsequiousness in a petition begging to be adopted as a son, and asking for permission to appear at court. Compiègne, whither the imperial pair soon returned, was crowded with royal personages, with the most distinguished diplomatists, and with the couriers bearing congratulatory despatches from persons of consequence throughout Europe.

CHAPTER XXI

RIGORS OF THE CONTINENTAL SYSTEM

MEASURES OF ECCLESIASTICAL PROCEDURE—REFORMS IN THE CHURCH
—NAPOLEON AS SUZERAIN OF THE POPE—METHODS OF DEFYING THE
CONTINENTAL SYSTEM—MEASURES TO ENFORCE IT—REARRANGEMENT
OF GERMAN LANDS—NAPOLEON AS A SMUGGLER—"SIMULATED
PAPERS"—EVASIONS OF THE IMPERIAL RESTRICTIONS—VISIT TO THE
NETHERLANDS—NAPOLEON AND HIS BROTHER LOUIS—THE LATTER
DEFIANT—LOUIS'S NEGOTIATIONS WITH ENGLAND—FOUCHÉ'S INTER-
FERENCE—HIS COUNTERPLOT.

THE consolidation of Napoleonic power appeared to be progress-
ing rapidly. In February a decree of the senate had declared
the Papal States to be divided into two French departments, under
the names of Rome and Trasimenus. The Eternal City was to give
her name, as second city of the Empire, to the imperial heir. The
Pope, endowed with a royal revenue of four millions, was to have a
palace in each of several different places, and reside, according to his
choice, in any one, or in all in turn. He was to swear that he would
never contravene the judgments of the Gallican Church, and his suc-
cessors were each to be similarly bound on their accession to office.
Daunou wrote a book, which was published at the Emperor's expense,
maintaining the two theses of Machiavelli: first, that the court of
Rome had always used its spiritual power to increase its temporal estate; secondly, that its efforts had always been directed against the
temporal power strongest at the moment in Italy. Unconquerable as
was the resistance of Pius VII. on the whole, he had nevertheless
surrendered temporarily at the beginning of what might be called the
second quarrel of investitures, by inducting into their offices the bishops
nominated by Napoleon. After he had been thrown into captivity,

201

however, he flatly refused to continue, and the Emperor cut the knot by installing in the bishoprics, as they fell vacant, men of his own choice, under the style of "vicars of the chapters."

This was but the initial step to an entire destruction of the administrative scheme devised and perfected by the Roman hierarchy. The college of cardinals had first been brought to Paris, and its members then banished in pairs to the great provincial towns; the ecclesiastical courts, with all their archives, were likewise transplanted from Rome to the French capital; the thirty episcopates of the two new French departments were reduced to four; the army of foreign prelates which had been supported by the papal system was dispersed into the various lands from which its members had come. The number of Roman parishes, too, was reduced, and all the convents were secularized. Such of the discharged priests as were ready to swear allegiance to the Emperor and the Gallican Church received a small pension; the rest—and they appear to have been in a majority—saw their personal as well as ecclesiastical goods confiscated and were themselves exiled.

These or similar measures being applied likewise to Piedmont, Liguria, Tuscany, Parma, and Placentia, the sums of money raised from confiscated estates became enormous. A large proportion of these funds flowed of course into the imperial coffers, and to this fact, as well as to the restored public confidence, was largely due the rise in prices on the stock exchange which occurred on the consummation of the Austrian marriage. These sweeping changes were of great service to true religion and to the lands in which they were made, breaking as they did the chains of an ecclesiastical oppression under which the populace had been reduced to poverty, ignorance, and apathy. Unfortunately the new rule, while more economical than the old, was not less arbitrary—military despotism being as little fitted for the development of a people as the rule of a corporation. Men looked aghast as the papacy and papal influence crumbled together, while the seat of real ecclesiastical power was removed from the banks of the Tiber to those of the Seine. Time seemed to be taking its revenge. Seven centuries earlier Lothair had been the vassal of Innocent II.; Napoleon was now the suzerain of Pius VII. So contemptible had the Pope become, even in the eyes of devout Catholics, that De Maistre called the inflexible but supine pontiff a punchinello of no importance.

It had been clear since Trafalgar that though France might domi-

LOUIS BONAPARTE
KING OF HOLLAND, COUNT OF SAINT-LEU

nate earth, air, and fire in Europe, she could not gain the mastery of the sea and its islands, at least by the ordinary means. The Emperor's infatuation with the plausible scheme of destroying England's commerce by paper blockades and by embargoes on British goods had not been diminished either by his inconclusive struggle in Spain or by his victory over Austria. It was in vain that he had changed his naval policy from one of fleet-fighting to one of commerce-destroying; that he had seized and was continuing to seize neutral vessels laden with British wares; that he had expanded his political system by conquest until he was nominally master of the Mediterranean, Atlantic, and Baltic harbors. Since 1805 English trade with the Continent, so far from diminishing, had steadily increased in the hands of contrabandists and neutral carriers, until it had now reached annual dimensions of twenty-five millions sterling. In spite of the Tilsit alliance, even French soldiers occasionally wore English-made shoes and clothing, English ships carried naval stores out of Russian harbors, and colonial wares found their way from the wharves of Riga to the markets of Mainz. But the chief offenders in defying Napoleon's chimerical policy were the Dutch and Hanseatic cities. The resistance elsewhere in the Continent was passive compared with the energetic smuggling and the clandestine evasion of decrees which went on under the eyes of the officials in places like Amsterdam and Hamburg.

These facts had not been concealed from the Emperor of the French at any time, and he now made ready to enforce the threats which he had uttered in the agony of the late wars. It had come to a life-or-death struggle between the policies laid down respectively in the imperial decrees and in the British orders in council. Neither measure was in the strictest sense military, but it is easy to see that the two were irreconcilable in their intent, while the success of either one meant the ruin of the land which upheld the other. It was for the sake, apparently, of waging this decisive though unwarlike contest that Napoleon renounced leading his victorious legions into Spain for the expulsion of English troops from the peninsula. What he himself called the "Spanish ulcer" might weaken the French system, and one hundred thousand good troops, together with the imperial guard, were to be sent to heal it by overwhelming the great English general who had been made Duke of Wellington, and by seizing Lisbon. But the English commerce with the peninsula was slender in comparison with what she carried on with the Baltic and with Holland through the connivance of governments which were nominally her foes. The Continental system, therefore, must first be repaired, and it was to convert a nominal acquiescence into a real one that Davout was despatched to hold the fortresses from Dantzic westward, while Oudinot was to coerce Holland.

With such purposes in view, the lands taken from Austria were apportioned among Bavaria, Italy, Würtemberg, and Baden. Each of these vassal states was made to pay handsomely for its new acquisitions. The principality of Ratisbon was given to Dalberg, the prince-primate, and he in turn delivered that of Frankfort to Prince Eugène. The King of Westphalia received Hanover and Magdeburg, promising in return about ten millions a year of tribute, and engaging to support the eighteen thousand French troops who occupied his new lands. The gradual evacuation of South Germany began, and before long the entire coast land between the Elbe and the Weser was held by soldiers who had fought at Essling and Wagram. Hamburg, Bremen, and the other Hanseatic towns, East Friesland, Oldenburg, a portion of Westphalia, the canton of Valais, and the grand duchy of Berg were destined very soon to be incorporated with France in order to round out the imperial domain. It might be possible for southern Europe to substitute flax and Neapolitan cotton for American cotton, chicory for coffee, grape syrup or beet sugar for colonial sugar, and woad for indigo, but the North could not. Like Louis, though in a less degree, Murat and Jerome, sympathizing with their peoples, had sinned against the Continental system, and were soon to do penance for their sins by the loss of important territories. But for the present the ostensible compliance of the Northern dependencies was accepted.

It is a curious and amusing fact that the great smuggler and real delinquent was Napoleon himself. Even he felt the exigencies of France to be so fierce that, by a system of licenses, certain privileged traders were permitted to secure the supplies of dye-stuffs and fish-oil essential to French industries by exporting to England both wine and wheat in exchange. The licensed monopolists paid handsomely for their privilege, not only in the sums which they publicly turned over, but in those which lined the pockets of unscrupulous ministers like Fouché, who winked at great irregularities not contemplated by the immunities secured from Napoleon.

An evasion of the British orders in council analogous to that of the French decrees was extensively practised, and licenses to neutral traders were also issued by the English government. But it practised more discretion, and the regulation of the extensive commerce which resulted was not attended by those court and private scandals so rife in France. The worst feature of the English procedure was its adoption of the so-called "neutralization" system. Dutch, French, and Spanish trading vessels had long been provided by their owners with forged papers certifying a neutral origin, generally Prussian. To these both captains and crews swore without compunction when searched by British cruisers. This system England made her own, issuing not merely to real, but also to sham, neutrals licenses which insured them against search when laden with wares for or from English ports. The firms which engaged in the trade — and after the removal of the non-intercourse restrictions many of them were American — compounded morality with legality, considering themselves perfectly reputable, even though they continued to furnish "simulated papers"— that is, prepared forgeries — to their ships as part of the regular outfit.

Such immoralities, inequalities, and absurdities were the necessary consequence of a fight for the means of subsistence between two combatants one of which had no hands and the other no feet. So extensive was the traffic, however, that although England had found it necessary, in consequence of the Spanish rebellion, to restrict her paper blockade to the coasts of Holland, France, and northern Italy, she nevertheless doubled her importations of naval stores during the season of 1808, while the prices of wool, silk, and colonial wares gave temporary promise of a revival of manufactures. As long as Napoleon's energy was elsewhere engaged, the ubiquity of English war-ships on the high seas rendered the use of "simulated papers" inordinately profitable; and even after he began to give his undivided attention to policing the harbors and guarding the coast-line, it continued to be fairly so. It must further be remembered that in the treaty which Russia made with Sweden on September seventeenth, 1809, the latter country promised not only to cede Finland, but also to shut out from her harbors all British ships except such as brought salt and colonial wares. In January, 1810, Napoleon had made an agreement with the same power that he would hand back Pomerania, but in return Sweden was to import nothing but salt.

The Austrian marriage having now been consummated and Austria having been added to his system, Napoleon was ready in June to open his novel campaign and begin the commercial warfare which eventually furnished one of the most important elements in his overthrow, the other two being the national uprisings and the treachery of his friends, so called. But the zenith had not even yet been reached by his star. It was with undimmed sagacity and undiminished power that, accompanied by his bride, he set out about the end of April from Compiègne, to visit the Dutch frontier, his object being to observe how far Holland's well-nigh open contempt for his cherished scheme would now justify the destruction of her autonomy and the utter overthrow of her government. The nominal purpose of the journey was to please the young Empress, and to gratify the peoples of Belgium and Brabant by a sight of her charms. This aim was observed in all the arrangements, but in well-nigh every town visited the sun's first rays saw the Emperor on horseback inspecting troops, ships, fortifications, and arsenals; and when its last beams faded away the unwearied man was still holding interviews with the local authorities, in which every detail of administration was revised and strengthened. To all appearance the end of the journey was as prosperous as its inception. Favors were distributed with lavish hand, the people displayed a wild enthusiasm when the affable but distant Empress showed herself, and nothing occurred to mar the outward state in which the Emperor returned to Paris. But the condition of his mind cannot be depicted, such was his rage and humiliation in regard to a revelation of treachery made inadvertently and innocently by Louis on the eve of their separation. To explain what had occurred a short retrospect is necessary.

From earliest childhood certain qualities of Louis had endeared him to Napoleon. The school of poverty, in which the younger brother had been the pupil of the elder, was likewise a school of fraternal affection. Throughout the Italian and Egyptian campaigns they stood in intimate relations as general and aide-de-camp, and one of the earliest cares of the First Consul was to bestow the beautiful Hortense de Beauharnais on his favorite brother. In 1804 Louis was made general, then councilor of state, and finally in 1806 he was elevated to the throne of Holland. His child until its untimely death was cherished by Napoleon as a son destined to inherit imperial greatness. But, like the other royal Bonapartes, the King of Holland regarded his high estate not as a gift from the Emperor, but as a right. He ruled the land assigned him, if not in his own interest, at least not in that of the Empire, and from the outset filled his letters with bitter complaints of all that entered into his lot, not excepting his wife. Napoleon admonished and threatened, but to no avail. The interests of his own royalty and of the Dutch were nearer to Louis than those of the Empire.

At last the Emperor hinted that the air of Holland did not agree with its monarch, indicating that circumstances required it to be incorporated with France. In March, 1808, he offered the crown of Spain as a substitute. A little later the suggestion was made that Louis might have the Hanseatic towns in exchange for Brabant and Zealand. Both propositions were scouted. When we remember who the potentates were, by whom such offers were made and refused, we seem forced to dismiss all notions of patriotism, uprightness, and loyalty as the motives of either, and must attribute Louis's course to petulance. Napoleon was highly incensed. On the failure of the Walcheren expedition, both Brabant and Zealand were occupied by French troops, and Louis was summoned to Paris. His first desperate thought was one of resistance, but on reflection he obeyed. On his arrival he learned that his fate was imminent. Napoleon announced to the legislature that a change in the relations with Holland was imperative. The Minister of the Interior explained that, as being the alluvium of three French rivers — namely, the Rhine, the Meuse, and the Scheldt—that land was by nature a portion of France, one of the great imperial arteries. Louis sought to fly, but was detained. He at once despatched the Count de Bylandt with orders to close the Dutch frontier fortresses and defend the capital against the French troops. This was done, but Louis's defiance was short. After signing a treaty which bound him, among other things, to open his fortresses, seize all "neutralized," and even all neutral, vessels in his harbors, including those of the United States,—a document which thus left him only a nominal throne,—he was permitted early in April, 1810, to return to Amsterdam.

Napoleon's subsequent course was dictated by what might appear to be a sudden change of view, but was in reality a revival of his perennial hopes for peace with England. Having in mind the annexation of Holland, it occurred to him that by desisting from that measure he might wrench from Great Britain the lasting peace which she had thus far refused. Accordingly he ordered his brother to open a negotiation with London and represent his kingdom as in danger of annihilation unless the British government would consent to a cessation of hostilities and an enduring treaty of peace. This was done, and though Labouchere, Louis's agent, had so little to offer that his propositions were farcical, yet there was at least the show of a diplomatic negotiation. At this juncture the superserviceable Mephistopheles of the Empire, Fouché, intervened. By an agent of his own he approached the cabinet of St. James with an offer of peace on the basis of restoring the Spanish Bourbons and compensating Louis XVIII. by a kingdom to be carved from the territories of the United States!

The agent of Fouché reached London somewhat ahead of the one sent by Louis. He was firmly sent to the right-about. Labouchere was then told that before entering further on the question, a proposition for peace must be formulated and presented, not by the King of Holland, but by the Emperor. The failure of the Walcheren expedition had exasperated England, Canning had fallen, and Lord Wellesley, his successor, represented a powerful sentiment for the continuation of the war. Napoleon replied, therefore, by a note suggesting not a definite peace, but a step toward it. If England would withdraw the orders in council of 1807, he would evacuate Holland and the Hanseatic towns. His note closed with a characteristic threat. If England should delay, having already lost her trade with Naples, Spain, Portugal, and the port of Triest, she would now lose that with Holland, the Hanseatic towns, and Sicily.

Nothing dismayed by his first rebuff, the audacious Fouché again intervened. This time he selected Ouvrard, a friend of Labouchere's and of his own, a man well known as a stormy petrel of intrigue, to operate insidiously through the accredited envoy, who innocently supposed his friend to be representing Napoleon's own views. There was consequently but little sense of restraint in the renewed negotiation. Virtually the entire Continental situation was considered as open, and Fouché's pet scheme of an American kingdom for Louis XVIII. was further amplified by the suggestion of an Anglo-French expedition to establish it. Labouchere having returned to Holland, much of the negotiation had been carried on by letter, and Napoleon, getting wind during his Belgian visit of Ouvrard's presence at the Dutch court, suspected trickery and called for the correspondence. Its very existence enraged him; that such matters should have been put in writing was

compromising to his entire policy. Ouvrard afterward declared that
he personally informed the Emperor of what was going on, but he
could never prove it; the only possible basis which can be found for
his statement consists in the seizure and confiscation about this time of
some hundred and thirty American vessels lying in Continental harbors; but, base as that deed was, it proves nothing and was due to another cause. It is not easy to determine whether this deed was a
well-considered measure of French diplomacy, intended to arouse the
pugnacity of the United States, or a temporary shift to fill empty
coffers. In either case it was not intended to have a direct bearing
on irregular diplomatic negotiations between England and Holland.
The circumstances were a direct result of the Berlin decree.

CHAPTER XXII

THE CONTINENTAL SYSTEM COMPLETED

THE BAYONNE AND RAMBOUILLET DECREES—FOUCHÉ REPLACED BY
SAVARY—ABDICATION OF KING LOUIS—CONDUCT OF LOUIS AND LU-
CIEN—HOLLAND INCORPORATED IN THE EMPIRE—NAPOLEON'S RELA-
TIVES UNTRUE TO HIS INTERESTS—FRENCH EMPIRE AT ITS GREATEST
EXTENT—THE CONTINENTAL SYSTEM AS PERFECTED—DISCONTENT IN
RUSSIA AND SWEDEN.

THE American Embargo Act of 1807 had been for manifest reasons
entirely to Napoleon's liking, as is proved by the Bayonne decree
of 1808, which ordered the seizure and sale in French harbors of all
American ships transgressing it. The Non-intercourse Act of March
first, 1809, was, however, quite another thing. It was passed by the
Democratic majority of Congress in defiance of Federalist sentiment,
and prohibited commercial intercourse with both Great Britain and
France. Napoleon declared that French vessels had been seized under
its terms in United States harbors; and it was nominally in retaliation
for this, which was not a fact, that, according to the Rambouillet decree, issued on March twenty-third, 1810, American vessels with their
cargoes, worth together upward of eight million dollars, were seized and
kept. In reality Napoleon regarded or pretended to regard the Non-
intercourse Act as one of open hostility to himself, and used it to fill
his depleted purse, exactly as he used the substitutes passed by Congress in the following year to bring on the War of 1812. Owing to
the general use of "simulated" American papers and seals, the non-
intercourse system introduced British goods into every Continental
harbor. A vessel holding both a French and a British license and
"simulated papers" of the United States or any other neutral state
might by unscrupulous adroitness trade in English goods almost with-

A DAY OF REVIEW UNDER THE EMPIRE. PLACE DU CARROUSEL

out restriction, and this was far from Napoleon's intention. Between 1802 and 1811, nine hundred and seventeen American vessels were seized by the British and five hundred and fifty-eight by the French in their harbors; the number seized in the ports of Holland, Spain, Denmark, and Naples was very large, but it is not definitely known. The dealings of Napoleon with the United States in this matter, like those of England, were irregular and evasive; but there is nothing in them to show that the Emperor of the French contemplated either the dismemberment of the American republic or the abandonment of his Continental system.

Having traced the whole English-Dutch conspiracy directly to Fouché, Napoleon contemplated bringing the treacherous minister to trial on the charge of treason. Fearing, however, the effect not merely in Europe, but particularly in France, of such a spectacle, and the revelations which must necessarily accompany it, he contented himself with degrading and banishing his unruly henchman. The important office of Police Minister was filled by the appointment of Savary, an equally unscrupulous but more obedient tool. The murderer of Enghien, and the keeper of Ferdinand as he now was and had been since Talleyrand's return to public life, was both feared and hated in Paris. "I believe," he says in his memoirs, "that news of a pestilence having broken out on some point of the coast would not have caused more terror than did my nomination to the ministry of police."

Louis, within the narrowed sphere of his activities, continued quite as incorrigible as before. He refused the perfect obedience demanded, and even treated the French diplomatic agent in Holland with indignity. Napoleon's scorn burst its bounds. "Louis," he wrote in a letter carefully excluded from the authorized edition of his correspondence, "you do not want to reign long; your actions reveal your true feelings better than your personal letters. Listen to one who has known those feelings longer than even you yourself. Retrace your steps, be French at heart, or your people will drive you out, and you will leave Holland, the object of pity and ridicule on the part of the Dutch. Men govern states by the exercise of reason and the use of a policy, and not by the impulses of an acid and vitiated lymph." Two days later, on hearing of a studied insult from his brother to the French minister, he wrote again: "Write no more trite phrases; you have been repeating them for three years, and every day proves their falseness.

This is the last letter I shall write you in my life." In a short time French troops were marching on Amsterdam. Louis summoned his council and advised resistance; but the councilors convinced him how useless such a course would be. The dispirited King at once abdicated and fled.

For some days Louis's whereabouts were unknown. There was much talk, and Napoleon was agitated. He wrote beseeching Jerome to learn where the fugitive was and send him to Paris, that he might withdraw to St. Leu and cease to be the laughing-stock of Europe. In ten days it was known that Louis was at Teplitz in Bohemia. A circular was at once addressed to the French diplomatists abroad, explaining that the King of Holland must be excused for his conduct on the ground of his being a chronic invalid. Inasmuch as about the same time Lucien found the air of the French department of Rome not altogether to his liking, and besought his brother's leave to expatriate himself to the United States, the family relations of the Emperor were published throughout Europe in a most unbecoming light. The ship in which Lucien sailed was captured by an English frigate, and he was taken to England, where he remained in an agreeable captivity until 1814.

The "Moniteur" of July ninth, 1810, published a laconic imperial decree stating that Holland was henceforth a portion of the Empire. "What was I to do?" the Emperor exclaimed at St. Helena. "Leave Holland to the enemy? Nominate a new king?" It is difficult from his standpoint to answer these questions except in the negative. Louis had viewed his royal task as if he had been a dynastic king, which of course he never was, though much beloved by many of his subjects. He had moved the capital from The Hague to Amsterdam, had reformed the Dutch jurisprudence by the introduction of the Code Napoléon, had patronized learning and the arts. In all this he had not followed his brother's leading, and the results were excellent. But the Dutch merchants suffered exactly in proportion to the enforcement of the Continental blockade, riots of the unemployed became frequent, and the King, forgetting the ladder by which he had climbed, became the friend and the ally of his people. His fate was a natural consequence of his conduct. As a portion of the French empire, Holland was divided into eight departments, her public debt was scaled down from eighty to twenty millions, the French administration was put upon a basis of the most rigid economy, and for the ensuing four years the

Dutch found what consolation they might for the loss of their independence and their trade in a tolerable physical well-being, in the suppression of all disorders, and in an enforced calm such as Louis, by reason of his false position, had not been able to secure for them — a boon which, it must be confessed, their placid dispositions did not undervalue. When, however, opportunity was ripe, they bravely rose to assert once more their nationality.

In this connection it is interesting to note the effect which the conduct of the Emperor's family had finally produced in his mind. Brothers and sisters alike had come to consider their changed fortunes as having introduced them into the royal hierarchy of the old absolutist Europe, which their narrowness and ignorance led them to regard as still existent. Their behavior was distinctly that of the old dynastic sovereigns, whose lives were their model. The Emperor at last saw his mistake. " Relatives and cousins, male or female," he said in September to Metternich, "are all worthless. I should not have left a throne in existence, even for my brothers. But one grows wise only with time. I should have appointed nothing but stadholders and viceroys." This policy he thenceforward adopted. Carrying out the threat made in response to Joseph's complaints, Spain as far as the Ebro had been annexed to the Empire in March, 1810; in December the whole North Sea coast as far as Lübeck was likewise incorporated into the Empire. Jerome was deprived of a portion of Hanover, which he had received only in January, and the Duke of Oldenburg, who had married that favorite sister of Alexander for whose hand Napoleon had tentatively sued, was dethroned.

The same year Valais, the little commonwealth which had been separated from Switzerland and made independent in order to neutralize the highway into Italy, was likewise annexed. This new department, called that of the Simplon, together with the four erected out of the coast-line of the North Sea, brought the limits of Napoleonic empire to their greatest extent. The Illyrian provinces and the Ionian Isles were not under direct civil administration from Paris, being held as military outposts. Biscay, Navarre, Aragon, and Catalonia were each likewise held as military governments. Murat was made king of Naples, Louis's infant son became grand duke of Berg, Elisa was already grand duchess of Tuscany and princess of Lucca and Piombino. It will be remembered that Pauline was duchess of Guastalla, Jerome

king of Westphalia, Joseph king of Spain, Berthier prince of Neuchâtel, Talleyrand prince of Benevento, and Eugène viceroy of the kingdom of Italy. These states, together with the Confederation of the
Rhine, the Helvetic Republic, Bavaria, Saxony, Würtemberg, and Denmark, with Norway, were all vassal powers. But Rome, Genoa, Parma,
Florence, Siena, Leghorn, Osnabrück, Münster, Bremen, and Hamburg
were now capitals of actual French departments, the total number of
which reached one hundred and thirty. They were directly administered by a central bureaucracy as autocratic as any military despotism.

Thus at last was carried out the program of the Revolution, whose
leaders had determined in 1796 to close the Continent to English commerce. What republican idealism had imagined imperial vigor at least
partially realized. According to the Trianon decree of August fifth,
1810, and that of Fontainebleau, issued on October eighteenth of the
same year, French soldiers crossed the frontiers of the Empire, seized
every depot of English wares within a four-mile limit, and burned all the
contents except the sugar and coffee, which were transported to the great
towns, and sold at auction for the Emperor's extraordinary expenses;
the smugglers themselves were hunted down, captured, and handed over
to the tender mercies of a court created especially to try them. From
the Pyrenees to the North Cape the "licenses" devised by the Directory and issued by the Empire were the only certificates under which
English goods could be introduced into the now nearly completed system. Denmark, which still held Norway under its sway, had neither
forgotten nor forgiven the bombardment of Copenhagen in 1807; and
her king, Frederick VI., hoping that in the chapter of accidents Sweden too might fall to his crown, was only too willing to assist the
Emperor and close his ports to all British commerce, even to "neutral"
ships carrying English goods. The popular fury against England made
the people willing to forego all the comforts and advantages of free
trade in colonial wares.

It was with jealous eyes that Napoleon saw Russia's growing lukewarmness and marked her evasions of her pact. He knew also that in
spite of his decrees and his vigilance English goods were still transported
under the Turkish flag into the Mediterranean. But direct and efficient intervention on the Baltic or in the Levant was as yet impossible.
To complete one portion of his structure, a cordon must first be drawn
about both Sweden and Spain. The former was apparently secure, for

NAPOLEON AT COMPIEGNE.

Gustavus IV., having nearly ruined his country by persisting in the English alliance, had made way for his uncle, who now ruled as Charles XIII. under the protection of Napoleon. The new King, being childless, had selected as his successor Marshal Bernadotte, whose kindly dealings with the Pomeranians had endeared him to all Swedes. The estates of Sweden, remembering that he had married a sister of Joseph Bonaparte's wife, and recalling his long association with Napoleon, believed that in him they had a candidate acceptable to the French emperor, and therefore formally accepted him. They did not know the details of his unfriendly relations to Napoleon, nor with what unwillingness consent was given by the Emperor to his candidacy. The bonds of French citizenship were most grudgingly loosed by the Emperor, for there rankled in his breast a deep-seated feeling of distrust. But he was forced to a distasteful compliance by the fear of exposing unsavory details of his own policy. The new crown prince himself was well aware of the facts. He coveted Norway and asked for it, that on his accession he might bring Sweden a substitute for the loss of Finland; but Napoleon would not thus alienate the King of Denmark. The Czar was not hampered in the same way, and in December, 1810, offered Sweden the coveted land as the price of her alliance. When we recall the early republicanism of Bernadotte, his repeated failures in critical moments,—as on the Marchfeld and elsewhere,—the impatient and severe reproofs administered to the inefficient and fiery Gascon by his commander, we are not amazed that the crown prince Charles John, as his style now ran, began immediately after his installation at Stockholm to vent his spleen on Napoleon. Though there was no declared enmity, yet this fact augured ill for the steadfastness to the French alliance of the land over which he was soon to reign.

CHAPTER XXIII

THE COURSE OF THE PENINSULAR WAR

Napoleon's Plans for Spain—Character of the Troops Sent
Thither—Conflicting Policies in England—The Battle of
Busaco—The Lines of Torres Vedras—Soult's Dilatoriness—
Consequences of the Spanish Campaign—English Opinion Op-
posed to Wellington—Difficulties of Spanish Warfare—
Marmont Replaces Masséna—French Successes—Their Slight
Value—The French Character and the Spanish Invasion.

BUT matters were much worse beyond the Pyrenees, where there
was open warfare. The seizure of the northern provinces marked
the commencement of a new policy, nothing less than the incorporation of all Spain in France. Azanza, the envoy of Joseph at Paris,
could scarcely trust his senses when, after long and fruitless efforts to
persuade Napoleon that the troubles of Spain were due to the rapine
of the French generals and the quarrels of their unbridled soldiery, and
that the new King's moderation would be a perfect remedy if left to
work its effects, he was finally shown his master's carefully written
abdication, only waiting on events for publication, and was harshly told
in reply to his intercessions for the integrity of his country that it
was merely "the natural extension of France." It was Talleyrand who
originally said that Italy was the flank of France, Spain its natural
continuation, and Holland its alluvium.

Spain was to be conquered step by step, and by a season of military
administration each new acquisition was to be made ready for the
eventual dignity of a French department. A manifesto setting forth
this policy was prepared and was to be duly issued to the Spanish
people, but it never reached Madrid. The courier who carried it was
captured by a guerrilla, and the proclamation was at once printed in a

popular journal and copied thence into the "London Courier." It is not difficult to imagine how its perusal intensified the ever-growing national passion of the insurgent Spaniards for emancipation from the French yoke.

This spirit was England's powerful ally and Masséna's destructive foe. The great marshal, second in ability only to his imperial master, had succeeded to the command in the peninsula. The Imperial Guard was the mainstay of the reinforcements despatched thither in order to end the military conflict and inaugurate the new peaceful warfare by enforcing the Continental system of commercial embargo for humiliating England. Besides the guard there were, however, some of those regiments which had quailed at Vienna before the supposed approach of the Archduke John's army from Hungary after the battle of Wagram, by no means the flower of the Emperor's troops. These newcomers, together with the forces already in Spain under Suchet, Augereau, Reille, and Thouvenot, and the remnant of those troops which had been under Soult, were quickly organized for offensive warfare, first against the Spaniards and then against the English under Wellington who were still holding Portugal. The three army corps which were collected in Leon ready for advance were commanded respectively by Ney, Junot, and Reguier. Their number on paper was eighty thousand; in reality there were not more than fifty thousand effective fighting men. By the arrival of Hill's corps to reinforce Wellington the English numbered nearly if not quite as many.

For three years public opinion in England had been divided, some sustaining on the one hand Canning's policy of striving to defeat Napoleon by rousing the Continental nations and furnishing them with subsidies for warfare, others preferring that of Castlereagh, which advocated the sending of English forces into the Continent. The latter theory had temporarily prevailed. Three expeditions, one to Portugal, one to Walcheren, and one to Sicily, had been entire or partial failures. But Wellington's victory at Talavera having kept the peninsular ports open to English trade, his older brother, Lord Wellesley, who was now secretary for foreign affairs in the new cabinet, and who ardently believed that thus alone could England win, managed continuously to reinforce the army in Portugal until at last it was strong in numbers and efficient as a fighting machine.

From beginning to end Masséna's campaign was marked by unexpected disaster. Such were the zeal and endurance of the Spaniards that the old, ill-constructed fortress of Ciudad Rodrigo held out from the beginning of June until the ninth of July. Owing to the great heat and the preparations necessary in a hostile and deserted land, Almeida, which next blocked the way, was not even beleaguered until August fifteenth, and it held out for nearly a fortnight. Finally, on September sixteenth, Masséna crossed the Portuguese frontier, and Wellington, who lay near by but had not ventured to assume the offensive, began a slow and cautious retreat down the valley of the Mondego, devastating the country as he went. At last he made a stand on the heights near Busaco, over against a gorge where the river breaks through the hills into the plains below. Masséna attacked on September twenty-seventh, and was repulsed with a loss of four thousand five hundred dead and wounded. His division commanders showed at once a spirit which soon developed into unruliness: they had declared from the outset that their force was not sufficiently strong for the task assigned to it, and they now demanded a retreat. But the veteran Masséna stood firm: his scouts had brought word of a certain unprotected vale or rather depression of the land on the English left, which, having apparently escaped Wellington's observation, was not fortified, and the French commander determined to outflank his foe on that line. The movement was thoroughly successful, and the British began a rapid retreat southward before the advancing French.

Masséna found easy sustenance for man and beast in the rich lowlands about Coimbra, and halting in that town for a short time to recruit his strength and nurse his sick, started at last in the full tide of success for Lisbon and the sea, to drive the English to their ships and complete the Continental embargo. As one day succeeded another, his hopes grew higher until at last he overtook and began to skirmish with the English rear-guard. But after a final dash on October eleventh, that rear-guard suddenly vanished. Two days later the French were brought suddenly to a standstill before a long, perfectly constructed, and bristling line of fortifications of whose existence they had known absolutely nothing. These were the famous lines of Torres Vedras, constructed by Wellington in his recent enforced vacation, to guard his eventual retreat and embarkment, provided Sir John Moore's unfortunate campaign and the last Austrian war should find a climax in a similar French victory over all Spain. These lines effectually protected

MARSHAL LOUIS-GABRIEL SUCHET
DUKE OF ALBUFERA

the right bank of the Tagus. They consisted of one hundred and fifty-
two redoubts, equipped with seven hundred guns and manned by thirty
thousand English, thirty thousand Portuguese, and eight thousand
Spaniards. As Masséna now had but forty-five thousand men, there
could be no question of storming such a fortress, and nothing was left
but to await reinforcements and plan a strategic movement by which
he might cross the Tagus, threaten Lisbon from the left bank, draw off
the foe to its defense, and thus perhaps, having weakened the garrison,
secure the possibility of a successful attack on the fortified lines in front.

The notion was not visionary. Soult had been despatched with a
strong force southward into Andalusia, with orders to crush out the resistance of that province; he was then to turn westward, join Masséna
in Portugal, and coöperate with him under his orders for the expulsion
of the English. The belated expedition had not arrived, but in spite of
delay and disappointment it must surely come at last; and if the Emperor would but consent to order up the troops lying in Castile, the
quickly formed and brilliant plan of Masséna would be feasible. But,
alas for the scheme, what was apparently jealousy on the part of Soult
had quenched all ardor in the Andalusian invasion. He was at this
moment before Cadiz, carrying on a siege in which either the Spanish
were displaying great courage or the French but little heart. His sluggish progress was not unobserved at Paris, and finally under pressure
he left half his force before the walls of the "white city," while with
the other he advanced and captured the fortress of Badajoz. There he
paused of necessity, being falsely informed that Masséna, who had only
withdrawn toward Santarem, was in full retreat, but being correctly
notified that the portions of his own force left before Cadiz were not
able to hold their own. Having been virtually defeated in his attack on
Sir John Moore, his invasion of Portugal in 1809 had been temporarily
successful; but he had occupied Oporto only to conspire like Junot for
the crown of the country, and he had been driven out without difficulty
by the English. Made commander-in-chief after the empty victory of
Wellington at Talavera, he had won a great battle at Ocaña on November nineteenth, 1809; but since then his time had been virtually
wasted, for his bickerings with Joseph and his jealousy of Masséna
made all his successes, even this last one at Badajoz, entirely useless.
In a short time he returned to Cadiz, and the French before Lisbon
remained therefore without their auxiliaries.

Both these checks displeased Napoleon bitterly. It is often stated that it was because he felt contempt alike for the Spanish guerrillas and the English infantry that he delegated the conduct of affairs in the peninsula to his lieutenants. Quite the reverse appears to be the truth. Foy, Masséna's envoy, reached Paris about the end of November, and found the Emperor in something like a dull fury. His personal experience had now the confirmation of that undergone by Masséna and Soult, two of his greatest lieutenants. He had himself found the rugged and ill-cultivated country unable to support large armies. It was a discouraging fact that neither Soult nor Masséna had succeeded better than the great captain himself, and Napoleon was thus convinced that the Continental system could not be enforced against such dogged persistency as that of the unreasoning, disorganized, but courageous and frenzied Spaniards, assisted by the cold, calculating, and lucky Wellington: at least not without terrible cost in life and money. Accordingly Masséna was left without immediate reinforcement, while on December tenth, 1809, was promulgated the decree incorporating the North Sea coast into the Empire. Alexander chose to regard this fateful act as merely disrespectful, remonstrated with the French envoy at St. Petersburg, and sent a circular to the powers reserving the rights of his house over Oldenburg; he refused the petty indemnification of Erfurt offered by Napoleon, and a year later, in December, 1810, issued a ukase which laid prohibitive duties on French silks and wines, while at the same time it favored the "neutral" traffic in English wares. But at the moment he bore the affront without any menace of war, and merely called attention to the common obligations of friendship between sovereigns. If the breach were to occur, it must be plainly and manifestly Napoleon's doing.

Napoleon's failure to reinforce Masséna left the situation before Lisbon precarious. It cannot be proved that he understood all the difficulties in Wellington's position, but it is not unlikely that he did. Lisbon was overcrowded with fugitives, and demanded speedy relief by offensive operations. If Masséna had opened a bombardment from the opposite bank, its inhabitants would have risen in rebellion against the English general. The opposition party in Westminster used what seemed in England to be the perennial and everlasting delay of the younger brother as ground to attack the older one's conduct and to arraign the entire ministerial policy. The English people had heard of the Spanish insurrection with wild delight, but the inefficiency and stubbornness of the insurgent leaders, together with the untrustworthiness of the provisional governments, had cooled their ardor, and after the defeat at Ocaña — a battle which the vainglorious Spaniards had fought in direct opposition to Wellington's advice — they were loud in abuse of their allies. Lord Liverpool openly attacked Wellington, popular discontent was heightened by the opposition taunts, and it seemed for a time as if the ministry must abandon the expedition or fall.

But if Wellington required all the force of his will and the compulsion of a higher necessity to make him deaf to the clamor of his allies for an advance, Masséna had equal need for strength to sustain his forces, and to resist the clamor of his own generals for retreat. Foy finally brought back the necessary orders for reinforcements to come in from Castile; but, as a large proportion of the men stationed in that province existed merely on paper, only nine thousand could be spared from those who actually were there. Still Masséna stood like a rock. Wellington wrote home that with all his money, and assisted by the good will of the inhabitants, he could not have maintained one division where all the winter long Masséna found sustenance for sixty thousand men and twelve thousand beasts. This tribute to the campaigning powers of the French reveals incidentally the exaggerated conception of their strength entertained by the enemy.

The return of Soult to Cadiz emboldened Wellington to advance into Spain. After various movements on the part of both sides, Masséna was beaten at Fuentes de Onoro and Almeida was retaken by the English. Badajoz was beset by the English, and Soult once more advanced to its assistance. He, too, was defeated in a battle at Albuera, but succeeded finally in effecting a junction with Masséna, so that Wellington felt compelled to retreat again into Portugal before the united army. The exasperation of Napoleon at the failure of Masséna in the battle of Fuentes de Onoro led to the disgrace of the old marshal, and Marmont was sent to replace him. Such was the difficulty which the French experienced in securing commissary stores from an impoverished land that Wellington seemed content to let want fight his battles. The season of 1811 was marked by inactivity on both sides except in the east, where Suchet captured Aragon and Valencia, annihilating the Spanish army under Blake. But at the close of the year Soult was compelled to withdraw southward toward the coast, in the hope of securing indispensable supplies. The Spanish guerrillas of central Spain harassed the French soldiers and took the heart out of them. Wellington at once resumed the offensive; Ciudad Rodrigo fell before him on January twelfth, 1812, and on April eighth, after one of the bravest and bloodiest assaults recorded in English annals, Badajoz also was carried.

Marmont drew back for concentration, and the English advanced to the Duero. Thereupon the French turned again, Wellington retreated on Salamanca, and there made his stand, defeating his enemy on July twenty-second, in a brilliant engagement. The French commander then marched to Burgos, but his opponent, instead of following, turned toward Madrid, in order first to drive Joseph from his capital. By that time Burgos had been made so strong that all efforts to capture it proved unavailing. Soult at once abandoned Cadiz and turned northward to aid Joseph. The English were thus between two foes, and such was the demoralization of the British soldiery when they understood their danger that Wellington could with difficulty lead them back into Portugal. At the close of 1812 the French were in control of all Spain except the south, which had been freed by Soult's northward movement. Cadiz became the capital of the nationalists, but they could not restrain their revolutionary impulses long enough to form a respectable or trustworthy government, and Wellington was once more relegated to inactivity. His enforced leisure was occupied by the consideration of plans for the great successes with which he crowned the following season.

Viewed from a military standpoint, the French warfare in Spain appeared utterly disastrous. Regiments melted away like ice before an April sun; desertions became ominously numerous, and disease laid thousands low. Guerrilla warfare demoralized the regular forces. The new conscripts at first showed a noisy zeal, but they had been torn too young from their home nurture, and had neither strength nor power of resistance. The troops from vassal kingdoms and newly annexed territories were dismayed by the sufferings they had to endure, and beheld with interest the national uprising of the Spaniards, which, in spite of local jealousies, of rabid and radical doctrines that could lead to nothing but anarchy, of disastrous failure in government, of feebleness and falsehood in the temporary rulers, seemed likely to render of no avail the efforts and successes of a great Empire.

Yet in some respects the French character appeared in a stronger

AQUARELLE MADE IN 9. THE CENTURY CO.

THE CANTINIÈRE OF THE 26TH REGIMENT
CLIMBING THE ROCKS AT BUSACO

light throughout the disasters of the Peninsular war than at any other

time. Marbot's tale of the beautiful young cantinière, or woman sutler,
of the twenty-sixth regiment, who after Busaco rushed unhurt through
the English outposts in order to alleviate the sufferings of the captured
general of her brigade, and who returned on her donkey through the
lines without having suffered an insult, reflects equal credit on the
unselfish daring of the French, which she typified, and on the pure-
minded gallantry of the English. The same writer's narrative of the
French deserters who, under a leader nicknamed Marshal Stockpot,
established themselves as freebooters in a convent not far from Masséna's headquarters at Santarem, and of the general's swift, condign
punishment of such conduct, graphically delineates the straits of the
French, which led them into the extreme courses that devastated the
land, but it also displays the quality of the discipline which was exercised whenever possible. Nor should it be forgotten that the two
most splendid writers of France's succeeding age were profoundly
impressed with the terrible scenes of the French invasion of Spain.
George Sand was in Madrid as an infant for a considerable portion of
1808; Victor Hugo passed the year 1811 in a Madrid school, fighting
childish battles for "the great Emperor," whom his Spanish school-
mates called Napoladron (Napo the robber). Upon both the fact of
their connection with the repulse of Napoleon's armies left a profound
impression. The former was irresistibly drawn to revisit the country;
the latter recalled his impressions in some of his noblest verse.

CHAPTER XXIV

BIRTH OF THE KING OF ROME

ENGLAND UNDER THE CONTINENTAL SYSTEM—END OF CONSTITUTIONAL GOVERNMENT IN FRANCE—NAPOLEON'S PERSONAL RULE—WEALTH OF HIS HIGH OFFICIALS—LITERATURE AND THE EMPIRE—MME. DE STAËL'S ASPIRATIONS—HER ATTEMPTS TO WIN NAPOLEON—HER GENIUS SAVED BY DEFEAT—THE DECENNIAL PRIZES—PREGNANCY OF MARIA LOUISA—THE HEIR OF THE NAPOLEON DYNASTY.

IT would be idle to suppose that during the winter of 1810–11 the Spanish situation was not thoroughly appreciated by the imperial bridegroom at Paris, or that he underrated the ultimate effects of what was taking place in the Iberian peninsula if the process were to go on. Still less is it probable that with the direction of all his energy toward that quarter he could not have quenched the uncertain and spasmodic efforts of Spanish patriotism, either by arts of which he was a master, or by making a desert to call it a peace. No; every indication is that his eye was still fixed on England at her vital point, and that he took his measures in the North to deal her such a stab that the life-blood which sustained the Peninsular war would either flow inefficacious, or be turned away altogether from Spain, and change the ever-doubtful success of Wellington into assured disaster. Wealthy as England was, it was certain that her credit could not long hold out in view of the lavish subsidies she was constantly granting to Continental powers, while the expeditions to Spain, Holland, and Sicily were even more costly, inconclusive as they had so far been. In 1810 English bank-notes were twenty per cent. below par, and the sovereign could be exchanged on the Continent for only seventeen francs instead of the twenty-five it usually brought. Business failures were becoming ominously frequent in London, and panic was stalking abroad. What must be the necessary result if the Continental embargo were more thoroughly enforced? The enormous contraband trade of the North was now virtually at an end. Where English merchants had so far been able to secure at least half of the prices obtained from the consumers by smugglers, they could now no longer secure even that doubtful market at any price; the incorporation of Holland and the North Sea shores into France left virtually no opening into Europe for them except through Russia. The fate of England and of the world seemed to hang on how far the Czar could or would keep the engagements which he had made at Tilsit.

This might not have been so completely true if the French finances had been desperate; but they were not—that is, the Emperor's personal finances were not. After the legislative assembly met in December, 1809, it was soon clear to France that the farce of constitutional government under the Empire was nearly played out. Not only were the members of the senate, who should have retired according to the constitution, kept in their seats by a decree of the body to which they belonged, but an imperial edict appointed the deputies for the new departments without even the form of an election. Fontanes retired from the presidency of the senate to become grand master of the university; the grand chamberlain of the palace was appointed in his stead. The Emperor had already sold to private corporations the canals which belonged to the state; the legislature ratified the illegal act. The penal code was now ready. It contained the iniquitous and dangerous penalty of confiscation for certain crimes, thus punishing the children for the faults of their sires, and opening a most tempting avenue to the courts for indulgence in venality under legal forms. There was little debate, and the code was adopted in its entirety as presented.

The reason for this paralysis of constitutional government is clear. Even the immense war indemnities taken from conquered states did not suffice for the maintenance of the enormous armies which covered Europe like swarms of locusts. The marshals and generals were insatiate, and the greed of the civil administrators was scarcely less. From the top to the bottom of the public service every official stood with open hand and hungry eyes. This state of things was directly due to Napoleon's policy of attaching everybody to himself by personal ties, and in giving he had the lavish hand of a parvenu. The recipients were never content, hoarding their fees, and becoming opulent, pursuing

all the time each his personal ambitions, and ofttimes returning inso-
lence for favors. To meet these enormous expenditures there had been
inaugurated throughout Europe a system of what may be termed private confiscations, the vast dimensions of which can never be justly
estimated. German princes and Spanish grandees, English merchants
and the Italian clergy, had all been wrung dry; timorous statesmen,
crafty churchmen and sly contractors, unprincipled financiers and ambitious politicians, not one was forgotten or overlooked in the accumulation of hoards which, having long been called the army chest, were
now erected into the dignity of an "extraordinary domain."

Kept so far in a decent obscurity, these ill-gotten possessions, which
belonged, if not to their original owners, then to the state, were, in the
low condition of public morality, not merely recognized—they were actually increased from new sources of supply. The confiscated palaces,
forests, lands, and fisheries, the proceeds from the sale of American ships,
values of every kind, were all made the private property of the Emperor. If any of these rills of revenue should run dry, the criminal code
with its legislation of confiscation might be relied on to supply a menace strong enough to express inexhaustible treasure from storehouses
yet untouched. One orator declared this barbaric fund to have been in
the Emperor's hands a "French Providence, which made the laurel a
fertile tree, the fruits of which had nourished the brave whom its
branches covered." Napoleon had found the crown moneys sufficient
for himself. Berthier now had a revenue of one million three hundred
and fifty thousand eight hundred francs, and Davout was scarcely less
regal with one of nine hundred and ten thousand; Ney had only seven
hundred and twenty-eight thousand, and Masséna five hundred thousand; Soult was ambitious to increase his income of three hundred and
five thousand by securing the Portuguese crown. What with the great
public charities endowed from this extraordinary fund, what with the
great public works in Paris and elsewhere which had been carried on
by its means, the total expenditures had been more than four hundred
and thirty million francs. The total receipts had risen to about seven
hundred and sixty millions, and there were therefore still in the Emperor's purse upward of three hundred millions. He could not be
called destitute or even poor.

The same years which saw the extinction of the remnants of legislative independence saw likewise the establishment of six state prisons,

MARSHAL NICOLAS-JEAN-DE-DIEU SOULT
DUKE OF DALMATIA

in which were to be confined those disaffected persons who were too powerful to be left at liberty, but whose trials in open court would have revealed troublesome facts. The censorship of the press was likewise reëstablished with iron rigidity, and the publishers purchased the meager immunities they were permitted to enjoy by the payment of whatever pensions the Emperor chose to grant to needy men of letters. Chénier the poet, Bernardin de Saint-Pierre, the author of "Paul and Virginia," and others enjoyed, in addition to decorations of the Legion of Honor, substantial incomes that were virtually paid by their fellow-craftsmen; while a chosen few—including Gros, Gérard, Guérin, Lagrange, Monge, and Laplace—were elevated to the new baronage. Even Carnot did not hesitate to accept employment and place from Napoleon. At first he solicited a loan for the relief of his urgent necessities. This the Emperor made unnecessary by ordering the War Office to pay all arrears in his rations and other perquisites, by giving him a commission to prepare a volume on fortification, and by according him a pension of ten thousand francs. The ponderous sledge-hammer of the censorship was apparently forged to kill a gnat. Nothing is known to the history of literature so subservient and humble as the conduct of the great majority of French writers and artists under the Empire.

There was one exception — Mme. de Staël. That overestimated woman had gained the halo of martyrdom by the so-called persecution of the Emperor. But the persecution was, in the opinion of keen observers, more on her part than his. The Committee of Public Safety had found her an intriguer, and had called upon her husband to remove her from Paris; the Directory kept her under watch at Coppet, and ordered her arrest should she return to France. Her aspirations were boundless, and Mallet du Pan, royalist agent, said that she shamelessly flaunted her charms on public occasions. In 1796, aspiring to rule the country through her friends, she wrote to Bonaparte, who was in Italy, that the widow Beauharnais was far from possessing the necessary qualities to supplement those of a genius such as he was, and on his return to Paris she at once made suspicious advances to win his favor. Bourrienne declares that he saw one of her letters to Bonaparte, in which she flatly stated that they two, she herself and her correspondent, had been created for each other. Mention has elsewhere been made of the coldness with which Bonaparte treated her when by her own request she was presented to him in Talleyrand's drawing-room. Not long afterward, at the reception given by the Minister of Foreign Affairs to the conqueror of Italy, the indefatigable seeker for notoriety addressed the latter once again.

The scene is given in the memoirs of Arnault. At first she plied her suit with fulsome compliment. Bonaparte listened coldly, and the conversation flagged. In despair she blurted out, "General, what woman could you love the most?" "My own," was the stinging reply. ("Quelle femme?" "La mienne.") Woman and wife being the same word in French, Napoleon's retort was a disdainful pun. "Very well; but which would you esteem the highest?" she persisted. "The best housekeeper." "Yes, I understand; but which one would be for you the foremost among women?" "She who should bear the most children, madame," was the icy rejoinder, as the harried and disgusted soldier turned on his heel. Somewhat later she said to Lucien in a melting voice, "I am but a fool in my desire to please your brother. I am at a loss when I wish to converse with him. I choose my language and modify my expressions; I want to make him think of me and occupy himself with me. It ends in my being and feeling as silly as a goose." When the complacent Lucien reported the language his brother replied: "I know her thoroughly. . . . She declared to one who informed me that since I would neither love her nor permit her to love me, there was nothing left but for her to hate me, as she could not remain indifferent. What a virago!" In a letter to Joseph, dated March nineteenth, 1800, the future Emperor wrote: "M. de Staël is in the depths of misery, and his wife is giving dinners and balls. If you should continue to see her, would it not be well to have the woman allow her husband one thousand or one thousand two hundred francs a month? Have we already reached a time when, without any protest from decent people, not merely morality but the most sacred ties which bind children to their parents can be trampled under foot? Suppose we judge Mme. de Staël as we should a man,—only, of course, as a man inheriting the fortune of M. de Necker,—one who had long enjoyed the prerogatives of a distinguished name, and who should leave his wife in misery while he lived in abundance: could we associate with a man like that?"

Soon afterward the battle of Marengo was fought. All her passion being now turned into hate, the scheming woman openly desired Bonaparte's defeat. Thenceforward she was an avowed and bitter enemy; he would have called her a conspirator. The ten years of her banishment, as she herself declared, were occupied in wandering from court to court in England, Russia, Prussia, and Sweden, engaged in the task of undermining the Emperor's name and fame, and in fomenting the coalitions which eventually ruined him. As Bonaparte became an ultra-imperialist she became an ultra-liberal. Her book on Germany, published in 1810, was a laudation, in the main just and fair, of a regenerated land; but it held up to France as a model the achievements of the country which was now her bitterest foe. The censors gave it a fictitious renown by ordering its complete suppression.

When, in November, 1810, the decennial prizes, instituted as a spur to literature and science, were distributed, the judges could find nothing in science later than 1803 worthy of their favor; but the prize-winners, old as they were, were all men of real distinction. The names of the literary men who were crowned are now known only to the student of history. Napoleon demanded why the name of Chateaubriand had been omitted from the list, as it was. He may have remembered, as one of his detractors suggests, that in that writer's great book the Roman doctrine of obedience to constituted authority was attractively presented; or else, and more probably, he may have wished his list of authors to be more brilliant. The Emperor may have instituted those prizes, as his apologists declared he himself said that he did, to keep active minds from occupying themselves with politics; but the exhibition of how the Empire had crushed out originality and fecundity in the French brain must have appalled him, whatever were his thoughts.

During the winter of 1810-11 Napoleon's private life was virtually devoted to beneficence. In addition to the favors granted to Carnot, he lavished money on other objects, some not so worthy. Canova, who had been called from Rome to make a portrait-statue of the Empress, obtained a substantial grant for the learned societies of that city. Chénier, like Carnot, had been a pronounced adversary of the Empire. He now sought employment under it, and was made inspector-general of the university, an office which he did not live long to enjoy. All the old favorites were remembered in a general distribution of good things. Talleyrand having just lost an immense sum by the failure of a trusted bank, the Emperor came to his relief by purchasing one of his minister's most splendid palaces for more than two million francs. The court resided sometimes at St. Cloud, sometimes at Rambouillet, sometimes at the Trianon, but for the most part at Fontainebleau, where the ceremonious life, to which all concerned were now well accustomed, was marked by none of the old awkwardness and friction, but ran as brilliantly as lavish expenditure could make it. The pregnancy of the Empress was celebrated with great festivities, during which Napoleon performed one of his most applauded acts—the endowment of a vast maternity hospital. The Empress was brought into great prominence as the president of a society consisting of a thousand noble ladies under whose patronage the charity was placed.

The unconcealed and ecstatic delight of the prospective father found vent in delicate and tender attention to the mother of his child, and until her deliverance he was a gentle, devoted, and considerate husband. His whole nature seemed transformed. When in the early morning of March twentieth, 1811, word was brought that the Empress was in labor, and that a false presentation made it of instant necessity to choose between the life of the mother and that of the child, the feelings of the Emperor can better be imagined than described. If the expected heir should die his dynasty would be jeopardized, his enemies would once more be making appointments over his grave, the hopes of a lifetime might be shattered. But there was not a moment's wavering. "Think only of the mother," he cried. The fears of the attending physician were vain, after all, and the man-child, coming without a cry into the world and lying breathless for seven minutes as if hesitating to accept or decline his destiny, finally gave a wail as at last he caught the breath of life. Napoleon turned, caught up his treasure, and pressed it to his bosom. A hundred guns announced the birth, and the city burst into jubilations, which were reëchoed throughout Europe from Dantzic to Cadiz. Festival succeeded festival, and for an interval men believed that the temple of Janus would be again closed. No boy ever came on the earthly stage amid such splendors, or seemed destined to honors such as appeared to await this one. The devotion of the father was passionate and unwavering. It lasted even after he had been deserted and betrayed by the mother, after the child had been estranged and turned into an Austrian prince.

CHAPTER XXV

TENSION BETWEEN EMPEROR AND CZAR

MENACES OF WAR — NAPOLEON'S "EXTRAORDINARY DOMAIN" — RUPTURE
OF THE CONCORDAT — THE PROSPECT OF WAR — THE EMPIRE PRE-
PARED FOR A COMMERCIAL SIEGE — NAPOLEON'S SELF-DECEPTION —
THE EMPIRES OF OCEAN AND CONTINENT — THE CZAR'S HUMILIA-
TION — POLAND AND THE FRENCH EMPIRE — ALEXANDER'S APPROACH
TO FRANCIS — SPURIOUS NEGOTIATIONS.

AMONG other bodies which sent deputations to congratulate the
Emperor on the birth of his child was the Paris Chamber of
Commerce. Their address was sufficiently adulatory, but it contained
a suggestion that the trade and commerce of the country were not all
that could be desired. Napoleon replied in language which attracted
attention throughout Europe. There was some irritability in his tone,
but there was an unqualified assurance with regard to the future. He
said, among other things, that England was depressed. This was true;
the new measures taken to enforce the Continental system had told.
British harbors were glutted with the products of all the colonies — not
only of her own, but of those she had seized during the Napoleonic
wars. The storehouses could hold no more; and as colonial trade was
conducted by barter, all the products of English industry must remain
at home for lack of an export market. Business was at a standstill,
and the specter of English bankruptcy stalked abroad. As to France,
the Emperor declared that he was in no sense the successor of either
Louis XIV. or Louis XV., but of Charles the Great; for the present
Empire was but the continuation of the old Frankish dominion. In four
years, he said in substance, I shall have a navy. When my fleets shall
have been three or four years at sea we can hold our own with the
English. I know I may lose three or four battles; very good, I will

lose them. But we are ever courageous, ever booted and spurred, and we shall succeed. Before ten years have expired I shall have beaten England. No state of Europe will any longer have intercourse with her. It is my custom-houses which do the greatest harm to the English. Her blockade has injured herself the most by teaching us how to get on without her products, her sugar, her indigo. A few years longer, and we shall be thoroughly accustomed to it. I shall soon have enough beet-root sugar to supply all Europe; for your manufactures there is an open market in France, Italy, Naples, and Germany. At the close he added words to this effect: The Bank of France is full of silver, while that of England has not a white sou [five francs]. Since 1806 I have taken over a milliard francs in contributions. I alone have money. Austria is already bankrupt, and Russia and England will be. There exist three versions of this famous allocution. In one of them are the words: "I showed mercy to the Emperor of Russia at Tilsit in return for promises of help; but if those promises are not kept, I will go, if need be, to Riga, to Moscow, to St. Petersburg."

Three points of the utmost significance demand attention in this, a typical deliverance of the "imperator," uttered at the flood-tide of imperial success: two of them, both negative, are ominous; the third is positive and plain. There is no reference to the financial condition of France, or to the ecclesiastical situation. Russia was openly threatened. The boast of wealth referred to Napoleon's own "extraordinary domain." About this time Metternich reported to his government that France was the richest country in Europe, but that her treasury was empty. The budget of 1811 had nine hundred millions on the credit side, but it had also nine hundred and fifty-four millions on the debit. The previous year had required five hundred and ten millions for army and navy, the present required six hundred and fifty millions. It was a fixed principle of the Emperor to make each generation pay its own expenses. The only source of supply he could find was an increase of the indirect taxes and the institution of a state monopoly in tobacco. His remedy would have been adequate but for two causes — the drought of the ensuing summer and Russia's hostile attitude in regard to French silks and wines. The year 1811 closed with a deficit of forty-eight millions. This fact had a bearing on the political situation because in general the Emperor's remedy for an empty treasury was a new war.

The ecclesiastical situation had now become acute. As one bishop-ric after another had fallen vacant, bishops had been nominated by the Emperor; but the Pope, who was still sitting in captivity at Savona, had from the moment of his incarceration steadily refused to institute them. For a time, as has been explained, the difficulty had been ingeniously avoided by the process of ecclesiastical law, according to which the chapters of the various dioceses elected the imperial candidates as vicars capitular, and thus enabled them to perform episcopal functions without regard to institution. But this could not go on forever, and every effort had been made to induce the prisoner of Savona to yield. In response he took a firmer stand, and indicated to the chapters both of Italy and France that they should no longer elect the imperial nominees as vicars capitular. This was, and was so regarded by Napoleon, a rupture of the Concordat. The attitude of all pious Catholics was becoming uneasy, and this new declaration of war by the Church could only serve to heighten the bellicose humor of the Emperor. The Pope was eventually brought to terms, partly by increasing the rigors of his imprisonment, partly by terrorizing his agents in France, but chiefly through the representations made to him by the ablest ecclesiastics of the realm, and by the summoning of a church council, which turned out nearly as subservient to the secular authority as the Jewish Sanhedrim had been.

With reference to the third point, it seems impossible to determine whether the menace to Russia was actually made, as one version of the reply has it, or whether a later speech at the opening of the legislature in June, and the report on the situation of France issued in the same month, have not both been confused with the Emperor's talk in March. In either case the result was identical, for France and Europe instinctively took in the situation, and clearly understood that the Emperor was not indisposed toward the renewal of war in northern Europe. This third point was of course the most noteworthy of the three, for it could be only a question of time when the storm should burst.

If it were possible at that epoch of the world's history to distinguish between Napoleon the man and Napoleon the embodied political force of Europe, the aspect of the former would abound in human interest. Filled with paternal tenderness, his sole ambition appeared for a time to be that of retaining what he had gained, the leadership of a Western empire as splendid as that of Charles the Great. To make sure of this acquisition and hand it on to his heir, he seems for a moment to have dreamed of standing forth as the pacificator of Europe. He actually withdrew the mass of his troops from Germany for use in Spain, leaving only enough to watch Prussia and guard Westphalia; with the former power he finally formulated his pecuniary demands, as if thus to put an end to strife. The "rebellion" in Spain he intended to crush out by the pacific operations of a commercial warfare with England, which he felt certain would bring Great Britain to terms, now that for the first time since the outbreak of hostilities the blood of her soldiers "was flowing in a stream." He was probably strengthened in this conviction by the reluctant consent of the cabinet of St. James to open negotiations for the exchange of prisoners on the very basis he had suggested long before. Believing, moreover, that European princes had by this time lost their delicate sensibility, it seemed no monstrous crime to consolidate his Empire for its commercial siege by the simple expedient of removing the Duke of Oldenburg from his hereditary domains which bordered on the ocean and offering him the inland sovereignty of Erfurt, or by adopting the alternative expedient of leaving him to enjoy the former under French protection. It seems presumptuous to attempt any revelation of his feelings, but surely he might hope that then, controlling every inlet to European commerce from Corfu around by Triest, Italy, Spain, and the Texel as far as Lübeck, his wall of protection for French manufactures would do its work, that in a few years France would be the industrial and commercial center of continental Europe. With Paris the capital of a new Western empire, the true relation between the secular and ecclesiastical heads of the world would be reëstablished, as it could not be while the papacy had its seat at Rome, and all things would work together under a strong hand to humble the island empire of England, destroy her ascendancy on the mainland, and thus bring in a moral and material millennium for the civilized world.

But alas for such self-deception, if, indeed, it ever existed. Nature is too complex and habit too strong for such sudden sublimations of purpose. Had the true, complex Napoleon in his supposed communing asked the question, What then? sincerity would have compelled him to reply, More beyond. Men remembered to have heard him use the expression "Emperor of the Continent" in these very days, jocularly, perhaps, but still with significance. Orders were issued in March, 1811, to fit out vessels for two expeditions, one against Sicily and

ALEXANDER I
EMPEROR OF RUSSIA

Egypt, one against Ireland; if these were successful he could then
work his will at the Cape of Good Hope and ultimately in the East
and West Indies. "They want to know where we are going, where I
shall plant the new pillars of Hercules," he said. "We will make an
end of Europe, and then, as robbers fling themselves on others less
bold, we will fling ourselves on India, which the latter class have mas-
tered." About the same time the Bavarian minister, pleading for
peace, received the retort: "Three years more, and I am lord of the
universe." When Mollien advised against war, on account of the fiscal
disorders, the reply was: "On the contrary, the finances are falling
into disorder, and for that very reason need war." Behind Napoleon
the father was the ambitious and haughty statesman combined with
the self-reliant general, the embodiment of French ambitions as they
had consolidated in the old régime, and had been transmitted through
the Revolution, the Directory, and the Consulate, to the Empire.

But there were two other gladiators in the arena: England, hard
pressed but still undaunted in her mastery of the seas which flowed
around her majestic colonial empire; Russia, grimly determined to hold
an even balance with France in Europe while reëstablishing by the
overthrow of Turkey the eastern counterpoise to Napoleon's western
dominion. The Czar of Muscovy would fain have passed for a philosopher. Fourteen years earlier, when in his eighteenth year, he had
fallen under the charm of Prince Adam Czartoryski, a youth of about
his own age, whom the Empress Catherine had taken as a hostage after the final dismemberment of Poland in 1795. Trained by his grandmother to play her own rôle of enlightened despot, the young ruler,
still in those early years when generous impulses rule, conversed with
his friend, the representative of a downtrodden land, about the possibility of a restored and regenerated Poland, avowing his secret detes-
tation of all that he was compelled in public to profess. We may picture
the joy of the noble Pole at the thought of his country made whole
once more, even though it were destined to be but semi-autonomous as
a member of the Russian empire. But years rolled by, and Czartoryski,
though preferred to place and honor by the Czar, heard less and less of
the young philosopher's scheme. In 1805 he finally wrung from Alexander a promise that he would begin to act; but it was very soon
withdrawn, and Czartoryski retired to his estates. The realities and
selfishness of life eclipsed the man of sensibility and developed the des-

pot. For a time, however, he essayed the rôle of European mediator, with what success Tilsit is the witness.

Disgusted from the practical point of view with the old dynasties and their chicanery, Alexander had not only eschewed the idea of a reconstructed Poland, but had become indifferent to the territorial lines of all ancient Europe, and momentarily dreamed of Napoleon as his twin emperor. To this end he too must likewise be a conqueror. Finland he had gained, but at the price of adhesion to a commercial system which was gradually ruining his people. The exhausting, slow-moving war with Turkey was still dragging on, and neither Moldavia nor Wallachia was yet acquired. Oldenburg was incorporated in France. The grand duchy of Warsaw was not merely the specter of a restored Poland: the addition of Galicia to its territories had given it solidity and substance. The Franco-Austrian alliance was a menace to all the Czar's aspirations on the Balkan peninsula. It was clear that he must choose between keeping his engagements to the letter and an open rupture. He had been beaten and humiliated at his own game.

The first steps toward a rupture had already been taken before Napoleon's second marriage. In the last days of 1809 Alexander had negotiated with Caulaincourt, the French ambassador at St. Petersburg, a treaty requiring from his ally a formal promise that Poland should never be restored and the name never officially used. It is certain, from the language used at the time, that the two questions of Poland and the Russian marriage were not connected; the former he could raise merely as an ally with a just expectation of a favorable reply. It is of course possible that Alexander hoped Napoleon might connect them, and thus sign the Polish treaty in the hope that his request for the grand duchess would be granted as a return. In that case the Russian emperor could still have refused his sister's hand, putting his ally's compliance in regard to Poland on the ground of existing political relations. He might then have laughed in his sleeve at his outwitted dupe. Be that as it may, Napoleon was the craftier. He replied that he would sign, not this document, but one slightly different, though quite as satisfactory to Russia. Accordingly he drew up, executed, and forwarded to Russia a counter-project promising "never to give help or assistance to any power, or to any internal rising whatsoever, looking to a restoration of the kingdom of Poland." A few days after its arrival at St. Petersburg came the news of the Austrian marriage.

Two courses were now open to the Czar. One was to take advantage of the strong Russian party which existed among the Poles in Warsaw, promise a restoration of Poland with himself as king, and enter on an offensive campaign against France. This scheme is contained in an extant letter addressed to him by Prince Galitzin. The other was to negotiate further and await events. After dallying for a time with the former idea, the Czar at length told Czartoryski that he could never consider giving up provinces already incorporated in Russia,—which meant of course that he would not restore the integrity of Poland,—but that he might accept the crown of the grand duchy of Warsaw as it was, including Galicia. Secret agents were thereupon despatched to sound the Austrian court. If the partition of Turkey should take place, as was already determined, could not Russia and Austria join hands to secure each her own interests against France? In view of the fact that Napoleon had rejected the idea of destroying Turkey because Russia had displayed jealousy of Austria and had refused her any share in the Turkish lands, this was a virtual declaration of hostilities.

Alexander's overture was unheeded at Vienna, at least for the moment, because Metternich was in Paris wooing Napoleon's good will. Simultaneously and openly, therefore, the fencing between Paris and St. Petersburg went on. A rejoinder to the counter-project was laid on Napoleon's desk, containing the identical words "that the kingdom of Poland shall never be restored." This persistence angered the recipient, and seemed capable of but one interpretation. If Alexander did not consider the guarantees given by France after Friedland and Wagram to be sufficient, could Napoleon see in this reiterated demand anything more or less than a determination of the Czar not to abide by the engagements of Russia unless new ones were given by himself? He returned therefore a softly worded, non-committal reply, and began to make unmistakable preparations: a journey to Flanders for the purpose of rousing public opinion on his behalf, the strengthening of certain fortresses, and a general rapprochement to Austria in all his relations. The negotiations continued a little longer, Russia insisting on the phrase as first written, France declaring that its use would be a confession of the insinuation contained in it, and therefore incompatible with her dignity. Any other equivalent language she would use, but not that.

CHAPTER XXVI

THE ARRAY OF NATIONS

ESTRANGEMENT OF FRANCE AND RUSSIA — PREMONITIONS OF WAR — ALEXANDER'S SECRET POLICY — THE VARIOUS FACTORS IN THE SITUATION — BERNADOTTE — THE EVE OF A GENERAL CONFLAGRATION — ENGLAND AND PRUSSIA — AUSTRIA AND PRUSSIA — ALLIANCE BETWEEN SWEDEN AND RUSSIA — ENGLAND AND THE UNITED STATES — THE CONFEDERATION OF THE RHINE — THE STATE OF FRANCE.

MEANWHILE Metternich, confident that in the partition of Turkey better terms could be obtained for Austria from Napoleon than from Alexander, was doing his utmost to embitter the relations of France and Russia. A strong Russian party in Vienna was in close touch with the numerous Poles in Warsaw who looked to Alexander for the restoration of their country's integrity. In both places there was much talk of the restoration of Poland, in Warsaw especially, and the phrase was constantly in the newspapers. Alexander's ambassador in Paris made urgent representations concerning "a persistent rumor that the Emperor intends to restore Poland." Napoleon retorted in fury, and threatened war, but immediately wrote a soothing assurance that he was still true to the engagements of Tilsit, and as to the treaty itself he would agree to changes, but would never brand his own memory with dishonor. On July first, while the lines were in the copyist's hands, there occurred the incident which many thought at the time changed the course of history. During a magnificent festival given by the Austrian ambassador, the decorations in an open court took fire, and the conflagration spread, enveloping the entire embassy. All the important guests escaped unhurt except Kourakine, the Russian ambassador, who was so injured that he could no longer perform his official duties. It appeared to throw a strong light on Napoleon's character as a man that almost immediately his humor seemed to change; his personal obligations to the much-abused but well-bred envoy could not now be wiped out by a gentle reply to the master; hence, apparently, he curtly dismissed the Russian chargé d'affaires, and ended the negotiation. It was when this news reached St. Petersburg that Alexander a second time offered Norway to Sweden.

The real cause of Napoleon's abrupt manner was the news communicated by Metternich that the Russian army had advanced successfully to the Danube. On July seventeenth Francis despatched an envoy requesting his new son-in-law to join him in a protest against the aggressions of the Czar; in other words, to throw the agreements of Tilsit and Erfurt to the winds. Napoleon returned an unhesitating and honorable refusal, but said significantly to Metternich: "If Russia quarrels with us she will lose Finland, Moldavia, and Wallachia," adding that if the Czar, contrary to his engagement of 1808, should seize anything south of the Danube, then he himself would intervene on Austria's behalf. But all Europe seemed convinced that war was inevitable. In all the watering-places the talk was of nothing else. The Russian party in Vienna grew bolder; Pozzo di Borgo, Napoleon's lifelong foe, who had been temporarily under a cloud in Russia, appeared in Vienna in his Russian uniform, courted and oracular. A French interpreter on his way to Persia was stopped by him, and bribed to enter the Russian service. In a terse personal note written by his own hand, Napoleon called Alexander's attention to the facts, but without awaiting the reply he went further. Kourakine, partly recovered, was leaving Paris for home. Through him the Emperor poured into his ally's ear a long exposure of the situation, saying in substance that war was to be avoided, that he had not the slightest intention of restoring Poland, and that if the Czar would write what was desired as a guarantee in the form of a newspaper article, the words should be inserted unchanged in the "Moniteur." At the same time orders were sent commanding Caulaincourt to end all negotiation, and the Poles were peremptorily enjoined to silence. Simultaneously schemes for a new naval campaign were gradually being perfected, so that they might be realized the following year.

Something of Alexander's secret diplomacy must have leaked out, but he appeared unmoved. He was steadily preparing for war, strengthening his fortresses, and locating fortified camps in the district between the Dwina and the Dnieper. But his chief concern was with Poland. Relying on the Jesuit influence at Warsaw for support against the jailer of the Pope, he again took up his old scheme of restoring the country as an appanage of the Russian crown, and wrote to Czartoryski. The plan was dazzling: a national army, a national administration, and a liberal constitution. But that nobleman, after a long residence in his native land, had learned how strong was the conviction of his countrymen that Napoleon would give them a more complete autonomy than the Czar, and sent back what must have been a discouraging reply, although it has never been found. Alexander on its receipt determined that the coming war should be defensive on his part, and immediately opened communications with England and Sweden concerning the Continental system. Finally, in the closing days of the year, he issued a ukase excluding wines, silks, and similar luxuries from France, but facilitating the entry of the colonial wares in which England dealt. This was an act of open hostility to his old ally, a declaration of commercial war. Prussia immediately made semi-official advances to the Czar, but they were repelled.

It is not easy to estimate Napoleon's responsibility for what had happened and was about to happen. He was persistently domineering, contemptuous of national feeling and dynastic politics, over-confident in the unswerving devotion of France, inflexible in his policy of territorial aggrandizement, ruthless in applying his peculiar conceptions of finance and political economy, and pitiless in his own self-seeking. On the other hand, Alexander, having received Prussia's autonomy as his part, had proved an untrustworthy ally from the outset. Having seized Finland, he would not pay the price, but first evaded the Continental system, then rejected it, and finally declared commercial war on France; in the latest conflict between France and Austria he had actually wooed the latter's favor. Procrastinating in the marriage affair, he was furious when the suppliant turned elsewhere, and at once displayed an insulting mistrust concerning Poland; finally, he declared diplomatic war by his overtures to England and his secret machinations in Vienna; there was but a final step in the evolution of complete hostility, the declaration of military war. Austria, too, had done her utmost to bring on a conflict, hoping to find her account in the dissensions of the two empires. Her policy demanded her territorial aggrandizement at the expense of Turkey; in a war between France and

Russia she was sure to find her account, and there was nothing in Metternich's dealings with Napoleon which tended to preserve the peace of Europe.

Sweden, under Bernadotte, was manifestly anxious to find a cause of offense, being defiant in temper, and ready to do anything for the purpose of strengthening the hands of Alexander and escaping from French protection. So feeble was the titular King of Sweden that the adoptive crown prince speedily became the real ruler, and his personal desires were soon the public policy. It was a strange transformation which took place in the man. He had been generous and kindly in the difficult positions he held as a French general. Avowedly a revolutionary democrat of the most radical stripe, he was nevertheless a true Gascon and failed to display his great abilities wherever his heart was not engaged. He had, moreover, basked in the sunshine of imperial favor, and in an age of atheism had remained in the fold of the Roman Church. Having himself schemed against Napoleon under the promptings of personal ambition, he often gave aid and comfort to the Emperor's enemies. When adopted into the royal family of Sweden it cost him little effort to profess Lutheranism; his republican sympathies were quenched, and he developed into a beneficent despot anxious to put Sweden in line with Russia. He never was able to win the affections of his people, and when before the close of his life they demanded a liberal constitution, this democratic sovereign, brought up under the illumination of French revolutionary doctrines, held back until the paper had to be wrung from him. The phases of Napoleon's life are scarcely more startling than those of this rather commonplace actor on a stage which was provincial when compared with the cosmopolitan scene of the Emperor's life-drama.

In the spring of 1811 all Europe knew that war was inevitable. "It will occur," wrote Napoleon on April second of that year, " in spite of me, in spite of the Emperor Alexander, in spite of the interests of France and those of Russia. I have already so often seen this that it is my experience of the past which unveils to me the future. . . . It is all a scene in an opera, and the English control the machinery." A week later he notified Alexander that he was aware of the movement of Russian troops toward Poland, and declared that he himself was likewise preparing. Lauriston was sent to replace the too pacific Caulaincourt at St. Petersburg, and Champagny was removed from the Foreign Office to make way for the fiery Maret. There was much to be done before the actual outbreak of hostilities. England's history is the story of her struggles for nationality, for religious, civil, and political liberty, and for mercantile ascendancy. Her inborn longings for the highest civilization were not inconsistent with her grim determination to resist a system that stood on the Continent for progress, but which she had come to believe meant national ruin for her. Prussia, with a new vigor born of self-denial, education, and passionate patriotism; Sweden, restless and uneasy under the yoke of Napoleonic supremacy; Denmark, friendly, but independent in her quasi-autonomy; the United States, chafing under the restrictions of her commerce; Turkey, sick to death, but then as now pivotal in all European politics — the relation of all these powers to the coming conflict was still a question, and during a year much might be done in a diplomatic way to determine it. The whole civilized world was to be in array, although the life-and-death struggle was to be between two insatiate despotisms, one Western and modern, the other Oriental and theocratic. Napoleon grasped the tendency of his own career but dimly. Goethe said of him, "He lives entirely in the ideal, but can never consciously grasp it." Unconsciously, too, Alexander the Great had fought for the extension of Greek culture; Cæsar, to destroy the stifling institutions of a worn-out system; Charles the Great, to realize the "city of God" on earth; Napoleon for nationality, individual liberty, popular sovereignty. What was personal and petty in the work of these Titans, being ephemeral, disappeared in the death of each; what was human and large has endured and will endure. The creative ideas of the revolutionary era with which Napoleon's name is so closely connected are no longer called in question; his own career was now verging to its decline, but in his fall the fundamental conceptions of the epoch were firmly established.

In January, 1812, Wellington, as has been mentioned, stormed Ciudad Rodrigo; on April sixth Badajoz fell. On April eighteenth Napoleon offered terms of peace, Spain to be kept intact under Joseph, Portugal to be restored to the house of Braganza, Sicily to remain under Ferdinand, and Naples under Murat. Considering all the circumstances, the offer was worthy of consideration; but the English cabinet refused it. The possibility of peace with Great Britain being thus extinguished, Napoleon considered what course he should pursue toward

MARIA LOUISA AND THE KING OF R

the other great Protestant land, which also felt itself to be struggling for life. Some well-informed persons asserted that at first the Emperor contemplated destroying the Hohenzollern power utterly. If so, he quickly dismissed the idea as involving unnecessary risk. With the reforms of Stein and Hardenberg successfully accomplished, with her educational system completed and her army reorganized, with her people electrified at last into true patriotism, Prussia was again a redoubtable power. Her influence permeated all Germany, and the secret associations which ramified everywhere labored for German unity, their members already dreaming of the Jura, Vosges, and Ardennes as the western frontier of their fatherland. At first Frederick William made overtures to the Czar, offering an army of a hundred thousand men. Alexander, desiring a purely defensive war, was cold; but late in 1811 he agreed, in case of an attack on Prussia, to advance as far as the Vistula, "if possible."

Meantime Austria had at first contemplated neutrality, but she abandoned the policy when convinced that, whichever side should be victorious, Prussia would be dismembered. Francis saw Alexander's continued successes on the Danube with growing anxiety, and, learning that Napoleon would put four hundred thousand men into the field, made up his mind that France must win. Accordingly, in March, 1812, a treaty was executed which put thirty thousand Austrian troops under Napoleon's personal command, and stipulated for Austria's enlargement by Galicia, Illyria, and even Silesia, in certain contingencies. During these negotiations Frederick William had learned how stupendous Napoleon's preparations were, and, with some hesitancy, he finally sent Scharnhorst to sound Austria. The result was determinative, and on February twenty-fourth, 1812, a treaty between France and Prussia was signed, which gave Prussia nothing, but exacted from her twenty thousand men for active service, with forty-two thousand for garrison duty, and afforded the French armies free course through her territories, with the right to charge up such requisitions as were made against the war indemnity. To this pass Alexander's narrowness had brought the proud, regenerated nation; its temper can be imagined.

French diplomacy, triumphant elsewhere, was utterly unsuccessful with Sweden. Alexander offered Norway as the price of alliance, with hints of the crown of France for Bernadotte somewhere in the dim future. Napoleon temptingly offered Finland for forty thousand Swedish soldiers. But the new crown prince was seemingly coy, and dallied with both. This temporizing was brought to a sudden end in January, 1812, when Davout occupied Swedish Pomerania. On April twelfth the alliance between Sweden and Russia was sealed. It carried with it an armistice between Russia and Great Britain. This was essential to the Czar, for he would be compelled to withdraw his troops from the Danube for service in the North, and to that end must make some arrangement with Turkey. He offered the most favorable terms; Napoleon, on the other hand, demanded a hundred thousand men if he were to restore to the Sublime Porte all it had lost. England threatened to bombard Constantinople if there should be too much hesitancy, and on May twenty-eighth, 1812, the Sultan closed a bargain with Russia which gave him the Pruth as a frontier.

In spite of Turkey's submission, Great Britain was not to be left passive. The neutrality of the United States had, on the whole, been successfully maintained, but their commerce suffered. On May first, 1810, Congress enacted that trade with Great Britain should be forbidden if France revoked her decrees, and vice versa. Madison and the Republicans believed that this would relieve the strain under which farmers as well as merchants were now suffering. This enabled Napoleon, in those days of slow communication, to make a pretense of relaxing the Berlin and Milan decrees, while continuing to seize American ships as before. England was not for a moment deceived, and enforced the orders in council with added indignities. This conduct so exasperated the American people that they demanded war with the oppressor, and on June nineteenth the war of 1812 began. Napoleon's diplomatic juggling had been entirely successful.

A year earlier the princes of the Rhenish Confederation had received their orders. Their peoples were unresponsive, but the zeal of the rulers overcame all opposition. The King of Saxony was grateful in a lively sense of favors to come, and his grand duchy of Warsaw became an armed camp, the Poles themselves expecting their national resurrection. The prince primate's realm was erected into a grand duchy for Eugène, whose viceroyalty was destined for the little King of Rome, and under the stimulus of a fresh nationality the people gave more than was demanded. Würtemberg and Baden learned that Napoleon "preferred enemies to uncertain friends," and both found means to supply their respective quotas. Jerome, true to the fraternal in-

ARRESTING DESERTERS.

stincts of the Bonapartes, hesitated; but his queen was a woman of
sound sense, and both were alive to the uncertainties of tenure in royal
office, so that, receiving a peremptory summons, Westphalia fell into
line. Bavaria and Switzerland furnished their contingents as a matter
of course. Among the Germans, some hated Napoleon for his dealings
with the papacy, some as the destroyer of their petty nationalities;
some devout Protestants even thought him the antichrist. But the
great majority were in a state of expectancy, many realizing that even
the dynastic politics of Europe had been vitalized by his advent; others, liberals like Goethe, Wieland, and Dalberg, hoped for the complete
extinction of feudalism and dynasticism before his march.

This had already been accomplished in France, and for that reason
the peasantry and the townsfolk upheld the Empire. In Paris the upper classes had never forgotten the Terror, and were ready for monarchy in any form if only it brought a settled order and peace. There
were still a few radicals and many royalists, but the masses cared only
for two things, glory and security. They enjoyed the temporary repose under a rule which protected the family, property, and in a certain sense even religion. Family life at the Tuileries was a model, the
Emperor finding his greatest pleasure in domestic amusements, playing
billiards, riding, driving, and even romping, with his young wife, while
his tenderness for the babe was phenomenal. Still he was no puritan,
and the lapsed classes could indulge themselves in vice if only they
paid; from their purses fabulous sums were turned into the Emperor's
secret funds. Under the Continental system industry was at a standstill, and every household felt the privation of abstaining from the free
use of sugar and other colonial wares. There was, however, general
confidence in speedy relief, and there were worse things than waiting.
The peasantry were weary of seeing their soldier sons return from
hard campaigning with neither glory nor booty, and began to resent
the conscription law, which tore the rising generation from home
while yet boys. Desertions became so frequent that a terrible law was
passed, making, first the family, then the commune, and lastly the district, responsible for the missing men. It was enforced mercilessly by
bodies of riders known as "flying columns." Finally, every able-bodied
male was enrolled for military service in three classes — ban, second
ban, and rear ban, the last including all between forty and sixty.
Nevertheless, and in spite of all other hardships, there was much en-

thusiasm at the prospect of a speedy change for the better. In March, 1812, Napoleon could count not far from four hundred and seventy-five thousand men ready for the field. Berthier was retained as chief of staff. In the guard were forty-seven thousand picked men, the old guard under Lefebvre, the young guard under Bessières. Davout's corps numbered seventy-two thousand, all French; Oudinot's thirty-seven thousand, French and Swiss; Ney's thirty-nine thousand, French and Würtembergers; Prince Eugène's forty-five thousand, French and Italians; Poniatowski's thirty-six thousand, all Poles; Gouvion-Saint-Cyr's twenty-five thousand, all Bavarians; Reguier's seventeen thousand, all Saxons; Vandamme's eighteen thousand, Hessians and Westphalians; Macdonald's thirty-two thousand, Prussians and Poles. Murat commanded the cavalry reserve of four corps under Nansouty, Montbrun, Grouchy, and Latour-Maubourg respectively, and numbering in all forty thousand. In addition to this majestic array there were thirty thousand Austrians under Schwarzenberg, and the ninth corps of thirty-three thousand French and Germans under Victor was to follow. "I have never made greater preparations," the Emperor wrote to Davout.

MICHEL-LOUIS-ETIENNE

COMTE REYNAUD DE SAINT-JEAN D'ANGÉLY

CHAPTER XXVII

THE CONGRESS OF KINGS

FOREBODINGS — NAPOLEON AND MARIA LOUISA — THE CZAR'S ULTIMA-
TUM AND THE EMPEROR'S CHOICE — NAPOLEON'S LAST DIPLOMATIC
MOVE — THE IMPERIAL COURT AT DRESDEN — NAPOLEON AND POLAND
— THE HEALTH OF NAPOLEON — HIS STRATEGIC POWERS UNDI-
MINISHED.

READY, at least to outward appearance, Napoleon was in truth
ready as far as equipment, organization, commissariat, strategic
plan, and every nice detail of official forethought could go. But how
about the efficiency and zeal of men and officers? There had been mur-
murings for some years past. It was remarked that Napoleon's studies
in 1808 were the campaigns of Rome against the Parthians from the
days of Crassus onward; from his death-bed Lannes had warned his
chief in 1809 how ready many of his most trusted servants were to betray him if he continued his career of conquest; Decrès, another true
friend, expressed his anxiety in 1810 lest they should all be thrown into
a final horrid elemental crash; and in 1811 Regnaud de Saint-Jean-
d'Angely exclaimed, " The unhappy man will undo himself, undo us all,
undo everything." The Emperor heard neither of these last forebodings, but is doubtfully reported to have himself declared, "I am driven
onward to a goal which I know not." Caulaincourt made no secret of
how his anxiety increased as he knew Russia better. He was recalled
because, having learned Russia's pride and Russia's resources, he made
no attempt to conceal his aversion to the final arbitrament of bloodshed. Poniatowski believed Lithuania would refuse to rise against her
despot; Ségur and Duroc foresaw that France, if degraded to be but one
province of a great empire, would lose her enthusiasm; even Fouché,
having been permitted, on the plea of ill-health, to return from his exile

in Italy, ventured to draw up a vigorous and comprehensive memorial against war, and instanced the fate of Charles XII. The contents of Fouché's paper were divulged to Napoleon by a spy, and when the author presented it he was met by contemptuous sarcasm. The Emperor believed Prussia to be helpless, chiding Davout for his doleful reports of the new temper which had been developed. Jomini declared, but long afterward, that the great captain had avowed to a confidential friend his eagerness for the excitement of battle.

But in spite of the anxiety felt by a few leading Frenchmen, there was general confidence, and it was not until after the catastrophe that details like those enumerated were recalled. It is customary to attribute Napoleon's zeal for war to the fiery counsels of Maret. But there is no necessity to seek any scapegoat. In reality the outlook in 1812 was better than in 1809. Napoleon's spirits were higher, his conscripts were not visibly worse than any drafted since the beginning of the Consulate, and the veteran Coignet's remark concerning the march to Russia is that "Providence and courage never abandon the good soldier." As to the commander-in-chief, he had largely forsaken his licentious courses, partly from reasons of policy, partly because of his sincere attachment to wife and child. Throughout the years of youth and early manhood he had indulged his amorous passions, but until his second marriage not a single woman had been preferred to power, not even Josephine. Maria Louisa, however, was an imperial consort, for whom no attention, no elevation, was too great. Pliant while an Austrian archduchess, she remained so as empress, apparently without will or enterprise. Men felt, nevertheless, that, remaining an Austrian externally, she was probably still one at heart, perhaps a mere lure thrown out to keep the hawk from other quarry. There was much in her subsequent conduct to justify such suspicions, but the utter shamelessness of her later years argues rather the self-abandonment of one in revolt against the rigid social restraints and personal annihilation of early life. The hours which Napoleon spent with her were so many that he laid himself open to the charge of uxoriousness. The physician attendant at the birth of the infant King of Rome declared that the mother would succumb to a second confinement, and the father exercised a self-restraint consonant with the consideration he had displayed at the birth of his heir. He was the squire and constant attendant of his spouse, her riding-master even, and often her playfellow in the

romps of which she was still fond. Scenes of idyllic bliss were daily
observed by the keen eyes of the attendants. The choice of gover-
nesses, tutors, and servants for the little prince was personally superin-
tended by his sire, and every detail of the feeding, dressing, and airing
of the prospective emperor was the subject of minute inquiry and regulation. When it was clear that war was imminent, Napoleon seemed
for the first time ready to abandon his abhorrence for female gover-
nance. Certainly his domestic happiness had not sapped his moral
power; possibly it rendered him over-anxious at times, and, perhaps
in revulsion from anxiety, over-confident.

During two years of diplomatic fencing the initiative had been Russian, the instigation French. For the war which followed no single
cause can be assigned. Some blamed Napoleon, claiming that with his
scheme of universal empire it was inevitable; Metternich said Russia
had brought on war in an unpardonable manner. The Tilsit alliance
was personal; the separation of the contracting parties inevitably
weakened it. The affiliations of the Russian aristocracy with the Austrian; the smart of both under the Continental system, which rendered their agriculture unprofitable; England's stand under Castlereagh;
the Oldenburg question—all these were cumulative in their effect.
With Alexander, Poland and the Continental system were the real
difficulties; the marriage question was only secondary. On January
twelfth, 1812, the Czar with mournful and solemn mien declared his
hands clean of blood-guiltiness and laid down his ultimatum. To
the concentration of Russian troops Napoleon had replied by sending
his own to Erfurt and Magdeburg. Alexander formally stated his
readiness to take back his own move if the Emperor would withdraw the French soldiers; he would even accept Erfurt for Oldenburg, and permit Warsaw to be the capital of a Saxon province. But
he said not a word about the Continental system, being fully determined not to yield one jot, and for Napoleon this was the primary
matter. Alexander's ultimatum by its clever form compelled his ally
either to abandon the scheme of Western empire or to fight. Both parties to the Tilsit alliance understood that with European harbors shut
to English trade, Great Britain must cease to support the Spanish
insurrection, which in that case a few thousand troops could hold in
check. Then the great scheme of revolutionary extension which had
been inaugurated by the Convention and logically developed by Na-

poleon step by step in every war and treaty since Campo Formio, would in a few short years be complete. But two real powers would thus remain in Continental Europe, France and Russia. They could by united action crush British power both by land and sea. To dash this brimming cup from his lips was for Napoleon an insupportable thought. With the hope, apparently, of securing from the Czar the last essential concession, he set his troops in motion toward the Vistula on the very day after his treaty with Prussia was signed.

The natural countermove to Napoleon's advance would be the invasion of Warsaw; although the new Poland was fortified for defense, yet it might be overwhelmed before assistance could reach the garrisons. Moreover, there were ominous signs in France at the opening of 1812. Food supplies were scarce, and speculators were buying such as there were. Napoleon felt he must remain yet a little while to check such an outrage and to strengthen public confidence. Ostensibly to avoid a final rupture, but really to prevent the premature opening of war, he therefore summoned Czernicheff, the Czar's aide-de-camp, who, as a kind of licensed spy, had been hovering near him for three years past, and offered to accept every item of the Russian ultimatum, if only an equitable treaty of commerce could be substituted for the ukase of December, 1810; in other words, if Alexander would agree to observe the letter and spirit of the Continental system. During the two months intervening before the Czar's reply not a Cossack set foot on Polish soil, while day by day Napoleon's armies flowed onward across Europe toward the plains of Russia, and a temporary remedy for the economic troubles of France was found. When, late in April, the answer came, it was, as expected, a declaration that without the neutral trade Russia could not live; she would modify the ukase somewhat, but, as a condition antecedent to peace, France must evacuate Prussia and make better terms with Sweden. On May first the French army reached the Vistula; on May ninth Napoleon and his consort started for Dresden, whither all the allied sovereigns had been summoned to pay their court as vassals to the second Charles the Great.

The surge of German patriotism had nearly drowned Napoleon in 1809, but for manifest reasons it had again receded. The Austrian marriage had withdrawn the house of Hapsburg from the leadership of Germany; the imperial progress to Dresden, and the high imperial court held there, were intended to dazzle the masses of Europe, possibly

HUGUES-BERNARD MARET

DUKE OF BASSANO

to intimidate the Czar. The French were genuinely enthusiastic; the Germans displayed no spite; princes, potentates, and powers swelled the train; all the monarchs of the coalition, under Francis as dean of the corps, stood in array to receive the august Emperor. From the spectacular standpoint Dresden is the climax of the Napoleonic drama. Surrounded by men who at least bore the style of sovereigns, the Corsican victor stood alone in the focus of monarchical splendor. At his side, and resplendent, not in her own, but in his glory, was the daughter of the Cæsars, the child of a royal house second to none in antiquity or majesty, his wife, his consort, his defiance to a passing system. Maria Louisa was as haughty as the Western Empress should be, patronizing her father and stepmother, and boasting how superior the civilization of Paris was to that of Vienna. It was during these days that she first saw Neipperg, the Austrian chamberlain, who was later her morganatic husband. Napoleon appeared better: self-possessed, moderate, and genial. His vassals and his relatives, his marshals and his generals, all seemed content, and even merry. The King of Prussia had lost his beautiful and unfortunate queen; he alone wore a sad countenance. Yet it was rumored that the Prussian crown prince was a suitor for one of Napoleon's nieces. Beneath the gay exterior were many sad, bitter, perplexed hearts. The Emperor was seldom seen except as a lavish host at public entertainments; most of the time he spent behind closed doors with the busy diplomats. As a last resort, Narbonne was sent to Russia, ostensibly to invite Alexander's presence in the interest of peace; actually, of course, to get a final glimpse of his preparations. The Abbé de Pradt was despatched into Poland to fan the enthusiasm for France.

This unparalleled court was dismissed on May twenty-eighth, the Empress returning by way of Prague to Paris, Napoleon hastening by Posen and Warsaw to Thorn. The Poles were exuberant in their delight; they little knew that their supposed liberator had bargained away Galicia to Francis in return for Austrian support. For this betrayal, and his general contempt of the Poles, he was to pay dearly. Had he labored sincerely to organize a strong nucleus of Polish nationality, a coalition of Russia, Prussia, and Austria such as finally overwhelmed him would have been difficult, perhaps impossible. But the founder of an imperial dynasty could not trust a Polish democracy. When the Diet, sitting at Warsaw, besought him to declare the existence of Poland, he criticized the taste which made them compose their address in French instead of Polish, and gave a further inkling of his temper by sending his Austrian contingent to serve in Volhynia, so that neither French nor Polish enthusiasm might rouse the Russian Poles. When he reached Vilna he found that the impassive Lithuanians had no intention of rising against Russia, and no attempt was made to rouse them. If, as appears, his first intention had been to wage a frontier campaign, that plan was quickly changed. Retaining Venice and Triest for use against the Orient, with Austria virtually a member of his system, he determined to force Russia back on to the confines of Europe, perhaps into Asia, and then — Who can say ? It seems as if Poland was to have been divided into French departments instead of being erected into another troublesome nation, vassal state, or semi-autonomous power.

At the opening of the Russian campaign the gradual change which had been steadily going on in Napoleon's physique was complete. He was now plethoric, and slow in all his movements. Occasionally there were exhibitions of quickened sensibility, which have been interpreted as symptoms of an irregular epilepsy; but in general his senses, like his expression, were dull. He had premonitions of a painful disease (dysuria), which soon developed fully. His lassitude was noticeable, and when he roused himself it was often for trivialities. In other campaigns he had stolen away from Paris in military simplicity; this time he had brought the pomp of a court. He planned, too, to bring theater companies and opera troupes to the very seat of war. Above all, he was deeply concerned with his imperial state, having in his trunks the baubles and dress he had worn at his coronation in Notre Dame. His bearing was proud, but there was no sparkle in his eye; he seemed spiritless and ailing; he showed no confidence in his magnificent army.

The haughty, exacting mien of 1812 was very different from the half-jocular, half-sarcastic curl of the lip and sparkle of the eye which had inspired his followers in former days quite as much as his stirring, incisive harangues. Yet careful study will prove that his sagacity as a great captain was in no way dimmed; his military combinations were greater than any he had ever formed. As no parallel to the numbers engaged in this enterprise can be found in European story, nothing comparable to its organization can be found in the history

NAPOLEON AND THE EMPRESS OF AUSTRIA AT DRESDEN

of any land or age. Every corps had its ammunition-train, and great
reserves of supplies were stored in Modlin, Thorn, Pillau, Dantzic,
and Magdeburg. In the two last-named arsenals were siege-trains for
beleaguering Dünaburg and Riga. There were pontoons and bridge
material in abundance; one thousand three hundred and fifty field-
pieces, and eighteen thousand horses to draw them. The commissary
stores were prodigious, and there were thousands of ox-wagons to
transport them. The cattle were eventually to be slaughtered and
eaten. In various convenient strongholds there were, besides, stores
for four hundred thousand men for fifty days. Knowing Russia, he
had prepared to conquer streams and morasses, to feed the army without fear of a devastating population, and to trust the seat of war for
nothing except forage. His strategic plan was amazing, containing,
as it did, the old elements of unexpected concentration, of breaking
through the opposing line, of conclusive victory, and occupation of
the enemy's capital. It was carried also to successful completion,
and in one respect the execution was fine. The obstacles to be sur-
mounted made every movement slow, and while a vast, complicated
military organization may be reliable for weeks, to make it work
for months requires qualities of greatness which increase in geometri-
cal ratio according to the extension of time. Twice Napoleon bared
his inmost thought, once to Metternich in Dresden, once to Jomini at
a dinner-company in Vilna. The first season he intended to seize
Minsk and Smolensk, winter there, and organize his conquests. If
this should not produce a peace, he would advance in the following
season into the heart of the country, and there await the Czar's surrender. To his army he issued an address as direct and ringing as
that which had echoed sixteen years before across the plains of Lombardy. Its substance is that the second Polish war would bring the
same renown to French arms as the first, but the peace would be such
as should end forever the haughty interference of Russia in European
affairs. It seemed to those who heard it as if Russia's hour had struck.

CHAPTER XXVIII

THE INVASION OF RUSSIA — BORODINO

SUCCESS AND FAILURE.—THE STRUGGLE WITH SUMMER HEAT—NAPOLEON
AT VITEBSK—THE RUSSIANS OVER-CONFIDENT—THE FIGHT AT SMO-
LENSK—TECHNICAL VICTORY AND REAL DEFEAT—NAPOLEON'S FATAL
DECISION—THE RUSSIANS AT BORODINO—THE BATTLE ARRAY—NA-
POLEON'S VICTORY—RUSSIAN EFFORTS TO BURN MOSCOW.

WHEN Napoleon left Dresden his force was so disposed that the Russians could not tell whether he meant to strike from north or south, and accordingly they divided theirs, Barclay de Tolly, with a hundred and twenty-seven thousand men, standing before Vilna; Bagration, with sixty-six thousand, ensconcing himself behind the swamps of the upper Pripet in Volhynia. Barclay, hoping to strike a sharp, swift blow, and open the campaign with a moral victory, was soon convinced of the danger, and called in Bagration, who was to be replaced by an auxiliary force. But before the long Russian line could be drawn together Napoleon struck the first decisive blow. Disposing his army in echelon, with beautiful precision he suddenly turned against the enemy's right, crossed the Niemen, and seized Vilna. This turned the Russian flank, and Barclay fell back to the fortified camp which had been established at Drissa in order to cover St. Petersburg. If, then, Jerome's division had promptly advanced from Grodno, Bagration would have been cut off and annihilated. The plan failed, partly because Napoleon did not superintend its operation in person, partly because Davout did not coöperate with sufficient alertness, but chiefly through Jerome's ignorance, slowness, and self-assertion. Bagration turned back, and, descending the Dnieper, placed himself beyond pursuit. For a moment Napoleon contemplated a junction of Ney and Eugène against Barclay, but the former had pushed on to seize Düna-

THE FRENCH ARMY CROSSING THE NIEMEN.

burg, and was out of reach. This scheme, like the other, came to naught; Bagration, by a long, painful detour, was able to establish communication with Drissa, and seemed likely to effect a junction with Barclay on the road to Smolensk. As in these movements both the Russian commanders had lost many men, there would be only a hundred and twenty thousand in their united force, a beggarly showing in view of the two years' preparation necessary to bring it together. Consternation reigned in the Russian camp. The Czar could raise no money, Drissa was painfully inadequate as a bulwark, and the people grew desperate. The nation attributed its sorry plight to the bad advice of the Czar's German counselors, and such was the demoralization at the capital that Alexander was compelled to hasten thither in order to avert complete disaster. In spite of his personal unpopularity, he met with considerable success. The nobility and burghers of both St. Petersburg and Moscow caught the war fever, opened their coffers, equipped a numerous militia, and by the end of July all Russia was hopeful and eager for battle.

This, too, was the earnest desire of Napoleon. The advance from the Vistula to the Niemen and from the Niemen to the Dwina had been successfully carried forward — but at what a cost! "Since we have crossed the Niemen," wrote the artist Adam, who was at the viceroy's headquarters, "the Emperor and his entire army are occupied by a single thought, a single hope, a single wish — the thought of a great battle." Men talked of a great battle as of a great festival. If the Russian army in its own territory shriveled as it did before the summer heat by sickness and desertion, it may be imagined how that of the French dwindled. Their terrible sufferings could be ended only by a battle. Heat, dust, and drought wrought havoc in their columns; the pitiless northern sun left men and animals with little resisting power; the flying inhabitants devastated their fields, the horses and oxen gorged themselves on the half-rotten thatch of the abandoned huts, and died by the wayside; the gasping soldiery had no food but flesh. Dysentery raged, and soldiers died like flies. For a time Saint-Cyr's Bavarian corps lost from eight to nine hundred men a day, and it was by no means a solitary exception. Such facts account for the dilatoriness of Napoleon's movements in part; for the rest, his imperial plans demanded that he should organize all the territories in his rear, and he gave himself the utmost pains to do so. Besides, he had never before had a task so heroic in all its dimensions, and every detail of military and political procedure required time and care in fullest measure, the more so when preparing for a decisive, uncommon battle.

Vitebsk and Smolensk occupy analogous positions on the rivers Dwina and Dnieper, the former of which is to the westward and flows north; the latter, farther inland, flows in the opposite direction into the very heart of Russia. Barclay had planned to await Bagration at Vitebsk, and Napoleon, arriving on July twenty-seventh, hoped for a decisive battle there. But Davout's movements drove Bagration farther eastward, and Barclay, instead of waiting, hurried to Smolensk, where the junction was effected. This compulsory pursuit had, as communications then were, thrown the extreme wings of Napoleon's army virtually out of reach, the Prussians being near Riga, and the Austrians in Volhynia. The long, thin line of his center must be, therefore, drawn in for safety; and since the character of the country had improved, he determined to concentrate near Vitebsk, and recuperate his troops in the comparatively pleasant land which environs that city. Both commander and officers were at first so disheartened that they contemplated remaining for the season, Murat alone remonstrating; but Napoleon said three years were necessary for the Russian war. Such counsels did not long prevail; with new strength came the old daring, and orders were sent both to Macdonald and the Prussians on the left, and to the Austrians under Schwarzenberg on the right, which were indicative of a great project. Napoleon's prestige among the Poles had in fact shrunk along with his army. The latter he could not recruit, but the former he must repair at any hazard; this could be done only by what he designated to Jomini as a "good battle." The success of the minor engagements to right and left, incident to concentration, was encouraging for such a speedy and overwhelming triumph.

The Russians at Smolensk were vainglorious at having outwitted Napoleon, and longed to fight. Barclay alone was uneasy, but, in deference to the prevalent sentiment, he advanced to offer battle, and on August ninth there was a skirmish between pickets. Napoleon at once set his army in motion, but as neither general was really well informed or prepared, Barclay pushed on to the right, and the two armies lost touch. Once aroused, the French spirit brooked no further delay, and it was determined to seek the "good battle" before Smolensk, which, lying on the right, or north, bank of the Dnieper, could be reached

only by crossing the stream. This manœuver was brilliantly executed.
Barclay was a day's march distant on the south bank when Ney and
Murat deployed on the other side for action on August sixteenth.
Bagration, nearer at hand, threw one corps across the river into the
town, and then hurried his main force down-stream to oppose its
passage by the French.

Smolensk, called from its site the Key of Russia, and designated
from its importance as a shrine, "The Sacred," was then a town of
about thirteen thousand inhabitants. Around the inner city was a line
of thick but dilapidated walls, and these were surrounded outside by
densely built faubourgs. The first attempt of Ney to storm the walls
failed, and a bombardment was ordered. By evening of the seventeenth the French army were all drawn up on the north bank between
the city and the river; the Russians were opposite on the heights.
During the night of the seventeenth the Russian army began to cross
the Dnieper by the permanent bridge, which they held; a fresh garrison was thrown into Smolensk, and at four in the morning of the
eighteenth the van began to retreat toward Moscow. Napoleon, foiled
in his attempt to carry Smolensk by storm, had hoped that Barclay
would offer battle under the walls of the town. He, therefore, waited
until afternoon for the expected appearance of his foe, but in vain.
Puzzled and uneasy, he then determined to force the fighting by a fresh
assault. The suburbs were captured late in the evening, but the walls
were impregnable. Barclay then set fire to the quarter opposite that
attacked by the French, and in the resulting confusion safely drew out
his garrison; the next morning saw his rear well beyond Napoleon's
reach, with the bridges destroyed behind it. On the twenty-third he
halted and drew up for battle behind the Uscha.

Technically Napoleon had won, since an important frontier fortress
was captured; but he had not fought his great battle, nor had he cut
off his enemy's retreat. Ney and Murat were despatched in pursuit,
but it is charged on good authority that they acted recklessly, without
concert, and gave the first exhibition of a demoralization destined later
to be disastrous. In another land and under ordinary circumstances
the fight at Smolensk would have been, if not a decisive victory, at least
an effective one. But while Russia is despotic politically, socially she
is the least centralized of all lands, and a wound in one portion of her
loose organism does not necessarily reach a vital point or affect the seat

CH. XXVIII
1812

of life and action. This Napoleon perfectly understood. He could either summon back the patience he had vaunted first at Dresden, then at Vitebsk, or he could yield to his impulse for swift action and go on to Moscow in the hope, before entering the capital, of fighting the "good battle" for which he so longed. The older officers with long memories compared the Russian Smolensk with the Syrian Acre. Murat had foreseen that an affair at Smolensk would amount to nothing, and had begged Napoleon to avoid a conflict. Rapp came in after

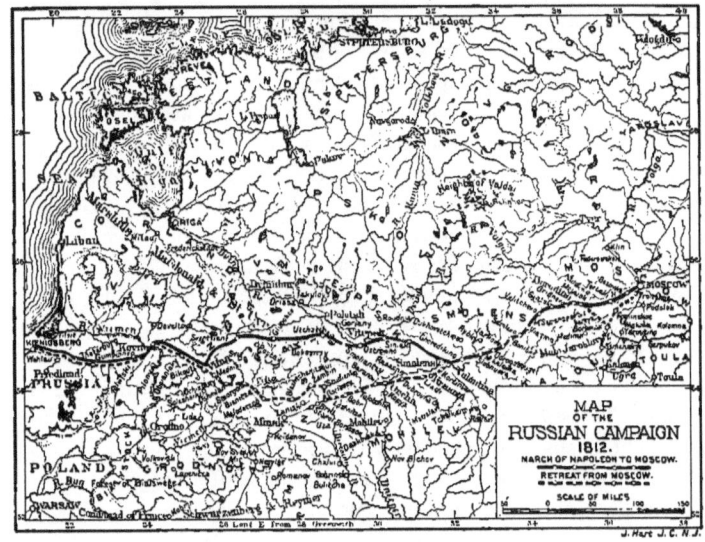

MAP OF RUSSIAN CAMPAIGN.

the victory, and recalled the scenes of distress which had marked every step of his long journey from the Niemen: the numerous victims of dysentery and typhus who lay dying along the roadsides, the desperate bands of marauders and deserters who were eking out a doubtful existence by ravaging the villages, the maddened hordes of peasants and tradespeople who were shooting or striking down the enfeebled stragglers from the army like bullocks in the shambles. Recounting all these horrors, he pleaded with the Emperor to desist. But Napoleon remembered that his transport barges had been wrecked on the river bars, and that his wagon-trains were without horses or oxen to draw

COUNT JEAN RAPP

FROM THE PAINTING BY EDOUARD LIBIG

them. The counterfeit paper money he had brought from Paris would
no longer pass; where was he to find sustenance for his still numerous
force of a hundred and eighty-five thousand men at least?   Only by
pressing on to some populous city; and on the twenty-fourth his army
was in motion eastward.   If Alexander could be brought to terms, he
would yield more quickly with one of his capitals in the enemy's grasp.
In the attempt to form a calm judgment concerning this conclusion it
must be remembered that the French base was secure; there were garrisons of about fourteen thousand men each in Vitebsk, Orscha, and
Mohileff; another was left at Smolensk.   The line from the Niemen to
Moscow was very long, yet Schwarzenberg was on the right to prevent
Tormassoff from breaking through, and Napoleon felt sure that Wittgenstein on the left was too weak to be a menace.   If the great captain had
halted at Smolensk and strengthened himself on the double line of the
Dwina and Dnieper, as was perhaps possible in spite of all difficulties,
he would have been quite as strong in a military way as before Austerlitz or Eylau.   But had Russia learned nothing from these two experiences, and would she come on again a third time as on those two
occasions to certain defeat?   To have acted on the affirmative hypothesis would have been to expect much.   The Czar would rather take time
to raise the whole nation; if need be, to organize, discipline, and drill
his numerous levies; to wear out the patience of the invaders and strike
when the advantage was his, not theirs.   Making all allowance for
troops to be left in garrison, Napoleon would still have a hundred and
fifty-seven thousand men, hardened veterans who, though murmuring
and grumbling after the soldier's manner, were nevertheless altogether
trustworthy, and would turn sulky if compelled to retreat.

If this were Napoleon's reasoning, it proved to be fallacious, because
the Russians were constantly increasing their strength, while that
of the French, both on the base of operations and on the line of
march, was diminishing.   The Austrian troops, moreover, behaved
toward Russia as the Russian soldiers had behaved toward Austria in
the last campaign; that is, as a friendly exploring guard, and not as
hostile invaders.   It is now easy to say that to lengthen the French
line of operation was a military blunder.   It was certainly wrong.   The
reasons are, however, not altogether strategic; they are chiefly moral,
and were not so clearly discernible then.   In the face of national
feeling, before the march of national regeneration, a single man, world-

conqueror though he may have been during a period of national disorganization, is an object of microscopic size. The French emperor
did not know the strength of Russian feeling, the great revolutionist
was ignorant of the Europe he had unconsciously regenerated. If he
blundered as a strategist in not confessing defeat at Smolensk, he
behaved like a tyro in statesmanship when he courted an overthrow
at Moscow.

Barclay was charged by the old Russians with being too German
in feeling, with manœuvering timidly when he ought to fight, and—
sacrilege of sacrileges!—with leaving the sacred image of the Virgin at
Smolensk to fall into hostile hands. Yielding to the storm of popular
feeling, Alexander appointed in his stead Kutusoff, the darling of the
conservative Slavonic party; but Barclay was persuaded to remain as
adviser, and his policy was sustained. The Russians withdrew before
the French advance, until, on September third, their van halted on the
right bank of the Kalatscha, opposite Borodino, to strike the decisive
blow in defense of Moscow. On the fourth Napoleon's van attacked
and drove before it the Russian rear, which was just closing in. He
had a hundred and twenty-eight thousand men at hand, and six thousand more within reach. That night he issued a ringing address:
recalling Austerlitz, he summoned the soldiers to behave so that future
generations would say of each, "He was in that great battle under
the walls of Moscow." Next morning a courier arrived, bringing a
portrait of the little King of Rome. The Emperor hung it before his
tent, and invited his officers to admire it. But at night the sinister
news of Marmont's defeat at Salamanca arrived. Napoleon said
nothing, but was heard in self-communing to deplore the barbarity of
war. All night he seemed restless, fearing lest the Russians should
elude him as they had in other crises; but, rising at five, and dis-
cerning their lines, he called aloud: "They are ours at last! March
on; let us open the gates of Moscow."

The Russians, roused by religious fervor, and elevated by a fatalistic
premonition of success, had thrown up trenches and redoubts at advantageous points on their chosen battle-field. In their first onset
they advanced like devotees, with the cry, "God have mercy upon us!"
and, as each forward rank went down before the relentless invaders,
those behind pressed onward over the bodies of their comrades. But
it was all in vain; throughout the fourth and fifth of September one

outpost after another was taken, until at ten in the evening of the latter day the whole Russian force was thrown back on its main position, stretching from the bank of the Moskwa on the north, behind the Kalatscha, as far as Utizy on the south, such portions as were not naturally sheltered being protected by strong redoubts. There were a hundred and twenty thousand in all, of which about seventeen thousand were un-uniformed peasantry. Opposite stood the French, Poniatowski on the right, Davout, with the guard, in the rear, then Eugène; behind Davout, to the left, Ney; and farther behind, in the same line, Junot. The orders were for an opening cannonade, Poniatowski to surround the Russian left, Eugène to cross the Kalatscha by three bridges thrown over during the night, and attack the Russian right; while Morand and Gérard, his auxiliaries, should move on the center, and storm the defenses erected there.

The battle was conducted almost to the letter of these orders, but such was Russian valor that, instead of being a brilliant manœuvre, it developed into a bloody face-to-face conflict, determined by sheer force. At six in the morning the artillery opened. Poniatowski advanced, was checked, but, supported by Ney, stood firm until Junot came in; they two then stood together, while Ney and Davout dashed at the enemy's center. Eugène having acted in perfect concert, Poniatowski then advanced alone, and his task was completed by nine. But he was so weakened by his terrific exertions that he could only hold what he had gained. At ten Ney and Davout, reinforced by Friant, seized the central redoubts; but they, too, were exhausted, and could only hold the Russian line, which bent inward and stood without breaking. Eugène then massed his whole division, and charged. The resistance was stubborn, and the fighting terrific, but by three his opponents yielded, his artillery opened, and he held his gains. About the same time Junot reached Poniatowski, and their combined efforts finally overpowered the Russian left. So superhuman had been the exertions of both armies that they rested on their arms in these relative positions all night, the Russians too exhausted to flee, the French too weary to pursue. But early on the seventh the flight of Kutusoff began, and the French started in pursuit.

Between the generals of the Russian rear and those of Napoleon's van an agreement was made that if the former were left to pass through Moscow unmolested, the latter should gain the city without a blow.

The contracting parties kept their pact ; but the governor of Moscow rendered the agreement void. Great crowds of the inhabitants joined the Russian columns as, six days later, they marched between the rows of inflammable wooden houses of which the suburbs were composed; and, while they tramped sullenly onward, thin pillars of ascending smoke began to appear here and there on the outer lines. But when, two hours after the last Russian soldier had disappeared, the cavalry of Murat clattered through the streets, the fires attracted little attention, nor at the moment was Napoleon's contentment diminished by them, as, from the "mount of salutation," whence pious pilgrims were wont to greet the holy city, he ordered his guard to advance and occupy the Kremlin, that fortress which enshrines all that is holiest in Russian faith. Kutusoff, boasting that he had held his ground overnight, had persuaded the inhabitants of Moscow, and even the Czar, that he had been the victor, and that he was withdrawing merely to await the arrival of the victorious and veteran legions from the Danube, when he would choose his field and annihilate the invaders.

CHAPTER XXIX

THE EVACUATION OF MOSCOW

THE REASONS FOR NAPOLEON'S ADVANCE — THE IMPORTANCE OF MOS-
COW — THE BURNING OF THE CITY — THE FRENCH OCCUPATION — THE
MILITARY SITUATION — ALEXANDER'S STEADFASTNESS — NAPOLEON'S
IMPATIENCE — THE STRATEGIC PROBLEM — THE EXAGGERATION OF THE
FACTORS — THE PLAN OF RETREAT — MALOJAROSLAVETZ — NAPOLEON'S
VACILLATION.

SOME insight into the state of Napoleon's mind may be secured by
contemplating his conduct during and after the battle of Borodino.
That conflict was, on the whole, the bloodiest and most fiercely contested
of all so far fought by him. The French losses were computed by the
Emperor at twenty thousand men, those of the Russians were not less
than double the number. Yet the day was not decisive. Napoleon, suffering from a severe cold and loss of voice, displayed an unwonted lassitude. Setting a high value on his personal safety, he did not intervene
at crucial moments, as he was wont to do and as he asserted was essential in the new science of war, for the purpose of electrifying officers and
men. His scheme of rolling up Kutusoff's line by a double attack on
left and center consequently failed, in the opinion of the greatest experts, because he did not throw in the guard on the center at the decisive moment. This failure was due to a disregard of his own maxim that
"generals who save troops for the next day are always beaten"; not
divining a complete cessation of hostilities by Kutusoff, he thought his
reserve might be required on the morrow. It seems, too, as if he were
gradually becoming aware of the dangers attendant on the prolongation
of his base to Moscow. At Mozhaisk he halted three days, doubtless
with the hope that Alexander would open negotiations to prevent the
sack of his sacred capital. During this pause careful orders were is-

sued for the concentration of a strong French reserve at Smolensk. Victor was summoned to bring in his thirty thousand men from the Niemen so as to be ready in an emergency to advance even as far as Moscow. It seems like a case of wilful self-deception that on the tenth Napoleon wrote to Maret as if convinced that the exposure of his flanks would escape Kutusoff's notice, saying that the enemy struck in the heart was occupied only with the heart, and not with the extremities. This would have been a justifiable confidence had Borodino been decisive. But it was not decisive, since the Russian army, far from being annihilated, drew off with its files, companies, and regiments so far intact as to be easily available for the quick incorporation of new recruits. This it was which gave verisimilitude to Kutusoff's boast and made the French occupation of Moscow a matter of doubtful expediency.

Yet the temptation was irresistible. Mother Moscow, as runs the caressing Russian phrase, is indeed the source of all Muscovite inspiration. Watered by the winding stream of the same name, its heart is the Kremlin, a citadel of Russian architecture, Russian orthodoxy, Russian authority, and Russian learning. From its churches are promulgated the authoritative utterances of the Greek Metropolitan, within its triangular walls is found the most characteristic Muscovite architecture, behind its portals stand the largest bell ever cast and the largest cannon ever founded until the most recent times; statues of Russian heroes adorn its open spaces, the splendors of its palaces are lavished with Muscovite profuseness, the edicts of the White Czar thunder over untold millions of subjects from its walls. Clustered about the Kremlin are the various quarters of the town, which cover a space equal to the area of Paris, and contain about one fourth as many inhabitants. The epithet of "holy city" is amply justified by the sanctuary-citadel, but its aptness is further sustained by the three hundred and sixty churches, each with its tower and onion-shaped cupola, which are scattered through all the districts. In the beginning of this century Moscow from within appeared like a congeries of villages surrounded with groves and gardens, each with its manor-house and parochial church. Around the whole was a girdle of country-seats, and the beauty of the scene as viewed by the approaching traveler was such as to kindle enthusiasm in the coldest breast. The inhabitants had hoped that the "victory" of Borodino would spare their home the shame of foreign

occupation. When the governor announced that in a council of war it
had been decided to abandon the city, there was first dismay, then
fury, then despair. The long trains of departing citizens wailed their
church hymns with sullen mien and joyless voices.

The surrender was marked by barbarous conduct on the part of the
civil authorities. It has been recounted that by a military convention
the Russian rear-guard had been permitted to withdraw unmolested
after Borodino, in return for a promise not to destroy Moscow. Yet
on September fourteenth, the day of the French occupation, as has
also been told, fires had been kindled in the suburbs, whether by accident or design cannot be determined. Besides this, on receipt of the
notice to evacuate, such stores as in the short interval could be reached
were destroyed; the prison doors were opened, and a horde of maddened criminals was set free in the streets. Nevertheless, there was
fair order throughout the fifteenth. Next day a raging conflagration
burst forth. At the time, and long afterward, this was attributed as a
deed of dastardly incendiarism to the invaders; with the growth of
modern ideas about ruthlessness in warfare, Russian historians have
begun to attribute it to the inhabitants as a heroic measure. It is now
asserted that the governor cast the first brand into his own country-
seat. More probably, the fanaticism of the populace, heightened by the
criminal rage of the escaped prisoners, led to the almost simultaneous
firing of many buildings in various quarters. A possibility of method
in the destruction of the city begins to dawn, however, when it is remembered that the devastation of the surrounding country by the
fleeing Russians was equally thorough, and was carried out according
to a carefully devised plan.

The entry of the French into Moscow has been compared to the
appearance of great actors before an empty house. When the conflagration broke out, every effort was made to stop it, and eight hundred
fire fiends were summarily punished. But as the burning walls of the
storehouses fell, the rabble seized the barrels of spirits thus revealed,
and drank themselves into blind fury; the French soldiery pillaged
with little restraint, not sparing even the Kremlin. Finally, the flames
were checked and order was restored, but not until three quarters of
the city proper were destroyed; the Kremlin and the remaining fourth
were saved. On the evening of the fourth day the French army was
disposed in rude comfort within or about the site of Moscow, and

Murat's riders began to bring in reports concerning Kutusoff's army. To soothe the peasantry of the neighboring districts, one of the old insidious proclamations was issued, appealing to their manhood against the tyranny of their rulers. " Die for your faith and the Czar!" was the answering cry, as they seized the French stragglers, surprised the garrison of Wereja, and beset the Smolensk road. Day by day the people labored, the townsfolk helping to gather the peasants' goods, both classes waylaying the French supply-trains, and hiding every article of use in vast underground chambers constructed for the purpose. Consternation filled the invaders, and their plight became desperate when they learned of the Russian military dispositions, and understood how Kutusoff already menaced their safety.

Instigated by Castlereagh, Bernadotte had released the Russian corps placed at his disposal for conquering Norway, and Wittgenstein, on the Russian right, thus suddenly acquired a force of forty thousand wherewith to menace Napoleon's outlying left on the north. By English mediation, also, a peace was arranged between Turkey and Russia, thus releasing Tchitchagoff, who promptly joined Tormassoff, and opposed Schwarzenberg on the extreme French right with nearly two to one. Meanwhile Kutusoff had taken a position at Tarutino, where he commanded the left flank of the main French army, and daily received new recruits, who flocked to fill his depleted ranks. Napoleon had, since Borodino, been in daily expectation of some communication from the Czar. His critical situation made him impatient, and on the twentieth he wrote, informing his strangely silent foe that Moscow was burned, a misfortune which might have been averted had negotiations been opened after Borodino. There was no response. On October fifth Lauriston was despatched to Kutusoff's camp, nominally to secure an exchange of prisoners. The latter said that the affair must be referred to St. Petersburg ; but the French general learned that the Russians had extended their line south toward Kaluga to secure the fertile base behind, and further threaten the long, weak French flank.

Alexander's silent steadfastness was, indeed, remarkable. Hitherto in every crisis — as, for example, after Austerlitz and Friedland — he had yielded. Why was he now so firm? Stein, the Prussian patriot, was at his side; but so was the trusted Rumianzoff, leader of the French party, which was for peace. The Old-Russian party, demoralized by Napoleon's advance to the heart of the empire, was also clam-

orous for peace negotiations. An English embassy, composed of Lord
Cathcart and the body of English officers under Sir Robert Wilson sent
to reorganize the Russian army, had so far been able to accomplish
little, for by all accounts their influence was slight. The improved
military situation no doubt accounts for much, but the best information goes to show that Alexander moved and talked like one dazed,
feeling himself to be a storm-tossed child of fate. Destitute of self-
reliance, he appears to have been drawn toward Galitzin, whose piety
was eminent, and verged upon mysticism. It is certain that in those
days the Czar for the first time became an ardent Bible reader, and
frequently exclaimed, "The hand of God hath done this!" On
leaving St. Petersburg at last for the seat of war, his parting act was
to found the Russian Bible Society. It was with but small reliance on
the military situation, and with a feeling of providential guidance, that
he determined to renew the conflict.

Thus passed five weeks. Interminable they seemed to the anxious
conqueror at Moscow, who yawned even at the theater; who forgot
the stern abstemiousness of his table habits, and, like a gourmet, spent
hours at his meals merely to kill time; who threw himself into vicious
ways, and contracted a loathsome disease; who lost all interest even in
his troops, and finally, unkempt, preoccupied, and feverish, seemed indifferent to everything. The crown, scepter, and robe wherewith he had
hoped to be invested as Emperor of the West, were not unpacked from
the camp chests. The pompous ceremonies of military occupation
were scrupulously performed; drills, parades, and concerts followed in
due succession; but the Emperor's interest was languid. At last the
dreary waiting became intolerable, the season, although neither early
nor severe, was rapidly advancing, the predatory excursions of the soldiers into the surrounding country were growing longer, more difficult,
and less fruitful of results with every day. The elements of danger
were hourly increasing in an appalling ratio. Daru advised turning
Moscow into an armed camp and wintering there. "A lion's advice,"
said Napoleon, but he put it aside. The question of retreat would soon
be imperative, and that he sometimes discussed, but only languidly,
until, on October eighteenth, without warning, a truce made by Murat
was broken, and his command driven in. Then at last the captain in
Napoleon awakened, the emperor vanished, the retreat was ordered,
and universal empire, a dependent Czar, the march from Tiflis to the

Ganges, England humiliated, and the ocean liberated — all were forgotten in the presence of reality. Robe, scepter, and crown were never seen again.

Political considerations prompted a movement of withdrawal toward the northwest, as if against St. Petersburg, but military considerations prevailed, and between the two alternatives — a direct retreat to Smolensk through a devastated land, or a circuit southwestward, through fertile districts, toward Kaluga, as if to attack Kutusoff — the choice fell on the latter. The reason is clear. The seat of war was within a triangle marked by Riga, Brest-Litovski, and Moscow; from Riga to Moscow, the left flank, is five hundred and fifty miles; from Riga to Brest, the base, is three hundred and seventy-five miles; from Brest to Moscow, the right flank, is six hundred and fifty miles; the perpendicular from Moscow to the base, which was the shortest line of retreat, is therefore about five hundred and seventy-five miles. These distances are all enormous; on the left were only forty-two thousand men; on the right, about thirty-four thousand; along the line, forty-two thousand. The diagram, if drawn, will display all the peculiarities of Napoleonic formation in mass, abstractedly considered, but it will likewise display the fact that with the highest and most perfect army organization then known, it would have been well-nigh impossible to work the combination. Neither of the monstrous flanks could be held by the comparatively scanty forces available; the line of operation was equally weak. What safety was there for the army in retreat? None.

There will never be complete agreement as to the causes of Napoleon's disaster in Russia. A comparison of the relative values of mass-formation, tactics, and organization in modern warfare, which uses railroads and telegraphs, with the distances practicable in present-day operations, must nevertheless reveal the chief cause — that the Napoleonic organization had not kept pace with the development of Napoleonic strategy. The emperor had overweighted the general, the former having soared into an ether which would not sustain the pinions of the latter. The well-used plea of an "act of God" will not stand. The autumn of 1812 was mild, the winter late in opening. Neither cheerless steppes, nor phenomenal cold, nor unheard-of snows, nor any reversal of nature's laws,— not even the motley nationalities of the grand army, or an unhistoric migration from south to north,— none of these was the chief cause of failure, which is to be found in the attempt monstrously to exaggerate the factors of a strategic system evolved for national, but not for continental, proportions.

The first and natural thought of a direct retreat to Smolensk was momentarily entertained; but it had to be abandoned because, with weak flanks and a bare country, the distance was too far. The same was true in regard to the move toward St. Petersburg—the distance was too great for the conditions. The circuit toward Kaluga was first considered as a feint to throw the Russians off the scent; it became a necessity when they assumed the offensive in the unforeseen and unexpected attack on Murat. The Emperor did not dare to expose his flank and rear to an advancing foe, and accordingly his army was assembled on the road toward Kaluga. Should he advance or await a further movement of the enemy? Evidently the former, otherwise the entire moral effect of the first offensive would be lost. A long march had to be extended still farther, partly for strategic reasons, but chiefly in order to secure an additional advantage of the first importance, to wit, sustenance from the country when the distances were too great for the workings of any feasible commissariat department. If the Russians should even momentarily be deceived into believing that the French had resumed the offensive, a line from Kaluga direct to Smolensk would still be open for retreat while the enemy was preparing for action.

The report was spread in Moscow that Napoleon was going out to overwhelm Kutusoff and then return. Mortier, with eight thousand of the young guard, remained behind, his orders being to blow up the Kremlin before leaving. The main army advanced across the river Pachra and moved toward the Lusha. There was as yet no word of the enemy; possibly he had been misled and was advancing directly on Moscow. Napoleon, therefore, turned westward in the hope that he might reach Kaluga without opposition. On the twenty-fourth the Russian van appeared. Had Kutusoff acted on his correct information and thrown forward his whole army, a decisive battle might have ended the invasion. As it was, Eugène, after a bloody conflict at Malojaroslavetz, remained master of the field, and the timid Kutusoff drew back his force. Meantime the truth leaked out in Moscow. Suspicion was excited, as the resident French observed not merely the immense booty packed in the officers' baggage, but also the loads of Muscovite art treasures under which the government wagons groaned. They were quick to act, and soon, accompanied by women and children, they joined the march with all the paraphernalia of their household goods. From the first this throng, uniting with the usual horde of stragglers and camp-followers, prevented all rapid movements by the army; in fact, but for them the half-senile Kutusoff would not have been able to show even his van to the French line. Mortier's effort to destroy the Kremlin failed, and served no purpose except to exhibit the thirst for revenge of a savage nature brought to bay.

In short, every plan of Napoleon's seemed ineffectual, and indecision marked his every act. Eugène's terrible struggle had resulted in a list of wounded numbering four thousand. The old Napoleon would have abandoned them and then have attacked Kutusoff even in the forest defiles where he was ensconced; or else he would have pressed on past Kaluga, or would have swiftly wheeled to regain the northern road toward Smolensk. The harried, sick, exhausted man of 1812 did none of these things, but called a council of war, and weighed the arguments there presented for nearly a week, when, finally, he decided, and with forced marches drove his columns toward the northern road to Smolensk. He wrote to Junot that his motive for delay was to provide for the suffering from his depot at Mozhaisk, but, in fact, he had not waited long enough materially to assist the wounded, and had secured no advantage from the bloody battle. In the absence of trustworthy information he took (when once he did move) a long, circuitous road. As yet there was no cold except the usual sharpness of autumn nights; but the summer uniforms of the troops were tattered and their shoes worn. Germans, Italians, and Illyrians began to straggle, and the horrors of the approaching cold, as depicted by Russian prisoners, sank deep into the minds of the dispirited French, so far away from their pleasant homes.

END OF VOLUME III.

www.ingramcontent.com/pod-product-compliance
Lightning Source LLC
Chambersburg PA
CBHW020234110726

47898CB00004B/1256